J...
and the
GREATER
GAME

❧

Being an account of certain
dramatic events that recently unfolded
on the Subcontinent,

and

of several amazing revelations
about the discovery of Annapurnite
and the nature of reality,

as experienced by

a Lady, Miss Janisha Chatterjee.

Also by Eric Brown

Novels

Murder at the Chase

Salvage

Satan's Reach

The Serene Invasion

Murder by the Book

Starship Seasons

Helix Wars

The Devil's Nebula

The Kings of Eternity

Guardians of the Phoenix

Cosmopath

Xenopath

Necropath

Kéthani

Helix

New York Dreams

New York Blues

New York Nights

Penumbra

Engineman

Meridian Days

Novellas

Famadihana on
Fomalhaut IV

Starship Spring

Starship Winter

Gilbert and Edgar on Mars

Starship Fall

Revenge

Starship Summer

The Extraordinary Voyage
of Jules Verne

Approaching Omega

A Writer's Life

Collections

Rites of Passage

Strange Visitors

The Angels
of Life and Death

Ghostwriting

Threshold Shift

The Fall of Tartarus

Deep Future

Parallax View
(with Keith Brooke)

Blue Shifting

The Time-Lapsed Man

ERIC BROWN

Jani and the GREATER GAME

SOLARIS

First published 2014 by Solaris
an imprint of Rebellion Publishing Ltd,
Riverside House, Osney Mead,
Oxford, OX2 0ES, UK

www.solarisbooks.com

ISBN: 978 1 78108 205 8

10 9 8 7 6 5 4 3 2 1

A CIP catalogue record for this book is available
from the British Library.

Designed & typeset by Rebellion Publishing

Printed in the US

To Jack and Katrina Stephen

CHAPTER ONE

Mr Gollalli displays his wares –
The dowager to the rescue – The Russians attack –
"Show a bit of mettle under fire..."

JANI WAS ABOARD the *Rudyard Kipling*, somewhere over the Hindu Kush, when the Russians attacked.

For much of the journey from London she had remained in her cabin, reading a volume of poetry and composing a letter to Sebastian. Her peace of mind was in tatters, torn by her affection for Sebastian, her interrupted studies at Cambridge, and the terrible communiqué from Delhi informing Jani that her father was gravely ill. She had last seen him almost a year before, when government business had brought him to England. He had seemed so full of life then, so vibrant with energy and ideas, that it was almost impossible now to imagine him stricken. He was not yet sixty; surely, she thought, the wonders of modern medicine could do *something*... Had she believed in any of the plethora of gods so popular these days, she would have prayed for his health. Her refusal to do so had upset Sebastian whose Christian faith, she thought, was less a matter of committed belief than a nebulous notion of good form.

She pushed thoughts of Sebastian from her mind and stared through the porthole of her cabin. The sun was going down and spreading a tangerine glow over the foothills of the Hindu Kush. The fires of scattered villages glowed in counterpoint to the stars just appearing overhead. In a few hours the airship would be docking at Delhi air-terminal, and Jani would step out onto the dusty soil of her homeland for the first time in five years.

She realised that she was crying. She dried her tears, picked up her book, and slipped from her cabin.

She had dined in her cabin earlier, avoiding the forced sociability of the dining room, and now made her way to the observation lounge on the second level. The lounge was a vast area of pile carpeting, with ornate brass-work and a plethora of potted plants and ferns like an airborne Kew Gardens. Padded velvet *chaises longues* and armchairs occupied booths around the perimeter, each with a porthole that looked out across the curving expanse of the land. The lounge was occupied by perhaps fifty passengers, mainly middle-aged and elderly Englishmen and -women – servants of the Raj returning to their postings in the subcontinent after holidays in Blighty. She was the only Indian in sight, discounting the servants and bar-staff; not that she was in any way discommoded by the fact. She had become accustomed to being the only brown face in a sea of white, the perceived exotic amidst the mundane.

She caught sight of Lady Eddington with her crocheting on her lap – the dowager looked up and smiled at Jani, perhaps expecting the courtesy of her company. Jani acknowledged her, but decided that she could do without the old lady's well-meaning solicitations and crossed the lounge to an unoccupied booth.

She sat on the sprung cushions of the *chaise longue*, ordered a juniper cordial from a passing waiter and stared through the window. Night had come on apace, rendering the folded foothills all but invisible; only the occasional village fire showed. She sat back, lulled by the thrum of the engines – a dozen Annapurnite-powered turbos, Sebastian had announced with wonder at the sight of the de Havilland at the London airyard two days ago. She opened her book and tried to read, but Wilfred Owen's latest collection failed to hold her attention and her gaze wandered to the scene far below.

"There you are!" cried a familiar voice. "Seeking refuge behind the cover of the aspidistra! But you won't mind if I intrude upon your privacy, Miss Chatterjee?"

She fixed a smile in place and looked up at the roly-poly figure of the irrepressible Mr Gollalli, at the same time setting her open book down on the cushion beside her to deter unwanted intimacy. "Not at all," she smiled.

Mr Gollalli beamed – a great spread of ivory and gold in a rubicund face – and squeezed his bulk into the armchair opposite. As ever he carried his valise, which he placed at his feet with great care.

"You were not at dinner, Miss Chatterjee."

"I elected to dine alone this evening, Mr Gollalli."

"I was hoping to take up our little conversation where it was interrupted this morning," he went on. He was a grossly overweight man whose huge face was forever dewed with beads of perspiration. He carried a pink bandana and mopped his brow and cheeks at regular intervals. "Though perhaps the occasion of dinner was not quite the appropriate time at which to demonstrate my..."

Jani smiled politely.

"Whereas," he went on, "now is the perfect opportunity," and so saying he leaned over the bulge of his stomach and snapped open the hasp of his valise.

Mr Gollalli had introduced himself at dinner on the first day of the voyage. He was, he informed her proudly, the managing director of Gollalli and Chandra – one of the premier film studios in Bombay. "Perhaps you are familiar with our films?"

Jani had admitted her ignorance, claiming that she had been too busy with her studies to attend the cinema. She had elected not to mention that she had heard of the studio, and that the type of film they made – horror and supernatural shockers – were not to her taste.

Whereupon Mr Gollalli had proceeded to recount to her, and everyone else present around the table, the plot of Gollalli and Chandra's latest release.

"But as I was saying," Mr Gollalli said now, "I was in London on a very special errand, and one which I could not entrust to any minion, oh, no! This trip required my especial attention, let me tell you. You see, I was visiting the capital in order to show my colleague in the business the latest developments made at our Dadar laboratories. Now, as a medical student, I would like your honest opinion."

Jani took a sip of her cordial, trying not to exhibit her unease. "I have barely begun my very first term," she said.

"But you informed me of your desire to go into surgery," Gollalli said. "You must therefore have attended autopsies, no? Post-mortems?"

Jani's smile became strained. "Not yet," she murmured, wondering where all this might be leading.

Mr Gollalli pulled a fat ledger from his valise, and it appeared to take all his strength to lift the volume from the floor and lodge it, with a grunt, on his expansive lap.

"No matter," he said breezily. "I would still be interested in your opinion of the fidelity of my... ah... *samples*."

He opened the ledger, its cover like some great trapdoor, and flipped through what appeared to be a thousand transparent leaves with blood-red slivers compressed between them.

He beamed at Jani, a golden incisor catching the light of the chandelier, and proceeded to roll up the sleeve of his left arm. "Now, Miss Chatterjee, what do you think of this?"

Quickly he slipped what looked like a sliver of bacon from between the transparencies and slapped it on the bulging flesh of his exposed forearm.

Jani stared. Mr Gollalli's left arm now appeared to sport a deep and bloody wound, stomach-turning in its realism. What was quite remarkable was the illusion of depth achieved by the artificial wound. Jani swore that she could make out the white gleam of the bone beneath.

"Remarkable," she murmured.

Mr Gollalli beamed in delight. "I thought you would appreciate it!" he chortled. "I developed the process myself. It is all about utilising enamel paint on layered, micro-thin vinyl. But I have more..."

He whipped off the ersatz gash, slapped it back between the transparencies, and turned the pages until he came to another example of rendered flesh. "Now behold this one, Miss Chatterjee!"

He peeled off the vinyl wound and draped it across the underside of his forearm, and Jani gasped at the verisimilitude. It appeared for all the world as if a long gash on the man's arm had been badly stitched and had become infected. The petroleum iridescence of gangrenous flesh glinted in the electric light.

Jani's stomach heaved. She put a hand to her lips and turned away.

"You see," Mr Gollalli went on, oblivious, "it is the fidelity of these and other samples that make the films of Gollalli and Chandra so popular in India. I was hoping to impress my colleagues in Britain, and in this I have succeeded. Let me tell you that my order book is now full! Soon, my dear, all the Empire will be shrieking in horror at the realism of films supplied by my company, oh, yes!"

Jani was trying to think of a polite way to absent herself from his company when a shadow fell across the booth.

"Mr Gollalli! What on earth are you showing the girl?"

Mr Gollalli's smile became ingratiating. "Why, Lady Eddington. What an unexpected pleasure! I was just displaying..."

"I can see very well what you are displaying, my man, and let me tell you that severed arteries and the like have no place in polite company, and are certainly not for the eyes of a girl of such refined sensibilities. Now, if you will excuse us, I have more important matters to discuss with my young friend. Janisha, if you would care to accompany me..."

Jani smiled at Mr Gollalli who, open-mouthed, watched her accompany Lady Eddington across the observation lounge. "Thank you for saving me," she murmured.

"Think nothing of it, child," said Lady Eddington. "Really, the audacity of the man!"

"I'm sure he's well-meaning, Lady Eddington."

"That is hardly the point. The man has no sense of decorum. Fancy his flagrant exhibition of those appalling *samples*, as he calls them – and to one of your tender years! Do you know, he had the poor taste to display his wares to the Captain on the very first day. I'm surprised he wasn't made to walk the plank!"

Jani settled herself into an armchair across the lounge from Mr Gollalli. She smiled to herself. To be saved from Mr Gollalli's excesses only to suffer those of the dowager... She wondered whether it was her age, her sex, or the colour of her skin which allowed people the presumption of superiority.

She recalled Sebastian's father, Lord Consett, and his patronising attitude to her – and his poorly disguised horror at his son's attachment to someone he referred to as 'a subject of the Raj'...

"Do you know," Lady Eddington said now as she settled her crinolines around her on the *chaise longue*, "I do envy the youth of today. The thought of it, a girl entering the medical profession! Such a thing was unheard of in my day."

Jani smiled. "Society has changed, little by little," she said. "And I must admit that it does help that my father is in a position of influence in the Indian government. Not that I am saying that this got me into Cambridge," she added, hurriedly. "It was more that his influence on me, on my sensibilities, allowed me to think that there was nothing of which I might not be capable."

Lady Eddington peered at Jani through a lorgnette. "You are, if you do not mind my saying, a most remarkable young woman. How refreshing it is to meet a gal with the strength to face the world on its own harsh and unremitting terms. You will go far, my child; of that I am sure."

Jani was casting about for a suitably modest rejoinder when a burst of raucous laughter sounded and a dozen young subalterns barrelled into the lounge. They appeared to be applying the rules of Twickenham to the airship and, in lieu of a rugby ball, were tossing around the cockaded turban of a young servant boy who appeared behind them in the entrance and looked on helplessly.

Jani wanted more than anything to jump to her feet and remonstrate with the rowdies, but fear of their reaction kept her rooted to her seat. Undaunted, Lady Eddington rose to her considerable height, puffed out her chest, and with a murmured, "Excuse me," to Jani propelled herself across the lounge.

"Just what in the name of decency do you think you young scallywags are playing at?" she bellowed, then admonished the leader of the ruck in lowered tones.

The effect was instantaneous. To a man, the subalterns stood to attention, saluted the dowager and proceeded, with metaphorical tails between their legs, to scurry to the bar – but not before returning the servant's headgear with muttered apologies.

Lady Eddington returned, all but dusting her hands in a gesture of accomplishment. "Some might call such a display merely high spirits," she said. "But I call it downright *rude*."

Jani smiled. "You certainly put them in their place."

Lady Eddington peered across at the subalterns who were now drinking in a nearby booth. She laid a frail hand on Jani's arm. "Come, let us repair to my carriage. The tenor of the lounge has taken a turn for the worse."

Jani finished her drink and followed Lady Eddington across the lounge to the elevators.

As they dropped to a lower deck, Jani said, "Did I hear you correctly, Lady Eddington? Did you say your 'carriage'?"

"Your hearing is not at fault, child. Carriage is indeed what I said."

The elevator bobbed to a halt and the doors parted to reveal a corridor. This one was neither carpeted, nor wallpapered, nor equipped with the ubiquitous potted palms, nor any other signifier of luxury. Jani followed the dowager along the corridor towards a pair of double doors, guarded by an armed officer.

"Good evening, Stubbs. I have a guest I wish to escort to my carriage, now there's a good man."

She passed the officer a half crown, and Stubbs saluted and stepped aside.

Jani followed Lady Eddington into a vast chamber and halted on the threshold. "But where are we?" she asked. She was reminded of an airship hangar, but one filled with railway rolling-stock.

"I think the technical name is the 'garage' or some such, but this way."

They walked beside a length of railway track on which stood three Pullman carriages end-to-end. The overpowering stench of axle grease and engine oil filled the air. Jani could well believe that she was in some siding of Paddington Station, but for the wall to her left, the ribbed metal punctuated by a line of portholes.

Taking in the racing green livery of the carriages, picked out with gold filigree scrollwork, Jani realised that although she had lived a life of relative affluence, both in India and in England, there was an order of privilege above and beyond that to which she was accustomed.

"And this one is mine," said Lady Eddington, pausing before the vertical steps of the central carriage. She climbed them with surprising spryness and Jani followed.

"But I never knew such things were possible," Jani said once she was ensconced in the Pullman's buttoned-velvet couch and Lady Eddington was preparing Assam tea.

"Anything is possible if one possesses three important attributes, child, and those are money, influence, and the confidence with which to carry off the desires of one's heart. And do you know, I often think that the third might be the most important."

Jani smiled to herself as she sipped her tea: only a truly rich person could make such a striking declaration.

"I like to travel in style *and* comfort," Lady Eddington went on. "You see, my husband ran the Calcutta-Bombay Railway Company, and this carriage was a gift from the board when he retired. I have it transported almost everywhere I go these days, though the Americas are something of a trial – much of the railway gauge, you know, does not conform to Empire standards."

Jani almost replied, "What hardship..." but stopped herself just in time.

"Of course, technically speaking we are breaking the rules by being down here. Safety regulations, don't you know. What tosh! But Sergeant Stubbs and I have a little arrangement."

Jani smiled and looked around the palatial carriage. "It must be wonderful to be able to take your home with you, as it were."

"I suppose it is, at that," the dowager said. "I am spending a week in the sub-continent, Janisha, visiting old friends for the last time. I am eighty-five next month – though I know that's hard to believe – and one does not last for ever. I moved back to England five years ago after a lifetime in India. I have a little place in Mayfair, so as to be in the thick of things, you know."

"Do you miss India?"

Lady Eddington gave a thin smile. "Of course I do, child! I was born in Delhi; the place is in my blood – but so, too, in an odd way, is England. The strange thing is that I miss India when I am in the Old Country, but when I'm in India I miss England. I suppose one is never satisfied, is one?"

"I know what you mean." Jani blew on her tea, smiling. "I missed India and my father terribly for the first few years I was in England. But five years ago I returned, and yes, I did miss England then." She almost went on to say that she felt torn between the two countries, being the product of both places, with an Indian father and an English mother, reared in India by a nanny, then packed off to boarding school in Chichester at the age of eight. She had felt like the proverbial fish out of water for many years in England – and then for three months, at the age of thirteen, had felt oddly out of place back in India. She had felt too English, too accustomed to the different ways of the Old Country.

She almost told Lady Eddington all this now, but something stopped her; she did not want the dowager to think her presumptuous by claiming to be fifty percent English, which after all was her right – and as soon as she thought this, she resented her inhibition. Lady Eddington was right, she thought: what was most important was *confidence*.

"But enough of me," Lady Eddington said. "I do hope you will visit while I'm in Delhi, and again when I return to England."

"I should like nothing more."

"Did I hear you mention, yesterday, that your father was a member of the Indian government?"

"He is a minister in the Senate," Jani replied with a note of pride, "with the portfolio of State Security."

Lady Eddington arched her eyebrows. "Indeed? But what a responsibility these days, with our enemies bearing down on every side," she said. "I'm sorry, but I didn't quite catch your surname when we were introduced on the first day."

"Chatterjee," Jani said, "and my father is Kapil Dev Chatterjee."

Lady Eddington lowered her cup, striking the saucer with a tintinnabulation of fine china. "Kapil Dev Chatterjee? But then your mother was none other than Eleanor Markham, the concert pianist?"

Jani beamed. "That's right."

"But my child, I had the good fortune to attend her very first concert in Delhi. 1901, if I'm not mistaken – my word, almost a quarter of a century ago! But what a virtuoso! What divine playing."

Jani felt a glow of pride. "Thank you."

"I followed your mother's career with interest, child. And my, didn't she cause a furore when she fell for your father and they married! Ruffled quite a few feathers, and no mistake – but feathers that needed ruffling, mark my word. I've met some outrageous stuffed shirts in my time, I can tell you."

"They were ostracised by both communities at first – by the English in Delhi *and* by Indian society."

The dowager shook her head and endeared herself to Jani by saying, "Prejudice is a petty though invidious sin, child. Never allow it to get its talons into you, mm?"

Jani smiled. "I'll do my best not to."

"And I was so saddened and shocked when I read of your mother's passing. Of course, you would be too young to recall."

"I was three. I can't remember Mother. Or rather I have faint memories of a tall, dark-haired woman, strikingly beautiful. But I have no way of knowing if these are *true* memories or my recollections of photographs that were around the house when I was growing up."

"But how tragic, to be without a mother at such a tender age. My dear, she would be proud of what a fine young woman you've become."

Jani blushed modestly and took refuge in a sip of tea.

The dowager began to say something, but stopped at a sound from outside. Jani made out the tattoo of marching feet. "Ah," said Lady Eddington, "the changing of the guard."

"But who is being guarded?" Jani asked.

"That, my dear, is a secret no one is prepared to divulge. But I have little doubt that the prisoner is important, if the level of security surrounding him is any indication. Observe." Lady Eddington pointed through the window.

Jani made out a double file of uniformed troops in the dim light of the 'garage.' They marched past the carriage towards what looked like a cube constructed from some dull grey metal. Jani saw a door in the face of the cube, inset with bars. There was no sign of anyone within the cell.

The cube was surrounded by a dozen armed soldiers, who saluted their relief guard, formed ranks and marched from the chamber. The new guard took up their positions around the cube with arms at the ready.

"My word, but how do they think a prisoner might escape from such a secure box?" Jani asked.

"Perhaps they fear that some *outside* element might attempt to effect his escape," Lady Eddington surmised.

"Ah... you think he might be a Russian spy, or Chinese?"

"One or the other, I suspect, though..." She trailed off ruminatively. "What flummoxes me is the dashed level of security. It's almost as if they're transporting a wild animal, with the measures they take. The cell is never without at least a dozen guards armed to the veritable molars, and it was transported aboard the ship when we docked at Athens with an escort of a hundred troops *and* a Churchill tank fore and aft. I saw it all with my own eyes, child, and that's a fact."

Jani found herself wondering if her father might be in a position to know anything about the prisoner, then was pole-axed by the thought that such considerations as state security would probably be beyond his consideration at the moment.

Lady Eddington was replenishing Jani's cup when the carriage gave a slight jolt. Tea spilled into the saucer and the dowager apologised. "A little more turbulence

– but wasn't it frightful as we passed over Albania? We're just above the Kush, now, which is known for its erratic weather... And there we go again!" The airship lurched and the gondola swung like a pendulum. Jani reached for the mahogany arms of the chair and held on as the airship shuddered.

"You see," Lady Eddington went on, gamely pouring a second cup despite the conditions, "the garage is at the very bottom of the gondola, so the severity of the swing is exaggerated."

Jani was just about to suggest that perhaps they should ascend to the main deck when a frenzied tattoo sounded on the door, followed by Sergeant Stubbs shouting, "Lady Eddington! I think we should–"

The carriage lurched and interrupted Stubbs' advice. He hauled open the door and peered in, holding the frame for support. Red-faced, he called out, "Follow me, Lady Eddington! Easy does it, and hold on tight!"

Jani followed the dowager, who reached the door and grasped Stubbs' hand. Jani lowered herself from the carriage and, tottering this way and that, followed the pair across the chamber towards the double door. She glanced quickly over her shoulder. The guards around the grey cell were facing it, their rifles at the ready as if expecting the prisoner to break out at any second.

They hurried from the chamber and along the corridor to the elevator, sliding the last few yards as the airship tilted. Jani thought that the 'ship was climbing. As they were about to step into the lift, Lady Eddington said, "What the blazes is going on, Stubbs? I thought the established practice was to *descend* out of a storm if at all possible?"

Sergeant Stubbs licked his lips and said, "That's as maybe, ma'am, but we ain't in no storm, you see. We're under attack."

He turned and retraced his steps along the corridor before Lady Eddington could question him. The lift doors closed and the elevator whisked them up into the body of the airship.

Jani's stomach flipped, and the sensation had nothing to do with the elevator's ascent. "Attack?" she said.

Lady Eddington took her hand in a tight grip. "The Russians have been known to aim their pea-shooters at passing ships in the area, child – but they've yet to down one of the Empire's finest."

The elevator bobbed to a halt and the doors swished open onto the relative normality of the observation lounge. Passengers were gathered in knots around the portholes, peering out and exclaiming with 'oohs' and 'aahs' as if at a particularly impressive firework display. The posse of subalterns cheered the airship's every pitch and yaw with the bravado of the inebriated, and liveried servants transported trays of drinks across the lounge with admirable élan.

The dowager led the way to an unoccupied booth and Jani peered out.

She gasped, wondering for a second how something so beautiful could be dangerous. Tracer fire hosed up from the ground like the luminescent tentacle of some deep-sea creature. For its part, the ship was returning fire: great gouts of flame spouted from the underbelly as missile after missile was launched towards the Russian positions below. She could see now why the light-show was attracting such gasps of wonder; it really did resemble some extravagant fireworks display.

Jani heard a woman's scream as the airship rocked violently.

"But what I don't understand," she said, "is how the Russians can launch an attack from British territory?"

Lady Eddington peered through her lorgnette at Jani. "The Captain was explaining this at dinner," she said. "The Russians make incursions into Afghanistan from time to time and cause as much mayhem as possible. This is a lightning strike, after which they'll skedaddle back over the border like frightened rats. I shouldn't worry if I were you, child."

"I'll try not to," Jani said, gripping the arm of her chair as the airship rolled like a sailing ship caught in a tempest.

Mr Gollalli had crossed the lounge to view the attack. He sat in the neighbouring booth, mopping his face with his bandana and looking petrified as he clutched his valise to his chest. He caught Jani's glance and tried to smile.

Jani returned her attention to the attack as a parabola of Russian artillery shells rose from the foothills below, whipping out and catching the underside of the airship. The resulting explosion rang through the lounge and the ship bucked and listed. In the ringing aftershock of the impact Jani heard cries and screams from startled passengers. The ship had tipped and seemed to be falling with increasing momentum. She looked *up* the carpeted slope of the floor and watched as potted palms, untended trolleys, passengers and bar-staff alike slid inexorably to starboard. Fortunately the *chaises longues* and armchairs were bolted into position; she held on for dear life.

"We're falling!" Mr Gollalli cried. "We're going to crash!"

"Be quiet, my good man!" Lady Eddington snapped. "Show a bit of mettle under fire, why don't you? The dashed Russians have yet to down one of our airships, and this one won't be the first!"

Jani gripped the arms of her chair, peered through the porthole into the tracer-stitched darkness, and wished she shared the dowager's confidence.

Passengers were sobbing all around her. Those individuals not secure in armchairs found themselves piled in the corner between the floor and the wall and were struggling to extricate themselves. The off-duty subalterns, having passed through the stage of regarding the attack as a bit of a lark, now attempted to come to the aid of the distressed passengers. They slid down the incline of the floor but only succeeded in adding themselves to the struggling melee.

Jani flinched as another explosion rang through the vessel. She heard the crunch of rending metal and distant screams. Something flew past the porthole – a section of superstructure bearing the colours of the union flag, which tumbled, end over end, off into the darkness.

She thought of her father, on his deathbed in Delhi, and hoped he would be spared hearing the news of the crash.

The last thing she saw, before the lights went out, was Mr Gollalli clutching his valise to his ample stomach and murmuring frantic prayers – and Lady Eddington sitting upright in her seat and smiling with otherworldly serenity. She just had time to smile back, and then the lounge was pitched into absolute darkness.

Oddly, the darkness was accompanied by a matching silence as the cries and screams ceased momentarily. All Jani could hear was the wind tearing through a breach in the hull, and then a flash of fire ripped through the lounge. Through the porthole she made out the land, lit by the fall of the airship, coming up to meet them with terrifying speed.

She saw bodies, some alive and some obviously not, flying through the air. Then the floor seemed to fold like a closing book, threatening to press the passengers like so many bloody petals. She flinched, drawing up her legs instinctively, as a settee rushed towards her and pinioned her own seat so that she was trapped within like the meat of a clamshell.

Then the airship hit the ground and Jani knew no more.

CHAPTER
TWO

~∞~

Alfie drowns his sorrows –
Fracas in Allahabad – Tomlinson the irredeemably stupid –
"They're all pink where it matters..."

In Delhi, Lieutenant Alfie Littlebody slumped at the bar of the Officers' Club and stared into his G&T.

A fan turned lazily on the ceiling, the blades not so much cooling the air as stirring the humidity. White-liveried servants moved among the officers and their wives and dance band music played on the wireless. Alfie's glass was beaded with condensation, matching the perspiration that stippled his round, overweight face. For perhaps the fiftieth time that evening he mopped his brow and cursed the heat.

The damned thing was that he loved the country – it was just the climate he couldn't stick. He liked the vibrant colours of the place, the amazing diversity, the odd amalgam in the Indian race of pragmatism and spirituality. He liked the incredible variety of the food and the geographical beauty of the subcontinent, especially the hill stations and highlands north of Delhi. He had dreamed as a young man of joining the army and coming to India, and it was all he'd ever hoped it would be: exotic, beautiful and mysterious. His father had expected Alfie to follow him into the Church, but he'd told his father that he wanted to be part of the Raj, to bring a little British fair play to the subcontinent. His father had smiled, in his wisdom, and given his only son his head. Alfie often recalled that tolerant smile, and the look in the old man's eyes that knew the truth – a truth that had taken Alfie two years to work out for himself.

Those two years had seen a gradual erosion of his dreams. The British were not here to ensure fair play but to subjugate the country and its people. It had dawned slowly on Alfie that his fellow officers despised the average Indian. They ruled with a fist of steel in a velvet glove of ostensible decency. He had done his best to ignore the comments, the jibes made by his fellow officers at the expense of the educated Indians allowed into the Club on sufferance. He had turned away when his compatriots had sworn at and sometimes struck servants for perceived misdemeanours. He had never condoned their behaviour, but had done nothing to challenge it either.

And then the incident at Allahabad on Friday...

He drained his G&T, slammed it down on the bar and ordered a fourth.

"There you are, Littlebody!" Tomlinson cried, slapping him on the back. "Still moping?"

Alfie almost collapsed under the blow. "Christ, can't you pack it in for once?"

"I say, I'm sorry, old man. Touched a raw nerve?" Tomlinson hitched himself onto a stool and called out, "Scotch on the rocks, Ali, and make it a bloody big one."

Alfie winced. The old bar-tender's name was Rajiv; he was Hindu.

"Look, moping about it isn't the way, Alfie. Put it behind you. Chalk it up to experience and move on. We've all tasted the funk from time to time. Don't let the fact that you ran away get you down."

Alfie stared at the fatuous oaf. Tomlinson was an Old Etonian, which proved that while money could buy an education it could do nothing to instil intelligence.

"I was not," Alfie said, "moping about the fact that I ran away."

Tomlinson pursed his lips and nodded sagely. "Ah, say no more. I get the picture."

Alfie blinked. "You do?"

"Of course!" Tomlinson took a swig of whisky and smacked his lips. "You've got the jitters because Sergeant Travers *saw* you skedaddle, what? Brigadier Cartwright'll have your balls for breakfast!"

Alfie gripped his drink and knocked back most of it. He felt very drunk and very angry. "Listen, Tomlinson, you were there. You saw what happened. Good God, you were right beside me."

"And I'm man enough to admit that when I saw that the natives were armed, I said a quick bloody prayer!" Tomlinson laughed. "But, you see, I had *confidence*."

"Confidence?"

"Confidence, Alfie," Tomlinson said, leaning forward and prodding Alfie in the chest with his forefinger, "in the efficacy of a little lead."

"No, no..." Alfie began. "You don't get my point. That's not what I meant at all. I mean, look... I didn't run away because I was *frightened* – though I admit that I was..."

It was Tomlinson's turn to blink in confusion. "What? I'm afraid you've lost me, old boy. You were frightened, so you turned tail and ran."

"Yes. No. I mean, I was scared, yes, but I ran because I... because I didn't want to be a part of it."

"Exactly. You thought the mob was about to get bolshy and attack and you thought, 'every man for himself,' and high-tailed it, what?"

Alfie closed his eyes. He wondered if it was his own drunken explanation that was not allowing Tomlinson to get the point, or if his fellow officer was irredeemably stupid.

"No, Tomlinson. Listen here, I ran only after *we* began firing, don't you see? There we were, a platoon of heavily armed infantry up against, what? Fifty Nationalists armed with a few old Enfields, the odd revolver and a few scythes? It was a slaughter. We should never have opened fire. Christ, we should never had confronted the protest in the first place. It was sheer provocation."

"I say, old boy, that's going a bit far, isn't it?" Tomlinson was visibly non-plussed, like a child being told that Father Christmas does not, in fact, exist. "I mean, they were a bunch of bloody armed natives. Nationalists, moreover. They got what was bloody well coming to them."

Alfie murmured, "We killed thirty-five of them, Tomlinson."

The officer slapped Alfie's back again. "Well, in my opinion that's thirty-five less of the troublemakers to worry about in future, hm?"

Alfie sipped his drink. "Did you see the look in their eyes?"

"Of course I did. They hate us, Alfie. Hate what we're doing for them. They'd rather we left so they could take this damned hellhole back to the dark ages."

Alfie focused on Tomlinson's smiling face. "I mean – did you see them *after* we opened fire? The fear on their faces as they were slipping and sliding around in all the blood and trying to get away... My God, it's something I'll never forget."

Tomlinson laid a solicitous hand on Alfie's shoulder. "Look here, Alfie. A word of advice. When Cartwright drags you over the coals, not a dickey bird about all this 'shouldn't have opened fire' business, hm? Better he thinks you're a coward than a wog-lover, what?"

Alfie shook his head and downed his drink. "I don't know..." At nine in the morning he was due to report to Brigadier Cartwright, and he despaired at the thought.

Tomlinson caught sight of Second Lieutenant Kemp across the mess and called out, "I say, Kemp. Over here, if you please. A word in your old shell-like."

Kemp, a jolly roly-poly artillery officer from Devon, approached the bar and draped his arms around Tomlinson and Alfie's shoulders. He was very drunk and used the pair to lodge himself upright.

"Whassat?"

"Young Littlebody here's in a bit of a funk. Thinks the little fracas in Allahabad was bad form. Thinks we shouldn't have shown the natives the old lead."

Kemp looked incredulous. "What? The bastards were asking for it, *begging* for it, f'you ask me! Wanted... wanted to be made martyrs of, and all that."

"You see?" Tomlinson said, nodding to Alfie as if Kemp's dictum was the last word on the subject.

"But," Kemp went on, massaging the supporting shoulders, "thass not why I'm here. Y'see, I'm planning a little trip down Thompson Street tomorrow. Men's night out, get my meaning? And I thought... thought you jolly good chaps might like to come along. How about it?"

Alfie drained his glass and tried to slip out from under Kemp's pressing arm. "Not for me thanks, Kemp."

"What? Don't tell me you don't like the whores, Alfie? Granted, they might be darkies, but... but they're all pink where it matters, y'know?"

"I really must be going. I'll see you tomorrow. Good night Tomlinson, Kemp."

"Hey!" Tomlinson said, "Don't run away like that!" He found the line incredibly funny and repeated it as Alfie hurried from the mess. "*Don't run away...!*"

He left the club, the hubbub of conversation and dance music diminishing behind him as he stepped down from the verandah and wended his way homewards.

A full moon was out and the night was hot. A breeze, freighted with the heady scent of some tropical bloom, wafted down the quiet street. A rickshaw-wallah pulled up alongside him.

"You like ride, sahib? I make very good price, yes?"

"Thanks awfully, but it's a very... a very short walk home."

He considered, as he rounded the corner and approached the bungalow he shared with three other officers, the first and last time he'd accompanied Kemp and the others whoring on Thompson Street. He had found himself in a flimsy cubicle with a beautiful girl barely out of school... if she'd ever been to school in the first place. He'd given her ten rupees and tried to explain, when she attempted to unzip his flies and take him in her mouth, that he really didn't want her to do that.

He reddened now, a year later, when he recalled his discomfort and subsequent embarrassed flight.

He saw the girl's face now, demure and ineffably beautiful in the rose light of the bedside lamp.

He stopped in his tracks when he came upon a military police jeep parked outside the bungalow. A young officer was coming down the steps, tapping his thigh with his swagger stick.

"I say, Lieutenant Littlebody?"

Alfie's stomach turned and he almost discharged the evening's G&Ts at the feet of the policeman. "Yes?"

"Good show. Thought I'd missed you. Word from the Brigadier. He had to dash off on some emergency up north and he'll be gone for a day. He said he'd see you at nine A.M. sharp, the day after tomorrow."

"Thank you," Alfie said. A stay of execution, he thought – though he'd rather, on reflection, have got it out of the way in the morning.

Groaning, Alfie let himself into the bungalow and hurried to bed and the welcome oblivion of sleep.

CHAPTER
THREE

∽

Search for survivors – The strange creature –
The arrival of the Russians –
"We'll kill the old lady..."

THE FIRST THING Jani noticed was the sunlight.

She was still seated in the armchair she had occupied last night, though now imprisoned beneath a settee that had closed over her like a lid. To her right, through the gap between the two clasped pieces of furniture, a piercing arrow of sunlight warmed her skin.

She heard birdsong, a sweet high trill, and thought she had never heard a sound so beautiful.

She was alive. The idea passed through her consciousness in an incredulous litany: *I am alive, I am alive...*

She felt a dull throbbing pain in her right ankle, and another in the small of her back. She wondered if she had passed out with the impact and spent the night unconscious, or if she had somehow slept.

Experimentally she flexed her legs, stretching them as far as the opposite settee would allow. She was about to kick out at the settee above her head, in an attempt to escape from the accidental enclosure that had in all likelihood saved her life, when she heard a voice.

"Help... Please help me..." The plea was frail and heart-rending.

She turned to the gap. The first thing she saw, amid a tumble of wreckage that made no sense to her notions of order and symmetry, was Lady Eddington lying on her back and smiling up at her. The sight of her struck Jani as oddly beautiful, something triumphant about the fact of her survival.

"Jani... are you...?"

Jani struggled through the gap, lowered herself to where the old lady lay amid the debris of chandeliers, shredded carpet, and a... Jani stared at the object for some seconds before realising what it was: a severed foot and ankle, shod in a stout army boot, standing bizarrely upright beside the dowager's disordered crinolines.

Jani cried out, clutched the boot and cast it behind her, sickened by its surprising weight. It was imperative that Lady Eddington was spared from seeing the thing.

She knelt beside the dowager and clutched her hand.

"My leg, my dear, feels as though it has been amputated..." she began, then clenched her jaw against the pain.

Trembling, Jani lifted the old lady's dress.

The thin, ivory-white right leg was broken just below the knee, but Jani was relieved to see that the flesh was unbroken. The lower leg lay at an odd angle, and Jani knew she must set the fracture immediately.

She squeezed Lady Eddington's hand. "It is broken, but not too badly. You'll be fine, Lady Eddington. But I must straighten the leg." She bit her lip, looking around her at the smouldering wreckage scattered over the sloping hillside.

Only now, as she took in the disorganised lines of the ship's tortured architecture, did she make out the bodies. The haphazard impact of the ship had shown no reverence to the passengers: bodies and body parts – severed arms and legs, heads and torsos – occupied places where they had no right to be. She made out the bloodied corpses of men and women crushed beneath girders and impaled high up on the broken skeleton of the ship's triple envelopes.

She had to find the surgery... but where to begin amidst such devastation? She recalled that every deck had first-aid posts, white boxes painted with red crosses. If she could find one of those... She turned in despair, and everywhere she looked her gaze was met with death and destruction.

She saw a brass rod lying amid tussocks of grass, and not far away a blood red cummerbund that no longer contained the girth of its owner. She fetched both and hurried back to Lady Eddington. She ripped the cummerbund into strips and turned to the dowager who was watching her with an odd smile on her aged face.

"This will hurt a little, Lady Eddington, but I must straighten your leg."

She reached out, took hold of the old lady's lower leg – the flesh cold and clammy to the touch – and pulled it forward and around. She felt bone grate and Lady Eddington gave a startled scream.

When she judged that the bone was aligned, she lay the rod beside the fractured tibia and began to wind the shredded cummerbund around both rod and shin. Five minutes later, accompanied by the occasional moan from Lady Eddington, the job was done. She mopped the dowager's brow with the remaining material from the cummerbund and lodged a cushion beneath her head.

"I'm sure the authorities will be searching the area as I speak," Jani said reassuringly. "We'll be rescued in no time. When you are well," she went on, "we must dine out at the Union restaurant on Connaught Circus."

Lady Eddington smiled, her gaze looking beyond Jani. She murmured, "Poor Mr Gollalli... I must admit that I found his company more than a little wearing, but his... his enthusiasm for his vocation was endearing, don't you think?"

Jani stared at her. "Mr Gollalli?"

Lady Eddington lifted a frail hand and pointed.

Mr Gollalli, in a macabre semblance of life, sat propped against a potted palm, beaming across at them. A great rent bisected his chest, parted to reveal ribs and, lower down, a spill of iridescent intestine. The strange thing was that the hideous wound seemed much less realistic than those which he had exhibited to Jani just yesterday evening. In death, his right hand still clutched his precious samples case.

Jani looked away, tears welling in her eyes.

She took in the wreckage that tumbled down the hillside, then looked back at the old lady. "There might be other survivors. I really must go and... perhaps I might be able to do something to help."

Lady Eddington clutched her hand. "You go, child. Do what you must."

"I'll look for food and water, and then I'll be back."

She stood and, wondering where to begin – and wondering, too, what she might be able to do to help the severely injured she might stumble across – she limped through the wreckage.

It was hard to credit that the airship, vast though it had been, could occupy so much space on this lonely, deserted hillside. Everywhere she looked, near and far, she saw the wreckage of the craft. Much of the debris was unrecognisable, broken and twisted, often burning; other parts were intact and all the more poignant for being familiar: she saw a Pullman carriage on its side, and a hundred yards away a great cross-section of cabins like a devastated doll's house, with some of the cabins occupied by dead passengers.

Over the scattered wreckage loomed the skeletal spars of the triple hulls around which the skin of the balloons had been stretched. Denuded now, with blue sky and clouds showing through the reticulations, the mighty de Havilland looked insubstantial, and Jani wondered how the gas-filled envelopes had managed to keep the many decks airborne.

The ship had come down in the saddle of a high valley slung between two lofty, snow-capped peaks. She looked for any sign of villages or townships, but saw none: the Hindu Kush was sparsely populated, and they were high up. She shivered, despite the warmth of the sun, and hoped that the authorities would locate the wreckage by sunset.

She avoided the burning corpses as she moved down the hillside, and the larger fires whose heat was like the blast from a furnace. She looked around her, hoping to come across the halt and the lame but again and again finding only the dead.

She must have walked for two hundred yards before she happened upon another section of the observation lounge, somehow parted from the area she had occupied. She saw that the subalterns had died together, their corpses piled in the angle of the floor and the outer wall; arms and legs poked stiffly from the khaki mass, and she was touched to see that many of the young men had drawn their revolvers, in a gesture of defiance as pathetic as it was futile.

Averting her gaze, she passed on. She stepped over the sprawled corpses of servants and bartenders; she recognised the young Tamil whose turban the subalterns had used as a rugby ball. Nearby she saw a boy and a girl, the six-year-old blonde twins she had spoken to on the first day of the voyage; they had been going to India, accompanied by their nanny, to visit their mama and papa... She felt a strange emotion then, a burning that seemed to rise through her chest to overwhelm her. She felt anger towards the men who had done this, the Russian military who had so casually brought down a ship carrying almost a thousand innocent men, women and children.

She moved on through the debris. Evidently the airship had ploughed into the hillside nose-first and scored a deep furrow for five hundred yards towards the head of the valley, shedding bits of itself as it went. She passed a wide pit where the nose of the gondola must have hit first, with scattered cabins to either side.

It was in one of these cabins that she found a survivor. A young Englishwoman sat hugging herself in the lee of a wall. She appeared catatonic, and hardly registered Jani as she approached. The front of the woman's dress was soaked with blood from a gash to her forehead, but Jani thought the wound minor. She knelt and laid a hand on the woman's arm.

She looked beyond the woman, and saw the reason for her grief: a young man – her husband or beau? –

lay on the slope, decapitated. His head, a yard away, regarded the blue sky with open eyes.

Jani gasped and whispered, "Come with me. You're safe now. We'll find food and water. A rescue party will soon be here."

The woman stared at her, then pushed Jani away with surprising strength. "Leave me alone! Go! Chalo!" she cried in Hindi, dismissing Jani as if she were a servant girl.

"I'll be back with food and water," Jani murmured.

She limped through the wreckage. She passed more corpses, hundreds of them, men and women who had been on the threshold of their own unique futures, with hopes and dreams to lighten their days. She grimaced at the thought, almost word-for-word a line from a scrap of poetry she had written in her last term at school.

At last, lying beside what looked like a crushed wardrobe spilling assorted clothing, she made out a gleaming, white-painted first-aid box, dented into a parallelogram with the impact of the crash. She sorted through its contents, creating a bag from a nearby dress and stowing bandages, sticking plasters, antiseptic salve, ampoules of diamorphine and intravenous needles.

Slinging the makeshift bag over her shoulder, she moved up the slope and veered right, towards where she thought she might find the restaurant and kitchen.

Ahead she saw a Pullman carriage, its stencilled name plate reading: *Lady Antonia Eddington*. The carriage had lost its cambered roof, and every window along its length was shattered. She climbed aboard and found an unbroken bottle of Malvern spring water amid the tumble of possessions. She took a long drink, stoppered the bottle, then climbed back down.

She came to another carriage, this one lying on its side, the grease of its undercarriage catching the light of the sun. She gasped at the corpse of a soldier, his legs and lower torso crushed beneath the coachwork. She recognised Sergeant Stubbs, drew a shocked breath and hurried on.

The chamber housing the Pullman carriages had buckled outwards and split vertically so that it resembled a Chinese lantern – although light cascaded *in* through the rents, not out. Jani moved through the chamber, passing from columns of bright sunlight to areas of dark shadow. There was a strange hush in the air, a cathedral calm, which made the experience of coming upon the next lot of corpses all the more shocking. She stopped when she made out the first of the guards: the private had evidently been thrown across the chamber and had impacted with the bulkhead, his skull shattered so that little now remained of his head. All around him, she saw, were his compatriots, each one dead through impact with the same wall.

She recalled the grey cell they had been guarding, and wondered at the fate of the prisoner.

She looked around the sun-pierced gloaming of the chamber. A hundred yards away was the blocky shape of the cell. It had fetched up at an angle like a rolled die against the far wall. Jani made out a dark rent – in the shape of forked lightning – in the front wall of the cell.

She wondered whether she should hurry from the chamber, attempt to locate the restaurant and kitchen and then return to Lady Eddington – or obey her instinctive curiosity and approach the cell. She wanted to know who the soldiers had been guarding, and whether or not the prisoner had survived the crash.

Certainly, confined in the box, he would have suffered broken bones and concussion at least.

Her step slowed as she came to the split in the leaden grey wall. She drew a breath, paused before the cell, and peered in through the rent.

The cell was empty.

She stepped back. She had expected to see the prisoner within, dead or badly injured.

She turned and looked around her. To her relief she appeared to be alone in the chamber.

Then, just as she had decided to move on and continue her search for provisions, she heard a voice.

"I am here," it said.

Her first thought, once she had recovered her wits and calmed her breathing, was to wonder how he had known of her presence.

The voice had issued from around the far side of the cell. She wondered whether to turn and run, but had second thoughts. She carried with her medical supplies; what if the prisoner were in need of aid?

As she moved with purpose towards the corner of the cell, she thought what an irony it would be if the prisoner turned out to be Russian.

She began quickly, "I have medical supplies with me, should you need them..." and stopped when she made out the prisoner squatting before her.

She had seen many terrible sights that day – a catalogue of horrors it would take her years, if ever, to expunge from her consciousness – but not one was equal to what she set eyes on then.

The man sat on his haunches, his back against the wall. At least, she thought it was a man, and then revised her opinion.

The creature was naked but for the tattered blue trousers of what might have once been a uniform. It was long and thin, its skin deathly white. In fact, had it not spoken, she would have assumed it dead, as it sat with its head tipped back against the wall and its eyes closed.

The head was skull-like, with white skin drawn over the bone – as tight and pale as canvas stretched around a frame. Its features were almost human, in that it had two eyes, a nose and a mouth, but the mouth was almost lipless, the nose flattened and splayed, and the eyes huge.

The eyes opened and the head turned, and Jani received another shock. Its eyes were flat and grey, without any whites at all.

Jani found herself saying, "What are you?"

She remained standing before the creature, clutching the bunched medical supplies to her chest.

The thin mouth elongated in a travesty of a smile. "My name," it said in barely a croak, wincing with pain, "is unimportant."

He shifted his position against the wall, and Jani took fright and backed away. The creature gestured. "Do not be afraid. I wish you no harm." He spoke English as if it were not his first language.

"Why..." she began, "why were you imprisoned?"

"Because... because they feared me? I was in the custody of the Russians. They tortured me." He held up his right hand, which was missing two fingers, the stumps badly amputated and ill-stitched. With the mangled hand he gestured to his bare torso, and Jani made out a herringbone pattern of stitched scars. "I escaped and fled south, only to be found by the British in northern Greece and incarcerated once again."

She gazed at the creature and found herself stating, "You are not human, sir."

"Perspicacious."

"You patronise me."

"I'm sorry. To date I have dealt with human beings driven by base motives. I must remind myself not to judge all you people so cynically."

You people, she thought. "What are you?" she asked again.

"I am an intelligent, sentient being. They call my people the Morn."

"And your own name? Or do you still refuse to tell me?"

"Very well. My name is Jelch."

"And where did you come from?" she asked.

He stared at her, his flat, grey eyes somehow penetrating; she felt, then, as if he were looking deep into her being.

"You wouldn't," he said, "believe me if I told you."

"Again, you patronise me, sir."

"Sir!" the creature laughed again. "You call me 'sir.' You are indeed a singular... human."

She had an inkling, then, of the creature's origins. She had heard stories of wildmen living far from human habitation in Siberia and Tibet... Could this Jelch be one of these?

The creature winced in pain. Jani said, "I have diamorphine. Painkiller. If you will allow me to..."

"Your painkillers," he said, "would have no effect on me. But I thank you for your concern."

Jani watched the creature. "Well," she said at last, "will you tell me where you come from?"

He took a breath and said, "The less you know, the better. I come from far away, so far away that your mind could not encompass the concept."

"So you are not going to tell me?"

"Correct," he said. "You are young. Your mind is... unformed. You have assumptions, cultural, racial, that it would be cruel of me to undermine. Perhaps, in time..." – he stared at her – "perhaps then you might be comfortable with the facts."

She wondered if these words were the gibberings of a madman, someone driven to the edge of sanity by the ministrations of the Russians.

The creature – Jelch – stiffened and bent his head as if listening. He said, "People approach."

Her heart leapt. "A rescue party?"

"Or the Russians responsible for this. I cannot tell."

She stared through a rent in the chamber and looked down the valley. She made out a single track leading through a distant pass. "I see no one," she said.

"They are ten miles distant, at least, and anyway are coming here in an airship."

"Ten miles... How can you tell?"

"I can hear it," he said.

She listened, and heard only the soughing of a warm wind through the chamber and the distant sound of birdsong.

"If they are Russian..." she began, seized by panic.

"Then hide. They will be merciless with survivors."

"Then you, too, must hide."

"Or run. I must not be found, by either the Russians or the British. Time is of the essence."

"Are you fit enough?"

He inclined his head. "I *am* fit enough, and I am touched by your concern."

"But where will you go?"

"Eventually, to Nepal."

He coughed, a racking bark that belied his claim of fitness. He placed a hand before his mouth and retched again and again, and, watching him, Jani was reminded of a dog forcing up a bone that had lodged in its throat.

He wiped his hand on his ragged blue trousers, smearing shiny phlegm and mucus. He rose slowly to his full height and Jani backed away in alarm – for, although she had guessed that he was much taller than her, now he towered over her, over six feet tall and perilously thin, with something in the articulation of his legs that put her in mind, once again, of a dog.

"Look among the wreckage for food and water," he said, "and then secrete yourself."

"I will do that." She hesitated, then said, "Tell me, why did the British incarcerate you? Are you... are you our enemy?"

"I am an enemy of no one," he said. "I came here in peace, to help you, but unfortunately your people chose to disbelieve my motives."

He reached out to her. She thought he was about to take her hand in an oddly formal shake, but as their fingers touched she felt something warm being transferred to her palm.

Then Jelch turned and in an instant was tearing away across the chamber, dodging debris with an alacrity she had hardly expected from one so seemingly feeble.

He gained the outer wall of the chamber, leapt through a vertical rent in the metal, and was lost to sight.

Jani found herself standing alone in a shaft of sunlight, her heart pounding.

Then she recalled the thing Jelch had given her, and opened her hand.

A coin sat on her palm, a small silver coin, no larger than a farthing and etched with a curious spiral of words in no script Jani had ever seen before.

She slipped the gift into the tiny pocket beneath the waistband of her dress, then hurried across the chamber towards a gaping hole where the elevator shaft had once been. She stepped out into dazzling sunlight and picked her way up the hill through a scree of personal possessions, strewn clothing, books, and a teddy bear.

There was no sound of any vehicle approaching, airship or otherwise, and she wondered if Jelch had been mistaken.

Five minutes later she came upon the concertinaed remains of what had been the restaurant. Sandwiched between the engine-room below, and the cabin deck above, the contents of the restaurant and kitchen had spilled across the ground in a great wave of assorted food, glinting silver cutlery and shattered porcelain. Large birds with colourful plumage danced amongst the accidental feast, taking off in fright as she approached.

She found three unbroken bottles of spring water, slabs of cheese still in their greaseproof wrappers, and a dozen loaves of bread strewn across the grass. She gathered up what she was able to carry and struggled up the hillside towards the remains of the observation lounge. She would attend to Lady Eddington first, and then attempt to find other survivors.

Lady Eddington was propped upright against a cushion, her head tipped back; she looked for all the world as if she were taking the sun on the Brighton seafront. Her right leg was terribly swollen.

"There you are, girl! I was beginning to wonder if you'd ever return."

Jani placed her finds on the grass. "I found one other survivor, and..."

"Yes?"

And a creature that I thought wasn't human...

"What a marvel you are, child, and you've found food! My word, but I am famished."

Jani passed the dowager a loaf of bread and a slab of cheese. "I'm sorry, I forgot knives, forks and plates." She found herself laughing at her apology.

"Do you hear me complaining, Janisha? This is a feast indeed."

While Lady Eddington broke off a heel of bread and nibbled at the cheddar, Jani unpacked the medical provisions. She found the diamorphine and a hypodermic and glanced at the old lady.

"This might hurt a little," she said.

"Not as much, my dear, as the gyp my leg is giving me at the moment. You could say that I fell on my feet when I made your acquaintance."

Jani smiled as she drew the diamorphine into the chamber of the hypodermic and administered a small dose – 10 milligrams, she thought, would be adequate – to her patient. Lady Eddington winced, then smiled her thanks.

Jani was eating bread and cheese – only then realising how hungry she was – when she heard the sound.

She stopped eating and listened. The regular thumping thrum of an engine sounded faintly in the distance. The creature had been right; someone *was* approaching.

"My word," Lady Eddington said, "I do believe I feel a little better already. Do you know, I can hardly feel my leg. What is it, child?"

"I can hear an airship."

Lady Eddington beamed. "Succour at last, and not a second too soon!"

Jani kept her reservations to herself and stared down the valley. She recalled what Jelch had said about the Russians being 'merciless with survivors...'

She made out a tiny dot in the distance and wondered at the creature's sense of hearing. He had detected the approach of the airship a good fifteen minutes ago. Oh, please, let it be the British...

The dot grew larger, taking on the shape of a twin-propped airship. The craft came in low, nose down, and as it banked she made out the hammer-and-sickle sigil on its flank. Her stomach flipped.

Lady Eddington was peering hopelessly through her lorgnette. She saw Jani's expression and said, "What's wrong, child?"

"I am afraid it isn't a British craft, Lady Eddington. It's Russian."

"Blast their eyes. And what might they want with us?"

"I dread to think," she murmured.

She looked about her. There were numerous nooks and crannies where she might conceal herself, though moving Lady Eddington, with a broken leg, would prove difficult.

The rhythmic thumping of the airship's rotor blades became deafening. She watched it land half a mile away down the hillside. At least, she thought, they would have time to hide themselves among the debris.

"I've heard bad things about the Russians' sense of fair-play, girl, but I assume we can presume upon their better natures to lend us a helping hand."

"With respect, Lady Eddington," Jani said, "I think that might be a mistake."

A minute later she heard the first shot. It rang out in the silence and Jani felt the sickening, cold weight of dread in her stomach.

She recalled the woman she had found further down the hillside.

The shot was followed, shortly, by further sharp reports.

She was about to tell Lady Eddington that she would attempt to carry her into the cover of a nearby engine cowling – and hope that the Russians would not investigate too scrupulously – when she saw movement amid the wreckage further down the slope.

Three soldiers, in drab green uniforms and fur-lined hats, were moving methodically through the wreckage. She judged they were a hundred yards away and heading towards where she and Lady Eddington were cowering. Her gaze dropped to the seated form of Mr Gollalli, his limbs stiffened and ridiculous now with rigor mortis.

She whispered urgently to Lady Eddington, "Be very still, and forgive me for what I'm about to do. There is a method in my madness, as my father is fond of saying."

Before the dowager could question her further, Jani leaned forward, took a handful of the old lady's dress and ripped it, exposing a sunken expanse of ancient stomach.

"Have you taken leave...?" the dowager began.

"Shh!" Jani hissed.

Dropping to her belly and out of sight of the approaching Russians, she scrabbled across the tussocky ground and grabbed Mr Gollalli's samples ledger. Opening it at random, she tore out a section of transparencies and scrambled back to the old lady.

The Russians had stopped to light cigarettes. Seconds ago, she thought, they had been killing innocents – and now they were enjoying a leisurely smoke.

She flipped through the transparencies, selected a suitably gory-looking wound, pulled it free and draped it across Lady Eddington's exposed stomach.

"Now lie still and when they approach, hold your breath!"

"Are you sure...?" Lady Eddington began.

Jani examined her handiwork. The wound appeared fresh and fatal; she only hoped that the Russian soldiers would give it no more than a cursory glance.

The dowager clutched her hand suddenly and squeezed. "I'm frightened, Jani!"

"If it's any consolation, Lady Eddington, so am I. Now don't move a muscle!"

She slipped the facsimile of a long gash from the transparencies, concealed the remainder beneath her skirts, and ripped at the chest of her bodice. Peering down, her heart thumping, she spread the wound across her throat and the swelling of her breast, then lay back on the ground and flung out her arms.

She closed her eyes and waited, a sick feeling in her stomach.

Only then, as she mimicked death, did the throbbing pain in her ankle and back return.

She heard a Russian voice – what an ugly language it was! – and the sound of footsteps crunching through the debris. The soldiers were chatting casually among themselves, and Jani would have loved to know what they were talking about. Were they homesick for a bleak Moscow, or missing their sweethearts, or crowing at the British deaths their actions had brought about?

The footsteps came closer. She held her breath, drawing in her stomach and hoping the thickness of her dress might conceal any inadvertent movement. She thought then that an eagle-eyed soldier might notice the ticking pulse at her throat – but there was little she could do about that now.

She only hoped that Lady Eddington would play her part and keep still.

The Russians' conversation seemed only yards away. She could smell the reek of cheap cigarettes, and then a waft of body odour. A Russian soldier laughed and the sunlight – showing venous red through her closed eyelids – was blotted out as he stepped between her and the midday sun.

The shadow remained, and Jani wondered if the Russian was looking down on her, examining her wound, wondering why it appeared *not quite right...* Or was he standing with his back to her, examining the 'corpse' of the dowager?

She longed to open her eyes, quell her curiosity, but knew that to do so might spell her death.

She heard another round of gunshots, a long way off, and it was all she could do to prevent herself from giving an involuntary start.

At long last the shadow moved away from her, and the red light resumed.

She heard the scraping of metal and wondered what the soldiers were doing now. She heard the sound of conversation, not far off. The odour of tobacco wafted her way again. Unable to stop herself, she fluttered open her right eye minimally.

The soldiers were ten yards away; they had righted a *chaise longue* and an armchair and were sitting down to finish their cigarettes.

She could not help herself; unbidden, a tear escaped her right eye and slid down her cheek.

Whether it was the tear that betrayed her, or Lady Eddington's sudden, small indrawn breath, she would never know.

She heard a Russian exclamation, and hurried footsteps, and then someone kicked her in the ribs and she cried out in pain and opened her eyes. Lady Eddington screamed as another soldier assaulted her; a third, she saw, was kicking at the corpse of Mr Gollalli in an attempt to discern if the dead film-maker were part of the duplicity.

Terrified, Jani scrambled over to the old lady and they held each other as the Russian soldiers bent down, picked something from the ground, and passed it around with quizzical comments: one of Mr Gollalli's fake wounds.

Then the trio faced Jani and the dowager, and their grins were almost identical: venal and libidinous, and accompanied by a look in their eyes that Jani would never forget.

They whispered to each other, staring at her exposed chest, and Jani was too petrified to move a hand and cover herself.

"Be brave, child," Lady Eddington murmured, then cleared her throat and addressed the soldiers.

"I doubt whether you speak English, so I am reduced to employing your mother tongue. H'hem..." She stared at the soldiers and spoke a short sentence in Russian.

In an aside to Jani, she said, "I've asked to speak to their commanding officer."

The tallest of the soldiers grinned, then laughed uproariously and said something to his comrades. The trio laughed with him.

He knelt so that he was level with Lady Eddington and said deliberately, "I speak a little English. Our orders, to kill all who survive the crash. But my commanding officer... he say nothing about... how you say... having a little fun?" He turned to his comrades and smiled. "But first of all," said the soldier, "we kill the old lady."

He stood, drew a revolver – prolonging the torture by checking that the chamber was fully loaded – then stood back and raised the weapon.

Jani wept, too frightened to move a muscle.

Lady Eddington, fixing the soldier with her steely gaze, recited, "The Lord is my shepherd..."

Jani saw the soldier's trigger finger tighten. She wept and closed her eyes.

The expected detonation never came. She heard a grunt, and when she opened her eyes she saw the soldier slumped on the ground, his head twisted at a strange and unlikely angle. There was a blur of motion and the second soldier screamed as something attacked him, twisted his neck with a snap and discarded him like a rag doll.

The third soldier backed off, terror in his eyes, as Jelch advanced. The soldier fumbled with his weapon, raised it and tried to find the trigger. He was too slow. Jelch yanked his rifle from his grip, reversed it and, as the Russian stared in horror, the creature stepped forward and drove the weapon through his sternum with a terrible crunch of breaking bone.

A silence sealed itself over the suddenly motionless tableau, broken after a second by the beautiful singing of a song bird.

Jelch turned and stared at Jani, its deathly white, flattened face expressionless. Then it took off at speed and was soon lost to sight amidst the wreckage of the airship.

Jani felt a hot flush spread from her chest and rise into her head. Her ankle throbbed as if someone was prodding it with a red hot poker, and the pain in the small of her back surged.

Lady Eddington, eyes shut tight, was still reciting the Psalm.

Jani wanted to tell the dowager that her prayers had been answered, but she felt a sudden and overwhelming nausea.

Clutching Lady Eddington's hand, she passed out.

CHAPTER FOUR

Das addresses his followers –
The perfidy of the British – The age of Kali –
"Obey my commands..."

DURGA DAS SAT in the shade of the banyan tree, in a square on the outskirts of Delhi, and addressed his followers.

It was late afternoon on a punishingly hot summer's day and even the dogs had not yet ventured from the shadows. The only sounds were the distant hum of the city, the occasional thrum of an airship as it passed overhead, and the mellifluous drone of Das's voice as he stressed to the crowd the iniquitous nature of British rule in India.

He was a huge man swaddled in the tangerine robes of a high priest, his belly hammocked in his lap. A garland of marigolds hung around his neck, lost in the cataract of his grey beard. On his broad forehead was painted a single word in Hindi, *Kali*... For Durga Das was a follower of Kali, the goddess of time and change and the consort of Shiva.

For two hours he had worked the crowd into a fervour of indignation, and then rage, as he outlined the crimes committed by the British. "They came to our great land," he said in Hindi, "and posed as traders, beneficent people with only the buying of spices in mind. They persuaded our forefathers with sweet words – but is it not written that the vicious, despite their honeyed words, have poison in their hearts? And very soon they showed their true colours; when their evil agents had gained our trust, worked their wiles on our gullible leaders, then little by little they exerted their considerable powers, dividing and conquering, setting maharajah against maharajah, nawab against nawab; and then they sent in their soldiers – for our protection, they claimed – and the rot had set in. For it is written that the cruel are feared even by the wise. From then on, the story has been one of relentless conquest, rape and pillage, as the British took what is rightfully ours and imposed their decadent ways on our people…"

They were a simple crowd, composed mainly of stall-holders, street-hawkers and the unemployed; he could get away with half-truths, generalisations, and the occasional quote from holy texts. If challenged, he would say that he would use any weapon in his armoury against the British oppressors, even lies; if lies were the means to a desired end, then so be it. What mattered was that he instil in the hearts of the people the basic truth, that India belonged to the Indians and the British were not wanted here.

"Down the decades," he went on, "they have shown their hatred of our people by massacring innocent men, women and children. They are no better than the Russians and the Chinese whom they constantly rail against! Consider, if you doubt my word, the most recent atrocity committed by British soldiers in the city of Allahabad. There our brothers, the Nationalists, staged a peaceful demonstration – and what did the British do?"

Several people, planted and paid for by his acolytes, shouted out, "They shot dead fifty of our people!"

"The dirty British killed us like dogs!"

"They began firing upon innocent protestors who had fired not one shot! One hour later, over fifty men, women and children lay dead in the square!"

Durga Das raised his hands. "All," he went on, calming the tide of outrage spreading through the crowd, "to put down our fellow Nationalists, to quell the *peaceful* voice of dissent – to keep their powerful stranglehold on the country they stole from us!"

He allowed the protests to swell again, then raised his hands – relishing his power as he played the gathering like an expert conductor. "But what is it that they really want from us?" he asked, eyeing the front row of the gathering. Eager eyes returned his stare, hanging on his every word. He saw individuals shake their heads, their lips moving silently as they asked him what it was the British really wanted.

"I will tell you, my children. The British do not want to rule over us because they take from our great country spices and tea, coffee and all manner of exotic foodstuffs they are unable to grow in their own frost-bound homeland – though they gladly steal such produce from us by the by. No, the true reason they subjugate our great nation is to get their greedy hands on what they call Annapurnite."

A scandalised murmur passed through the seated crowd.

Das raised his arms. Silence fell. He went on, "But I can tell you, my friends, that there is *no such thing* as Annapurnite!"

A collective indrawn breath raced through the crowd like wildfire, followed by a hubbub of frenzied comment. Durga Das called for order and said, "Be patient, my friends, and I will explain... I come from a long and venerable line of Holy Priests – my father was a Priest, and his father before him, and his father too, all the way back, over five hundred years – and having its source, like the holy Ganges itself, in the foothills of the Himalayas, from where my family hailed. Now fifty years ago, so the British claim, an English prospector discovered in the foothills an ore of such tremendous power that from it could be derived the means to create a fuel with which to drive all manner of technology. But I will tell you this..." He paused, his commanding gaze sweeping over the gathering, ensuring their obedient silence before he went on triumphantly, "I tell you this – the British were lying!"

When the outcry had abated, Das continued. "There was no such prospector! There was no such ore! There is no such thing as Annapurnite! It is yet another lie the British use in their armoury of treachery to subjugate our great nation!"

A stooge called out, "But how do you know this?"

Das silenced him with a stare. "I know this because my great-grandfather was a holy man in the village of Lokhara in the year of 1875. I know because my grandfather told my father, who passed down the story to me... There was no British prospector scrabbling greedily in the foothills of the holy mountains. In 1875, my friends, the goddess Kali came to Earth and conferred upon my great-grandfather the wisdom of the gods and bestowed upon him an amulet of such power that only the holiest of the most holy of men might be blessed with its safe-keeping. However, the perfidious British soon learned of Kali's coming, and her great gift, and wrested it from the possession of my great-grandfather. From it they extracted the means to enrich their nation, and power their evil ways – and concealed it beneath the lie of Annapurnite!"

He smiled to himself as the crowd digested this, and outraged comment passed back and forth. Of all the lies he had told today, oddly enough, this was the one that most nearly conformed to the truth. The truth, if he told it, would not be believed – it was beyond the grasp of these simple people; and if the British got wind that he knew the truth, then he had no doubt that they would arrange for his swift despatch. The crowd would have to make do with metaphors, which, after all, had always been the way that holy men and great seers had made the unbelievable believable.

He stood and addressed them. "We live in the Age of Kali, my friends, my people, my brothers and sisters. We live in the Age when Kali will again set foot upon the hallowed soil of our great nation and help us drive from our land the despicable foreigners who rule us with such disdain. Kali will rain destruction upon those so deserving, but from that destruction I tell you that renewal will come to pass."

Someone shouted, "But what can we do about this evil, baba-ji?"

Durga Das smiled beatifically. "We bide our time, we defy the British, but peacefully. We give them no reason to kill even more of us. To the peaceful and the patient comes the just reward. We it is who will reap the benefits when Kali once again walks the Earth."

A great cheering roar went up, started and stoked by his stooges, and Durga Das turned, sweeping his robes about his considerable bulk, and was led by his minions down a street to a waiting car.

Minutes later he was in the flat, arid countryside north of Delhi and approaching the oasis of his ashram, surrounded by tall poplars and fed by a small stream. As the car swept into the lawned grounds, where sprinklers cast diadem fountains across emerald grass, Durga Das grunted to his driver, "My dak, and I want no interruption. At six bring a meal to me, ah-cha."

"Very good, baba-ji."

The car crawled around the main building, where his disciples queued for their evening meal, and along a track towards a small, whitewashed building set amid long grass and shaded by plane trees. This was his retreat, where he studied, meditated, took his meals alone, and, once a week, commenced his devotions to his goddess so that he might be blessed with her manifestation.

He eased his girth from the car and dismissed the driver with a wave, and as the car pulled away he waddled up the path and unlocked the door. He lit a lamp to illuminate the cool, darkened interior, and moved to a small room which was his sanctuary, spread with rush matting and decorated with hand-painted scenes from the Upanishads. Against the far wall was an altar with a figurine of a dancing Kali.

Grunting, Das lowered himself to the floor, bowed his head and murmured blessings. He lit three incense sticks and inhaled their perfumed fragrance. He felt the tightness of anticipation in his chest, the weight of expectation. He felt light-headed. Soon would come the time he had awaited for so long. Various auspices had convinced him that Kali would manifest: the moon was full – and his father had told him that Kali had last showed herself on the night of a full moon – and just that afternoon he had witnessed two holy cows kneel before a clay statue of Kali in the Delhi square.

Cross-legged, he pulled up the material of his robe, exposing a slab of thigh and his bulging belly. He kept a folded square of silk on a cord about his groin, and he pulled it from the sweaty fold between his belly and upper leg, rearranged the robe over his knees, and carefully – murmuring prayers all the while – unfolded the moist silk.

The coin sat on the material, glinting silver in the lamplight. He stared at it, open-mouthed – as ever, in its presence, reduced to a state of awe. The coin had been passed down through his family, from holy man to holy man, since the gods had bequeathed it to his great-grandfather almost fifty years ago.

He picked up the disc with trembling fingers, raised it to his eyes and stared at the words spiralling from the coin's edge towards its centre. The words meant nothing to him, but thirty years ago his father had pronounced the sounds and told him, "Recite this mantra when the moon is as full as a pregnant belly, and, when the time is auspicious, then Kali will come forth..."

Durga Das closed his eyes and, from memory, recited, "*Anghra dah tanthara, yangra bahl, somithra tal zhell...*"

For thirty years, on the occasion of every full moon, Das had sequestered himself and chanted the holy words, praying that one day his devotion would reap dividends.

His father had told him, "Kali came to Earth and bestowed upon my grandfather the gift of the coin, and explained its significance. It has been in our family ever since. The coin is a *tithra-kuñjī*, a holy amulet that allows access between Heaven and Earth, and when the time is right, Kali will step forth."

Das came to the end of the mantra, repeated it, then intoned the words a third time, still with his eyes shut tight. He felt a lightness of being, and something like a charge of electricity within the room.

He felt a source of heat before him, at the altar, and when he came to the end of the mantra for the third time he opened his eyes... and gasped. He wept in wonder and steepled his hands before his face in prayer.

A shimmering oval hung in the air a yard from his face, and within the oval, framed as if in a mirror, was the countenance he had dreamed of every day of his life and to which he had devoted his every thought.

The face was hazy – almost pulsing and fading from vision, then becoming stronger as it stared out at him.

He mouthed the words, "Oh, Kali..."

The face was blue, and he strained his eyes to make out the features. His heart beat fast and he willed himself to calmness. He saw a long face, a wide, inhuman mouth, and great slanting eyes – but it was the words that brought forth an amazed cry from his throat. The goddess leaned forward and spoke in Hindi...

"You will bide my words, my servant, and obey my commands. The time of change is upon us. The portal between the worlds will open anon. You will be called upon to leave your city and head east, into another country. You seek the second tithra-kuñjī, and after that the third. You will be visited by someone with news concerning the second coin, and in your wisdom you must act upon it." The goddess waited, staring out at him, and Durga Das could only weep at the import of the words as Kali continued, "The success of my coming to your world is entirely dependent upon the success of *your* actions over the course of the next few days. Do you understand?"

Das nodded, then found his voice and murmured that he understood, and the vision of Kali hanging before him gradually faded from sight, leaving only the fug of burning incense in the air.

Durga Das pitched forward in a dead faint.

CHAPTER
FIVE

∽

Aboard the Peshawar-Madras Mail –
An interview with the Brigadier – Home at last –
"The answer to her prayers..."

THE TRAIN RACED south.

From the foothills of the Kush, the Peshawar-Madras Mail tore through the northern plains like a scintillating silver lance. The pride of the Raj, it could complete the fifteen hundred mile journey in a little over twenty hours, powered by a great Annapurnite engine which hauled twenty passenger carriages and as many cargo containers. In terms of cutting-edge technology, it was second only to the famous London-Nairobi Bullet which, crossing the bridges at Dover and Gibraltar, made the journey to Kenya in just over two days. The Peshawar-Madras Mail, however, unlike its European counterpart, was equipped with armoured gun-carriages fore and aft, as defence against attack from Russian terrorists in the badlands of the border with Afghanistan.

The journey, on this blisteringly hot summer's day in early July 1925, had passed without mishap, though the crack platoon of Gloucestershire Rifles was ever vigilant.

Pausing only for an hour to deposit and collect passengers at Karachi, the Mail began the central leg of its journey across the parched wastes of the Gujarati desert to the capital city of Delhi. The fourth carriage along from the hulking engine, bracketed by the buffet car and a first class compartment, was the hospital carriage, its cambered roof marked with a red cross.

Jani felt the comforting thrum of the engine and the cooling waft of the overhead fan as she lay in bed. Through the window she had a magnificent view of the rolling desert; to her right was a sliding door which gave onto a passage along which nurses in bright white uniforms bustled back and forth.

She recalled the crash of the airship and the chaotic aftermath, her meeting with the creature called Jelch and how it had saved her life.

She sat up. A passing nurse saw her and entered the room, smiling. The nurse wore a starched white pinafore dress marked with a red cross and a strange paper hat like an elaborate example of origami.

"So you're awake at last, my dear. And you surviving that terrible bump, a little dot like you. Those Russians have a lot to answer for, and no mistake."

"They have indeed."

The nurse took her temperature and pronounced herself satisfied. "And how are you feeling? You have a bruised back and a swollen ankle."

"My back is fine, thank you," Jani answered. "My ankle..." She turned her foot under the sheets. "Only a little sore. Where am I?"

"You're aboard the Peshawar-Madras Mail, my dear, and I'd guess we're just a couple of hours from Delhi."

My father, she thought. "What date is it? How long have I been unconscious?"

"It's the 5th, my sweet. You were brought aboard just last night. Oh, you were delirious, I can tell you. But you don't remember?"

"Not a thing. Delirious?"

"Raving and ranting about monsters and such, fair set my blood a-curdle. But after what you went through, I wasn't a bit surprised. I gave you something to put you to sleep for a while. You must be hungry."

"Ravenous. What time is it?"

"Almost twelve. I'll go and fetch you some soup. Mulligatawny it is today, with freshly baked white bread."

The nurse hurried out and Jani gazed through the window at the passing land. The desert was featureless, and the bright blue sky almost so, except for the cigar-shape of a small airship, its envelope marked with a bold union flag.

The nurse returned bearing a tray, and Jani struggled upright. The soup smelled wonderful. As the nurse was about to leave, she asked, "And my friend, Lady Eddington?"

The nurse smiled. "Oh, her Ladyship gave me an earful on the way to Karachi. My word! Brave soul, but she put me in my place and no mistake, demanding to see a commanding officer so that she could arrange for her carriage to be taken down to Delhi and repaired." The nurse laughed. "She was transferred to the hospital at Karachi to have her leg set."

Jani smiled. "I'm pleased to hear that."

"And she was full of stories about your good self, my sweet. Sang your praises and called you a real heroine!

Oh, before I go... I was told to ask if you were up to being interviewed."

Jani halted, her spoon part way to her mouth. "Interviewed?"

"A certain Brigadier Cartwright is boarding at the next station. He wishes to talk to you about your ordeal." She consulted the watch pinned to her bib. "We're due into Chandigarh in a little over one hour."

"I'd like to get dressed first, if I may?"

"Of course. We had your clothes washed last night, though your dress is a little the worse for wear."

In due course the nurse left. Jani spooned her soup and devoured the crusty roll, and it was the finest meal she'd tasted in a long time.

She could guess what this Brigadier Cartwright might wish to question her about, and she wondered, as she ate, how she might respond to his probing.

The nurse returned with her clothing and Jani finished her lunch and dressed. She was surprised to find that she could stand and walk on her injured ankle with hardly a limp. She looked at her reflection in the wall mirror. She had no recollection of hitting her head, but her brow sported a minor gash, evidently not deep enough to warrant a dressing, and her right cheek was bruised. How odd, she thought, that she had felt hardly a thing in the aftermath of the crash.

One hour later she settled herself on a small wicker chair beside the bed as the train pulled into Chandigarh station. This was her first sight of urban India in over five years, and the busy platform filled her with a satisfying sense of homecoming. Passengers hurried back and forth and food vendors called out their wares, "Chai, chai!" and, "Mooli!" She saw a snake charmer surrounded by a posse of fascinated street urchins, and a legless, ash-covered holy man propelling himself along the platform on a homemade cart. Above the ornate Victorian architecture of the station was the bulbous envelope of a British Army airship, a fan of guy-ropes securing it to a docking rig.

Ten minutes after arriving, the train pulled out of the station and was soon racing at speed through brilliant green rice paddies dotted with bent workers and plodding oxen.

Her nurse appeared in the doorway, smiled at her and stepped aside. "Miss Chatterjee, Brigadier Cartwright."

"I'm delighted to meet you, Miss Chatterjee," the brigadier said as he side-stepped into the compartment and removed his peaked cap.

Jani shook his hand. "I'm pleased to make your acquaintance, Brigadier."

He was a tall, willowy gentleman in his sixties, Jani estimated, who with his long, scholarly face looked more like a retired Oxford don than an officer in the British Army. He looked around, found a wicker chair, and sat facing Jani.

"What a terrible business; the attack, etcetera. By all accounts you acquitted yourself with flying colours, my dear. But before we go into all that, I have some news." He smiled at her and went on, "Your father's out of the old sick-bed – up and about, don't you know – and looking forward to seeing you."

Jani's heart leapt. "He is? But, oh... but that's wonderful! The last I heard..."

Cartwright raised a hand. "I know your father well – we liaise a couple of times a year. Security and all that, y'know. I must admit that the last time we met I didn't hold out much hope. Death's door. Thin as a rake, poor blighter. That was a month ago. But his secretary told me that he's rallied, put on weight. Capital news, hm?"

"I don't know what to say. I must admit that I was preparing myself for the worst."

She imagined entering the study of her father's house in New Delhi and flinging herself into his arms, and it was all she could do to hold back tears of joy.

She considered Sebastian and her friends back in London, and asked the brigadier if there was some way they might be contacted and told that she had survived the attack.

The brigadier gestured. "All in hand, my dear. Your father had his secretary cable the Consetts just as soon as he heard you were alive. No need to bother yourself on that score."

Jani thanked him, and made a mental note to contact Sebastian when she reached Delhi.

"Now, the attack..." Cartwright said diffidently, as if not really wanting to broach the matter. "Terrible business. But what do you expect from the Russians, hm? Barbarians. Attacking a ship full of men, women and children like that. Makes one's blood boil."

"Were there many survivors? Apart from Lady Eddington and myself, that is?"

"Three, after the Russians had had their way. A couple of businessmen and a serving girl – hid themselves away in the wreckage when the Ruskies showed up. They'll pull through, thanks be, so I'm told."

"Just three..." she murmured.

"Now I know this can't be pleasant to think back on, Miss Chatterjee. Raking over old coals, never good for the equilibrium. Fact remains... this is a dashed odd business all the way round, from beginning to end."

"Odd?"

"Decidedly." He caressed his long jaw, lost in thought. He looked up. "I say, how rude of me. Would you care for a cup of tea while we're chatting?"

"That would be most pleasant, thank you."

The brigadier poked his head into the corridor and called out, "I say, nurse. D'you think you could rustle up a pot of Darjeeling, by any chance?"

In due course, china cup and saucer in hand, Cartwright said, "Where was I? Ah, the attack... Bizarre. Most odd. Y'see... we've had our investigators go over the crash site with the proverbial fine TC. How we reckon it went is like this: the Russians came over the border with an artillery piece, or several, and went at the airship all guns blazing. The engine-room took a direct hit and down she comes. Not many survivors then, twenty or so, we reckon. Anyway, the Ruskies turn up in one of their airships loaded with troops and... well, to put it bluntly, go through the wreckage and account for the survivors. Hellish business. They'll pay, mark my word."

Jani sipped her tea, watching the brigadier. He stared into his cup, biting his lip as he marshalled his thoughts. "Now... I know this can't be easy, reliving the event. But I'd like to ask you what you recall of the attack – or rather the aftermath. It's what happened on the ground that we're really interested in, y'see."

Jani finished her tea and set aside the cup. "Well, I must have passed out when we came down," she began. "The first thing I recall is waking up in the morning..."

She recounted finding Lady Eddington and helping her, then setting off in search of medical supplies, food and water, and other survivors.

"And what did you find, Miss Chatterjee?"

"I came upon just one survivor, and located a few medical supplies, food and water. Then I returned to Lady Eddington and did my best to splint her broken leg." She was not wholly sure why she had omitted her discovery of the prisoner.

The prisoner... For the first time she recalled the coin that Jelch had given her. Under Cartwright's scrutiny she felt unable to move her hand to the pocket beneath her dress's waistband.

"And can you recall what happened then," the brigadier asked, "if it's not too painful?"

"I heard gunshots, and then I saw three soldiers approaching. I knew that I had little hope of concealing myself and Lady Eddington... and then I saw Mr Gollalli."

She told the brigadier about the film-maker and his singular ledger of faux wounds. "It was our only hope, you see. I told Lady Eddington to play dead and applied a wound to her, and then did the same to myself."

"Extraordinary! Quite remarkable... And it fooled the blighters, hm?"

Jani hesitated. "Well, for a minute or so, yes. But one of them must have noticed something, and... and then..."

"In your own time, my dear. No need to rush these things."

"And then they threatened us, and a soldier drew a revolver and was about to shoot Lady Eddington. I closed my eyes, expecting to hear the gunshot at any second."

"Only...?"

"Only... Well, it never came, and when I opened my eyes, some time later, the three Russian soldiers lay dead."

Cartwright was absently stroking his chin and nodding his head. "I see, I see... And – I'm sorry to press the point – but are you sure that you didn't see how the three met their end?"

Jani shrugged and held the brigadier's gaze. "I assumed at the time that... that rescue had arrived and accounted for the soldiers. I must admit that I didn't look too closely. In fact, I think I pretty much passed out again at that point."

"Just so, and there's no shame at all in that, considering your ordeal. Hmm..."

"I'm sorry. I wish I could be of more help."

"Don't fret on that score, Miss Chatterjee." He stared at his fingers as they drummed a tattoo on his thigh. He looked up.

"You see, I'll be quite frank with you... Fact is, something odd happened up there in the Kush. When we turned up a few hours later we found every man-jack of the Russians dead. Some had been shot, others... well, I won't go into detail in polite company. But it wasn't pretty, by all accounts. And I was wondering, as you made your way through the wreckage looking for medical supplies and food and what have you... if you saw anything?"

She stared into his eyes. "Anything?"

"Or rather *anyone* – anyone who might have occasioned the Russian casualties?"

"I'm quite sure I saw no one, Brigadier," she said.

Cartwright nodded. "Of course not. And why should you? Just thought I'd ask, on the off chance, you know?"

Jani smiled.

"Well, I've wasted enough of your time already, Miss Chatterjee. I'll leave you to get some well deserved rest. We should be in Delhi in less than an hour. Please pay my respects to your father when you see him, and thank you so much for your time."

He stood, bowed, and slipped from the carriage.

Jani sat very still on the wicker chair for a time, then slid shut the door to her compartment. She went over what she had said to the brigadier. The worrying thing was that she could not adequately explain, to her own satisfaction, why she had decided not to tell Cartwright about her meeting with the bizarre prisoner, their conversation, and his subsequent actions in saving her and Lady Ellington's skin. It was almost as if she had been willed to silence by some outside force – which was, of course, ridiculous.

She looked through the window panel in the door, glancing up and down the corridor to ensure that she was unobserved. Then she resumed her seat and slipped a finger into the tiny pocket beneath her waistband.

Her breath caught as she moved her finger back and forth.

The tiny coin that Jelch had given her was gone.

But did that mean the authorities had been through her clothing and discovered the coin? Or might there be some simpler explanation to account for the disappearance? Might the coin have been stolen, or lost when her dress was washed?

Jani was still dwelling on this, fifty minutes later, when the train pulled into Delhi station.

*   *   *

HER FATHER'S PERSONAL driver, Mr Rai, met Jani at the station and drove south to the select area where Government officials lived in relative luxury. The streets were wide and very un-Indian: the boulevards and manicured parks reminded Jani of Paris, which she had visited last year with a fellow student.

Mr Rai eased the car down a side-street and turned into the driveway of a sprawling bungalow set amid extensive lawns. Jani felt her throat tighten at the thought of meeting her father.

A houseboy met her at the French windows that opened onto the lawn, a tall gangling youth with a mop of unruly hair and a bright white grin.

Janisha stared at him as he diffidently held open the door. "Anand?" she cried. "Is it really you? No! It cannot be! But yes, it is! Anand Doshi! How you've grown!"

Where was the stunted, frail-limbed houseboy she had last seen five years ago? He was still as thin as a policeman's lathi, yes, and his hair was evidently still as resistant to the tines of a comb, but she could never mistake his winning grin for that of anyone else.

"I am sixteen now," he announced proudly. "And I have a part-time job in the factory of Mr Clockwork!"

Jani passed from the searing afternoon heat into the cool shadows of the dark-timbered lounge, where a tall, ticking grandfather clock sedately calibrated eternity.

"Mr Clockwork?" she asked as Anand trotted alongside her.

"Oh, a master craftsman of the clockwork art!" Anand sang. "But Janisha-ji, you should see the wonders of his workshop! The marvels! You see, I have always been good with my hands – Mr Fix-it, your father calls me – and when... when, that is..."

Jani smiled. "When my father fell ill."

Anand swallowed and nodded. "Ah-cha, when papa-ji fell ill he arranged for me to start an apprenticeship with Mr Clockwork. And Mr Rai, he will become the driver of Mr Cholmondley, the Home Secretary, and all the cleaners and gardeners, too, have jobs to go to." He stopped chattering suddenly, his eyes downcast, and then murmured, "I'm sorry..."

Jani found herself unable to reply, moved that her father, ill and facing the end, had thought of what his death would mean to his faithful household staff.

She moved to her father's desk and picked up his fountain pen, its ivory shaft worn by his thumb and forefinger. "Where is my father now, Anand?"

"He is taking a bath, Janisha-ji, but he will be finished presently. He was told what time you would arrive, and asked me to give you a drink on the verandah."

"That would be lovely. Do you have any of Zeena's homemade lemonade?"

Anand beamed. "She made some especially for you, Janisha-ji."

She moved out onto the verandah overlooking exquisitely manicured lawns on which peacocks strutted.

Her father had saved the tousle-haired Anand, an orphan, from the streets when he was three and Jani five. Until Janisha left for boarding school in England at the age of eight, she and Anand had been like brother and sister, inseparable. They had played with the peevish monkeys on the lawn, despite her father's repeated warnings, and ineptly knocked croquet balls into the head-gardener's prize herbaceous borders.

She leaned back against the cushions of the wicker settee as Anand poured her a tall glass of iced lemonade. He settled himself on the lacquered floorboards at her feet and asked, with downcast eyes, if she would tell him all about her time in England.

He listened to her with wide eyes, marvelling at her stories of Buckingham Palace, the river Thames, and Cambridge.

"Oh, Jani-ji, it is my dream one day to travel the world. First I would like to see my country, all India, north and south, east and west – and then I would like to take an airship to Europe and visit Great Britain!"

"And one day, Anand, you will do that."

He regarded her with his massive chestnut eyes. "Do you really think so? Do you think I might become an engineer or an inventor like Mr Clockwork and earn enough to travel far and wide!"

"If you apply yourself, Anand, study and work hard, then you can do anything."

"And you?"

"Me?" She sipped her lemonade.

"When... when you leave India, and go back to England and complete your studies... what then?"

She held the ice-cold glass and stared across the perfect lawn. "Then... I am not sure what I will do, Anand. A part of me would like to return to India, to work as a doctor among my own people, but..."

"But... you have met someone special in England, yes?"

She looked at the young boy, wondering at his perspicacity – or was he merely voicing his fears?

"There is someone, yes. A young man of twenty." She shrugged. "But I don't know where that might lead."

"Do you love him?"

She sighed. "I think I do, Anand. That is, when I'm with him I feel safe, secure, and when I am not with him I wish to be... So perhaps, yes, I do love him." She sipped her lemonade. "And you? Is there a young girl in Delhi who has won your heart?"

Anand coloured to the roots of his midnight hair. "Well, there is a servant girl at Mr Clockwork's workshop. She is my age and very, very sweet. Her name is Vashi and we have met once for chai on Rabindranath Road. I call her burfi, my nickname for her because she is so sweet."

Jani felt an inner glow, and it was as if she had never been away, much less spent years on the far side of the world.

The double doors onto the verandah opened, and a huge man like a genie appeared on the threshold. He wore baggy white trousers and a vest, in which the globe of his stomach hung like a sack of chapatti flour.

"Mr Vikram," Anand whispered, "your father's new nurse. He does not like me and is always shouting this and that."

Mr Vikram called out now, ordering Anand to make tea for papa-ji and, modulating his tone to address Jani, went on, "Your father will see you now, Miss Chatterjee. He is in his study."

Janisha clutched Anand's hand as he scrambled to his feet. "I will see you again, ah-cha. I will buy you chaat on Connaught Circus, yes?"

Anand beamed and scurried off.

Mr Vikram led Jani through the silent house. He opened the door to the study and stood aside, and Jani stepped through to greet her father.

A small, shrunken old man stood beside a desk in front of the French windows, the cascading sunlight illuminating his frail figure. As she hurried forward, Jani told herself that her father was only in his late fifties, hardly any age, and did not deserve the torture of the disease that was eating away at him little by little.

She came into his arms and they embraced, and he was light, no weight at all, and she found herself sobbing – a strange and welcome relief to be able to unburden all the pent-up emotion she had kept in check for weeks since learning of her father's illness.

"Jani, Janisha-ji! My beloved... You are here, here at last, despite all that fate does to conspire that we might never meet again."

She pulled away, and stared into the watery eyes, the whittled-down face, and saw his love for her shining through his pain at her distress.

He moved to his favourite leather armchair, walking with the aid of a stick, and sat down, wincing with pain. Once, he had dominated the armchair like a king enthroned; now the chair dominated him. He appeared tiny in its embrace, almost like a child in his trim white homespun suit and worn carpet slippers.

She told her father about the flight, and the Russian attack, but felt as though she were avoiding talking about what was really on her mind: his illness and the prognosis. The telegram from his secretary six weeks ago had merely stated that her father was gravely ill, and that she should come home to be with him in his final weeks.

Anand arrived with a tray bearing a silver teapot and two fine china cups. She poured, and added a little milk to her own – her father preferred his Darjeeling black – and thanked Anand as he hurried from the room.

"Is it not ironic, Jani-ji, that the problem that should be taxing my department most of late – the security of the north-western frontier – should be that which almost allowed the Russians to rob me of my daughter? I would take the shame with me to my grave. As it is, with the loss of the airship and so many lives..."

"Papa-ji..." She clutched his thin hand. "There was nothing you could do."

He looked pained, and Jani could not tell whether it was at his illness or the thought of the security breach. "For twenty-five years I have worked to keep my country secure. The job has become more and more difficult. If the enmity of the Russians was not bad enough, now we face the rise of the Chinese. We have enemies on every side." He smiled. "Well, perhaps I exaggerate. I am thankful that to the south of our great country there is only ocean."

Her father had created headlines, twenty-five years ago, by being the first Indian national to be elected to the government cabinet. The appointment of an Indian minister – in the security post, no less – had caused much adverse comment on Fleet Street. Those in power in Delhi, however, knew the worth of the man, his trustworthiness and unswerving loyalty to the Crown.

He caressed her hand. "My days might be short, Jani-ji, but I am content with the knowledge that I am leaving India stronger than it has ever been in all its long and illustrious history. The Russians might make incursions to the north, but these are minor irritations, a gnat biting the hide of a buffalo. And the Chinese might be marching into Tibet – but we can deal with all this."

She sipped her tea and smiled; he was sounding like the politician he was, issuing proclamations that would appear as headlines in the next day's newspapers.

"And you," he asked, "are you still passionate about independence as you were last year?"

She smiled and lowered her gaze from his. When he had visited London last summer she had – tentatively at first – voiced her thoughts that perhaps India would be better off, eventually, as an autonomous, self-governing entity with strong links to Britain, but with self-rule.

He had listened with tolerance, where many a father would have shouted her down or dismissed her. Instead he had replied, "It is a problem I have been wrestling with all my adult life," and they had debated the pros and cons long into the night.

She said now, "But I have been hearing rumours in London, papa-ji."

"Rumours?" He lowered his tea cup and smiled. "But you know what rumour is, my dear – rumour is the smoke from the fire of lies that obscures the truth."

"But they say that there is no smoke without fire."

He laughed. "And what are these rumours?"

She raised her gaze and looked into her father's old, mahogany eyes. "They say that Annapurnite was discovered not by a British prospector in Nepal, but by an Indian. They say that Annapurnite should belong to the Indian nation, not to Britain. By rights," she went on, feeling passion rise within her chest, "it should be India that is ruling three quarters of the globe, not the British; it should be India ruling the waves, not Britain waiving the rules!"

He threw back his thin head and laughed at the cheap wordplay. "You have the turn of phrase of a young politician in the making, Jani-ji, but take my advice and stick to medicine, ah-cha?" He patted her hand, and Jani felt a moment's fury, soon quelled.

"But am I not right? Annapurnite should belong to India."

He pursed his thin lips, contemplating. "Do you know what I think, my dear? I think that Annapurnite, and the power conferred by Annapurnite, is something of a cursed blessing. I acknowledge the many technological benefits brought about by... by its discovery, the advance on many scientific fronts that was the corollary, but I see also the terrible escalation in conflict that it has engendered. We – and I speak here of the British and Indian nations combined – have enemies where before we would not, even though the British have an unhappy knack at fomenting enmity."

"But I say that we should be the true and only possessors of Annapurnite and the power, and wealth, that it confers," she said.

"Do you know, I honestly think that it is right and proper that it should be the British to whom the dubious gift of Annapurnite fell. We would have all the enemies we have now, if we were sole possessors of the gift – but without the support of the British. And imagine the substance in the hands of the Russians or, fate forbid, the bloody Chinese, excuse my English. Imagine the state of the world if these nations were to wield the power now enjoyed by the British! You saw yourself what the Russians did to the survivors of the airship attack."

She stared at him. "You know?"

"Of course I know. I might be ill, my dear, and I might have given up many of my responsibilities, but my secretary keeps me well informed." He patted her hand. "You saw yourself the depravity of the Russians, and believe me, the Chinese are no better."

"But," she said, gesturing helplessly, "what about the massacre at Amritsar – and the quelling of the Nationalist riots last year in Lucknow? The British can be just as barbaric, no?"

He smiled, sadly. "Humans, Jani-ji, have a terrible and innate propensity for barbarity. It is the social systems that a society, a race, puts in place to keep a tight rein on this propensity which allow it to be judged civilised, or not. Amritsar and Lucknow were the responsibility of bad leadership and panic in the ranks – reprehensible, but not a sign of the greater corruption of the system. I would contend that, while the British are not perfect, they are the only race in the world who might harness the power conferred by... by Annapurnite with some measure of humanity."

Her gaze fell to her knotted hands, on which her father's hand rested like carved oak, his old skin worn to smoothness over the years. She murmured, "What you have just said is a terrible indictment of India and its people, papa-ji."

He drew a deep sigh, and Jani interpreted this as impatience. "My dear, believe me, there are those within the political set of our country who, if they were to rise to power, would make the Russian excesses seem like the misdemeanours of children. The Hindu extremists are, you must admit, an element to be reviled."

"I do not deny this, but I would contend that they are a minority greatly outnumbered by more fair-minded Indians, Hindu, Moslem and Buddhist alike."

"I speak here from experience, Jani-ji, when I say that the power wielded is often disproportionate to the numbers of those who wield it. It takes only a small fraction of fanatics to turn a nation. The metaphor of bad apples springs to mind."

Jani smiled to herself. It was often impossible to argue successfully with her father; he was, after all, a wily politician.

He said, "But all this talk of nationalism! Where is the little girl I packed off to boarding school all those years ago?"

"She grew up, papa-ji, became educated, read and experienced and talked to people."

"You have changed much in the last year."

"I..." She hesitated, then went on, "It may sound trite, but I have seen how the other half live."

"Ah, Sebastian."

She found herself blushing. Sebastian's family, the Consetts, owned a vast swathe of Warwickshire, with a great stately home and a host of servants. "I thought I lived a life of privilege here in India, but it was as nothing compared to the Consetts' wealth..." She smiled. "And while Sebastian is sweet, he is also ignorant in the ways of the world."

He laughed. "That is often true of the extremely rich. They are so well-educated they know nothing!"

"Do you know, papa-ji, I thought before I landed in England that poverty only existed in India, in the slums of Bombay, Delhi and Calcutta. It was something of a shock to discover that terrible poverty existed in London, in places like Manchester and Leeds and Glasgow. For all Britain's power and great wealth, those in power do little to alleviate the suffering of the masses."

"The 'masses'... You are sounding like something from Marx and Engels, now."

"Please, father, don't patronise me. I'm not seeking revolution, merely change. Equality. In London I met and spoke with Indian Nationalists, fair and educated people who put forward the case for Indian autonomy. And what they said seemed reasonable to me."

"And what did your aristocratic friend think of this?" her father asked.

She felt a sudden flare of irritation. "I was not in the least bothered by Sebastian's thoughts on the matter, father. My opinions are not shackled to my... to Sebastian's opinions and prejudices."

Her father sighed and squeezed her hand. "Jani-ji, Jani-ji... I am old and wear my experience heavily. There is much honesty, even truth, in what you think and say, but..."

"But they are the thoughts and words of callow, idealistic youth, is that what you are trying to say?"

He looked into her eyes and smiled his wonderfully loving smile. "I am trying to say that the world and its ways are far, far more mysterious, wonderful and terrible, than you might ever imagine, my darling. I would like to tell you everything I know, but..."

"But?"

"But I could not burden someone I love with such knowledge, Jani-ji."

She wanted to protest, but this was not the time to do so.

His eyes strayed to the occasional table beside his huge leather armchair, and the oval photograph in pride of place upon it. The sepia-tinted print showed a beautiful young woman in a long Victorian dress, holding a parasol and posing against a rose-covered bower in some cheap photographer's studio in Bromley.

He said, "You remind me so much of your mother, Jani-ji."

"In temperament? In character?" she asked. She did not look much like the woman who had given birth to her eighteen years ago, though perhaps she had inherited her mother's luxuriant raven hair.

"Yes, and in spirit. Do you know, I think Eleanor loved India even more than I did. She loved my country with the passion of the convert, a passion that blinded her to the many and obvious faults of the subcontinent – and this engendered in her a righteous indignation, even anger, at what she perceived as the faults of the Raj. She was an outspoken firebrand when I met her in Bombay in 1900. She was on a speaking tour of the Empire, spreading the suffragette message far and wide, aside from entertaining audiences with her music..." He laughed. "And then we met and fell in love, and Eleanor transferred her passionate conscience to the betterment of all things Indian."

"I wish I could remember her," Jani murmured.

"Oh, she loved you so much, Jani-ji. You were the answer to her prayers. We had been hoping for so long for a child, and belatedly you came along. And then, just three years later... when she learned that she was dying..." He stopped, his eyes pooled with tears, and Jani reached out and gripped his hand. "She grieved for herself, grieved at not being able to watch you grow to womanhood. She so much wanted to educate you, to see you flourish and prosper... I promised that I would do my best."

"And you *have*, papa-ji!"

"Your mother would be proud of you, just as I am more proud of you than words can express."

They sipped their tea in strained silence, Jani wanting to tell her father how much she loved him but unable to find the words to do so. A minute later the doors at the far end of the lounge swung open and Mr Vikram announced that it was time for Mr Chatterjee's afternoon medication.

Her father squeezed her hand. "I will see you for dinner at seven, my dear. At least," he went on, "I am still blessed with a healthy appetite. And I have ordered, for your homecoming, a veritable feast."

"I'll look forward to that, papa-ji."

"After my medication, I must rest a while, to prepare myself for dinner."

"And I can see you tomorrow?"

"I would like to spend as much time with you as possible. We will have breakfast together, after which I must work until late afternoon, when we will take tea."

She had much more to talk to her father about, not least whether he knew anything of the strange prisoner she had come across in the wreckage of the airship. Surely, as Security Minister, he would be privy to information regarding Jelch.

She watched as Mr Vikram assisted her father from the chair and guided him, slowly, from the room.

Jani left the lounge and made her way through the cool, old house, reacquainting herself with the once familiar furnishings, the oil paintings of the English countryside and the many faded family photographs. Nothing had changed since her childhood; she guessed that nothing had changed much in the house since her mother's death. The house was how Eleanor Markham had left it, a time-capsule reflecting the design and decoration of the Victorian era. Her father had neither the time nor the aesthetic sensibility to institute change, nor the desire to alter what was, after all, his wife's handiwork. The house was a memorial to her existence.

Jani went to her room and turned on the overhead fan. The wooden blades began to turn sluggishly, creating a pleasant cooling downdraught.

She lay on the overstuffed featherbed and looked around the room. The nursery wallpaper, the child's drawings on the wall, the rocking horse and wooden building blocks in the corner, all belonged to the little girl she had been before being whisked away to England and boarding school. She felt less of a connection to this room, oddly enough, than to the rest of the house. It was as if it had belonged to another little girl, not herself.

She drifted off, inhabiting that strange hinterland between wakefulness and true sleep in which dream images seem startlingly vivid and real. She was with her father and they were on the flight deck of an airship, laughing together at their adventure as the ship sped through the cloud cover.

Then these pleasant images were replaced by others, far less pleasant. She was running through the wreckage of an airship crash, following a strange creature she knew was Jelch, and Russian soldiers were chasing her.

She screamed as Jelch fell, his torso riddled with bullets...

CHAPTER SIX

∞

The summons – At her father's bedside –
Mr Chatterjee breathes his last –
"You must find Jani and warn her..."

"JANI! JANI, QUICKLY. You must come!"

She sat upright, rubbing her eyes. "What time is it?" She saw that darkness had descended outside and that the bedside lamp was glowing.

"Almost midnight, Jani. Your father has fallen ill again. They took him to hospital in an ambulance five minutes ago. Mr Rai is waiting in the car. He will take us now, Jani!"

His words had the instant effect of banishing whatever sleep still lingered. She slipped her bare feet into her sandals and stood up. "Midnight? I was due to dine with my father at seven." She had a sudden sense of a terrible injustice done to her. "But why wasn't I summoned?"

Anand rocked his head from side to side. "Your father was not feeling too well at seven, Jani, and when I came for you, you were sleeping soundly. Your father said that you were not to be disturbed."

"Ah-cha. Very well."

They hurried through the silent, darkened house, and Jani had the bleak thought that if her father was not to survive the night, then she would forever regret not dining with him one last time. As they stepped out into the humid night and crossed to the waiting car, she banished the thought. She was being maudlin and ridiculous; her father would rally and pull through and she would enjoy many more fine meals with him.

"Papa-ji felt unwell just before dinner, Jani!" Mr Rai said as he steered the car onto the quiet street and headed north. "He said he would eat nothing. I was a little worried and summoned Vikram, as your father has maintained a healthy appetite of late. Vikram was with papa-ji all evening, when just thirty minutes ago he took a turn for the worse and an ambulance was summoned."

"Do you know exactly what was wrong...?" she began.

"He was all hot and cold and then he was sick, Jani. That is all I know."

From the back seat, Anand said, "He was complaining of bad stomach pains at seven, Jani. But he has had these pains before, and once he was rushed to hospital and was kept in for one day, after which he was allowed home. The same will happen again, Jani, believe me."

"I hope so," she said as she watched the illuminated blur of traffic swing around Connaught Circus like the rides of a carousel.

Ten minutes later they came to the monolithic white block of the Queen Victoria Hospital set in acres of green lawn. Mr Rai left the car and guided Jani and Anand into the building, through a busy reception area and along interminable corridors crowded with shawled figures sitting on chairs or lying on the floor. They stepped from the building and crossed a lawn to a second, smaller building. Jani moved as if still in a dream, her senses muffled, the reality of the situation seemingly distant and relayed to her after a deadening lapse of seconds.

Mr Rai explained, "This is a special place set aside for government officials. Here your father will receive the very finest treatment."

He spoke to a nurse at reception. Jani noticed a few half-familiar faces seated around the reception area: her father's secretary, a couple of old men whom she thought were fellow politicians or government officials and other, younger men she assumed were reporters.

The nurse hurried Jani, Anand and Mr Rai along a corridor to a private room. "I will summon a doctor to talk to you immediately," she said and moved off along the corridor.

Jani entered the room, leaving Anand and Mr Rai seated in the corridor.

Mr Vikram, who looked more like a wrestler than a nurse, sat on a chair beside her father's bed. "If I could be alone with my father for a little while," she murmured.

The nurse, huge and impassive, nodded without speaking, rose and stepped from the room.

Jani took the vacated seat, reached out and gripped her father's thin hand.

Beneath his eyelids, which reminded her of tissue-thin liquorice cigarette paper, his eyes flickered back and forth – and Jani wondered at his dreams. Was he flying in an airship, with Jani by his side, laughing at the adventure they were having together?

She whispered, "I am here, papa-ji. I am with you."

She willed him to open his eyes and speak to her.

She jumped as the door opened and a grey-haired

British doctor hurried in, sat on the neighbouring bed, and glanced at his clipboard.

"I am Janisha Chatterjee," she said.

He introduced himself as Dr Hammond, and went on, "I've been treating your father, Miss Chatterjee. You can be proud of him; he's shown remarkable courage and resilience. His illness would have seen off most people months ago."

Jani didn't know whether to be cheered by this news or alarmed. "What exactly...?" she began, her voice catching.

"Your father presented three months ago with severe stomach pains. I performed an exploratory operation and discovered a massive tumour, unfortunately malignant. Though the procedure to remove the growth was successful, by then it had already spread. There are secondary cancers in your father's liver, lungs, and bones."

Her vision blurred. She made a conscious effort to pull herself together and found herself saying, "But... but just earlier today we were chatting and he seemed well and talked about working tomorrow."

Dr Hammond smiled. "That's your father all over, Miss Chatterjee. He will never admit defeat."

She stared at him. "And now?"

"Your father is very, very ill. I've been expecting him in here for the past month. We've sedated him, eased the pain."

"But?"

He reached out and laid a massive hand on her arm. "I'm afraid you must be very brave, Miss Chatterjee."

A cold weight plummeted from her chest into her stomach. "But he will regain consciousness?"

"Perhaps a little later, when the sedative has worn off. I'll send in his private nurse to be on hand."

Dr Hammond took his leave, and a minute later Vikram entered the room and eased his considerable weight onto the second bed. Jani stood and drew the curtain around her father's bed, not wanting to suffer Vikram's impassive, silent scrutiny.

She resumed her seat and took her father's hand. She could feel his weak pulse beneath her fingers.

A little later she dropped off, then woke suddenly, convinced that only seconds had elapsed but finding, when she consulted her tiny gold wristwatch – a present last year from her father – that two hours had passed. It was the early hours of the morning and the hospital was in silence.

Her father's eyes were open and he was looking at her, and Jani felt a surge of joy.

"Father!" she said quietly, not wanting to be overheard by Vikram.

His words were hardly louder than a breath. "Jani-ji. You're here."

She squeezed his hand, fighting back her tears. "I love you, papa-ji!"

His thin lips twitched into a smile. "And I love you too..." He took a breath and went on, "I'm sorry..."

"Sorry? For what?"

"Earlier... I so much wanted to dine with you. Cook had prepared mutter paneer and aloo palak with special chilli roti."

She pressed his hand to her lips. "When you get out of here, then we will have a feast!"

"I would like..." he whispered, and Jani had to bend close in order to hear. "I would like one last meal with my daughter."

It was as if a hand had reached for her throat and was squeezing. She could not bring herself to speak.

At last she said, "Are you in pain?"

His watery eyes regarded her. "No pain at all. I feel... wonderful. You are so... special to me. So beautiful."

"Oh, papa-ji."

He took several deep breaths and closed his eyes. Jani felt a stab of panic. He could not die now, not now, when she had so much to tell him. Frantically she felt for the pulse in his wrist, found it and whispered, "Papa-ji?"

"Jani, I need to tell you..." The effort seemed to exhaust him. After several seconds he went on, "I need to tell you..."

"Tell me what?"

"About..." His eyes focused on her with greater intensity. He gripped her hand. "About *everything*."

She smiled uneasily, alarmed that perhaps his mind was going the same way as his body. "Everything?"

"Nothing," he said, with renewed vigour, "nothing is as it seems."

She shook her head. "In what way?"

"Annapurnite," he said.

It seemed to be the extent of the sentence. "What about Annapurnite, papa-ji?"

"Annapurnite... What makes us great, what made the Empire what it is today, the greatest power the world has ever seen. We owe it all to Annapurnite – and to the fair play of the British, of course." He fixed her with his watery gaze. "Do you know what it is?"

"Annapurnite? It is a... a very rare precious metal, with remarkable properties. It can be... processed to act as a power source."

"And where do you think it comes from?"

"Why, the foothills of the Himalayas, in Nepal," she said. "It was discovered fifty years ago, and to this day the mining goes on, surrounded by the highest security."

He managed a smile. "The highest security!"

Nepal was a no-go area, the entire country closed off to outsiders, its population relocated over the decades to purpose-built villages and towns in northern India. She tried to imagine the logistical feat of moving over two million people from one country to another.

She frowned. "It does seem a little excessive, doesn't it, merely to protect British interests?"

"Not British interests solely. Our interests, Indian interests, and ultimately the Empire's interests. But no, these measures, and the security that surrounds the foothills to this very day, is not excessive, not in the slightest! Russia would stop at nothing to discover the secret of Annapurnite, and China too!" The speech seemed to exhaust him, and his head fell back to the pillow as he smiled at her.

"And the irony is, my beautiful daughter," he went on in a whisper, "the wonderful irony is that Annapurnite does not exist!"

She stared at him. Had he gone mad? Had the cancer spread from his torso to his brain? She fought the urge to weep. "Does not exist?" she said. "But how can that be?" She gestured hopelessly, the sweep of her hand taking in the length and breadth of the Empire, the super-fast trains, the vast airships, the jaggernath land-wagons, all powered by the miracle of Annapurnite. "But what powers all our machines if Annapurnite does not exist?"

He stared at her for a long time, and she wondered if he was about to admit that he was talking nonsense.

Instead he said, "What powers the wondrous machines of the Empire, the envy of all our enemies, is a process of harnessing the energy inherent in the smallest particle of matter – by annihilating that smallest particle!"

She shook her head, frightened now for her father's sanity. What he said made no sense at all.

He went on, "Annapurnite is simply an umbrella term for all the wonders discovered in the foothills of the Himalayas. Annapurnite is a word used to convince the gullible and to confuse our enemies."

"*All* the wonders?" she echoed. "There is more than one...?"

"Jani-ji, how do you think it is that we keep the Chinese and the Russians at bay along the long length of our borders?"

She was about to quip that, just the other day, the Empire had been unable to stop the Russians from crossing the border into India and striking a fatal blow to the airship. She held her tongue and said, "Tell me."

"We have super-weapons that make us almost invincible," he said.

"Yes, Annapurnite-cannons," she said.

He gave a feeble laugh. "A crude term, devised by politicians for public consumption. No, these weapons are lances of light that melt our enemies and their armaments. And we have more! Devices that render people and things invisible, devices that allow us to read the thoughts of selected subjects, and many, many more..."

Shaking her head, and wondering what to believe, she asked, "So where did all these wonders come from, if not from Annapurnite?"

He licked his cracked lips. She took a glass of water

from the bedside table and raised it to his mouth. He drank gratefully and sank back onto the pillow.

"They come from far, far away, Jani-ji. So far away..."

He seemed to find the concept amusing, and laughed to himself, then closed his eyes and fell into an exhausted sleep.

Jani clutched his hand. "Oh, papa-ji..."

A little later his breathing became ragged and, alarmed, Jani called out for Mr Vikram. Instantly he pulled the curtain aside, took one look at her father and hurried from the room.

Over the course of the next ten minutes Dr Hammond and three nurses came and went from the room, consulted with Mr Vikram, and at last administered an injection to her father's stomach. Dr Hammond placed the oxygen mask over her father's thin lips and in due course his breathing grew easier.

Alone with him in the curtained area, Jani clutched his hand and eventually, despite her best efforts, slipped into a fitful sleep.

When she woke much later she checked her watch and saw that it was almost four o'clock.

Her father's breathing was shallow now, and something told her that he would not live to see the dawn.

She held his hand and quietly sobbed.

"Jani-ji," her father whispered.

"Papa!" She leaned over and kissed his papery cheek, shocked at how cold it was.

"Brigadier Cartwright phoned me yesterday," he murmured.

"Cartwright?" She had trouble recollecting the name, out of context. Then she remembered and her blood ran cold.

"He told me that he had interviewed you."

"That's right."

"And... and he was concerned."

"Concerned?" Jani felt her pulse quicken. "About what?"

"About you. About what happened to you. About what you told him had happened to you. You see, he did not believe you."

Jani swallowed. "He did not believe me about what, exactly?"

"About you not witnessing... what happened to the Russians. He said that three dead Russian soldiers were found very close to you. He said it would have been impossible for you not to have witnessed what fate befell them."

She stroked her father's hand. "Papa-ji, I saw something terrible in the debris of the airship – and I mean apart from all the death and destruction. I saw someone who had been imprisoned and tortured by the Russians."

Her father tried to raise his head from the pillow, his eyes wide as he stared at her. "A pale creature, hardly a man at all?"

"That describes the poor creature I saw," she said. "You know about him?" She shook her head. "But why was he imprisoned aboard the airship?"

He squeezed her hand. "The Morn. We were bringing him from Greece to Delhi, where we would question him."

"But he was imprisoned like an animal!"

"Jani-ji," her father said in barely a whisper, "he was locked up as he was for his own safety, as well as that of the troops transporting him. He was insane when we found him; God knows what the Russians had done to the poor creature. He had to be restrained until we had him here and could sedate him, reassure him of our honourable intentions."

"He told me that he had come here in peace, though no one would believe him." She gripped her father's hand. "But do you know why the creature came here, and from where?"

He regarded her for a long time, his weak gaze steady. "He came here many years ago, accompanied by another of his kind. One fell into the hands of the Russians – the creature you happened upon. The other we discovered in London, in such a mentally parlous state that we could not decipher the truth of what he told us."

"There was a second creature?" she asked. "And where is it now?"

"The poor thing is insane, and kept locked up for its own safety."

She wondered at the relationship between the two – lovers, or family, or mere comrades – separated now by over four thousand miles. "Tell me, papa-ji, why did they come here?"

He licked his lips, and his breathing became laboured again. "The creature in London told us terrible stories, stories that we could not bring ourselves to believe, of vast invading armies bent on taking over the world..." His eyes grew large. "But Jani-ji, these were the rantings of an insane creature, who could not be held accountable for his words." He stopped and gripped her hand. "Tell me, Jani-ji – you saw what the creature did to the Russians?"

She bent her head and said, "I saw what he did. At least, I saw him kill the three Russian soldiers."

He said in a whisper, "And it killed, single-handedly, the remaining fifty-odd. It is truly a creature to be feared."

She recalled the creature and said, "But I felt no fear in its company, papa-ji, only compassion at what it had suffered. I... I tried to help it, to give it painkillers, but it refused. In return it gave me something."

"Gave you... what?"

"A coin. Or at least that's what I thought it was."

"You have it now?"

She looked at him. "No. I assume Cartwright or his men found it amongst my possessions, or that it was stolen or lost."

He shook his head. "He mentioned nothing of it to me," he said. "But then it was merely a courtesy call to a dying old man, to tell him that his daughter was fit and well following her ordeal. I wonder..."

"Yes?"

"I wonder why the creature gave you a coin?"

She said in a small voice, "A simple gift to thank me for my offer of help – perhaps it was the only thing of worth that it possessed."

"Perhaps," he said. "Oh, I implore you to be careful, my darling..." His words were less than whispers and his eyes fluttered shut and, within seconds, he was asleep.

Later, despite the furious thoughts crowding her head, despite the image of Jelch suffering torture at the hands of the Russians, she found herself giving in to exhaustion.

When she awoke, it was to find the room a melee of confusion. Dr Hammond was speaking hurriedly to a nurse while Vikram was slipping a hypodermic into her father's arm.

The tiny, frail figure of her father ceased its pained writhing, and the doctor and nurses fell silent and stepped away from the bed. Dr Hammond took her hand. "We have done all we can, Miss Chatterjee. Your father is no longer suffering."

One by one they slipped from the room, leaving her alone with her father.

She gripped his hand, and he turned his head and smiled at her. His lips moved, and Jani leaned even closer to make out his words. But she heard nothing, merely felt his warm breath on her cheek, and then not even that.

She pulled away in panic and stared into his eyes, and saw that they were gazing at her, glassy and blind.

She sobbed and kissed his face, then gripped his hand to her chest as if by doing so she might grant him some of her own vitality. She lowered her forehead to his chest and wept quietly.

Later Dr Hammond came up behind her and laid a hand on her shoulder, murmuring his condolences, and she dried her eyes and thanked him and asked that she might have a few more minutes alone with her father.

He withdrew from the room, and clutching her father's frail hand Jani recalled the many times in the past when his big, strong hands had held her, protected her, and she smiled at the memories.

She recalled little of the next half hour. She felt as if her senses had been insulated, somehow deadened against the enormity of her grief. She remembered Dr Hammond coming in and asking her something, and then she was stepping from the room. Mr Rai and Anand were before her, staring at her with tears in their eyes. Slowly she shook her head, and she watched as they wept. Mr Rai asked if he and Anand might say farewell to her father, and Jani smiled and murmured, "Of course."

She sat on a hard bench in the corridor while they were in the room, and someone brought her a cup of hot spiced chai – the first she had tasted in years. And this brought back a slew of memories, of drinking chai with her father on Delhi railway station and at Roopa's Tea Rooms. Her father was addicted to chai, and had had a constant supply of the milky, cardamom-spiced beverage ferried to him throughout the working day.

It came to her that she would never again share a cup of chai, a meal, or anything else, with her beloved papa-ji. Something vast and dark and cold opened up beside her, something which crying could not disperse.

Mr Rai and Anand came from the room, ashen-faced. Mr Rai said, with the formality of a speech rehearsed, "Your father was a great and good man, Jani-ji. Everyone loved him for his compassion and humanity. He was good to everyone he met, whether that be the Prime Minister or the chai-wallah. They were all equal in his eyes."

Anand, still weeping, said, "I loved your father like my own, Jani-ji. I am so sorry."

Jani smiled, choked by their words. "You are both very kind. It is good to have friends like you at a time like this."

"And now we will go home and you should go to bed," Mr Rai said. "You will feel a little better when you have slept."

They moved down the corridor to the reception area, and then outside. The night was passing and a rosy glow showed in the east. A knot of reporters was awaiting her exit, and she blinked at the flash of a camera, angry at the intrusion but working to keep her composure. How many times had she seen her father pounced upon by the press like this, and always he had maintained his enviable poise and equanimity.

A reporter asked, "Is it true, Miss Chatterjee, that your father has breathed his last?"

"How do you think this will affect security in the country?" another asked.

"Will your father receive a state funeral, Miss Chatterjee?"

She held up a hand and replied, "My father passed away, peacefully, just thirty minutes ago. I have every confidence that the government have matters in hand, and I am not aware at the moment of any funeral arrangements. Now, if I may..."

Escorted by Mr Rai and Anand, she pushed through the melee. "Is it true, Miss Chatterjee, that you survived the Russian attack on the...?"

Mr Rai snapped, "Do you not have any respect for the grieving, ha? Now cease your questions and let us through!"

It was five o'clock in the morning as she slipped into the car and was driven at speed from the hospital.

Crouched behind the wheel like an ugly temple monkey, Mr Rai said, "You do not wish to be troubled by this at the moment, Jani-ji, but your father left instructions regarding his funeral, and I have everything in hand."

"That's most kind of you, Mr Rai."

They drove on in silence. They passed through the higgledy-piggledy suburbs of Old Delhi, where every building appeared grey in the dawn light and the streets were clogged with traffic and pedestrians even at this early hour. The city of five million souls was coming to life and soon everyone would be listening to radio reports and reading newspaper articles about the passing of the Minister for Security.

They approached the airyard on Disraeli Street, a sight that always reminded Jani of a carnival. Once, at the age of six, she had accompanied her father to the terminal and had mistaken the dozens of cigar-shaped airships for children's balloons and the airyard for a fairground. Ever since, she had always associated airship termini with joy and excitement. She smiled now as she stared up at the tethered airships bearing the livery of a dozen different lines: the gold and green stripes of Empire Airways, the red and silver checks of the India Pacific Line, the black and white hoops of the Deccan Express, and many more besides. Taxis drew up outside the terminal and passengers alighted, and porters hurried hither and thither with luggage, and she thought of the many thousands of citizens taking flights today to all points of the compass. She watched a huge four-engined airship slip its moorings, turn slowly and head south.

She would stay for her father's funeral, she decided, and perhaps a few days afterwards, and then book passage back to London.

They left the airyard in their wake and burrowed through the narrow streets of Old Delhi. She caught the delicious scent of cooking food through the open window, and it came to her that she did not want to return to her father's house – so full of memories – and go to bed right now.

She wanted to stroll through the crowded streets of Old Delhi, as she had done as a child. She would find a café she and her father had frequented, and she would enjoy a breakfast of vegetable cutlets, chaat and salted lassi, just as she had done with her father all those years ago.

The idea became an obsession, and she would not let Mr Rai, for all his good intentions, talk her out of the notion.

"Mr Rai, I wonder if you might stop here and let me out."

He peered at her myopically. "Here, Jani-ji?"

"Right here."

"Very well. I will wait for you down this side-street, ah-cha?"

"That won't be necessary, Mr Rai. Please head home and I will make my own way back."

From the back seat Anand said, "Perhaps I should come with you, Jani?"

"No, Anand, thank you. I wish to be alone with my thoughts."

Mr Rai tried to protest again, but she was insistent. "My desire is to be alone with the memories of my father. Chalo. I will see you later today, Mr Rai, and thank you for all you have done today."

Mr Rai pressed his palms together and bobbed his head as she opened the door and climbed out.

She watched the car edge away through the crowds and felt a sudden and rather odd sense of release.

She recalled an occasion in London earlier in the year, when she had had an hour to spare before meeting Sebastian for lunch. She had strolled through Camden Town and Hackney, aware of the glances directed her way; she was a brown-skinned young lady, and alone, and as such a rare sight indeed.

Now she blended into the crowd that rushed about her. She felt a sense of remove from everything around her, and at the same time a feeling of belonging. This was her father's country, her mother's adopted country, and her own dear homeland. She relished the chaos of the street-scene, unmatched anywhere she had ever been: the headlong rush of pedestrians, the cries of street vendors, the thousand scents that assailed her from every direction. One moment, she caught a whiff of cooking garlic and ginger, the next the scent of rosewater from the hair of a passing Brahmin girl, overlaid then by the overpowering musk of dhoop, followed by wood smoke which in turn was superseded by the appetising aroma of masala dosa.

And the noise! The continual honking of car horns like a flock of importunate geese; the throaty warbles of hawkers advertising their wares, the blare of radio music and the ill-tuned tootle of pipe bands.

And in the skies, over all this, the intercity airships, the small dozen-berth craft flying from the capital to the other cities of India, to Bombay and Calcutta and Lucknow and Varanasi, hundreds of them crowding the skies in a dense, jostling pointillism.

If only her father had lived a little longer, so that they might have walked down this quintessentially Indian street together, hand in hand, and enjoyed a chai and a meal and chatted about everything and nothing at all...

She turned a corner and stopped suddenly, smiling.

And now she knew why some inner voice had told her to leave the car and walk through the streets of Old Delhi.

Before her, on the corner of the street, was the ancient establishment of Roopa's Tea Rooms, a timeless place of worn mahogany and soft-treading waiters, of silver cutlery and cotton tablecloths. It was neither English nor Indian, but some strange quaint amalgam of the two, where cucumber sandwiches could be had beside vegetable pakora, Earl Grey alongside Kashmiri scented tea.

It was – it had been – one of her father's favourite haunts in all the city, a quiet oasis where he could escape the stress of his job for an hour and pore over the *Times of India* while sipping his spiced chai. She and her father must have come here a hundred times before she left for England at the age of eight.

She hurried across the road, entered Roopa's ground-floor room cooled by lazily turning ceiling fans, and climbed the worn wooden staircase to the first floor tea room. With a sigh of familiarity, she stepped onto the verandah overlooking the bustling city.

She was alone on the verandah, which suited her reflective mood. She ordered salted lassi and chaat, and a vegetable cutlet, then sat back and thought of Sebastian. She wanted suddenly to tell him of her father's passing; she wanted to hear his calm words of love and condolence. She would call him just as soon as she returned home. It would be to her eternal regret that her father had not lived long enough to meet him.

Her breakfast arrived, served on a silver tray by a silent waiter in a white uniform and a maroon turban. He retreated with the same ghost-like glide as his arrival, and Jani dipped her vegetable cutlet into the spiced chaat and savoured her first mouthful of real Indian food for a long time.

As she ate, tears escaped her eyes unbidden and rolled down her cheeks.

She noticed movement in the doorway to her left and quickly dried her eyes. An overweight European gentleman stepped on to the verandah, eased his bulk behind a neighbouring table, and unfolded his copy of the *Times of India*. He was in his fifties, Jani thought, and sported a luxuriant walrus moustache. They exchanged polite smiles and the gentleman busied himself with his newspaper.

Jani sipped her lassi and recalled her father's last smile, the grip of his frail hand, and the strange things he had told her as he lay dying. She thought through what he had said, the bizarre claims he had made: no such thing as Annapurnite, and no heavily guarded mine in the Himalayas, and the revelations concerning the strange creature called Jelch...

Her thoughts were interrupted by the European. He flicked a hand at his paper and said, in heavily accented English, "I see poor old Kapil Dev Chatterjee is ill again. A good man, from what I've heard."

She found herself replying, "The newspaper is a little behind the times, sir. Mr Chatterjee passed away peacefully at six o'clock this morning."

"Aha. You have the advantage of me. That's where the radio surpasses the medium of print, yes?"

"I neither read the report nor heard the news on the radio. I was at Mr Chatterjee's bedside when he passed away."

The European stared at her. "You were? But..."

She smiled at his confusion. "I am Kapil Dev Chatterjee's daughter and I was at his side just two hours ago."

He folded his large face into lines of condolence. "But my dear... I had no idea. Please accept my apologies, and of course my condolences."

She thanked him and returned to her breakfast.

"Please allow me to introduce myself. I am Otto Kaspar, of the German Republic, here in Delhi on business." He rose from his table and, with German formality, approached her table and bowed. "And I wonder," he went on, "if I might have the pleasure of buying you tea? I see that your drink is almost finished."

"Your offer is most kind," she said, "but I must decline, thank you." She hoped that the German would get the message and depart.

He hesitated, then to her annoyance pulled out a chair and sat down across from her.

"Your father was a remarkable man, my dear. To hold such an exalted post, and for so long, and to perform the onerous tasks with such finesse and success." He spread his hands. "Why, your father was little short of a genius."

"That is so kind of you," she murmured.

"My business is in arms," Herr Kaspar rushed on. "My company supplies the Empire, and specifically India, with components of the MacArthur field gun. In my work I have contact with Indian civil servants, and their regard for your late father is of the highest."

She felt a tightness in her throat as she said, "My father was well loved. He was... he was a good man, Herr Kaspar."

Oh, please, *please* go away, she thought.

"Unfortunately I never had the good fortune to meet him; a fact that I regret."

She smiled at her. "Herr Kaspar... I'm sorry, but I really must be going. I am tired, and as I'm sure you can appreciate..." She made to rise to her feet.

Kaspar reached out and laid a meaty paw on the back of her hand. "One moment, please."

She sat back down, staring at him.

The German glanced over his shoulder, into the tea room, as if checking that they were unobserved. She watched him as he reached into his pocket and withdrew a rubber bulb of the sort used to apply perfume, and she wondered what on earth he might be doing.

Before she could react he smiled across at her and, with one quick movement, raised the spray and squeezed the bulb into her face. She gasped and tried to call out as an astringent, painful mist shot into her face and eyes.

She attempted to climb to her feet, but her vision swam and she felt herself swaying.

"I'm afraid she has taken a bad turn..." she heard Kaspar say in Hindi to a waiter. "I will take her..."

She wanted nothing more than to shout out, to alert someone that all was not well here, but she felt a sudden, sickening wave of nausea and then pitched forward across the table, unconscious.

ANAND STOOD IN the doorway and stared into the tiny bedroom.

A narrow charpoy stood in one corner next to a tea chest containing all his worldly possessions: a change of clothing, a wooden car from his childhood, and a pile of books: H. Rider Haggard, R. M. Ballantyne, Robert Louis Stevenson and H. G. Wells.

The bungalow had been his home for twelve years, the only real home he had ever known; but all that was coming to an end. He was sure he'd enjoy his new life living in the eaves of Mr Clockwork's emporium in Old Delhi, and working with the inventor in his workshop, but he would miss the bungalow, the routine he'd established over the years, and most of all he'd miss Kapil Dev Chatterjee. It was hard to believe that the man he'd come to see as a father was no more. His eyes prickled at the thought and raw emotion scoured his throat.

He would fetch a linen bag from the kitchen, pack his scant belongings, and say goodbye to Mr Rai, Zeena and the rest of the household staff. Then he would wait until Jani returned and make his farewells to her. First, though, there was something he had to do.

He left his room and hurried down the darkened corridor of the quiet house. He came to Mr Chatterjee's study and slipped through the door. He pulled it shut behind him, then stared into the shadowy room. It looked and felt like a museum to the great man. Sunlight pierced the drawn blinds with golden rapiers, illuminating motes of dust and the minister's vast desk. How many times had Anand delivered spiced chai to Mr Chatterjee as he sat at his desk, writing or poring over important papers?

Now he crossed to the desk, his heart pounding.

He paused before the solid oak monolith, his eyes skipping over the great man's fountain pen, his well-thumbed dictionary, and the many framed photographs. Catching his breath, he reached for what he had come here to claim as his own.

He had a choice: there were perhaps half a dozen photographs of Janisha in pride of place beyond the blotter. He selected the most recent, which she had sent to her father earlier this year. It showed Jani outside King's College, Cambridge, a radiant smile lighting her beautiful features.

Quickly he reversed the frame and prized back the small metal clasps. He withdrew the photograph with trembling fingers and stared into her smiling face.

His heart. He had missed her terribly when her father had sent her to England at the age of eight. Over the years, oddly, it was as if her absence had amplified her presence in his thoughts. Never a day had passed without him thinking of her, wondering what she might be doing in far away England.

Five years ago, when she returned briefly, he had awaited her return with an anticipation that had felt like a sickness; and when they had finally met, and played on the lawns as they had as infants, it was as if no time at all had elapsed: Jani-ji had been the same little girl she had always been, his best friend and confidante...

This time, however, she had changed; no longer was she a little girl: she had become a beautiful woman, and Anand, on first meeting her at the door yesterday, had found himself overawed in her glowing presence. His heart had thumped like one of Mr Clockwork's mechanisms, and he'd prattled on like a child, nervous but at the same time wanting to impress her.

In days, or at best weeks, she would be gone again. He would write to her, of course; but she would have her own life to lead in England, her studies to occupy her mind, and her young man to dote on. He doubted she would maintain their correspondence, and who would blame her? He felt a terrible emptiness in his heart, and realised that he was crying yet again.

But he would make the most of their time together now. He would suggest they go for coffee, like adult friends, and he would ask if she would like a conducted tour of Mr Clockwork's Fabulous Emporium. They would talk of her father, and he would tell her what a great man he was, and how much he was respected.

The thought reminded him of something he had overheard earlier this year. Mr Chatterjee had been dictating a memo to his secretary, and Anand had been sweeping ash from the hearth. He had heard the frontier mentioned, and something about the collusion of the local tribespeople with Russian insurgents.

The secretary had asked Mr Chatterjee if he intended to implement the Viceroy's suggestion, and Mr Chatterjee had replied, "I see no other way. The defence of the country is at stake. In normal circumstances there is no way I would authorise torture, but in this instance..." He had sighed. "Very well, give me the papers." And he had penned a hurried signature, adding, "Contact Major Bentley and have him round up the suspects."

Shocked, Anand had finished his sweeping and hurried from the study.

In the months that followed he had tried to forget what he'd overheard and, failing that, convince himself that the torture of the northern tribespeople had been necessary for the defence of the country.

He jumped at a sound from behind him.

A soft hand fell on his shoulder. He turned, blushing, and stared up into the benign, bespectacled face of Mr Rai. Anand could see that he, too, had been crying.

Mr Rai glanced at the photograph in Anand's hand, and smiled. "I haven't seen it," he murmured, "and anyway papa-ji has no need for it now."

"Thank you, Mr Rai," Anand said, slipping the picture into the pocket of his shorts. "You see, soon she will go back to England, and..."

"And you would like a memento?"

"She is very fair, no? I..."

Mr Rai smiled. "Tell me."

"I dream, Mr Rai. I dream one day that she will come back to India and that we will meet and fall in love, and..."

Mr Rai could have laughed at him for his childish fantasy, but he merely smiled and shook his head. "She is Brahmin, Anand, and half-English, and as is the modern way with women, she is educated also. You are a Dalit, boy, and you must know your place."

He realised that Mr Rai was attempting to be kind by gently stating the facts, but his pride bridled. "But she likes me, Mr Rai, we are friends. Maybe one day..."

Mr Rai smiled and shook his head.

Anand looked at the desk, at the photograph of Mr Chatterjee shaking the hand of the Viceroy. He murmured, "Mr Chatterjee was a good man, wasn't he?"

"Of course he was. And the gods know this, and will bless him."

"And..." Anand hesitated. He considered his words, then went on, "But do good men authorise torture, Mr Rai?"

The old man sighed. "Anand, Anand... You have much to learn about the world and the affairs of men. The facts are these: good men can authorise what you might consider to be bad things if the greater circumstances demand such action. Papa-ji was in a position of great authority, with enemies on every side, and he sometimes had terrible decisions to make. Not everyone would relish his position: only great men could fulfil his role, and papa-ji was a great man."

Anand considered the old man's words and wondered what other 'terrible decisions' papa-ji had had to make.

He was about to ask Mr Rai this when a loud knocking sounded at the front door.

Mr Rai sighed. "Go and see who that is, boy. No doubt the press..."

Anand hurried from the study and along the darkened hallway. When he opened the door, he was dazzled by a burst of blinding sunlight against which the caller showed as a tall, dark figure.

He blinked, and when his eyes adjusted he made out the smart uniform of a British officer – and not just any officer. He shrank back as he recognised Colonel Smethers, with his thin face, piercing blue eyes and sneering lips.

"Who's in charge here?" Smethers snapped, looking beyond Anand into the shadows.

"In charge?" Anand stammered. "Sahib, but Mr Chatterjee passed away just this morning."

"I asked who the hell's in charge, boy. Chalo. Fetch someone, quick smart."

Anand turned and ran to the study. "Mr Rai! It is Colonel Smethers, sir."

"And what might *he* want?" Mr Rai muttered as he left the study and shuffled down the hall.

Anand followed the old man and concealed himself behind the hat stand, listening to the exchange that took place.

"I am sorry, sir, but just this morning Mr Chatterjee–"

"I know, I know," Smethers said impatiently. "My condolences and all that. But it's the Chatterjee girl I need to see. Quick sharp, there's a good chap."

"Janisha?" Mr Rai said, sounding confused.

"Well, she's old Chatterjee's only daughter, isn't she? Of course Janisha."

"But... might I ask why you would like to see Janisha, sir?"

"Look, just bring her here pronto like a good man, ah-cha?"

"But... but Janisha is not at home, sir. When we left the hospital, she asked to be dropped off at... at Victoria Park. She said she needed to be alone with her thoughts in this time of grief."

Colonel Smethers grunted something and said, "Very well, then. When do you expect her back?"

"I really cannot tell, sir."

Smethers swore. "Right, I'll wait in here until the gel gets back. I'm dashed lathered, so fetch me a cold drink, hm? I'll be in the old man's study."

Anand shrank back into the shadows as Mr Rai stepped aside and the colonel strode down the hall and entered the study.

Mr Rai saw Anand and said, "You heard?"

Anand nodded. "But what does he want with Jani-ji, sir?"

Mr Rai murmured, "I dread to think, Anand. Smethers is a bad lot, according to papa-ji. You've heard the stories?"

Anand shook his head. "Yes, sir. Papa-ji hated the colonel."

"With good reason, Anand. Very well, you must find Jani and warn her. Tell her that for some reason Smethers wishes to question her. This will give her time to compose herself, ah-cha. And Anand, don't come back before noon. I think the colonel should be made to kick his heels for a while."

"But, Mr Rai, where will I find Jani-ji?"

The old man smiled. "She will be in one of three places, I think…"

Five minutes later Anand left the bungalow and took a rickshaw north to Old Delhi.

CHAPTER
SEVEN

Over the coals? – A pleasant surprise –
Alfie is tasked with a mission –
"The ferret after the rabbit..."

A MILITARY POLICE jeep drove Alfie Littlebody from his bungalow and through the canton to Brigadier Cartwright's office.

Alfie felt like a condemned man. He'd spent most of the previous day kicking his heels in the bungalow, and in the evening against his best intentions had weakened and taken himself along to the Officers' Club. Fortunately he'd not come across Tomlinson – out whoring with Kemp and his crowd, no doubt – and had proceeded to get thoroughly blotto. The drink had succeeded in wiping from his consciousness his fear of being hauled across the coals by the brigadier, but had left him this morning with a hell of a thick head.

The jolting of the jeep, as it passed the stands of bougainvillea surrounding the command complex, threatened to dislodge the contents of Alfie's stomach. His fear of the imminent meeting was starting to mount. As far as he could tell, he was well and truly for the high jump however it worked out. Either Brigadier

Cartwright had him down as a coward for turning tail and running from the massacre, or word had leaked to the brigadier from the mess that he'd gone native and had Nationalist sympathies.

It was another hot morning and Alfie was sweating in torrents. He mopped his brow. The sergeant in the driving seat glanced at him and said, "Head up, sir. Take it from me, old Cartwright's a pussycat. Mind your Ps and Qs, salute in the right places, grovel a bit and you'll be fine."

"I will?" Alfie said, and even to his own ears he sounded pathetically grateful.

"Mark my words," said the sergeant, braking outside the brigadier's office. "It's Cartwright's deputy, Smethers, who's the real bastard. Sadistic as they come. Good luck, sir."

Alfie thanked the sergeant, jumped down from the jeep and approached the ivy-draped office, a bungalow very much like his own, in a quaint, *faux*-English garden maintained by a troop of hoe-wielding Indians.

He was kept waiting for five minutes in an anteroom by a pretty Scottish secretary, then ushered into a capacious room more like a lounge than an office, with a scatter of chintz-covered furniture and a big desk positioned in the sunlit bay window.

Brigadier Cartwright sat behind the desk, shuffling papers absently. He had the air of a man whose thoughts were elsewhere.

"Ah, Lieutenant Littlebody, isn't it?"

Alfie snapped to attention and saluted. "Sir!"

"At ease, Lieutenant. Take a pew."

Alfie sat down on a stiff-backed chair across the desk from Cartwright. He was sweating again, despite the fan that ruffled papers on the desk, but was too nervous to fumble with his bandana and mop his brow.

The brigadier thumbed through a file and looked up at Alfie from time to time.

"How long've you been in Field Security, Lieutenant?"

"Eight years, sir."

"And in India for two years. What d'you make of the place?"

Alfie swallowed. He knew how a rabbit felt before the ferret pounced. "I... I'm enjoying my time here, sir, and finding the work rewarding."

Cartwright nodded. "Good reports from your senior officers, Littlebody. Involved in the Panaji clear out, I hear?"

"Yes, sir." Earlier this year he'd commanded a small unit that had travelled down to Goa and routed a cell of insurgents, arresting three Russians and half a dozen Nationalist sympathisers.

"Vital work you're doing. I've never underestimated the job Field Security carry out here. Some of my colleagues have you down as a bunch of pen-pushing busybodies, but I see what you people accomplish and I'm impressed."

Alfie croaked, "Thank you, sir." The compliments over, he thought, now would come the grilling.

"So..." Cartwright said, tapping the file before him with a nicotine-stained forefinger, "I've been reading all about this dashed Allahabad business." He leaned back in his chair, rather languidly, and looked across at Alfie as if expecting a comment.

Alfie said, "Yes, sir," in barely a whisper.

"Ghastly show, what?"

"Ah..." Alfie stammered.

"Bloody beastly, if you ask me."

Alfie swallowed, petrified. Was Cartwright referring to his, Alfie's, part in the business – the fact that he'd turned tail and fled – or to the massacre?

"Beastly," Cartwright went on. "I was livid when I found out. I said to myself, I'll flay a few damned carcasses before the week's out, what? Who was in charge–?" He riffled through the pages. "Ah, Frobisher. Might've known. I'll see the blighter dragged over the coals."

Alfie sat frozen in his seat, hardly able to believe what he was hearing.

Cartwright said, "So what's your opinion about the business, Lieutenant?"

"Ah, well..."

"Come on. Out with it, man." Cartwright leaned forward and said conspiratorially, "I'm on your side, y'know, Littlebody."

Alfie blinked. He felt like weeping with relief as he said, "I... Well, to be honest, sir, I felt the entire show was badly handled. In my opinion, we shouldn't have been there in the first place. It was a minor protest in the scheme of things. We should've let it blow over with a minimal police presence."

"Excellent. That's *exactly* what we should've done. Instead, Frobisher barrels in with all guns blazing." He leaned forward and clasped his hands on his blotter, looking for all the world like an elderly and rather benign headmaster. "And once you were there, facing the mob? What would you have done then?"

"Then..." Alfie began tentatively, "then I would have held fire, sir. You see, although the mob was waving a few weapons... I'm of the opinion that they wouldn't have used them. It was a token protest. I even think..."

Cartwright leaned forward. "Go on."

"I think that, perhaps, a faction of the Nationalist organisers might even have – dare I say? – welcomed what we did, sir."

"Hm. I don't disagree, Littlebody. In other words, Frobisher played right into their hands, what?"

"Well, yes, sir, in my opinion."

Cartwright nodded. "And your part in all this?"

Alfie considered his options for a split second – and decided that, in this instance, honesty would be the best policy.

"I wanted no part in the slaughter, sir, and effected a tactical retreat."

The brigadier harrumphed. "Word in the mess, Lieutenant, is that you pissed your pants – excuse my French – and fled."

"That is one opinion, sir."

The brigadier stroked the line of his jaw. "Between you, me and the gatepost, Littlebody, although you went against a superior officer's orders and refused to fire, you did the bally right thing."

Alfie thought he was about to pass out with relief. "Why... thank you, sir."

Cartwright tapped the file with the back of his hand. "Been reading up on your service record to date, Littlebody, and I've decided..."

Alfie blinked. "Decided, sir?"

"Something's come up. Delicate matter. Needs a light touch. Might be a storm in a tea cup kind of thing. You with me so far?"

"Ah... yes, sir."

"I don't know whether you've heard about the *Rudyard Kipling*?"

"I caught something about it in the club last night, sir. Terrible accident."

"But it wasn't an accident, Lieutenant. The Russians brought it down. Not only that, they went among the wreckage afterwards and shot most of the injured. Among the survivors was an old girl by the name of Lady Eddington and a certain Janisha Chatterjee."

"They were dashed lucky, sir."

"I'll say, Lieutenant. Now, the thing is, this Chatterjee gel – she's the daughter of Kapil Dev Chatterjee, the Minister for Internal Security. Or he was, until this morning. Poor blighter succumbed to a long illness. Now his daughter was at her father's bedside when he expired. An hour or so later her driver dropped her off in Old Delhi – she wanted a little time alone, which is understandable. Only, the damned thing is that she's vanished."

"Vanished, sir?"

"Completely. She was last seen at Roopa's Tea Rooms on Lal Singh Road around eight o'clock this morning, talking to some old European. According to witnesses, she took badly and was helped into a taxi by the gentleman. And after that, nothing. Now, as I say, it might be a typhoon in the old china, but I'd like you to look into it. See what you can dig up. We can't have the bereaved daughters of government ministers vanishing like this. Bad form. Doesn't look good."

"I understand, sir."

"I thought, this might be a job for Field Security. Lieutenant Bolton is up in Srinigar, isn't he, sorting out the bloody Kashmiris? So I took a look at your record and I thought, just the chap for the job."

He reached into a drawer, pulled out a folder and slid it across the desk. "This is the file on Janisha Chatterjee, and a report on what we know of her disappearance."

Alfie took the file. "Pretty substantial, sir."

"We like to keep a detailed record of our... subjects, Lieutenant. As you'll see, the filly is quite some girl. Bright as a button. Just started at Cambridge, studying medicine. Pro-British, as far as we can tell, though we do know that she has fraternised with a few Nationalists in London."

Alfie opened the file and slid a photograph from under a paper-clip. It showed a small, slim girl in a knee-length summer dress, her smiling brown face framed in a fall of long black hair. "And quite beautiful, too," he murmured.

"Don't see the attraction of the natives meself, Littlebody, but each to his own. Very well, you know the ropes. I want you to find where the bally hell she is, what she's doing."

"You don't think...?"

"What? That she has real Nationalist sympathies and has gone to ground with 'em?" he said. "Impossible to tell. Suppose it's possible, but I bloody well hope not. Wouldn't look good, what, if a minister's daughter threw in her lot with the other side, hm?"

"No, sir."

"So this is a priority job, Lieutenant. Drop everything and concentrate on finding the gel. And you'll be needing a bit of tech to help you along."

"Tech, sir?"

"High level clearance stuff. Top secret. Devices straight from our labs."

Cartwright unlocked a cupboard in his desk. He withdrew two items and set them on his blotter. One looked like a gold lipstick cylinder, the other a rugby skullcap.

Alfie looked up at the brigadier. "What are they, sir?"

Cartwright indicated the cylinder. "Bods in the labs call it a photon-blade. And this," he tapped the skullcap, smiling, "this is what the boffins term a VCA – or a Visual Camouflage Amplifier."

Alfie grinned. "I'm sorry, sir. I'm none the wiser."

"And nor was I when I pow-wowed with the scientists. In plain terms, Lieutenant, it allows the wearer to appear, to the onlooker, invisible – if one can 'appear' to be invisible, that is. You get my drift, anyway?"

Alfie felt dizzy. "Invisible, sir?"

"Quite invisible, apparently," Cartwright said, shaking his head in wonder at the skullcap. "Right, that's about it. Now take these bits and pieces over to the lab and a fellow there called Tennyson will show you the drill. Should only take an hour or so. And after that, you can start looking for the bally gel, what?"

Alfie sprang to his feet and saluted. "Yes, sir. Thank you, sir. Right away!"

He picked up the cylinder and the VCA, saluted again and turned to leave.

Cartwright said, "And don't forget the file, Lieutenant."

"No, sir!" he stammered, grabbed the report, saluted again, and marched from the office.

As he stepped from the building into the dazzling sunlight, Alfie felt as if he were walking on air.

*   *   *

BRIGADIER CARTWRIGHT SAT at his desk for a minute after Littlebody had departed, drumming his fingers on his blotter and humming a chorus from Gilbert and Sullivan's *H. M. S. Pinafore*. At last he pulled the phone towards him and dialled. "Smethers?" he said, "get yourself over here on the double."

He replaced the receiver and flipped through Littlebody's file again.

Two minutes later a tap at the door announced Smethers' arrival.

"Take a seat, Colonel. Won't keep you long. I've sent the ferret after the rabbit."

Smethers, a lean man in his forties, with intelligent eyes and a cruel lop-sided mouth, smiled like a hungry wolf.

Cartwright went on, "I'm not at all sure about young Littlebody. He might turn out to be top notch, but then again... Word in the mess is that he's a bit of a native lover."

"Nationalist leanings?"

"Hard to tell. My inclination is to think not, but I might be wrong." He stroked his jaw. "Anyway, I want you to tail him. Either make yourself known to him, or not – I'll leave that up to your discretion. I think he'll do a good job with the gel – just up his street, if his past record is anything to go by. And then, when he finds her..."

"You'd like me to take over?"

"Exactly."

"And...?"

"And try to find out if she was lying when she claimed not to have met the Morn, and if they did meet, what passed between 'em."

"Force, sir?"

Cartwright sighed. "Only if *absolutely* necessary, Smethers."

The colonel smiled. "Yes, sir."

"Oh – one other thing while you're here. I've had unconfirmed reports that that Russian pair, Volovich and Yezhov, have slipped into the country. Last bloody thing we want is that double-act stirring things up. Pair of psychopaths, so I've heard."

"I've read about what they did to the opposition in Warsaw, sir. Skinned them alive and tortured them for days. They used rather a lot of acid, so I'm informed."

Cartwright raised a hand. "Not before me morning tiffin, Smethers. Now there's a good chap."

"Sorry, sir."

"Liaise with Grey over at Intelligence, hm? See if there's any substance to the rumours." He nodded curtly. "That will be all."

Smethers rose, saluted, and quick-marched from the room.

Cartwright sat for a long time, frowning to himself and staring down at Lieutenant Littlebody's file.

Then he closed the folder, slipped it into a drawer, and turned his attention to other matters.

CHAPTER
EIGHT

In the taxidermist's warehouse –
A Russian threat – A visit from Jelch –
"I just don't understand any of this…"

JANI RECALLED ENTERING Roopa's Tea Rooms, ordering breakfast, and talking to the German about her father, and then… Then the German had sprayed some kind of anaesthetic into her face, and she had passed out.

She opened her eyes in panic.

She was in a vast chamber like the interior of a warehouse, imprisoned in a small cage; she could feel ice-cold stone through the straw beneath her. The chamber was dimly lit, but even so she could make out that she was not alone in her incarceration.

A veritable menagerie of animals occupied the floor: horses and donkeys and buffaloes and even a baby elephant – all of them examples of the hideous art of taxidermy. Racked upon shelves on the far wall were smaller stuffed animals: various birds – peacocks and macaws and parrots – as well as dogs, cats, rabbits, monkeys and snakes.

There must have been over a hundred specimens in the chamber, which was filled with the musty stench of old fur and the eye-watering reek of preserving fluid. On the lower shelves Jani made out large jars containing animal embryos, etiolated and malformed, either with congenital defects or from being squashed up against the glass. Sickened, she averted her gaze – and wished she hadn't.

More alarming even than the preserved embryos was what she looked upon then: the tools of the taxidermist's trade. In the centre of the room was a long bench laid out with various saws, knives, hooks and hammers, alongside a dozen bottles and jars of coloured fluids. The skin of a mandrill, removed from its flesh and skeleton, was laid out like a rug on the bench, its head facing Jani and its sightless, eyeless orbits staring at her.

Beyond the taxidermist's bench was another table. It reminded her very much of the autopsy gurney she had seen in the first week of her medical studies at Cambridge, all ivory and shining aluminium. A pipe led from its fluted underside to a large plastic container filled with some dark fluid like port wine.

She should have been more wary of Herr Kaspar, she told herself; the coincidence of his commenting upon the death of her father, his invitation to take tea with him... And his story of being a German arms dealer? A cover, obviously.

But what might he want with her?

The cage was tall enough for her to stand without having to stoop. She gripped the bars and peered right and left, taking in the extremities of the room. On the far wall to the left was a timber door. She looked up. A number of small skylights in the sloping ceiling allowed in meagre daylight. She saw a shadow through one of them – the fleet shape of a monkey passing high above its more unfortunate brethren.

She looked at her watch. It was still only ten-thirty; she had been in the cage for a couple of hours.

She shook the bars, or rather tried to. They were set solidly in the stone flags at her feet.

She entertained the terrifying notion that she was destined to be killed, laid out on the autopsy table, her skin flensed from her flesh and mounted on a frame, to take its place among the chamber's other exhibits. A complete collection: the fauna of the sub-continent, plus a native human.

She had led a safe, sedate life to date, the only small calamity of her existence being her relocation to England and the occasional name-calling at school. Now, in a matter of days, she had survived an airship crash, witnessed the death of her father, and been kidnapped by a lunatic taxidermist.

Was Herr Kaspar – though she was sure that that was a *nom de guerre* – the taxidermist in question, or had he been employed as the middle-man on the taxidermist's behalf?

She had an urge to call for help, but guessed it would be futile. And anyway she was averse to alerting her captors to the fact that she was awake; they would come in due course, and she feared that moment more than anything else.

She stepped forward and, taking a breath, turned sideways and eased her left shoulder between the bars, then smiled to herself at her futile optimism. She was slim, but not slim enough to force herself between the ungiving iron bars.

The door at the far end of the chamber creaked open, making her jump, and two men appeared.

Jani recognised the corpulent form of Herr Kaspar. The other man was younger and Slavic-looking, with a shock of dark hair and a broad brow. His dark, staring eyes struck her as cruel. The pair crossed the chamber, paused beside the autopsy table, and regarded her impassively.

They spoke to each other as they stared, but in tones too low for Jani to catch. There was something different about Herr Kaspar, aside from the fact he no longer wore a suit. Both men were garbed, she saw with heart-stopping alarm, in white knee-length surgeon's gowns.

The other difference was that Kaspar no longer sported that ridiculous walrus moustache.

She had the urge to ask what they wanted with her, but she stopped herself. To do so, she thought, would be to show her fear, to give the pair the upper hand... not that they didn't have it anyway. But she would remain defiant to the last, and take whatever opportunity arose to attack them.

The young man's broad face was almost simian, his brown eyes penetrating. The pair showed not the slightest trace of emotion as they stood discussing her as if she were a specimen in a zoo. The young man held his chin, nodding occasionally at what the older man said. It came to Jani that Kaspar could be relaying instructions: "*A cut here, an incision there... and finally mounted just so, do you agree?*"

She stopped that macabre line of thought in its tracks, gripped the bars and stared at them with all the defiance she could muster.

At last, breaking the tableau, they approached her. Kaspar plucked a wooden dining chair from behind the taxidermy bench, reversed it and placed it before the cage. He sat down carefully, straddling the chair back, and rested his arms along the curved rattan, watching her.

The younger man remained standing; he was so small that, even seated, Kaspar was the same height.

Jani gripped the bars, her heart thudding.

It was the young man who spoke first, and as soon as he did so Jani recognised the harsh, gutturally accented English: he was Russian.

"We will ask you a few questions, yes? The veracity of your answers will determine how we treat you."

She found her voice, "What do you want?"

"Simply the answers to a few questions," said the Russian. He looked at Kaspar, who nodded. Clearly the older man was in charge.

"We know you had contact with the... the prisoner aboard the *Rudyard Kipling*," the young man said. "Our intelligence informs us that you spoke with the creature."

She stared at him. "Then your intelligence is wrong. I spoke with no prisoner aboard the airship." But at the same time she wondered from what source they might have gleaned this information. She had told only her father, and no one else.

The old man whispered to his partner, who smiled slightly and said, "Then allow me to rephrase the question: we know that you spoke to the creature *after* the airship came down. What did you say?"

She shook her head. "I said nothing. I spoke to no prisoner." She licked her lips. "Who are you? You do realise, I hope, that I am a dual Indian-British citizen? What is more, as the daughter of a high-ranking government minister, I... I am under constant surveillance. My abduction will have been noted, and at this very minute the authorities will be working to rescue me. If I were you I'd release me now and run, before the police apprehend you."

Kaspar spoke to her for the first time since entering the chamber. He made no pretence, now, to affect a German accent: he was as Russian as the young man. "Miss Chatterjee," he said, "will you please cease your childish prattle? You are no more under surveillance than I am. I advise you to answer the questions, or suffer the consequences."

The young man smiled, with malice, and said, "What did the creature known as Jelch tell you?"

She swallowed. "What creature?"

"We know you spoke with it."

"You are mistaken."

"You will tell the truth or suffer the consequences."

"I am telling the truth, and it will be the pair of you who will ultimately suffer." She was shaking as she spoke, and her legs felt as weak as water, but she hoped she presented a brave face to her captors.

The young man said, "We know you discovered the creature amid the debris of the airship. You helped it, offered it medication. Later, you were found by Russian soldiers – and the creature appeared and saved your life, before going on to murder the remaining platoon."

She felt a sudden flare of anger. Maintaining her poise, she said, "Murder? I rather think he executed criminals in recompense for the crime they committed: the cold-blooded killing of a thousand innocent men, women and children."

"So you admit that you know about the creature's crimes?"

She smiled. "Of course I do – you just told me what he did."

She detected a very brief flicker of irritation in the eyes of the dark-haired Russian and allowed herself to feel a scintilla of satisfaction.

"Our informant also told us that you were given something by the creature, something which you mistakenly assumed at the time to be a coin. Now, what did you do with this object?"

Her mind raced. She had spoken to one person only about the coin – her father, that morning, as he lay dying...

She opened her mouth in sudden realisation.

She knew, then, the identity of their informant. There had been only one other person with them in the room – her father's nurse, Mr Vikram, beyond the concealing curtain, listening to every word that passed between her and her father.

She stared at the young Russian. "Now it is you who are prattling childishly," she said. "I was not given a coin, because I had no contact with any such creature."

At this, Kaspar raised a hand to silence the young man's next question. He reached into a pocket of his surgeon's gown and held up his right hand. Something filigree and silver twinkled in the weak sunlight falling through the skylights.

"Do you recognise this, Miss Chatterjee?" Kaspar said.

She shook her head. "No. No, I don't."

He smiled, his expression smug. "It's a rather clever British invention," he said, "which has recently fallen into our hands. It is what your oppressors have termed a Cognitive Wave Amplification Device. Or CWAD, as the British call it."

"It means," Jani said, "nothing to me."

"Then allow me to explain. A CWAD is an ingenious device which allows the operator – in this case myself – to read the very thoughts of the subject – in this case yourself. The process of having this implanted is exquisitely painful. Indeed some subjects have suffered agonising deaths during the implantation of the nexus and the subsequent retrieval of their thoughts."

Kaspar gestured to the autopsy table. "Now, we will not hesitate to fit this device to your pretty little head in order to learn what we need to know. In fact, my colleague here is relishing the experience. However, you might wish to forego the operation, and save yourself a lot of pain, by simply telling us what we want to know. What did you do with the object given to you by the creature?"

She allowed the seconds to elapse, each one marked by the loud thumping of her heart. She had little doubt that they would carry out their threats and affix the device... but even if she gave in and told them about the coin, would they believe that she had accepted the 'gift' from Jelch and then, somewhere aboard the train to Delhi, lost it?

She shook her head, slowly, and said, "I don't know what you're talking about, and... and even if I did, I would tell you nothing."

She looked from one man to the other, hoping they might see the hatred in her eyes.

Kaspar stood and approached the cage. Jani held her ground, though she felt the impulse to back off.

"We will give you a short while in which to reconsider your reply, Miss Chatterjee. After that we will return and perform the operation."

She watched the men as they turned and strode from the chamber. They passed through the door and slammed it resoundingly behind them.

A silence descended. At least, she thought, she was not destined to suffer the fate of these unfortunate creatures... though she had little doubt that the Russians would have no qualms about killing her if they did not get what they wanted... or even if they did.

She lowered herself to the floor, and the image of her father, smiling at her, filled her mind's eye, and she held onto it as if it were a treasure.

She looked around the chamber, searching for something she might use as a weapon. She might have known that they would have catered for that eventuality and cleared the area around her prison. On the autopsy table, however, she made out a collection of knives and scalpels – but would she be able to use them when the time came? It was the uncertainty of the situation that was so unsettling.

She crouched in the corner of the cage and shut her eyes. She wondered if Anand and Mr Rai had become concerned and called the police: but she had been gone no more than two hours, and they would not have the slightest concern that she had not yet returned.

She heard a voice saying her name, opened her eyes and stared in disbelief.

"How..." she managed at last in a whisper, "how did you get in here?"

It was as if the creature had not heard the question. He sat on his haunches, staring in at her. She took in his ragged breeches, his bare, elongated torso which she was sure, now, possessed more ribs than was the norm. Was she dreaming, she wondered? Was this yet another manifestation of her wishful thinking? "Jelch?"

"Janisha Chatterjee." Again his voice was barely a croak. "You have suffered much of late, and you will suffer much more before your journey is over."

"I only wish to be away from this place! Please, can you help me?"

He stared at her with eyes more fishlike than human, flat and grey and glaucous. "I cannot physically help you. That is beyond my present powers. However, I will advise you now, and again later, when you might be in need of my help."

She choked with something like despair. "I don't understand. How did you get in here? Surely you can get me out." She stared at the lock on the cage. "The cage!" she said, understanding. "You cannot open the lock!"

"I am, in one way, as helpless as yourself. You see, I am not really here, Janisha."

She managed a short laugh. "So I *am* hallucinating you!" she said. "There really is no hope..."

"There is always hope."

She stared at him; he seemed real enough. "So, if you are not here, then where are you?"

"I am running from the British, in the hills north of Delhi."

"But..." she began.

"I fear they will imprison me, ignore my warnings as they ignored those of my compatriot. Time is of the essence, Janisha, and I cannot risk being apprehended."

She recalled her father telling her about the Morn in London, its warning... She shook her head, close to tears. "I'm sorry... I just don't understand any of this."

"Be brave, Janisha. You will escape from here, be assured of that. Luck will be on your side. And when you do flee this terrible place, you must head east. Take the train from Delhi to the hill station of Rishi Tal."

"I 'must' head east? But I want nothing more than to return home, to attend my father's funeral."

"Please believe me when I say that you are in danger. Not only the Russians desire to apprehend you. Under no circumstances must you return home. You *must* go to Rishi Tal."

She shook her head, bewildered. "And there?"

"At Rishi Tal, with luck, I will meet you, and then guide you onwards to Nepal."

"Nepal? But that is restricted territory!"

"With my help, you will make your way to the foothills of the Himalayas."

She stared at him, incredulous. "And... and why *must* I do this?"

Jelch smiled, and it was as if his thin lips were not accustomed to performing the expression. "For the ultimate benefit of your planet, Janisha, and all who live upon it."

She blinked, but the creature remained squatting before her, as seemingly real as the bars of her cage.

"And where will I meet you in Rishi Tal?" she asked.

"You will know the place," he said cryptically.

She felt tears fill her eyes at the enormity of his words, at the hopelessness of her plight.

I have yet to escape from this prison, she thought to herself.

She started at the sound of bolts being shot, and stared across the chamber to the timber door. She turned back to Jelch, intending to exhort him to hide – but the creature had disappeared as if, all along, he had been no more than a figment of her optimistic imagination.

CHAPTER
NINE

The Russians return – Jani fights for her life –
The Mech-Man intervenes –
"The only pilot in India..."

SHE JUMPED TO her feet as Kaspar and his cohort entered
the chamber. She did not want to be seen crouching,
subservient, when they approached. She would face
them foursquare, proudly.

They came to a halt before the cage and Kaspar,
staring in at her with his piggy eyes, said, "Well?"

She took a breath. "I cannot change the facts. I met
no creature; I was given no coin."

The young man was carrying something; it looked to Jani
like the interior of an old wireless, stripped of its casing.
Two wires looped from the device and were connected to
the filigree nexus of the CWAD, which Kaspar held with
odd daintiness in his sausage-thick fingers.

The latter smiled, and both men turned and placed
the CWAD and its accompanying wireless device at one
end of the autopsy table. When Kaspar returned to the
cage, he was holding something in his right hand. At
first Jani thought it was a long cigarette holder, and she
wondered if he was about to enjoy a leisurely smoke

while he toyed with her again. She glanced at the young Russian; he was standing beside the autopsy table, examining the scalpels with evident anticipation.

Kaspar said, "You have had time to reconsider your lies. It would be much easier for you if you simply told the truth. All I want to know is the whereabouts of the device the creature gave to you, and then we will release you."

She stared at him. "How can I be sure of that? How can I be sure that you won't kill me to ensure my silence?"

"You have my word."

"Your word? The word of a Russian, whose soldiers were responsible for the deaths of a thousand innocent people?"

Kaspar merely shrugged. "In war, Miss Chatterjee, there are always innocent victims, on both sides. The British are not guiltless."

From the autopsy table, the young man snapped something in Russian. Kaspar replied, then turned to Jani. "Enough prevarication, Miss Chatterjee. Time is pressing. What did you do with the device?"

For a fleeting second she considered playing for time and admitting that Jelch did indeed give her something that looked like a coin, but that she had mislaid it. Then she abandoned the notion: it would gain her only minutes, if that, and would be met with disbelief.

She gripped the bars and looked Kaspar in the eye. "I was given no device," she said.

When they dragged her from the cage, she decided, she would be acquiescent until she reached the table – and then she would surprise them with her ferocity as she grabbed a scalpel and set about the pair.

Her heart sank as Kaspar raised the cigarette holder to his lips, and Jani realised that it was not a cigarette holder but a blow-pipe.

His cheeks inflated – two ridiculous little red apples – and he spat a dart through the bars at her.

She jumped back, shocked. The dart pierced the material of her dress, but, instead of pain, all she felt was a dull pressure. She stared down, and realised what had happened. The feathered tail of the dart protruded from the centre of her sternum, embedded not in her flesh but in the wooden frame of the tiny picture of her mother that her father had given her before her voyage to England...

Perhaps this was the luck of which Jelch had spoken.

She stared out at Kaspar, who was smiling with satisfaction.

She reached up and backhanded the dart from its moorings, so that they would not remove it and learn that it had failed to pierce her flesh. She wondered how long the drug would have taken to affect her; she had to be very careful, now, lest she give herself away.

She backed off and came up against the bars, then slipped down onto her haunches. She blinked. She would give it a minute before she closed her eyes fully. She felt a surge of hope, and at the same time a moment of panic: she was not free yet.

"What have you done...?" she asked with assumed drowsiness.

Kaspar said, "Merely a little sedative, Miss Chatterjee. I am sorry, but I did give you ample opportunity..."

She fluttered her eyes, allowed her head to drop forward. She lifted it suddenly, and opened her eyes briefly as if in a futile bid to stay awake, then let her head fall again and her eyes close.

She slumped against the bars, to all intents unconscious.

She heard a key in the lock, turning, and the door creak open, footsteps...

She felt tense, and willed herself to relax.

Grunting, the Russians took her weight and carried her from the confines of the cage. Her initial impulse was to fight, to spring into life and attack her abductors. But she knew that that would be a stupid mistake, and bided her time. Her head and arms dangling, she was ferried across the chamber to the hard, cold surface of the autopsy table and laid none too gently on her back.

The array of scalpels and knives were to her right. When she was sure that both men were close, she would reach out for a weapon, sit up and slash out at whoever was closest to her. Then she would leap from the table and attack the second Russian.

Kaspar spoke in his grumbling, ugly tongue, and the young man replied.

So Kaspar was to her right, the other to her left. She would attack the older man first, incapacitate him and then attend to the younger man.

She wondered what they were saying; their tone was conversational, casual. She wondered if she were just another innocent victim they would despatch without a qualm, for the greater good of their beloved ideology.

The thought incensed her, drove her to act.

She moved her right hand fractionally, felt the cold steel of a blade, and shifted her fingers towards the handle. At the very second her fingers curled around the handle of the knife, she sprang upright. One of the men grunted in surprise. She caught Kaspar's startled expression as she slashed out at him and missed. He backed off, tripping and falling onto his considerable bottom. The momentum of her swing carried her knife hand around, slicing towards the younger Russian who was frozen in place as if with shock. The blade slashed his face, bit deep, parting white flesh to the bone and shocking her with the resultant spume of brilliant red blood that slapped across her thighs. The man backed away, crying out in disbelief and pressing a hand against his lacerated face as if attempting to hold the torn flesh in place. He fetched up against the taxidermy bench, tripped and fell with a startled cry.

Jani jumped from the table, facing Kaspar as he struggled to his feet. With her left hand she fumbled on the tabletop and found a scalpel.

She took a step forward, clutching a weapon in each hand.

Kaspar was two yards away, crouched like a bear, watching her intently. All around him a silent menagerie of stuffed animals looked on. She felt the young man's blood soaking through her dress and drenching her thighs, hot at first then quickly cooling.

A weapon in each hand, she faced Kaspar. "Back off towards the door. Draw the bolts and open the door. Then move to the far end of the room."

"And if I refuse?"

"Then I will attack you."

He smiled, infuriatingly. "A little thing like you?"

"I don't think your friend would underestimate me, given a second chance. Now move towards the door."

She wanted him to show fear, but instead he merely smiled again as if it were he who had the upper hand and was toying with her. "You do realise, I hope, that even once through the door, you would not be free?

My people are in the ante-room, awaiting the success of the operation."

He was bluffing. He would have cried out by now, raised the alarm, if his cohorts had been nearby. "That's a chance I'll have to take. Move towards the door."

She was aware that the younger Russian was somewhere behind her. She had thought him too badly injured to get to his feet and attack her, but with a surge of paranoid fear she wondered if she were wrong. Not that she could risk a glance over her shoulder...

She danced nimbly forward again like a fencer and brought the knife in her right hand down in a great slashing arc.

She felt the flesh of Kaspar's belly part beneath the blade, and the material of his surgeon's gown bloomed with a slowly spreading carnation of blood.

He gasped and staggered back, skittling an antelope. It toppled, brought down a brown bear which crashed against a chimpanzee in a bizarre domino effect which in any other situation might have been amusing.

Kaspar clutched his stomach, staring at her with fury in his porcine eyes.

"You will die for this..."

She controlled her anger. Now was the time for a calm head, rational thoughts; she could not give in to her hatred of this man. Her heart pulsed. She was sweating. She recalled the other man and glanced quickly over her shoulder: there was no sign of him.

"Move towards the door and open it!" she said.

"For all the good it would do you..."

"I said move!" She leapt forward again, feinting with the blade in her right hand, and was gratified to see him scuttle back in alarm.

"Move!"

He looked over his shoulder, planning a route through the forest of animals. As he shuffled backwards, Jani matched his progress warily, on the alert lest he reach out and send a stuffed animal tumbling towards her.

He passed between a rearing brown bear and a panther. Jani slowed her advance. They were perhaps ten yards from the wall and the door. He continued backing carefully from her, occasionally looking over his shoulder to ensure that the way was clear.

He approached a magnificent pink flamingo. She imagined him catching it up and swinging the bird at her like a scythe. She slowed her pace, crouching even lower in readiness.

He passed the beady-eyed flamingo and came up against the wall.

She released a breath. "Now," she commanded in a steady voice, "move towards the door and open it slowly."

"I rather think not," Kaspar said, smiling.

As she contemplated darting forward again, slashing at him, his gaze flicked beyond her and his smile broadened. "Ah," he said, "I see that Mr Yezhov has recovered sufficiently to join us."

She broke out in a sudden hot sweat. He had to be bluffing. The small man's face had been sliced beyond repair...

"Mr Volovich," said a voice behind her, turning her blood to ice, "you seem to be in difficulty..."

Volovich glared at the younger man. "Miss Chatterjee has proven herself to be a worthy opponent, Yezhov, and one we were unwise to have underestimated."

"Between us, I think we will be able to subdue her," Yezhov said.

"And the subsequent operation," Volovich said, "and the reading of the thoughts in her pretty little head, will be made all the sweeter for her futile act of resistance."

She saw movement on the periphery of her vision. To her left, the young man, Yezhov, moved into sight, carrying a meat cleaver. He'd made running repairs to his face in the form of a bandage wound around his head. The white bindings, rapidly turning red, held the sliced flap of his cheek in place and covered his left eye.

He said something in Russian.

The older man replied in English, for Jani's benefit. "Perhaps, as you are armed and I am not, Yezhov, you should have the singular honour of subduing our guest. But go gently. We would not want any harm to befall the girl yet."

Jani backed off, stifling the urge to cry out. She would fight to the last, she resolved. After all, she was armed. If she could slice Yezhov again, then attend to Volovich...

She ran towards Yezhov and slashed at the arm holding the meat cleaver.

He backed off with the nimbleness of a ballerina, grinning at her.

Jani's advance had left her open to an attack from the rear, and Volovich pressed home his advantage. Before she could swing around and strike out, the older man had her arms pinioned – while the younger man, laughing now with satisfaction, danced forward and struck her head with the blunt edge of the cleaver.

She slumped, pain flaring across her skull. She felt strong arms lift her, bundle her like a sack across the chamber – toppling stuffed animals – towards the autopsy table. They dropped her without ceremony onto its cold surface; her head hit the steel and she moaned in pain.

They bound her hands, and then her legs, so that though she struggled, she was unable to move. She opened her eyes, stared up at the skylight overhead. From time to time the faces of her captors came into view as they prepared for the operation.

"Drill?" Yezhov asked.

"Check."

"Circular saw?"

"Check."

"Trepanning screw?"

"Check."

"Anaesthetic...?"

A silence. Then Yezhov said, "I think, in the circumstances, we might dispense with the anaesthetic."

"Considering the distinct lack of co-operation shown by our guest," Volovich said, "I think Miss Chatterjee has foregone the privilege."

A face came into view inches above her eyes. Volovich's great moon of a head, pocked with craters left by old boils and carbuncles, peered down at her.

"This will be painful, but not fatal, as that would defeat the object of the exercise. You have taken great delight in lying to us so far, but your lies are at an end. Within the hour, your thoughts will be laid bare for us to read."

"What should we do with her then?" Yezhov asked.

"When we have learned what we want from Miss Chatterjee's pretty little skull, I will take great delight in skinning her alive and mounting her chestnut Indian hide on a suitably svelte frame, if I can locate one amongst the taxidermist's stock."

Yezhov's grinning visage, swaddled in bloody bandages, came into view – all the more farcical for being bracketed by a pair of bulky ear-phones connected to the wireless-like CWAD.

Jani cried out, pulling at the ropes that bound her arms and legs. Her struggles rattled the table and she twisted back and forth. They would hardly be able to operate on her head if it were in constant movement.

Yezhov had a simple remedy, and brought the back of the meat cleaver down on her skull once again.

She moaned in pain and her head flopped. Semi-conscious, she felt cold fingers arrange her head. Something braced her temples, clamping tight, so that her head was held in place. She opened her eyes and stared at the sunlight slanting through the dusty skylights. She was beyond terror, feeling only a dull disbelief, a serene sense of remove; she wanted in some way to defy the pair, to strike some valiant last blow, but knew that she was incapable of doing so.

She stared up at Volovich as he lowered the flimsy wire frame of the CWAD over her face and made a minimal adjustment, lips pursed in concentration.

She felt pin-pricks on her cheeks and forehead. Volovich applied pressure to the frame and the spikes pierced her skin. Then he lifted the frame from her head and smiled down at her.

"Drill," he said.

She saw the drill pass before her eyes, and Volovich leaned over her again. "And now, using the frame's puncture marks as my guide, I will proceed to drill two dozen small holes into your skull. I would close your eyes, Miss Chatterjee, as this might be a little bloody."

She would be damned if she'd close her eyes. She remained staring at him and managed to say, despite her clamped jaw, "May you die in agony, Volovich!"

"But not before you, my dear."

He lowered the drill to her forehead, and despite her best resolve she closed her eyes and sobbed.

The explosion filled the chamber like a thunderclap, adding panic to Jani's terror. She heard Volovich and Yezhov exclaim above the din. She did her best to sit up, straining against the ropes and staring at the thing that was striding through the ruins of the far wall.

She had heard about these inventions, seen posters in London for an exhibition where Mech-Men would be on show. The photographs and illustrations had been impressive enough, showing mechanical men fully fifteen feet tall – all flashing lights and oiled metal carapaces – but the reality was altogether more startling.

The Mech-Man stomped through the tumbled masonry with legs as thick as girders, pushing aside drifts of brick and beams with hands like the scoops of mechanical diggers. Its torso was an amalgam of black boilerplate and ornately etched scrollwork – as if Aubrey Beardsley had gone to work on an invention by Isambard Kingdom Brunel – and polychromatic running lights threw the chaos of its arrival into crazed relief. Amidst the mayhem, the fur and feathers of a hundred stuffed animals filled the air in a whirling maelstrom.

The overpowering reek of formaldehyde made Jani gag as the Mech-Man crunched relentlessly through shattered specimen bottles, scattering the larger stuffed animals aside as it went.

Volovich and Yezhov backed off, their faces masks of alarm. Jani struggled to free herself, wondering whether she had been saved from one fate only to succumb to another just as lethal. The Mech-Man was heading directly towards her, and surely she would be crushed by its pylon legs or its great swinging arms? She yanked at the ropes that bound her wrists, but succeeded only in tightening the knots.

Yezhov sprinted towards the bolted door, yelling across the chamber in Russian. Obviously it was an instruction, for Volovich bounded towards the autopsy table and took up a knife. At first Jani thought he intended to strike her dead in a sadistic *coup de grace*, but to her amazement he began cutting at the ropes tying her arms. So even now they had not given up hope of extracting information from her; they would take her with them as they fled the Mech-Man's onslaught.

But not if she had any say in the matter.

Volovich cut through the rope encircling her ankles and instantly she kicked out, striking the fat Russian's jaw. He yelled and swung the blade. Jani ducked and rolled off the table, landing on all fours and scuttling through a jumble of stuffed animal legs.

She glanced over her shoulder. The Mech-Man reached down, swung a great arm and batted Volovich aside like a rag doll. He cried out and sprawled across the floor, fetched up against the wall and lay motionless.

Jani scrambled through the ruck of tumbled animals, then started in alarm as something clutched her arm. She whirled, finding Yezhov's bandaged face inches from hers. With his free hand he waved a scalpel at her and yelled, "If you resist, I'll kill you!"

He yanked Jani to her feet and dragged her across the chamber towards the door, their way impeded by felled animals and strewn bricks and beams, the air dense with choking plaster dust. Jani could hear the crunching steps of the Mech-Man and the bass grumble of its grinding engine as it stomped through the wreckage. She stumbled over an antelope, its legs as stiff as those of an overturned table. Her headlong fall freed her from Yezhov's grip, and on hands and knees she dived under the belly of the baby elephant. The Russian yelled and came after her, caught her by the elbow and swung her round. Facing him, his terrified face circumambulated by the bloody bandage, she gave a startled gasp and stared beyond her captor. Yezhov, seeing her alarm, turned and cried out.

The Mech-Man, towering over them, swung an arm like the boom of a crane. A great mechanical claw hung over Yezhov, then the pincer descended, plucked him with surprising delicacy by the collar of his surgeon's gown and tossed him halfway across the chamber.

Jani cowered, staring up at the mechanical monstrosity as it loomed over her. The great girder-like arm swung towards her, the pincer descending. She wept in fright and felt the pincer grab the collar of her dress. The next second she was being lifted into the air, dangling like a child's rag doll. She expected to be pitched aside just as the Russian had been, but as she was hoisted high into the air she was amazed to see the head and shoulders of the Mech-Man hinge open like a trapdoor to reveal the glittering chamber of its torso. Jani swung through the air, legs pedalling, and was dropped into the chamber. She landed with a thump, dazed, and sprawled behind what looked like a dentist's chair which bobbed and sighed pneumatically. The Mech-Man's head and shoulders, above her, clanged shut, plunging the chamber into an oily gloom relieved only by a constellation of flickering lights.

Then she was shaken this way and that as the Mech-Man straightened up and stamped through the debris, crunching bricks underfoot. She heard the deafening pounding of its footsteps, the grinding of its gears amplified as if the chamber were a sound box. She also heard, through the din, a high, thin voice crying out in delighted Hindi.

Dazed, hardly believing what was happening, she sat upright and collected her breath. Then cautiously, on her knees, she peered around the great bouncing padded chair and stared in amazement at the tiny figure ensconced there, hauling on levers and pulling gear-sticks and pumping pedals as if his life depended on it.

The Mech-Man's operator turned and grinned at her, his teeth fluorescent in his brown face, his shock of jet hair even more haywire than usual.

ANAND HAD NEVER felt more elated in all his life. The rescue had gone better than he'd dared hope, when the first inkling of the plan came to him on the rooftop of the warehouse more than an hour ago.

He stared at Jani, pride bursting in his chest. This would show her another side of him – not the houseboy she knew of old, but an adventurer who could knock down walls and save victims from evil-doers.

"But the Russians?" she cried. "Are they coming after us?"

He laughed. "The Russians are unconscious, Jani-ji. They will bother you no more." He hesitated. "But do you think we should return and arrest them?"

"No... No, the best thing is to be away from here."

Even in distress, with her long hair dishevelled and her face covered in dust, Jani looked beautiful. "Do not be alarmed!" he said. "You look like a frightened rabbit, Jani-ji! But you are safe now. Come and sit beside me."

She climbed up beside him as he steered the Mech-Man over the piled bricks of the erstwhile façade, grinning proudly at her. Jani was staring around her in wonder, and Anand saw the control cabin as if through new eyes. The chamber looked like the cockpit of an airship, with dials and verniers and levers and pedals which he pulled and pushed and pumped and adjusted with quick movements of his hands.

Directly before the seat, embedded in the chest of the Mech-Man, was a narrow view-plate through which he glanced from time to time as he guided the Mech-Man along the street.

"Mr Clockwork kindly taught me how to pilot Max," Anand told her.

"Max?" Jani laughed.

"Max – the Mech-Man. He is the star of Mr Clockwork's magnificent exhibition. There are only six of them in all the Empire – just think of that! And I am the only pilot in all India besides Mr Clockwork."

She stared at him as he manhandled the levers. "But... but Anand, how did you know where I was? How did you find me?"

He glanced through the view-plate. They were passing down a narrow alley between the grey walls of ugly warehouses.

"When we dropped you in Old Delhi, Jani-ji, Mr Rai drove home. A little later came a loud knocking at the door. Mr Rai thought it was the press, come to stick their noses into our grief. But no!"

"Who was it?"

He glanced at her. "It was the military, come to arrest you."

"Arrest me?" she said incredulously. "Surely not. But why...?"

"They did not say in so many words that they had come to arrest you, oh, no. But you see, the officer was Colonel Smethers. Now Smethers does the dirty work for internal security. Your father, bless his memory, hated Colonel Smethers. He said he was a thug and a bully who was responsible for the torture and deaths of many prisoners under his care. So you see, when Mr Rai saw Smethers, and he asked if you were at home, Mr Rai feared the worst. So he said that you were in Victoria Park, where you wanted to be alone with your thoughts at this sad time. Then Mr Rai told me to race to Old Delhi and find you, warn you that Smethers wanted to question you for some reason." He peered at her in the gloom. "But why does he want to question you, Jani-ji?"

She shook her head, looking perplexed. "I don't really know," she said. "It's a long story, and when we get out of here I will tell you." She gazed through the screen. "So Mr Rai sent you to Old Delhi to find me, but how did you manage–?"

Grinning, Anand interrupted. "He told me that you would be at one of three places – places which you visited with your father as a child: Roopa's Tea Rooms, Nazruddin's, or the Gwalior Café. I tried Nazruddin's first, because it was closest, but you were not there. Then I hurried across to Roopa's and the waiter told me that you had fallen ill and that a kindly old man had taken you off in a taxi. So I hurried to the taxi rank and asked every driver there if it was they who had taken you. None had, Jani-ji, so I waited and asked every driver who returned to the rank, and finally one man, who demanded ten rupees, told me that he had driven you and a European gentleman to an address to the north of the city. I took a rickshaw to this address and tried to find where they had taken you, but there were no windows in the walls, so I climbed a drainpipe and looked through a skylight, and there you were, Jani-ji, crouching in a cage like an animal."

She smiled. "I thought I saw the shape of a monkey up there, Anand."

"Ah-cha! That was me, climbing across the rooftop!" He shook his head, frowning. "But what did they want with you, Jani-ji?"

"Anand, something happened when the airship crashed. Now is not the time to recount my adventures. In fact..." She shook her head. "In fact, I don't know what I should do now for the best. Or rather..."

She appeared deep in thought.

"Jani-ji?"

"The British want to question me, and the Russians to torture me for something... I have only the clothes on my back, and a hundred rupees in my pocket."

Anand's heart skipped. He had an idea, and said tentatively, "Jani-ji, if I were you, with Colonel Smethers wishing to have words, and the Russians on your trail, I would get away from Delhi and hide for a while."

She stared at him and said suddenly, "Anand, I need to get to Nepal."

He looked at her, surprised. "*Nepal?* But Jani-ji...?"

"I know, I know... Nepal is a protected territory. But I need to make my way there, though first I must go to the hill station of Rishi Tal."

He stared ahead, concentrating for a time on manipulating levers and adjusting verniers. "I have an idea, Jani-ji," he said, bubbling with excitement.

"All your ideas have been capital so far, Anand."

He felt himself blushing. "Mr Clockwork has given me the job of taking Max north to Dehrakesh. A place is booked aboard the Chandigar Mail at noon. At Dehrakesh Mr Clockwork has a warehouse and an exhibition centre. I am to deliver Max there, where he will go on show, and I am due to return to Delhi with the Amazing Mechanical Elephant. My idea is this. I will deliver Max to the Old Delhi station goods yard and see him aboard the train – with you inside. Then, when we get to Dehrakesh, you will be part of the way to Rishi Tal." He hesitated. "But Jani-ji, getting into Nepal will be impossible!"

She asked, "How far from Dehrakesh is Rishi Tal, Anand?"

"Perhaps fifty miles. But why...?"

"I hope to meet someone there who will help me get into the protected territory, with a little luck."

He nodded, and glanced across at Jani as she laid her head back against the cushion and closed her eyes, exhausted. He concentrated on the controls and steered the Mech-Man towards the railway station.

By the time they reached the iron gates of the goods yard, the mechanical man had attracted a crowd of curious onlookers, mainly young boys to whom the arrival of the Mech-Man would be the highlight of their week. Peering through the narrow view-plate as he brought the vehicle to a halt, Anand made out a hundred gawpers staring up in wonder; some appeared amazed, others frightened. Ash-covered sadhus moved among the crowd with begging bowls and snake-charmers took advantage of the impromptu gathering and mesmerised their cobras with high, trilling tunes.

A station worker unlocked the gates and pulled them back, and Anand eased the Mech-Man forward, leaving the crowd in its wake. The same worker waved the mechanical man through the goods yard, across snaking tracks which Anand negotiated in great strides, towards a long line of rolling stock at the head of which was an old steam engine.

He steered the Mech-Man up a ramp and onto a long, low flat-bed, then lowered the Mech-Man into a seated position, its great metal legs looming on either side of the viewplate.

He jumped from the seat and climbed a ladder, opening the Mech-Man's head-and-shoulders lid. For the next ten minutes he shouted instructions to the porters, who were lashing guy ropes around Max and attaching them to lugs on the flat-bed. He glanced down at Jani as he shouted his commands, and her smile made him feel proud.

When Max was secure, he jumped down, closing the lid after him, and rejoined Jani on the seat.

"I have a cabin in the next compartment," he told her. "Mr Clockwork paid for my first-class passage – and the cabin has a shower and two bunks. So when we leave Delhi, Jani-ji, you can join me in my cabin and you can shower and sleep."

Jani reached out and clutched his hand. "Thank you," she murmured. "Thank you, Anand, for saving my life, for everything."

Embarrassed, he looked and turned away, his face burning.

He noticed movement through the viewscreen and stared out in alarm. A truck carrying six British soldiers pulled up beside the train, and three of the officers alighted and climbed a metal ladder into the adjacent carriage. The remaining three strolled towards where Max sat, tied down like Gulliver restrained by Lilliputians. They removed their peaked caps and scratched their heads, commenting to each other and laughing.

He saw Jani's alarmed expression and said, "Don't worry, Jani-ji. I will climb out and speak to these chaps. I will even ask them what all the hoo-hah is about."

Before he could do that, however, an officer climbed onto the flat-bed and approached the Mech-Man. Anand grabbed Jani's hand – so soft and hot in his – and pulled her behind the seat. They crouched side by side, peering through the gap between the seat and the head-rest.

The officer covered his eyes with his hand and peered in, then tapped the glass with his swagger stick and said something. Another white face appeared at the viewscreen, speaking to the first. The officer nodded, his eyes darting round the darkened interior of the chamber. He tapped the glass again, once, and then both faces vanished from sight. Anand gave a relieved sigh and grinned at Jani.

They watched the officers climb back into the truck and drive away.

"I wonder what they wanted?" Jani whispered.

He shrugged. "They were simply curious about Max," he said confidently. "Don't worry, Jani-ji, they were not looking for you, I'm sure."

"I hope so," she murmured.

One hour later the flat-bed lurched, and a succession of clankings sounded along the chain of the carriages as the train eased itself from the goods yard and through the station. Anand peered out at the platform, counting at least a dozen soldiers. He wondered if they were looking for Jani, and if so, why.

They left the grey, distempered northern suburbs of Delhi in their wake and were soon rolling through open countryside. Anand peered out at a flat, limitless expanse of maize and corn fields, at the tiny brown figures and their oxen toiling on the land.

He thought fleetingly of papa-ji, and the sadness he felt at his passing was soon eclipsed by the idea of the adventure he was embarking upon. He stared at Jani as she combed her fingers through her long, luxuriant fall of hair, and his heart beat like a tabla.

"Now, Jani-ji," he said, "will you please tell me what the bloody hell is going on?"

Jani smiled and, as the train steamed north on its hundred mile journey to Dehrakesh, Anand sat in amazed silence as she told a story of crashed airships, her meeting with a strange creature, and her abduction by the Russian spies...

CHAPTER
TEN

Alfie sallies forth – The wreckage of the warehouse –
In pursuit of the Russians –
"This is worse than I feared..."

ALFIE LITTLEBODY SAT in the back of the taxi and gazed out at the chaotic street scene. He was still light-headed with euphoria at the turn of events in Brigadier Cartwright's office. He had expected a dressing down at least – a court-martial at worst – but to gain the brigadier's tacit approval of what he'd done in Allahabad, and then to be tasked with tracing the missing Chatterjee girl, went beyond his wildest dreams.

He fingered the light-stick and the skullcap in his pocket, still marvelling at the demonstration of their capabilities he'd been treated to in the lab. The photon-blade was a marvel enough, but the invisibility skullcap – or the Visual Camouflage Amplifier, as the boffin Tennyson had insisted on calling it – was mind-boggling. Watching Tennyson touch the control on the chin-strap and vanish into thin air, Alfie had almost passed out in amazement. Then Tennyson had popped into existence again, on the far side of the room, and laughed at Alfie's reaction. "Always gets people the first time. Amazing, what?"

"I... I presume it's fuelled by Annapurnite?" he'd stammered.

Tennyson had chewed his lip for a time before replying. "Bit more complicated than that, old boy. But away you go. I haven't time to stand here chattering all day."

Now, in the back of the taxi as it sped north to Old Delhi, Alfie considered what Brigadier Cartwright had told him and the fact that he'd been entrusted with the photon-blade and the VCA.

He'd embarked on what he considered more important missions in the past, equipped with no more than a file report and his trusty Enfield revolver. Now he was trying to track down a missing girl, and had the very latest technology to help him do so. Granted, the girl was the daughter of the late Minister of Security, but Cartwright's line that it would be bad form if she went over to the Nationalists seemed a bit thin to Alfie. Was there more to the girl than Cartwright was letting on? Was that why he'd been equipped with the weapon and the skullcap? But why, then, had Cartwright sent him on the mission alone? Of course, Alfie didn't know for sure that he was working on this case alone. Perhaps Cartwright had other officers looking for the girl.

The whole affair was more than a little mysterious.

The taxi edged down Gupta Road, the thoroughfare blocked with pedestrians, street-vendors, wandering cows and bad-tempered rickshaw-wallahs wholly reluctant to give ground. The late morning heat was punishing, and to add to Alfie's discomfort the taxi driver insisted on thumping his car horn every three seconds. At last, his patience in shreds, Alfie leaned forward and tapped the driver's shoulders. "Ah-cha, baba. No problem," he said in his stumbling Hindi. "I'll walk from here."

He passed the driver five rupees and slipped from the cab.

He hurried down the road and turned right into a relatively quiet side street that had the added benefit of being in the shade. The fact that he was British, and in uniform, assisted his passage through the crowds, which parted for him as if he were contagious.

Roopa's Tea Rooms on Lal Singh Road was an ancient, timber-fronted establishment that had been a favourite – according to the report – of Janisha Chatterjee's father. It was also, according to a police report, the last place where the girl had been seen – in the company of a European gentleman.

He quizzed the owner of the Tea Rooms, a proud old Brahmin with a distracting array of gold teeth, who described the European. "He was very fat, sir. Very fat. So fat that he must be very wealthy. He was dressed in a white suit and spoke English very well, sir. He was also German."

"German?"

"I was talking with my good friend Mr Choudry and I overheard him telling the girl that he was a German businessman. Then the girl fell ill, and the German assisted her from the premises. But I am assuring you that it was not the produce of my respectable café that was making the girl ill, sir."

"I'm sure it wasn't," Alfie said. "And the taxi was one from the rank across the street?"

"That is correct, sir."

"And you didn't hear anything else the German and the girl were saying?"

"No, sir. Nothing more."

Alfie thanked the owner, left the tea room and crossed the street to the taxi rank. After asking half a dozen drivers whether they had picked up a European and an

Indian girl that morning, he was directed to a chair stall where a tiny Tamil in a brilliant white shirt was sipping chai and chewing betel nut.

"I am the driver, sir! I am the very man you want. I was driving the girl and the man from the tea rooms this very morning. The girl was very ill, sir. The big man had to be carrying her."

"And what time was this?"

"Approximately eight-thirty, sir."

"And where did you take them?"

"I was taking them to the Karnaka district."

Alfie nodded, pleased with his investigations so far but worried for the welfare of the girl. "Do you recall the exact address?"

The Tamil joggled his head. "Yes, sir!"

"Jolly good. Be a good chap and take me there straight away."

"Ah-cha! Hop in, sir!"

They crossed the road to the taxi rank and two minutes later were crawling along the packed by-ways of Old Delhi. The driver turned to him, grinning. "I was taking the gentleman and the girl to Mr Horniman's, sir."

Alfie repeated the name. "And just what is Mr Horniman's?"

"Mr Horniman is powerful personage, sir. He is very rich. Mr Horniman collects animals in his warehouse."

Alfie blinked. "Animals?"

"Yes, animals. I have delivered animals there myself."

"Mr Horniman runs a zoo?" Alfie asked, bemused.

"Not a zoo, sir. No. You see, Mr Horniman kills the animals, sir."

"Kills them?" Alfie was liking the sound of this place less and less.

Why should an elderly German, Alfie asked himself, take Janisha Chatterjee to a warehouse where the owner slaughtered animals?

Five minutes later the taxi halted. "The warehouse is down this street, sir. But there is some kind of commotion going on."

"I'll say there is," Alfie said, peering out.

A crowd had gathered at the end of the street, blocking access. Above the massed heads, in the distance, Alfie made out a great billow of what looked like smoke, and he wondered if the crowd was watching a factory fire.

"And the warehouse is along this street? Do you know what number?"

"Ah-cha, along this street. No number, sir, but it has very bright pink walls. You cannot miss it, sir."

"Very good." He paid the driver, climbed from the car and pushed his way through the crowd.

The curious bystanders had moved down the street until prevented from going any further by a roiling cloud of dust and debris. He hurried through the crowd, wafting a hand before his face and trying not to choke. The problem was not a fire, he realised now, but something else entirely. An explosion, a collapsed building?

Added to the choking dust was a terrible chemical stench that had him gagging. The reek was sickly sweet and acrid at the same time, and became ever more overpowering the further he moved along the street. Fifty yards on he came to a great pile of rubble and, beyond, a gaping hole in the façade of a cavernous warehouse. The few bricks intact, on either side of the maw, were pink – and Alfie felt a terrible sense of hopelessness. He pulled out his bandana and covered his nose and mouth, more to stem the appalling stench than the choking dust that obscured the sunlight.

He made out stuffed animals scattered among the masonry – deer and bears and monkeys – and shattered glass jars that had contained pickled lizards, geckos and salamanders. Now the terrible smell was explained; he wondered if the spilled chemicals might have somehow brought about an explosion.

Across the street, on top of a wall, sat half a dozen runny-nosed street kids, giggling to themselves and obviously enjoying the show. He was about to pick his way through the scattered bricks and question them when he heard the sound of movement from within the collapsed warehouse. He turned and peered through the miasma of plaster and masonry dust. Fifty yards away, on the far side of the piled bricks and girders, he made out two dishevelled figures. They were picking their way through the ruins, clutching each other for support. As he watched, they stumbled over the debris and moved away up the street.

His heart leaped. One of the figures was grossly fat and garbed in the tattered remains of a surgeon's gown. The other figure was thin and sported a bloody bandage tied around his head.

Alfie drew his revolver and stumbled through the debris after them, grimacing and side-stepping the grisly remains of stuffed or pickled fauna. He pressed his bandana to his face as he made his way over the bricks and girders, the reek of formaldehyde threatening to overpower him. His progress was slow, but then so was that of the pair up ahead. They were obviously suffering the effects of being caught in the blast – physical injuries as well as nausea from the airborne chemicals – which

Alfie reasoned should make his task of apprehending them a little easier.

He lifted his revolver as he ran towards the pair. He was perhaps ten yards behind them when he remembered the skullcap in his pocket.

He halted, pulled it out and arranged it over his head. He slid the switch on the chin-strap to 'on' – expecting to feel some change as he was rendered invisible. He felt nothing, and wondered if the device was working.

Ahead, the pair turned a corner. Alfie ran after them and cried out, "I say! Halt right there or I'll shoot."

The fat man turned, his dust-caked face registering astonishment as he searched for his interlocutor. Alfie fired a warning shot above their heads, which had the effect of galvanising the pair. They took off at a sprint. Alfie cursed and gave chase.

"I said halt or I'll shoot!"

The fat man turned again, growling something in a foreign language that turned Alfie's blood to ice. He was startled not by the content of the exclamation – which he couldn't comprehend anyway – but by the fact that it sounded Russian. Then the man drew a pistol and fired three times. Alfie dived into a recessed doorway. He peered out, fired again at the fleeing Russians but missed. The pair were careering around a corner, the fat man turning again to lay down a volley of warning shots.

Undeterred, Alfie gave chase. He came to the corner, turned and stopped dead, cursing his luck. He stared at the crowd surging down the wide street. The Russians were lost to sight. Alfie approached the corner and looked right and left, swearing to himself as he saw not the slightest sign of his prey.

He should have shot their blasted legs, he thought as he hurried back to the collapsed warehouse, winged the blighters and disarmed them, then interrogated them there and then in order to locate the Chatterjee girl. He had a dread suspicion, as he neared the warehouse, that he would find her among the debris, as dead as the hapless animals littering the area.

The children were still sitting on the opposite wall, gasping and laughing as if at a Punch and Judy show. He approached them and said in Hindi, "Do you know what happened here?" and only when expressions of bemusement crossed their features did he realise his mistake.

"Who said that?" a tiny girl asked.

Alfie ducked around the corner and, out of sight of the children, deactivated his skullcap. He pulled off the cap and re-emerged. "Did anyone see what happened to the building?"

The urchins stared at his uniform, sat up very straight, and all began jabbering at once.

Alfie held up a hand. "One at a time, please!"

He pointed to the little girl, who said, "We were playing kabaddi right here when the giant came!"

A bare-chested boy chipped in, "He came striding up the street. We were frightened, ah-cha, but we didn't run away!"

"We hid behind the wall and watched," said another.

The six urchins began chattering at once, each louder than the last. Alfie caught the odd word or phrase: "Crash!" and "hit the wall!" and "the girl..."

Alfie pointed to the tousle-haired boy. "Did you say 'the girl'?"

"Ah-cha!" said the boy. "The giant ate her!"

He stared at the six as they looked down at him, twelve bare legs drumming the wall in excitement. They were jabbering again, their volume escalating in a bid to be the one to relate the terrible story.

"Listen to me!" Alfie shouted above the din. "I will give each one of you five rupees if one of you, *one* of you, answers my questions. It doesn't matter who, just one of you. Now who will it be?"

"Five rupees?" said the tiny girl.

"Five rupees each," Alfie said.

They debated amongst themselves, shouting and gesticulating, until finally the tousle-haired boy was nominated as spokesman. He puffed his chest proudly and said, "We were playing kabaddi, sir. Kapil was winning, but he was cheating also. He always cheats–"

"No, I don't!" said a one-eyed boy.

"No arguments!" Alfie cried. "Now, what happened?"

"It was just one hour ago. The street was quiet, and then we heard a terrible crash!"

The little girl said, "Crash! Crash! Crash!"

"And we didn't know what it was. It became louder and louder. We hid behind the wall and peered over. Then we saw the giant!"

"The giant?" What on earth, Alfie thought, were they talking about?

"He turned the corner from the alley and walked towards Horniman's warehouse."

Alfie peered up at the raconteur. "He was a man, a big man?"

"No! He was a giant, a metal man, sir. He was taller than an elephant and had flashing lights on the front of his body and he walked like this..." The boy rocked from side to side and pumped his arms and legs like stiff pistons, even though he was sitting down. "He was a metal giant and he walked towards the warehouse and he didn't stop!"

Kapil leaned forward and interrupted, "He was the Mech-Man from Mr Clockwork's Fabulous Emporium!"

"Ah-cha," said the small girl, "he was the Mech-Man."

"Ah-cha!" said the spokesman. "The Mech-Man walked through the wall, sir, smashing it to bits with his arms and legs. He ripped the front of the warehouse away, and all the dead animals and bottles and bricks came tumbling down."

A mechanical man from Mr Clockwork's Fabulous Emporium?

Alfie looked at each child in turn, attempting to discern from their expression whether they were lying. They were all staring at him in deadly earnest, their eyes massive, and nodded along to the spokesman's account.

"And what happened then?" Alfie asked. "You said there was a girl...?"

"A girl was in the warehouse, and two men. The men were chasing the girl around and around. She was running away, and the Mech-Man marched into the warehouse and chased them. It was a madhouse in there, sir!"

"And then?" Alfie asked.

"And then the Mech-Man picked up one of the men and flung him away, and then he marched over to the girl, and he leaned over her and reached out with his big metal arm."

"And then," the little girl butted in, unable to contain her excitement, "the Mech-Man's head came off, and he lifted the girl up and popped her into his belly and ate her!"

"Ah-cha," the spokesman affirmed, "it is as Ana is saying. The Mech-Man ate the girl!"

"And what happened then?" Alfie asked.

"And then the Mech-Man marched away from the ruins, banging and crashing through the bricks. He went down the street and disappeared, and we didn't want to be eaten also, so we decided not to follow him."

"And you say that the mechanical man is from Mr Clockwork's Fabulous Emporium?"

The girl nodded. "Ah-cha. We have seen it. One day we snuck in and saw the Mech-Man. Only then he was not moving, just standing like this." She stiffened her hands at her side and stared straight ahead. "And it was not exciting. But today it *was* exciting!"

"Ah-cha!" Kapil said. "Today the Mech-Man ate a girl!"

Alfie withdrew the photograph of Janisha Chatterjee from his pocket and handed it to the first child. "And was this the girl?"

They passed the picture along the line, each urchin nodding in turn. "Ah-cha." "Yes, sir." "This was the girl."

Alfie returned the photograph to his pocket and pulled out his wallet. He counted out six five-rupee notes and passed them to the children, who accepted the notes in stunned silence. And then, in the blink of an eye, they jumped off the wall like a troop of temple monkeys and went whooping and yelling down the street.

Alfie made his way back along the thoroughfare, passing crowds of curious onlookers come to see the destruction of the warehouse. Once back on the main street, he hailed a taxi and told the driver, "Mr Clockwork's Fabulous Emporium."

He sat back as he was carried even further north into the decrepit slums and crumbling tenements of the

Karnaka district of Old Delhi. He had no doubt that the children had told him the truth – or the truth as far as they understood it. But far from eating the girl, Alfie surmised, the mechanical man had come to her rescue.

MR CLOCKWORK'S FABULOUS Emporium was a peeling stuccoed building situated between a barber's shop and a cinema bearing bloated images of Hindu film stars. It was a wholly unprepossessing frontage that bore no relation to its extravagant title painted on a panel above a khaki-coloured swing door.

Alfie pushed his way inside and found himself standing in a tiny foyer with a sticky red carpet and puce walls. A small door next to a ticket booth gave access to the emporium. He pushed the door open, stepped into the gloom, and stared around him in astonishment.

Aladdin's cave came to mind, and Madame Tussauds' waxworks, and even a railway museum. The emporium was an amalgam of all three, a fabulous chamber in which glittering vehicles of improbable design – part flying machine, part submarine – sat next to what looked like jewelled suits of armour, mechanical mannequins, improbable calliopes and impossible clocks, all glittering like treasure in the mysterious half-light.

"Can I help you, sir?" asked a voice in impeccable English.

Alfie whirled around. A tall, slim man emerged from between what looked like a four-legged grandfather clock and a gold- and glass-panelled gyrocopter.

Alfie introduced himself.

"And I am Mr Clockwork, sir, proprietor of this fabulous emporium and inventor extraordinaire. All the wonders you see before you, sir, began up here, in the humble abode of my cranium."

Mr Clockwork's appearance was as fantastical as his oratory. He wore curlicue Ali Baba slippers, a gold and tangerine striped dressing gown, and a fez. He had a thin, cunning face and a winning smile, and puffed a huge hookah pipe which rolled along behind him on a clockwork tea-trolley.

Alfie stared about him. "And I'm impressed," he said. "You invented *everything* here?"

"Everything, sir. Everything. But then I have been labouring at my craft – might I even say my art? – for almost half a century."

Alfie stared at the man. Granted, he had a full head of brilliantined hair, and the lighting in the emporium was low, but he would have guessed that Mr Clockwork was not a day over fifty.

Alfie remembered his mission. "And may I ask if you invented a device called, if I remember correctly, the Mech-Man?"

"Ah," said Mr Clockwork, "the Mech-Man. Yes, that is my latest, and I might say finest, brainchild."

Alfie considered how to phrase his next question. "And does it work of its own volition? That is–"

Mr Clockwork laughed. "Of course not, Lieutenant Littlebody. It is driven."

"Driven?"

"By a pilot seated within its chest cavity."

"Ah..." Alfie said. "I see now."

"But might I enquire as to your interest?"

"Of course. I was wondering if it has been... stolen, or if perhaps you yourself have used it in the last few hours? You see, it was seen in the Karnaka district this morning."

Enlightenment dawned on the inventor's hatchet face. "That would be Anand's doing. He took it early, bound for the Old Delhi railway station. You see, he is taking the Mech-Man by train up to Dehrakesh, where I have a second emporium – and where it will be on show for a month. I take it that nothing untoward has occurred?"

"Not at all. I was just curious; it isn't every day that something as... as distinctive as a mechanical man is seen marching the streets of Old Delhi. You said this Anand was due to take the Mech-Man to Dehrakesh by train – at what time, might I ask?"

"The train is due to leave the station at midday."

Alfie consulted his watch. It was fifteen minutes to twelve. If he set off in the next minute or two he might just apprehend the train before it departed.

"And who exactly is Anand?"

"My apprentice – my part-time apprentice, I should say. He is a most intelligent youth, wasted as a houseboy for the late Kapil Dev Chatterjee."

Alfie stared at Mr Clockwork. "He works for Mr Chatterjee, the Security Minister?"

The inventor inclined his head. "That is, he did, Lieutenant. But when Mr Chatterjee fell ill, it was arranged that Anand should become my apprentice when eventually the honourable Mr Chatterjee finally passed away. I heard the tragic news of his death on the wireless earlier this morning."

The pieces, Alfie thought, were beginning to fall into place. Anand had saved Janisha Chatterjee from the Russians with the help of the mechanical man, and they would soon be *en route* to Dehrakesh. Unless, of course, the Chatterjee girl had handed herself in to the safe custody of the nearest police station.

Alfie thanked Mr Clockwork for his time, shook the bemused inventor by the hand, and hurried from the emporium.

He hailed a taxi and a minute later was rolling through the streets of Old Delhi towards the railway station.

He would apprehend young Anand and quiz him as to the whereabouts of the girl. Alfie rather hoped that she would still be aboard the mechanical man, so that he could claim the plaudits for finding her. So swift a wrapping up of the case would look good on his record and please Brigadier Cartwright no end.

In the event, a traffic jam along Rajpur Road put paid to apprehending the noon train. It was almost five past the hour when he pulled up outside the ornate Victorian portico of the station, paid the driver and rushed inside.

Any hope that the train had been delayed was stymied by the admirable efficiency of the Indian Railway timetable. Mr Singh, the station master, informed him proudly that the Dehrakesh train had departed punctually on the dot of twelve.

Alfie was about to leave the office and arrange his own passage to Dehrakesh when, glancing through the window at the platform, he noticed a plethora of British army personnel. He wondered if they too were on the trail of the Chatterjee girl.

Mr Singh noticed his interest. "They are looking for Russian spies, Lieutenant, sir. Russians have been reported in the area, so I have been reliably informed. We have been on the alert all day."

Alfie left the station and considered his next move.

He found a phone box, got through to Cartwright's office, and asked the secretary to put him through to the brigadier. "Lieutenant Littlebody here, on urgent business."

Thirty seconds later Cartwright said, "Littlebody? What is it?"

He gave a resume of the morning's events. "And I have a lead regarding the Chatterjee girl," he said. "I was ringing in to see if she's turned herself in."

"No word at this end, Littlebody. I would've thought we'd've heard something by now, if so. I don't like the sound of this at all."

"Nor me, sir. And... and I understand that certain Russian agents are also on her trail."

Alfie heard the brigadier curse under his breath. "The Russians, hm? This is worse than I feared."

"I'd like to request an airship to take me to Dehrakesh, sir."

"Dehrakesh?" the brigadier drawled. "Not thinking of taking a holiday are we, Littlebody?"

"No, sir. I understand that she might be heading there."

"Very well, by all means requisition an airship. I'll contact the airyard right away. Good luck, Littlebody. Keep me informed."

"Yes, sir!" Alfie said.

Alfie considered returning to his bungalow and packing a few things for the journey north, then decided that, as time was of the essence, he would purchase whatever he needed once he was in Dehrakesh.

He took a taxi from the station and headed to the airyard.

CHAPTER
ELEVEN

∽

In the warehouse of wonders –
No such thing as Annapurnite – A rooftop conversation –
"Oh, let him come with me…"

JANI WOKE SUDDENLY, wondering for a second where she was. She recalled their arrival at Dehrakesh, then the Mech-Man's march through the town to Mr Clockwork's warehouse.

She opened her eyes and stared at Anand, who was peering down at her over the edge of the opening. She was reclining on the control seat, where Anand had left her a while ago to ensure that the way was clear.

"You can come out now, Jani-ji. The warehouse is empty."

Jani yawned and slipped from the seat, found the hand- and foot-holds and climbed out. She stood on the concrete floor of the warehouse and stared about her in wonder.

What sprang to mind was a story from *One Thousand and One Nights*. Truly she was in Aladdin's cave, a great chamber filled with all manner of jewelled trinkets and twinkling gems, golden gewgaws and scintillating treasures.

Anand laughed at her open-mouthed astonishment. "This is Mr Clockwork's workshop and warehouse, where he builds and tests his many inventions. Next door is the showroom where he exhibits his latest clockwork wonders before he transfers them to his emporium in Delhi."

Max stood to attention between a pterodactyl-like flying machine on one side, all gleaming golden spars, intricate cogs and scalloped wings, and on the other a spindly clock on legs, like some horological cross between the Eiffel Tower and Big Ben.

"Mr Clockwork calls this invention his Moon Clock," Anand announced proudly. "Because it tells the time on the moon."

Jani laughed as she stared up at the face of the clock, which was a faithful representation of the pitted lunar surface, with hands. "But how is that calculated?" she asked. "And the moon is a world like the Earth, so there would be many times all at the same time – if it were inhabited, that is!"

Anand frowned and shrugged. "That I do not know, Jani-ji. And this..." he said, moving on, "is what he calls his Criminal Aggravator."

She stared at a device which resembled a mediaeval village stocks equipped with an arrangement of rotary tennis racquets.

"You see, the ne'er-do-well is placed in here, the device is switched on and the bats paddle his backside!"

Jani moved around the warehouse. There were hundreds of inventions crowding the floor, mechanical animals and clockwork homunculi, strange vehicles like cars with great inflated tyres and spindly coachwork, improbable flying machines and a drill-nosed contraption which Anand explained was Mr Clockwork's Subterranean Excavator, which he intended to use to follow Arne Saknussemm to the centre of the Earth.

"But that was just a novel written by Jules Verne!" Jani said.

"Ah-ha, but according to Mr Clockwork, Verne based his novel on real events. Mr Clockwork plans one day to burrow deep under the Earth's surface, just as he plans to fly to the moon!"

Jani stared about in wonder; it was as if Heath Robinson and the engineer Robert Stephenson had collaborated to create all manner of devices which defied not only description but logic. Jani was amused by the whimsical phantasmagoria, the sheer insane bravado of Mr Clockwork's cornucopia of improbable machinery.

"He must be an amazing person," she said.

"Oh, Mr Clockwork is truly amazing. He comes from a long line of Brahmin priests, but he turned his back on the way of the spirits, so he told me, and devoted his life to 'the pursuit of the mechanical.'"

Anand took her hand and dragged her across the chamber. He stopped before a magnificent mechanical elephant, decorated with great iron cogs and flywheels, jewels and fabulously embroidered drapes – but twice the size of any elephant Jani had ever seen. It was as if a wealthy maharajah had decided to duplicate his finest bull elephant in brass and gold, with no expense spared.

"And this is Mr Clockwork's latest wonder!" he announced proudly. "This is the magnificent beast I have come to collect. I will leave Max here and take

Mel all the way back to Delhi, where he will go on show at Mr Clockwork's Emporium."

"You call him Mel?"

Anand laughed. "Why, of course! Mel – for Mechanical Elephant! He is extra-special, and powered by Annapurnite." He stared up at the invention, frowning. "The only trouble is that he is heavy and slow. You see, he is too heavy to travel by train, and so slow that it will take me two weeks to plod back to Delhi."

"You're taking him by road?" Jani asked, sad that soon they would be parted.

"I am due to set off tomorrow."

She moved around the warehouse, lost in thought as she took in marvel after marvel, mechanical monkeys and bizarre automata, and things that defied easy definition – something that might have been a calliope or a giant orrery, and another invention that combined the oiled black chitin of a giant stag beetle with the tracks of an ironclad. She recalled something that Anand had told her earlier.

"And you say that Mel is powered by Annapurnite?" she said.

"That is what Mr Clockwork claims, yes."

Jani smiled and strolled around the warehouse. "But Anand," she said, "I told you on the way here what my father said: that there was no such thing as Annapurnite. Oh, I wonder what he meant?"

The boy shrugged. "But how do you explain the super-fast trains, Jani-ji, and the airships, and the weapons employed by the British to keep the heathen Russians and Chinese in check?"

Jani smiled. "I don't know how to explain anything, Anand. My mind is in a total whirl."

Anand smiled at her. "Come, Jani-ji, I would like to show you something. And while we stare in wonder, we shall eat, ah-cha?"

"You've brought food?" she said, following him across the floor of the warehouse to a rickety flight of timber steps that disappeared up into the rafters. "How long was I asleep?"

"I was gone for over an hour, Jani-ji. First I had to talk to Mr Gopal, the warehouse manager, before he closed it up. I arranged a time to take Mel, and gave him Mr Clockwork's instructions regarding Max. Then I slipped into town and asked for directions to the nearest restaurant."

At the foot of the wooden staircase, Anand picked up a bag from which the aroma of hot spices issued. Jani realised how hungry she was.

She followed Anand up the staircase, wondering where he was leading her. At the top was a platform just beneath the eaves of the building, from which she had a view of the massed, twinkling artefacts in the warehouse down below.

"I come up here every time I visit the warehouse," Anand said, reaching up to open a skylight. He slipped through, and turned to help Jani after him.

She found herself standing on a narrow timber walkway overlooking the lights of the town and the distant forested hills. Far below, cars and rickshaws beetled along the main boulevard and the muted thrum of engines reached them as if from far away. Along with the sound came the many smells of the town, cooking food and wood smoke, diesel fumes and incense.

They sat side by side on the walkway, their backs against the raked tiles. Jani stared out across the town, taking in the sights and the sounds of her homeland and knowing in her heart – despite the many lures and attractions of England, of Cambridge and London – that this was truly where she belonged. India was in her blood, as her father had often said, and no one could take that away from her. Even death, she recalled him saying, when the blood was finally stilled, only brings about a return to the land that is home.

She realised that she would miss her father's funeral, and a dark, hopeless despair filled her chest and forced a muffled sob from her throat.

And Anand would be leaving her at sunrise.

But now the boy was busy beside her, all smiles as he unpacked their supper. Aloo gobi and vegetable phal wrapped in banana leaves, a pile of oiled puri, and bhaji and burfi, and a bottle of Henderson's lemonade.

They ate as if deprived of food for days, and Jani relished the curries of her homeland which she had missed – despite the occasional trip to Shafi's in London – for so many years.

At one point Anand paused, a piece of roti dripping masala before his lips. "But Jani-ji, tell me something... Do you trust this creature you told me about, this Jelch?"

She thought about it. She recalled coming across the being in the wreckage of the airship, and what he had told her. And how, later, Jelch had saved her life.

"He was strange, but I didn't fear him – even though he was like nothing I had ever seen before. He was not – and I know this might sound strange – but I didn't feel that he was threatening in any way. And then he gave me the coin, or whatever it was."

"And then," Anand said in awed tones, "the creature saved your skin, killed those bloody Russian soldiers."

"I owe Jelch my life," she murmured.

"And you saw him again, in the warehouse?"

She shook her head. "I dreamed I saw him, or I hallucinated his presence – or, who knows, by some fabulous means he showed himself to me? He told me that I would escape, and that I should head east."

"And go to Nepal." Anand shook his head. "But the danger, Jani-ji! The British are looking for you, and maybe even the Russians, and Nepal's border is very well protected. You would have difficulty in crossing. Also it is a long way. Rishi Tal is fifty miles from here, and the border with Nepal is a hundred miles beyond that."

As she thought about all these things, and considered the odds stacked against her, it was strange that she should feel such confidence and a sense of rightness. Where did this come from, this conviction that what she was doing was the only course of action she could take? And from where did she draw the strength to face the many obstacles in her path?

She shook her head. "Sometimes, Anand, you know what you must do; you know that it is right. And the odd thing is that I know my father would have wanted this, for all that he worked for the British all his life, for all that he respected and even loved those who ruled over us. I think... I think that was why he started telling me, as he lay dying, about Annapurnite. He wanted me to know the truth. And I think, Anand, that by doing what I am doing now, I will at some point learn the truth."

She glanced up from her food, at Anand, and saw that his big brown eyes were pooled with unshed tears.

She reached out and took his hand.

He rubbed at his eyes and said, "The question is this, Jani-ji: why did Jelch give you the coin, and why does he want you venture to Nepal? What can his motives be?"

"It would help if I knew why the British, and the Russians, thought Jelch so important that they had to imprison him. And the strange thing is, Anand, that Jelch told me he came here to *help* us."

"Help *us*? Help the Indian nation, do you mean, or the British?"

Jani frowned, thinking back to what the creature had told her. "I think he meant that he wanted to help us all, the human race in general."

He stared at her. "Jani-ji," he said in a small voice, "where do you think he came from?"

"I did at one point wonder if he was a yeti..."

"And now?" he asked.

She looked at him. "Now I honestly have no idea."

They ate for a long time in silence, accompanied only by the noise drifting up from the streets far below.

"Jani-ji," Anand asked a little while later, "what will you do tomorrow?"

She had already planned her day. "I need more clothing, and toiletries and so on. I will buy these in the morning and then think about getting to Rishi Tal. I am sure there will be a train heading there at some point."

He held the big bottle of lemonade in both hands, poised before his lips. "But how can you be sure that the British – or the Russians – will not find you? They must be looking for you everywhere by now, and the police will be on the alert."

She shrugged helplessly. "But what else can I do? I must get to Rishi Tal, and how else can I get there but by train? It will be a risk, yes; but I cannot walk!"

Anand tipped the lemonade and glugged. He passed her the bottle, wiping his lips on the back of his hand, and she took it and drank. The lemonade was cold and sweet, a perfect antidote to the fiery phal.

"Jani-ji," Anand said, "I have been thinking..." His big-eyed gaze was shy as he went on, "I have been thinking that after all we have gone through together, I cannot let you set off alone."

She stared at him, wanting suddenly to reach out and take this skinny boy's hand. "But Anand–" she began.

"Listen to me," he said. "I have two weeks before Mr Clockwork will be expecting me back in Delhi. He will not notice that I am missing until the end of that time."

"But I can't let you..." she said. "Anand, the British are after me, and the Russians – and for all I know the Chinese too! I can't let you put yourself at risk."

"Jani-ji, I owe my life to your father. He took me in when I had nothing. He gave me a life and an education. Thanks to him I can read and write; I can look ahead and plan great things!"

"Not if the British capture you with me!" she said – and yet, even as she spoke these words, there was a small defiant voice inside her that said *Oh, let him come with me; let him come!*

"Your father told you about Annapurnite on his deathbed; he wanted you to know the truth. And I also think that this poor creature, Jelch, also wishes you to know the truth. Also, *I* want to know the truth. It makes very good sense that we travel together, and have adventures evading the British and the Russians, and learn what is destined for us in Nepal, ah-cha?"

She turned away and stared at the blurred lights of the town, choked with emotion. "But," she said, a final token protest, "Mr Clockwork will sack you when you fail to arrive – and what about the mechanical elephant?"

He beamed at her. "Mel is coming with us!" he announced.

"But... but you said that Mel is slow. If it would take two or three weeks to get to Delhi, then think how long it would take us to reach Nepal!"

He shook his head. "But Jani-ji, I have a plan. You see, I know how to make Mel go faster."

"You do?"

He laughed and slapped his thigh. "Oh, Jani-ji, your face is so funny when you are confused. You frown, and your thick brows are pulled down, and your lips are like a monkey's that is eating tamarind!"

"It is you who more resembles a monkey, Anand!" she countered. "But if you wouldn't mind explaining yourself..."

"I will explain everything in the morning when I meet you outside town, after you have bought provisions. And now it is late, and we have much to do in the morning, and we must rest."

Her stomach was full, and after the trials of the day she was ready to sleep. She thought of her soft, deep feather bed in her father's house in Delhi, and did not relish a night on the couch in the belly of the Mech-Man.

But Anand had a surprise in store. He led her from the rooftop and back down into the warehouse. They crossed the chamber towards the chitinous beetle-tank, and Anand opened a door in its flank. He reached inside, fumbled with something and struck a match.

"Every time I come to Dehrakesh I sleep here. It is the most comfortable bed in town!"

He lit a candle, and in its flickering light Jani made out what looked like a padded boudoir within the belly of the beetle, with a sumptuous velvet divan at one end and a control console and a seat at the other. There was even, Anand pointed out, a basin with pumped water at which to wash.

Jani did so, then curled up on the divan and was asleep within minutes.

CHAPTER
TWELVE

∽

Das is called – The visitor Kali has mentioned? –
News of Janisha Chatterjee –
"An airship ride to Dehrakesh..."

DURGA DAS SAT in the shade of a plane tree in the
grounds of his ashram, eyes closed as he contemplated
his exchange with Kali the previous day. He had been
feverish with excitement ever since, an excitement it
had taken all his meditative powers to quell. An excited
mind was a mind unprepared, as the wise man said.
And he had to be prepared over the course of the next
few days so that he could follow Kali's command and
act with wisdom. The goddess had said he should head
east, into another country, and that other country could
only be Nepal – which the British had ruled out of
bounds and had shut off from the rest of the world. It
was fortune indeed that Durga Das, as a venerated High
Priest whose ancestors hailed from that very country,
had purchased a visa at great cost just last year.

Soon he would move to ensure that Kali's words
would come to pass; he would act to secure the second
tithra-kuñjī, and then the third, and in so doing bring
Kali once again to this realm. And then, as a reward for

all his work, he would request that Kali assist him in ridding his land of the despicable British.

His reflections were interrupted by a young acolyte who came scurrying across from the ashram. "Baba-ji, my apologies! There is someone phoning you and saying he has a most important message and that it is vital you are talking with him!"

Das's first impulse was to chastise the youth for the interruption, but then had second thoughts. If the 'important message' pertained to the tithra-kuñjī...

"Ah-cha. Tell whoever it is that I will speak to him presently. Chalo!"

He struggled to his feet, an operation that took some considerable effort and not a little time, and, panting, trudged across to the white-walled ashram. Acolytes salaamed at his passing, and he conferred blessings as he went, all the while wondering who might wish to speak to him.

"Yes? Who is this?" he snapped into the receiver when he reached his office.

"Mr Durga Das, sahib? It is Mr Vikram speaking."

"Vikram?" Das said querulously. "Do I know you?" The name brought no face to mind, but he knew so many people that it was hard to keep track.

"Mr Vikram," the caller went on, unperturbed, "your contact within the Kapil Dev Chatterjee household."

"Ah... *that* Mr Vikram!"

He had thought it wise, when learning of the Security Minister's illness, to insinuate one of his acolytes into the dying man's abode; he had tried on numerous other occasions, but to no avail, positions within the household being limited.

"Well, what do you want, Mr Vikram?"

"I have some very important news, sir. Very important."

Das's idea had been that, in having someone on the inside, he would be privy to the Raj's political machinations – intelligence which might be of use to his Nationalist contacts. He felt a flutter of impatience. His mind was on other, higher things now – not petty internal politics.

"I *have* heard that Kapil Dev Chatterjee is dead," he said impatiently.

"But, sir, that is not my news. It is the Chatterjee girl, sir, his daughter."

Das interrupted. "What about her?"

"This morning I overheard her speaking with her father. I was in the same room, attending Kapil Dev Chatterjee as he lay dying. I overheard something which I think you will find very much of interest."

"Which was, Mr Vikram? Please cease this prevarication. I am a very busy man, you know?"

"Ah... the matter is very delicate, sir, and not to be discussed over the phone. Also, there is the question of my expenses."

"Expenses?"

"I am still awaiting the payment of my expenses, and I was hoping that you might see your way to expediting the payment when I furnish you with the information, sir."

Das contained his anger. "Are you attempting to extort from me, Vikram?"

"Not at all, sir. But I know you will be interested in what I have to tell you. You see, sir, it concerns a creature called a Morn..."

Das's pulse quickened. "A Morn?"

His grandfather had told him about the Morn: creatures, he reported – verily demons – whose work it was to prevent the gods' triumphant return to Earth. He had heard rumours over the past few years that the British had a Morn in custody in London, and he had instructed his many contacts to keep an ear to the ground regarding any mention at all of these beings.

"What did she say?" he almost shouted now.

"Not over the phone, baba-ji. I will take a taxi and be with you in thirty minutes, ah-cha?"

The phone went dead and Das sat staring at the receiver, hardly able to believe his luck.

Was this the visitor Kali had mentioned, who would come to him with news of the second coin?

He hoisted himself from behind his desk and hurried into the dying light of evening. He ordered an acolyte to make Kashmiri tea, to be served in thirty minutes, and hurried back to his bungalow. There he sat on his reinforced wooden chair in the shade, working to calm his thoughts and slow his breathing.

Presently a taxi drew up outside the ashram and a squat figure stepped out. He wore brilliant white trousers and a white shirt, opened to reveal a string vest through which sprouted a profusion of body hair.

Mr Vikram trotted across the compound, murmuring apologies for his lateness and blaming the traffic north of Delhi. Das waved the words aside, told Mr Vikram to sit down, and snapped at a serving boy to pour.

When they were quite alone, Das eyed Mr Vikram. The man had a self-satisfied expression on his pudding face as he held a tiny china cup in a ham of a hand, his little finger extended ridiculously. Das decided that he didn't like the man.

"Now what of the Chatterjee girl and the Morn?" he said impatiently.

"The little matter of expenses..." Vikram began.

"I will expedite the payment of any monies owed when, and only when, you tell me what you know."

Vikram frowned. "I have considerably more information than that concerning the Morn, babi-ji. Information concerning the Morn will be covered by payment of my expenses. Further information, that concerning the whereabouts of the Chatterjee girl, will require a supernumerary consideration. You must understand that my wife is expecting our sixth child imminently, and with an extra mouth to feed..."

Das contained his anger and said, "The whereabouts of the girl? Explain yourself!"

"Shortly after her father died, and she left the hospital, Janisha Chatterjee was kidnapped."

"Kidnapped?"

"I followed her from the hospital. It was my intention to pay my condolences, and to question her further regarding what she had told her father. I assumed she would go straight home, which would make my job of apprehending her that much easier. However, she alighted in Old Delhi and I followed her to Roopa's Tea Rooms. A little later I saw her being carried unconscious by a Russian I have had contact with in the past."

"And where did the Russian take her?" Das asked, leaning forward over his stomach.

"To a warehouse in the Karnaka district, baba-ji. There I waited. It was my plan to enter the building and try to find out what they wanted with the girl. But the building was securely locked and I was forced to alter my plans. While I was outside, and wondering what to do next, the girl was saved."

Das stared at his informant. "Saved. This is becoming a more fantastical story by the second! What do you mean, saved?"

"A great mechanical man knocked down the wall of the warehouse and rescued the girl, babi-ji. I followed the giant to the station, where it was loaded onto a train. The girl was still within the giant, sir. Presently the train departed, bound for Dehrakesh."

Das sipped his tea and considered what Vikram had told him.

"And I wonder why," he said, more to himself, "first the Russian, and then whoever was piloting the mechanical man, were so interested in the Chatterjee girl?" He stared at Vikram. "You said that she spoke to her father about the Morn?"

Vikram smiled. "The following information, baba-ji, will come at a fee over and above that of my expenses."

Das began to argue, then stopped himself and said instead, "How much?"

"Five hundred rupees, baba-ji."

Das controlled his breathing. What was five hundred rupees, after all, when it might pave the way for the coming of the gods?

He inclined his head. "Tell me everything you know and I will expedite the payment."

"No, sir. I must insist. Payment now, and *then* I will furnish you with the information."

Das regarded the man. He withdrew a roll of notes from his robes and counted out two hundred rupees. "I will give you this only. The rest, when I have the information..."

Vikram grabbed the notes, hardly able to contain his greedy smile as he went on, "Janisha Chatterjee told her father about the attack on the *Rudyard Kipling*, which she was aboard. In the aftermath she happened upon a creature which her father called a Morn. When I heard this," Vikram, said, smiling, "I knew you would be interested. According to the girl, the creature gave her something."

"Something?"

"Something she described as a coin, baba-ji. A disc."

It was all Das could do not to shout out loud. He controlled himself for fear of fanning the fires of Vikram's greed. "A coin?" he said with all the casualness he could muster.

Vikram nodded. "A coin. That was all she said. But I guessed," he went on, eyes twinkling, "that it must be important."

The second tithra-kuñjī.

It was clear to Durga Das that there was only one course of action he might now pursue. It was imperative that he track down the Chatterjee girl.

"And you are sure that she was aboard the train bound for Dehrakesh?" he asked.

"With my own eyes I saw the giant take her, and she did not leave the mechanical man before it reached the station."

He would hire an airship within the hour, Das decided, and make straight for Dehrakesh. He struggled to his feet and hurried across to the ashram.

"And the remaining three hundred rupees?" Vikram asked, scurrying alongside him.

Das stopped, turned and stared at the man, a suspicion dawning. If he were correct, then he might work this to his advantage. "But what," he asked, "did the Russian agent want with the Chatterjee girl?"

Vikram joggled his head from side to side, his smile inane – and incriminatory. "That I cannot say, baba-ji."

Das shook his head. "You liar... You have had dealings with the Russians – you just admitted as much. Admit it, you phoned them just as soon as Kapil Dev Chatterjee died! You sold them the information, just as you're selling it to me!"

"But Baba-ji, the Russians are on our side! They are honourable men, fighting a common enemy!"

"You're a fool, Vikram – and what is worse, a greedy fool."

"But our agreement. I told you what you wanted to know! You owe me..."

Enraged, Das waved. "Chalo! Go to your Russian paymasters for your filthy rupees!"

"But sir...!"

Das took a step forward and bore down on the cowering man. "Already you have two hundred rupees. Be satisfied with that, you greedy cur."

"But..." Vikram began.

"If you do not leave now, Mr Vikram, then I shall be forced to have Mr Knives attend to you."

Vikram quailed. "Mr Knives?" he said, his voice trembling.

"Exactly, Mr Vikram, and you know what Mr Knives will do upon my instructions?"

Smiling, Das watched as Vikram turned tail and ran.

Das entered the ashram, and ordered one servant to call a taxi and another to arrange airship passage to Dehrakesh. He would make the journey and, with luck, arrive before nightfall – but he could not set out on the mission alone. He needed a trusted, capable companion, and there was only one such man suitable for the job.

He found Mr Knives – as he affectionately called the young fellow – lounging against a pillar on the verandah and cleaning his nails with a rather large dagger. He wore a sharp grey suit and possessed a face as thin as his favourite blades.

Last year Das had rescued Mr Knives from a street-gang, and a life of crime and certain imprisonment, and employed him as a bodyguard. The young thug came in useful when muscle needed to be applied in certain areas. Later Mr Knives had admitted to Das, when drunk one evening on cheap Bombay rum, that he had once killed a man with his beloved blade; it had been a rash boast to make, all things considered, for now the holy man had the reprobate just where he wanted him.

He snapped his fingers and said, "How would you like an airship ride to Dehrakesh, Mr Knives? Follow me!"

With luck, Mr Knives' expertise might not be required, but it was always wise to be prepared.

Thirty minutes later Durga Das and Mr Knives left the ashram aboard a taxi, and an hour after that were in the air high above Delhi, bound for Dehrakesh.

CHAPTER
THIRTEEN

~∞~

An accidental meeting –
Jani takes tea with the Reverend Carstairs –
A lucky escape –
"You're speaking in riddles…"

IT WAS TEN o'clock in the morning when Jani slipped from the warehouse and hurried along the busy street. She felt as if everyone who glanced her way knew of her secret, and she wondered how long it might be before the authorities traced her from Delhi.

As she left the warehouse behind her, heading for the main boulevard where the bazaars and stores were to be found, she saw a police jeep – carrying one British officer, with three Indian minions – edging its way through the press of humanity. The moustachioed officer looked impatient as he rapped on the frame of the windscreen with his swagger stick and shouted at the crowd to make way.

The Indian constables eyed the crowd with suspicion, and Jani hurried past, heart thumping.

She expected a harsh cry to arrest her progress – and only breathed a little easier when she turned a corner and hurried across the road towards the mock-Tudor frontage of a Hobson and Jobson department store.

As she was about to climb the three steps to the store's fan-cooled interior, a shadow crossed the face of the sun and she looked up. She squinted at a great airship passing sedately high above, a police vessel bearing the red, white and blue livery of the union flag on its cigar-shaped envelope.

She could not help but jump to the conclusion that reinforcements had been sent to Dehrakesh. The authorities in Delhi had discovered the remains of the shattered warehouse where she had been held, and traced the progress of the Mech-Man back to Mr Clockwork's premises. Then they had deduced that Max had been driven by one Anand Doshi, the houseboy of the late Minister of Security whose daughter they desperately sought... From this it was but a short leap of logic to assume that they had questioned Mr Clockwork and found that Anand had delivered Max the Mech-Man to the warehouse in Dehrakesh.

She felt dizzy with panic as she hurried up the steps to the department store.

So flustered was she that she collided with someone who was coming down the steps. She rebounded with a start and looked up to see her surprised expression mirrored on the round, moonlike countenance of an overweight young man in a beige suit, straw hat, and a clerical collar.

"I'm so sorry!" she began.

The young parson reached out, clutched her hand in a bid to steady her, and said, "My fault entirely, Miss. I was miles away." He raised his hat and smiled pleasantly. "Good day to you..."

Jani returned the nicety and hurried into the shadows of the store.

She found the clothing department and, for the next thirty minutes, worked to calm her nerves as she selected undergarments and a crimson shalwar kameez. The sales assistant attempted to interest her in a green sari which she said would complement the deep brown of her eyes. Jani smiled at the thought of fleeing through the jungle garbed in a flowing sari, and insisted on the more functional shalwar kameez. She changed into it, then stared at herself in a full-length mirror. It was the first time in five years she had worn Indian clothing, and the silk felt cool and comfortable against her skin.

She next bought toiletries in the same store, and a medium-sized valise in which to carry her purchases.

She would pay for the items and then find a tea room nearby, where she would take lunch and while away an hour before setting off to rendezvous with Anand at a pre-arranged meeting place in the hills. Thinking of the boy, she considered his ragged shorts and old shirt. She made a detour to the men's department and bought two pairs of shorts and two smart white shirts. It occurred to her that a map of the area might come in useful, and minutes later found a large-scale map of Uttarakhand.

She paid for her purchases and paused before the exit. The sunlight dazzled, and Jani thought of the police airship heading for the airyard. It would have landed by now, and disgorged its complement of officers intent on tracking her down.

She told herself she was being paranoid and plunged into the heat of the Indian day.

Across the street from the department store was the Oxford Tea Rooms, and she was about to cross towards it when she noticed, close by, the little English parson she had almost skittled earlier. He was leaning against a lamp post, a look of pain creasing his features as he reached down to massage his ankle.

He caught her gaze and winced a smile. "What did I say? Miles away! I was in such a hurry I missed a step and turned my dashed ankle – my Achilles' heel, don't you know? Old rugby injury."

"Can I...?" Jani began.

"I can hardly put any weight on the dashed thing," he explained, "and as my rooms are only just around the corner, I wonder if..."

Jani said unsurely, "Yes?"

"If you might possibly assist me to my room. It would be capital if you could. As I said, it's just around the corner. What a dashed nuisance!"

"But..." she began. She looked up and down the street, and at that second a policeman came striding around the corner. "It's no trouble at all," she said hurriedly; what could be better cover than playing the helpmate of a distressed English parson?

She took the young man's arm and assisted him as he hobbled, exclaiming in pain with every other step, along the pavement and around the corner to the Passmore Guest House.

A clanking lift carried them to the first floor and an old-fashioned suite of rooms with a balcony overlooking the main street. She helped him across to the verandah and into a rattan chair, and was about to take her leave when he said, "I'm most grateful for your help." He held out a small, podgy hand. "The Reverend Lionel Carstairs, by the way."

She thought fast, took the proffered hand in hers, and said, "Sita Nagar."

"I wonder..." he said. "I was about to take tea. It would be awfully pleasant if you'd consent to join me. I could have a tray sent up..."

She glanced at her watch. She had more than an hour to fill before she rendezvoused with Anand, and what better way to spend it than in the privacy of the parson's rooms, away from the prying eyes of the police?

"That would be most pleasant," she said. She noticed a bell-pull on the wall of the main room, stepped from the verandah and summoned service. Next to the hearth was a chest, its great lid standing open. She noticed that it was empty, and it struck her as odd that such a small man should possess such a vast travelling chest.

The servant arrived in due course and took their order for Earl Grey. Jani sat in the shade of the verandah across from the parson.

When their tea arrived, he poured. "If you don't mind my observing, Miss Nagar, your English is excellent."

She smiled and sipped her tea. She had often received the same compliment in England, the words always couched in the tone of someone expecting her to speak the King's English with an accent – or not at all.

"That's because, Reverend, I was educated in England, and just this past month took up my place to study at Cambridge."

The parson hid his surprise well. "Cambridge, no less. Well, well... But what brings you back to India, if I might enquire?"

She considered her reply before saying, "The passing of a close relative."

His face folded into lines of concern. Jani thought him no older than thirty, the typical parochial product of middle England, perhaps the third son of a prosperous businessman whose other sons had gone into law and the army. She had met many of their like in London, well-bred young gentlemen who oozed superiority and considered her something of an exotic specimen.

"I'm sorry to hear that, Miss Nagar. I can only say that I hope you find comfort and solace in the tenets of whichever belief..."

She interrupted him. "My father brought me up in a strictly secular household, Reverend Carstairs, an upbringing which the boarding school I attended in Surrey failed to dilute."

The Reverend smiled above his Earl Grey. If he was shocked, he failed to show it. "I take it that you are an atheist, Miss Nagar?"

"But whatever gave you that idea, Reverend? There very well might be a god, or a creator or whatever you might wish to call it – but that does not necessarily mean to say that any of the world's many religions can lay claim to represent him, her, or it."

The parson blinked. She could almost see the gears shift in his mentation, as if he were one of Mr Clockwork's automata, as he re-evaluated his assessment of the young woman sipping tea across from him.

"An interesting conceit," he said. "Your father must have been a remarkable man to have brought up such a strong-willed daughter."

"Indeed he was," she said, and was struck by a sudden and aching melancholy.

"And what brings you to Dehrakesh?" the parson said.

"I have friends in the area, whom I wish to see before returning to England to take up my studies."

He sipped his tea. "In what field, if I might ask?"

"Medicine. I hope, one day, to become a surgeon."

His eyes lost their focus, and he murmured something to himself, which Jani thought might have been *remarkable*. "My own father was a vicar, Miss Nagar, and he always wanted me to follow him into the profession."

"He must be pleased that you obliged," she said.

His eyes refocused and he stared at Jani as if in confusion. "What? Oh – oh, yes, of course! There I was, miles away again."

She finished her tea and placed the cup and saucer upon the table. "Thank you for the tea, Reverend. I have enjoyed our little conversation." She consulted her wristwatch. "And now, if you'll excuse me..."

He set aside his own cup and saucer. "I wonder if you would be so good as to do me one last small favour?" he said. "You will find a small vial of malaria tablets on the mantel-shelf. I wonder if you would be so good as to fetch them for me?"

She smiled. "Not at all."

She rose and stepped back into the room, crossed to the mantel-shelf and looked for the pill bottle among the many oddments and knick-knacks. As she was reaching out for the small brown vial, she was aware of movement behind her. She turned to find the Reverend Carstairs approaching from across the room.

He gave a sickly smile, and Jani saw that he had broken out in a sweat; perspiration beaded his round face. Also, he was no longer limping...

"Ah," he said, "those are the ones."

"Then here you are," she said, passing him the pills. "And I will be wishing you a good day."

"Ah... one moment, Miss Nagar. I wonder if I might have your opinion of this little watercolour I made the other day..." And he reached out to the mantel-shelf, his movement forcing her to step back so that her legs pressed up against the open travelling trunk.

In a fraction of a second she was aware of several facts: there was no watercolour on the shelf, the trunk was open to receive her, and the Reverend Carstairs was moving to push her into it.

She cried out and ducked under his outstretched hands. In desperation she dodged behind the parson and pushed him in the back. He gave a startled cry and pitched forward, tripping headfirst into the trunk. He struggled upright, floundering like a vaudeville comedy act, and Jani obliged by dashing forward, grabbing hold of the lid, and bringing it down on his head. He cried out and disappeared under its weight, and she lost no time in flipping over the brass hasp and securing the Reverend Carstairs – or whoever he might be – within the trunk.

She stared at the trunk in horror as his muffled cries and thumpings issued from within. So his twisted ankle, his invitation to tea, had all been an act to imprison her in the chest; in which, with wonderful irony, he now found himself.

But at whose behest was he working? The obvious answer, considering his nationality, was the British – but that did not necessarily follow. For all she knew he might be an agent of the Russians, or even the Chinese... Of one thing she was certain: by some means he had traced her here, and there was always the possibility that he was not working alone. In which case others beside himself would be aware of her presence.

She tamped down her panic; she had to think clearly and assess the situation. She had to get away from the hotel as quickly as possible, and not by the main entrance which for all she knew might be under surveillance.

Once outside she would hasten to where she was due to meet Anand.

She remembered to pick up her bag as she left the room, the parson's muted entreaties sounding in her wake. As she hurried down the staircase, it came to her that Carstairs and his cohorts, having traced her so far, might be aware of her involvement with Anand. Might they have the warehouse under observation too, and be waiting for his emergence upon the back of the mechanical elephant?

In the foyer, she turned from the entrance and hurried towards the back of the building, past a potted aspidistra, brass-framed mirrors and a drawing room full of guests reading the daily papers.

She felt a warm breeze and turned down a passage which she guessed gave onto a rear entrance. She came to an open door and hurried through, then turned left and sprinted, thinking that it was as well she was wearing a shalwar kameez and not a sari – or a European dress – as she tore down the alley.

She came to the main street and barrelled into a portly Sikh, bounced off him and almost tripped into the path of a passing water buffalo. Rolling along its bulging flank, her singular locomotion commented upon by a knot of laughing rickshaw-wallahs, she regained her balance and slowed to a sedate walk. Aware of a hundred staring eyes, she pushed her way through the crowd towards the far side of the street, then turned a corner and drew a relieved breath.

She would gain her bearings and make for the rendezvous point with Anand – but would not show herself immediately. She would observe his arrival, attempt to discern if he were being followed, and only when she had reassured herself that he had not inadvertently led the British to her would she show herself.

She felt calmer now, having marshalled her thoughts and devised a plan of action. Her father would have been proud.

She passed through a marketplace piled with a hundred different multi-coloured fruits and vegetables and, across the square, made out the peeling stucco frontage of the railway station. She glanced at her wristwatch. It was still only fifteen minutes to eleven. With luck, Anand had yet to leave the warehouse with the mechanical elephant.

She hurried past the station. As she turned the corner and stared down the street, she saw the great double doors of the warehouse part like the exit of an aircraft hangar and the magnificent clockwork pachyderm, its brass cogs and bejewelled ornamentation scintillating in the sun, trundle into view.

On its back, seated like a tiny monkey, was Anand.

The great elephant plodded along the street, bringing traffic to a halt as drivers stopped and stared, and attracting a gaggle of curious onlookers. Following at a safe distance, Jani scanned the crowds for any sign of the police or army. So far as she could make out, all the onlookers were civilian Indians. She willed Anand to gain speed and leave the city as fast as possible – a forlorn hope as this negligent, lazy amble appeared to be the elephant's top speed.

In due course Anand and his charge left the town in their wake, heading for the wooded hills that surrounded Dehrakesh. The crowds thinned; the small boys who had followed the elephant through the streets, whooping and yelling, fell away. Jani followed a hundred yards behind, keeping to the shadows and constantly looking over her shoulder for the first sign of pursuers.

The elephant plodded on, taking the road that climbed from the town in its careful, world-weary gait. As Jani followed, she marvelled at how lifelike the mechanical beast appeared; it was a construction of brass and metal, cogs and pulleys, and yet it moved with all the stolid imperturbability of an aged bull elephant.

They headed into the hills, fir trees, eucalyptus, and casuarinas on all sides. Ahead, the hazy foothills of the Himalayas showed on the horizon, a series of scimitar peaks whose summits were sheathed in scabbards of snow.

At the place agreed upon for their rendezvous, a roadside shrine to the goddess Lakshmi, Anand eased the elephant to a halt and looked around.

Jani hurried across the patched tarmacadam, waving up at him and calling out, "Take the elephant into the jungle, Anand! We need to get away from the road."

He stared down at her, and a second later started up the elephant and steered it through a stand of trees. Jani stood by the roadside, anxiously looking down into the town. Once the clockwork beast was hidden from view, she followed it through the ferns and trees.

"Jani-ji?" Anand called out with concern.

She climbed the cliff-face of the elephant's hindquarters, using rivets, flanges, and piston-heads as hand- and foot-holds. Breathless, she arrived on the broad back and flopped down.

"Jani-ji?"

"I... I must have been followed from the warehouse," she panted. "An Englishman invited me to tea." She recounted her meeting with the bogus clergyman, his attempt to capture her and her escape.

"So they must have followed us here!" he cried.

"They know about the Mech-Man, obviously – but perhaps not Mel," she said, patting its broad brass back.

Anand frowned in the dappled shade of the palm leaves. "We have one big problem, Jani-ji. On Mel we cannot make good speed to Rishi Tal and Nepal."

She stared at him. "So what to do? Back at the warehouse you said you had a plan."

Straightening his back proudly, he said, "So they know about Max... But by now, perhaps, they will have searched the warehouse, ah-cha, and failed to find us. That means that if I return, tonight, and leave with Max... then the job will be a bloody good one!"

She frowned at him. "Do you mean that tonight we will escape aboard Max, even though the British are aware of him?"

"You could say that," Anand said. "You will find out later tonight, Jani-ji."

"You're speaking in riddles, Anand." She reached out and gripped his hand. "I'll come with you."

"And run the risk of them capturing both of us? That would be foolish, Jani-ji. You stay here, and if I do not get back by dawn... then continue on to Rishi Tal and Nepal without me."

They waited out the rest of the day in the shade of the palm trees and at eight, as the sun went down over the hills and filled the valleys with its golden light, Anand climbed down from the back of the mechanical elephant and made his way back to Dehrakesh.

CHAPTER
FOURTEEN

∽

Smethers to the Rescue – To the warehouse –
Confrontation with the Mech-Man –
"You must know your place..."

ALFIE LITTLEBODY SQUATTED in the confines of the travelling chest, sweating inordinately and wondering if he would run out of air and suffocate to death.

Panic alternated with self-pity at his dashed ill-fortune. Things had begun to go wrong right at the outset yesterday, when his departure from the Delhi airyard had been delayed for thirty minutes – which should have been no problem as he was still scheduled to arrive at Dehrakesh well before Janisha Chatterjee's train. Then, midway through the flight, the pilot had called out that he was experiencing trouble with the port engine and had diverted to the airyard at Rishi Tal for running repairs. In consequence he had landed at Dehrakesh at midnight, some six hours after the Delhi train was due in.

Alfie had rushed to the address of Mr Clockwork's Dehrakesh warehouse on the edge of town, but found it locked, with no sign of the girl, her rescuer, or anyone else on the premises. As he was leaving the warehouse, however, he'd heard voices high above him.

Craning his neck, he had made out two small figures sitting up on the eaves of the building. In the moonlight he discerned a boy and a young woman.

Heartened, he'd returned to the centre of town, booked a room in a guest house, and in the morning bought a change of clothing. He'd affixed the parson's dog-collar, then hurried to the warehouse.

No sooner had he turned onto the street where the emporium was situated than the Chatterjee girl, looking as enchanting in real life as she appeared in the photograph, had slipped from the warehouse and hurried along the street. He'd followed the girl into town and effected their 'accidental' meeting.

And it had been going so well until he'd fouled up with the chest.

Now, for perhaps the hundredth time, he strained with all his strength against the lid, but to no avail. The catch held fast. He wondered how long it might be before a cleaner entered the room. He was sopping with sweat and frantic with panic. The proprietor might elect not to have the room cleaned, as he was still in residence... or would they knock and enquire? But that might not be for hours yet – and how much air was left in the chest? He cried out; rather the ignominy of being discovered like this, he thought, than a horrible death from asphyxiation.

And even if he did get out before he suffocated, he would have lost the trail of the precociously bright Chatterjee girl. She would have flown like a bird and might be anywhere by now. He groaned aloud at his situation. He'd said he would contact Brigadier Cartwright as soon as he landed in Dehrakesh, and bring him up to speed – which he'd signally failed to do.

How to explain the delay, and the subsequent failure of his lead, when he did get out?

Damn the girl! He cursed himself, yelled out again and thumped the wood above his head. The chest felt more and more like a coffin with every passing minute. He subsided, tried not to shed tears of self-pity, and in due course his thoughts returned to the Chatterjee girl.

He had to admit that she was something of a corker. He had always thought high-caste Indian women were amongst the most beautiful in the world, and to complement her looks Janisha Chatterjee had a piercing intellect and a comely manner. He'd found himself, as he'd sipped tea with her and traded thoughts, entirely smitten.

One thing that puzzled him, though – and one thing he could not have asked her outright – was why she had not turned herself in to the safekeeping of the police? That, to his way of thinking, would have been her obvious course of action after being saved from the heinous Russian pair. Why had she embarked on this perilous flight, in the belly of a mechanical man, all the way to Dehrakesh?

What, he asked himself, was she fleeing?

Into his mind's eye came the image of her smile, dazzling white against her brown skin, and something swelled within his chest. Her eyes were the biggest, brownest eyes he had ever beheld in his life, brimming with wit and wisdom.

His thoughts were interrupted by the sound of a door opening, followed by a male voice. "I say, Littlebody? Where the bally hell are you?"

His heart kicked. He didn't recognise the voice – but, whoever it belonged to, he was saved.

"In here!" he cried.

"In where? Dash it all, man, what the blazes are you playing at?"

"Here!" he yelled again, thumping the lid of the chest.

He heard fingers fumbling with the clasp and a second later dazzling sunlight flooded in as the lid was lifted.

"Am I glad to...!" The words died on his lips as he gazed up at the thin, sardonic face staring down at him.

"Oh," Alfie said, his heart sinking. "Colonel Smethers."

Smethers – or Sadean Smethers, as he was known in the Officers' Club – was perhaps the last person on Earth Alfie would have wanted to liberate him.

"What the bloody hell," Smethers said, pulling up an armchair and seating himself very precisely upon it, "what in the name of blessed creation, Lieutenant Littlebody, are you doing locked in a travelling chest dressed as a padre?"

Alfie knelt in the chest, sweat dripping from his face, gripped the rim and stared out at Smethers. "I can explain everything," he said pathetically.

Smethers nodded. He had a thin, rather cruel face, a lipless mouth, and ice cold eyes – the entire ensemble tailor-made to convey withering sarcasm. "This," he said, "should be interesting."

Alfie mumbled something approximating an abject apology.

Smethers held up a languid hand. "But first," he said, "why the fancy dress costume, Padre?"

"It isn't..." he began. He inserted two fingers behind the strip of white card he'd utilised as a dog-collar – an invention he'd been rather pleased with at the time. "You see, it was intended to gain her trust. No one suspects a vicar."

Smethers made a show of screwing his eyes shut, opening them and shaking his head. "Let me get this straight. In order to apprehend the Chatterjee gal, you dressed up as a vicar?"

"And it was my intention to incarcerate her within the chest – for her own good. You see, the Russians are intent on..."

Smethers raised a hand. "I know all about that pair."

"For some reason," Alfie continued, "she decided against seeking our help. I thought it best to use a modicum of force, rather than suggest she come into our custody of her own accord."

"And Cartwright didn't tell you why the girl's on the run?" Smethers asked.

"Not a word," Alfie said. "Do you know?"

"Let's just say that she's received something we would rather she hadn't, Littlebody. And thanks to your blithering incompetence, she's given us the slip."

"I'm sorry, sir."

"Oh, just wait until Brigadier Cartwright finds out about this!"

Alfie froze. "You... I mean, is there any need for him to know?"

A calculating look came into Smethers' Arctic eyes. "I suppose," he began, "that that depends."

Alfie felt a smidgen of hope. "Depends?"

"On how you conduct yourself over the course of the next few days as we attempt to track down the gel."

"We..." Alfie gulped, "we're working together on the case?"

"Well, you don't think I'm going to toddle off back to Delhi, put my feet up and let you exhibit the same level of incompetence as you've shown so far, do you? Of course we'll work together. And if you buck up your ideas, obey my every dashed order, mind your Ps and Qs and all the rest, then I might show a little lenience. But one step out of line, old boy, and I'll tip the wink to Cartwright and the old boy will make your life merry hell. Do you get me drift, Littlebody?"

"Yes, sir."

"Excellent." Smethers smiled sweetly. "Now, be a good chap and get out of that damned chest, why don't you? Oh – one further question: did you haul the chest all the way up here with the express intention of imprisoning the girl?"

Alfie stood, his muscles protesting. "No, sir. I... The idea came to me when I booked the room and saw the chest. It seemed the perfect way to detain her, sir."

Smethers shook his head. "When in fact what happened was that the slip of a thing turns the tables and incarcerates you."

"I... She took fright, sir; I overbalanced, and she pushed me."

Smethers stared at him. "I hope you feel as foolish as you look, Lieutenant?"

"Yes, sir."

"It's a bloody good job I was on the Chatterjee case meself, what, and traced you up here. Otherwise" – he laughed – "you might have suffocated to death."

"Yes, sir," Alfie said. "Ah... how did you find me, sir?"

"Used my grey matter, Littlebody. Knew you were in Dehrakesh and checked all the guest houses."

"Thank you, sir," Alfie said, sounding pathetic even to himself.

"Right." Smethers whacked his thigh with his swagger stick, business-like. "Now, how do you intend to proceed?"

Alfie looked past Smethers. Through the window he saw that twilight was descending. He'd been locked in the chest for hours.

"I... perhaps we'd better enquire at the railway station, sir, and the airyard."

"In my opinion I don't think the gel would be foolish enough to choose so obvious a mode of transport, Littlebody. Unlike some people, she's no idiot, what?"

"No, sir."

"I checked the warehouse earlier. No sign of the girl. Chances are she's miles away from here... But I suggest we return to the warehouse and have another quick shufti, hm? You never know, we might find something."

"Yes, sir."

"Now be a good chap, splash a bit of H_2O on your dial, change back into your uniform, and we'll be off."

In due course they left the guest house and headed across town, Alfie feeling like a kicked dog as he hurried to keep up with the long-striding Smethers.

The emporium, a big, ugly building like an airship hangar, bulked darkly against the jungle and the glow of the setting sun. Smethers rapped on the door with his swagger stick while Alfie moved from foot to foot next to him. From his elation at being entrusted with this mission, he was thrust now into a slough of despond at the thought of tagging along as the inept sidekick of the insufferably arrogant Smethers.

And what had Smethers meant when he said that the Chatterjee girl was in possession of something that the British – and presumably the Russians – wanted?

The sound of bolts being shot issued from behind the steel door, which opened a fraction. A thin face peered out. "Hello?"

Smethers said, "Open up, now there's a good chap."

A sing-song voice said, "But I was closing up for the night, sir."

"Well," Smethers said, "you'll just have to jolly well open up again, won't you?"

The single eye that Alfie could see in the sliver of open door narrowed in calculation. "Ten rupees," said the man.

"I'll give you 'ten rupees,' my good chap," Smethers said, and applied his shoulder to the door.

The man went reeling and Smethers stepped across the threshold, Alfie behind him.

Smethers stared down at the prostrated Indian. "And you are?"

"I am Mr Gopal, sir, the warehouse manager."

"Well pick yourself up, Mr Gopal," Smethers said, "and turn on the lights."

"But I was just about to close up, sir!" the Indian said, scrambling to his feet.

Smethers extended his swagger stick and hooked the man under the chin. "I said turn the bally lights on, hm?"

Looking daggers at Smethers, the man flipped a switch beside the door and rows of lights flickered on high overhead.

Alfie looked away, casting his gaze around the wonders twinkling dimly in the cavern of the warehouse. He hoped, by his body language, to dissociate himself from Smethers' high-handed actions.

"Now, my good man," Smethers said, "a few questions."

"Questions?"

"I presume you know what they are? They are words of mine to which you reply with the truth – d'you get me drift, my friend?"

The Indian's eyes shuttled from Smethers to Alfie and back again. "What questions?"

"The boy – Anand. Where is he?"

The man's eyes narrowed. "Anand? What has he done?"

Smethers tapped the man on the chest. "I'm asking the questions here. Where is the boy?"

The man shrugged. "He left here at midday. He is taking the elephant back to Delhi."

"The elephant? What the hell are you talking about?"

"I am talking about Mr Clockwork's Amazing Mechanical Elephant, sir."

"Was he taking it by train?"

"No, sir. By foot. Walking all the way to Delhi. It has been on display here for one month, and now it is returning to Delhi. In its place, I am displaying the Mech-Man."

"Ah..." Smethers said, casting his eyes around the emporium, "the fabled mechanical man. Where is it?"

The Indian pointed. "Over here, sir."

Alfie stared across the warehouse floor to the metal giant standing to attention under the apex of the corrugated ceiling. Now he could see why the street urchins he'd interrogated yesterday had been so impressed. The Mech-Man was a colossus, commanding even when motionless, its brass bodywork glinting in the overhead lights.

They stood and looked up at the giant. "Open it up."

"Sir?"

"I said open it up. I want to quick look-see inside, hm?"

The Indian moved around to the back of the Mech-Man and climbed, using spars and rivets as hand- and foot-holds. He fingered a catch and the head and shoulders tipped back.

The Indian climbed down and Smethers took his place, balancing precariously on a flange and peering into the giant's interior. "Not a bloody thing," he reported. "Not that I expected the girl to be hiding herself in there."

He jumped down and addressed the Indian. "And you say this Anand chappie skedaddled with a mechanical elephant?"

"Ah-cha. He left at noon for Delhi."

"And did he have a girl with him?"

The man blinked. "A girl, sir?"

"A girl. A young woman. You know what they are, don't you?"

"Ah-cha, sir. But no, there was no girl. He was quite alone."

Smethers stared down at the man, his gaze imperious. He reached out with his stick and tapped the Indian under the chin. "Now, my good man, if I find out that you've been lying to me, and this Anand fellow did have the girl with him... then you'll be for the high jump, ah-cha? I'll come back here and take a whip to your filthy hide, do y'get me drift?"

The man cowered away. "There was no girl, sir! Anand was alone, sir, very alone!"

Smethers nodded, smiling to himself. "Very well," he said, looking around the chamber. "Now make yourself scarce. You heard me, chalo. Oh, and before you go – the keys."

"The keys, sir?"

"We'll have a quick shufti and lock up when we've seen enough."

The man hesitated, grumbled something to himself, then handed over a big hank of keys. Smethers tossed them into the air, caught them and smiled. "Now chalo," he said, dismissing the man with a wave of his stick.

The Indian scurried across the warehouse and through the door like a fleeing rabbit.

Smethers tut-tutted. "India would be a fine place," he opined, "without the bally Indians, don't you know? They're either servile and arse-licking, or uppity and bolshy, what?"

Alfie kept his opinion to himself and moved around to the front of the Mech-Man, staring up at its engraved bodywork. The great domed head was imperious, the slit eyes inscrutable. He shivered.

Smethers joined him. "What did you make of what the chap said, Littlebody?"

"I think he was telling the truth, sir. As far as he was aware, the boy left for Delhi with the mechanical elephant."

"'As far as he was aware,'" Smethers repeated, looking down on Alfie. "What do you mean?"

Alfie shrugged. "The boy has helped her so far, sir, and I think he might still be doing so. My guess is that he didn't take the elephant back to Delhi but headed off somewhere else, accompanied by Janisha Chatterjee."

Smethers nodded. "That's a possibility."

The colonel strolled off, poking around the hundreds of mechanical exhibits as if he might find Anand and the girl skulking amidst them. Alfie joined him and they made a complete circuit of the warehouse.

"I think we've seen enough, don't you? It's too late to set off now, Littlebody, but at first light we'll commandeer an airship and scan the lie of the land east of here."

"East, sir? What makes you think...?"

Smethers silenced him with a glance. "Let's just say that I have intelligence, Littlebody, that the girl might be heading east, hm? As I said, we'll borrow an airship and have a quick look-see. If the pair are fleeing in a bloody mechanical elephant, it's my guess that the thing'd leave a hell of a trail, what?"

"Yes, sir. It probably would."

Smethers led the way to the exit, flicked off the lights with his swagger stick, and stepped from the building. Alfie followed, wondering why Janisha Chatterjee might be heading east, and what it was she possessed that was so dashed important.

East? A hundred miles away was the border with the restricted territory of Nepal. Why might she be heading in that direction?

Smethers halted outside the warehouse, shrugged, then tossed the bunch of keys into the darkness. Alfie was of a mind to retrieve them and lock the door, but Smethers was already striding away from the building.

Alfie hurried to catch up, then stopped.

"What is it, Littlebody?" Smethers asked, turning.

Alfie listened. He was sure he'd heard a sound coming from inside the warehouse. "I thought I heard something."

"Your imagination, Littlebody."

"No – there it is again."

He hurried back to the door, eased it open and peered within. He could see next to nothing in the darkness, but he heard the sound of footsteps and the clank of something metal. Smethers was beside him.

"By Jove, you're right," he whispered. "Easy does it now. Follow me."

Smethers stepped into the warehouse and led the way across the cavernous chamber. Alfie followed, his heart thudding. He almost jumped from his skin as he heard a great *clang*, and then the coughing din of an engine starting up.

"Look!" he cried, pointing.

Before them, limned in the light of the stars through a skylight, the mechanical man was coming to life. A sequence of lights flashed on its torso and the sound of meshing gears filled the chamber. As they stared up, transfixed, the giant took a great stride forward, then another, the sound of its engine deafening.

Smethers cried out, drew his revolver and fired. The bullet ricocheted off the bodywork with a sharp *ping*.

Had it not been for Smethers' rash shot, Alfie thought, the mechanical man – or whoever was driving it – might never have noticed them. As it was, the colossus swung itself in their direction and in one stride was upon them. Smethers, exhibiting a funk Alfie was delighted to behold, dropped his pistol and raised his arms before his face. Alfie was rooted to the spot, frozen with fear and fascination at what the giant did next.

As he stared, the Mech-Man reached out, plucked Smethers up by the front of his jacket and lifted him high. Smethers hung in the air, legs peddling ludicrously, as the great arm swung like the boom of a crane and carried the hapless colonel through the air.

At first Alfie feared that the Mech-Man was about to pulverise Smethers against the wall – and he wondered for a second if this was the janitor, come to exact his revenge for Smethers' arrogance. The mechanical man took a step, then another, and carried Smethers, wailing in fear, across the warehouse. It paused, gears grinding, and lowered the still struggling colonel into what looked like a great glinting jewel box. With its free arm, the Mech-Man closed the lid of the box and flipped a locking mechanism.

Then the giant turned ponderously until it faced Alfie, then began marching towards him.

Alfie overcame his fear, turned and fled through the open door. He looked over his shoulder, hardly believing what he saw as the mechanical man, without slowing down, ducked through the double doors and strode after him. Alfie whimpered, ran up the hill and threw himself behind a jacaranda tree.

He lay panting, hands clamped around his head, expecting a great metal claw to descend and pluck him up.

The sound of the giant's approach grew in volume, its engine deafening. Alfie scrunched himself into a ball – and, miraculously, the clashing, grinding, clanking cacophony of the Mech-Man drew level and passed by, gradually diminishing up the hillside.

At last Alfie screwed up his courage, sat upright and gazed around him. All was silent, or almost – the sound of the Mech-Man was faint, and growing fainter. He could see glinting metal in the starlight as it moved off, and Alfie was not inclined to give chase.

He took deep breaths and allowed the minutes to extend. At last, when the shaking in his limbs abated, he climbed to his feet.

He thought of Smethers, imprisoned in the jewelled box within the warehouse. He moved towards the building to free him, then halted.

He smiled to himself as it came to him that he should return to the guest house, spend a comfortable night abed, and then return and free Smethers at first light. He would claim, if the colonel asked at the delay, that the Mech-Man had incarcerated him, too.

He was about to make his way back to town when he saw something glinting on the ground.

He picked up the bunch of keys, approached the door, and dropped the keys on the ground where they would be found in the morning.

Then he turned and made his way back to the guest house.

ANAND CRIED OUT in delight, his laughter loud in the confines of Max's belly. He thought back to the expression on the face of the tall, thin officer as he plucked him off his feet and dropped him into the mechanical scarab. What a sight! The coward was wetting himself in fright! It was a pity he hadn't been able to find the second, dumpy little Britisher who'd scurried off up the hillside and concealed himself in the undergrowth.

What an adventure, Anand thought as he marched Max up the road and out of the town. It was like something from the most fantastical book he'd ever read – chased across the country by the damned British, the bloody Russians, and the gods knew who else! And all, he reflected with a warm glow in his heart, accompanied by the most wonderful girl in all the world. He felt a little guilty that he was having such a good time, so soon after the passing of papa-ji, but only a little... Papa-ji would be pleased that he, orphan houseboy Anand Doshi, was looking after his daughter so well.

As he clanked through the darkness and out of town, he thought back to something he'd told Jani-ji back in Delhi. He'd told her that he had a sweetheart at Mr Clockwork's factory, little Vashi who was as sweet as burfi; now, he wondered why he'd made up this story. Perhaps he'd wanted to impress Jani-ji, make her think of him not as the small playmate of old, but as someone old enough now to have a relationship with a girl...

But it was a mistake, he realised now. If Jani-ji thought he had a sweetheart, then she might never think of him as someone who... He felt himself reddening at the very thought, and considered what Mr Rai had told him yesterday: "*She is Brahmin, Anand, and half-English, and as is the modern way with women, she is educated also. You are a Dalit, boy, and you must know your place.*"

He sighed. Mr Rai was right. Jani-ji would never fall in love with him, no matter how long they were together. He was Anand, her houseboy playmate from childhood; a friend and nothing more.

But... but he was more than a houseboy now; he had proved himself. He had saved her life – she had said so herself – and in time her attitude towards him might change.

He would accompany her to the ends of the earth, and protect her from every evil that came her way, and in time he would tell her his true feelings, and maybe these feelings would be returned...

Heartened, he steered Max off the road and through the jungle.

Now he would impress Jani-ji again with his story of how he had bested the British officers – and then he would show her how he could make the mechanical elephant move so much faster.

His laughter echoed in the confines of Max's belly as he crashed through the foliage.

CHAPTER
FIFTEEN

❧

Anand returns in triumph –
On the way to Rishi Tal – Memories of a galloping horse –
"For the ultimate benefit of your planet..."

JANI CURLED ON a chesterfield inside the mechanical
elephant and waited for Anand to return.

She marvelled at the sumptuousness of the
accommodation – what Anand had called 'the living
quarters'. It was as if she were inside a great chocolate
Easter egg, an oval chamber constructed from polished
mahogany and brass fittings. A woven rug lay on the
floor and tapestries hung from the walls. Beside the
chesterfield was a small bookcase containing classics of
English and Indian literature. There was even a small
pot-bellied stove, for cold winter nights. Mr Clockwork
had thought of everything. "The room is on a gimbal,
Jani-ji," Anand had explained, "so that when Mel is in
motion it is rock-steady down here."

Jani tried not to look ahead, but to take each day as
it came. It was worrying that the British had followed
her so far, but at least she had foiled their attempt at
capturing her. She wondered at the wisdom of allowing
Anand to return for Max, and had tried to persuade

him to remain – but he was young, and stubborn, and would not be deterred.

She tried to read. She plucked a volume of poetry by Tagore from the shelf and read a page or two, but her mind would not settle. She set the volume aside, climbed the steps from the belly of the elephant and opened the trapdoor above her head. She climbed out and sat on the creature's broad back.

The jungle was still; she heard the distant call of bullfrogs, the chirrup of insects close by. A full moon rode through the treetops high above. Anand had estimated that, if all went well, they would reach Rishi Tal in a day. With luck, Jelch would be awaiting her there. She wondered why he wanted her to journey on to Nepal.

The night was warm, scented with the perfume of a hundred flowers. She lay on her back, her head pillowed on her laced fingers, and stared up through the jungle canopy at the pulsing stars. She made out Orion, and the bright star of Mintaka on the warrior's belt, and she was considering Jelch again when she heard a sudden sound.

She sat up quickly and listened.

She heard the sound of an engine, and then the crack of splintered wood. She stared through the jungle towards the road and made out the multicoloured constellation of the Mech-Man's chest panel.

Max stamped through the jungle towards her, the noise of its engine drowning out the insect noises and the calls of the frogs. The giant approached the elephant, its great domed head on a level with where Jani squatted, and a sudden silence fell as Anand stilled the motors. The head and shoulders tipped back and the boy popped out.

He stared at Jani with huge eyes. "Almost a disaster, Jani-ji. The British were waiting for me."

"But how did you get away?"

Anand laughed. "There were only two of them in the warehouse. I powered up Max and dealt with the first officer. I locked him up and chased the second officer away from the warehouse!"

"And did you catch him?"

"The coward hid himself, so I hurried away and came straight back here."

"And you're sure that they didn't follow you?"

"Tip-top sure, Jani-ji!"

"But now they know we have Max, and will be searching for him," Jani said. "Anand, it would be better if we left Max and travelled on Mel."

He was grinning at her. "But why do you think I went to get Max?"

"Stop your games. So that we could travel faster in him, of course. But as I said, they will be looking for Max..."

"Not 'of course', Jani-ji. Move aside and watch."

Confused, Jani scrambled to the rear of the elephant as instructed and watched as Anand closed the head and shoulders of the mechanical man and powered him up again.

The girder-like arms reached out and gripped the back of the elephant. Then the huge legs moved, finding footholds on the pachyderm's flank. The elephant swayed as it took the weight of the Mech-Man, and the latter hauled itself up.

A minute later Max straddled the elephant's broad back, and Jani stared in amazement as the mechanical man reached forward and opened a second trapdoor

– this one closer to the elephant's domed head. Then she blinked, as if at an optical illusion, as Max eased itself forward, legs first, and seemed to slide – with a loud meshing of gears and scrape of metal on metal – through the opening of the trapdoor and *into* the mechanical elephant. The trapdoor clanged shut and Max, the Mech-Man, vanished.

She heard the grumble of Max's engine, muffled, and a great series of internal clankings, whirrings, and assorted mechanical clangs and bangs.

She opened the trapdoor to the living quarters and tapped down the steps. Towards the front of the chamber she made out the broad back of the Mech-Man. As she watched, a hatch in his back swung open and Anand slipped out.

"Now Mel is powered by Max," he announced. "You see, Mr Clockwork conceived Max and Mel as one – he said that Max is Mel's mahout!"

Jani laughed and clapped her hands. "I see the method in your madness now, Anand."

The boy jumped back through the door into Max's torso control room, and Jani followed and sat beside him on the padded seat.

For the next ten minutes they pored over a map of Uttarakhand and the border of Nepal, plotting a route to Rishi Tal through the hills that avoided all the major towns and villages. They were fortunate that this was a sparsely populated area, covered by forest and jungle that would provide ample cover.

"I suggest we travel by night only," Jani said. "The British will be looking principally for Max, but of course they will question Mr Gopal, and when they find out that you were due to return to Delhi with Mel, then they will be searching for him also. We must be very careful."

"Careful will be my watchword!" Anand said, and reached out for the controls. He pulled a series of levers, thumped studs and turned a great wheel. The engine in Max powered up with a mounting drone and Anand cried out, "Hold on, Jani-ji!"

The view-plate in Max's torso corresponded with an identical horizontal observation port in the forehead of the mechanical elephant, and Jani made out the jungle illuminated by the beam of a searchlight set into Mel's forehead.

The control room lurched as Anand pushed a lever. The elephant took a great stride forward, then another. Jani heard the sound of rending and tearing as trees parted before the onslaught. They lurched along at speed, Anand laughing uproariously, Jani holding onto the padded arm of the chair as she swayed right and left.

She glanced at the boy. He was purse-lipped, wide-eyed, as he pulled and yanked at levers, adjusted slides and spun the wheel to control the pachyderm's headlong rush.

They marched up a wooded hillside, gained the peak and ploughed down the far side, guided by a vast compass set in a brass binnacle. The ride was far from smooth, and Jani was thankful for the thick padding of the control chair.

At one point, an hour into their journey, Anand said, "You must be tired. Go and rest on the chesterfield."

"I am not in the slightest bit tired, Anand. I will sleep when we stop for the day, ah-cha."

He grinned at her. "You remind me of your father, Jani-ji."

"In what way?"

"In many ways. He would not be told what to do. Mrs Chandra, our dragon of a housekeeper, she was always telling your father that he read too long into the night and should get to bed early. She even quoted Gandhi at him – 'early to bed, early to rise.'" He laughed. "But your father was having none of it! He called her 'that woman!' and read into the early hours anyway. You are stubborn, just like your father."

She smiled. "I hope he would approve of what I am doing."

"I think he would. He was so proud of you. He was always telling everyone about how you were doing so well in England. And when you gained a place at Cambridge, he never stopped talking about it."

"But what we are doing, Anand, defying the British..." She hesitated. "He was always on the side of the little man, Anand, the down-trodden and the oppressed. Although he was the Minister for Security, and responsible for the safety of the nation, I think he was fair and just."

Anand looked away. "I think so, too, Jani-ji," he said.

"I think, in many ways, my father saw the British through rose-tinted spectacles. He liked to think that with the Raj it was all cricket and fair play. He thought the... the killings and such like, were aberrations."

He stared at her. "And you? What do you think?"

"Oh, Anand, I don't know. I would like to have confidence in the British and their rule, but I know they are weak, like anyone else, and I do so wish that we Indians could one day rule our own nation. My father had worked too long for the British, and could not envisage life without them. But I can."

Beside her, Anand was silent.

"Have I shocked you?" she asked.

He shook his head. "No. Well, perhaps a little. I thought you believed what your father believed. I thought, with your English education... I thought you looked up to the Raj."

"Anand, in many ways I do. I see the good they've brought to the country, the bureaucracy, the order, the healthcare, the egalitarianism in trying to abolish the caste system... despite all their own inherent faults. But at the same time I think that we, as a nation, a people, are advanced enough to take over the reins of governance." She stopped, then laughed. "But listen to me, Anand! I am sounding just like a Nationalist pamphlet!"

She fell silent, confused in her own mind, and overwhelmed suddenly by the realisation, for perhaps the hundredth time that day, that she would never again see her father.

Six hours later the rising sun sent spears of light low through the jungle cover. Individual trees became defined, no longer the dark masses through which Mel crashed. Jani saw parakeets flash through the air like explosions of stained glass. Through a gap in the trees ahead she made out brilliant blue sky and a distant snow-capped peak.

Anand brought the elephant to a halt beneath the spreading shade of a baobab tree, and the sudden cessation of motion, after hours of jouncing this way and that, was disorienting. As the silence settled around them, Jani stretched and suggested they climb out to get some fresh air and something to eat.

They sat on the back of the elephant, picking at a selection of roasted nuts Anand had bought at the

Dehrakesh market, as the sun rose over the jungle and an orchestra of insects tuned up. Jani was too tired to appreciate the food and wanted only to curl up on the chesterfield and sleep.

Anand fetched the map and unfolded it before them, dropping a finger on their position. "We are halfway to Rishi Tal, Jani-ji, which is about twenty-five miles away now. There are no roads in the area, so with luck the British will not find us."

Jani stared at the map. "It is when we near Rishi Tal that I will become nervous."

"If we set off again when darkness falls, we will reach Rishi Tal tomorrow morning," he said. "Then we should leave Max and Mel well away from the town, hidden safely, and make our way there on foot." He looked up at her. "And then? Why do you think this Jelch wanted you to go to Nepal?"

She shook her head. "I honestly don't know, Anand—" She stopped speaking, cocked her head to one side and listened.

"What is it, Jani-ji?"

"Don't you hear it?"

Above the birdsong, the repetitive paddling sound of an airship's impellors made itself heard, growing louder.

Alarmed, Jani looked up, attempting to see the sky through the jungle canopy. At least, she thought, if she was unable to see the sky, then anyone up there would be unable to see the elephant.

Anand was scrambling down Mel's flank, and Jani followed him. They hurried through the jungle, following the rising gradient towards a bare hillock high above. The sound of the airship grew louder, became a din almost overhead. In due course they came to the last of the trees and stopped side by side, crouching in the cover of a fern and staring into the patch of bright blue sky.

Seconds later the shape of a two-man airship came into view. Jani's heart thumped as she made out, on its bulging hull, the union flag and the RAF roundel. The vehicle banked, veering north-east, and a minute later was a dwindling dot soon lost to sight.

She stared at Anand. "They cannot have been searching for us, surely?"

He shook his head. "I think it was just a routine patrol," he said.

She led the way back to the mechanical elephant, heavy of heart, and then curled up in the darkened interior of the pachyderm's belly and slept.

SHE LOOKED UP from her Tagore as the swaying motion of the elephant, like a galleon on the high seas, ceased and the engine began its long diminuendo towards silence.

She had joined Anand in the control seat for much of the last leg of this journey, and towards dawn had retired to the chesterfield to read. They had travelled throughout the night, and the journey had passed without incident.

The door in the Mech-Man's back swung open and Anand slipped out. "We are about one mile from Rishi Tal, Jani-ji. We will leave Mel here and walk the rest of the way."

Jani set her book aside. "I need to change, and you too. We will pass ourselves off as tourists, brother and sister, ah-cha, if anyone asks." And hope, she added to herself, we don't run into any policemen looking out for us.

"Tourists?" Anand gestured to his ragged shorts and shirt. "But these are the only clothes I have."

"I have a surprise." She reached for her bag and withdrew a new pair of shorts, a shirt and a pair of shining leather sandals.

"For me?" Anand said.

"In them you'll look like my younger brother. And remember, you must be respectful – and obey me at all times."

He squinted at her. "I think I do anyway, Jani-ji."

He took the clothes, returned to the control room and dressed, while Jani changed into clean underwear. Last night, before setting off, they had bathed in the icy water of a mountain stream, which had been all very well, but Jani looked forward to finding a hotel in Rishi Tal and drawing herself a hot bath.

Her bag slung over her shoulder, she climbed down from the back of the elephant and moved to its great head. She patted the sun-warmed trunk. "With luck, Mel, we will see you again in a little while."

They turned and walked through the forested glade, heading downhill towards the wide valley in which the town nestled.

"And where will we meet Jelch?" Anand asked.

"He did not specify a place, or a time. He merely said that I would know the place."

He glanced at her. "And do you?"

She smiled. "I must admit that I don't. But perhaps once we get there, ah-cha?"

"I'm curious to meet Jelch, Jani-ji. From what you said of him, he sounds like a monster."

"Perhaps physically, yes, though a very human monster. But in here..." she touched her brow, "in here he is... *humane* is the only word I can think of."

"And if we fail to meet him?"

Jani shook her head. "I don't know. We'll have to consider our options then, won't we?"

They walked on, and she wondered at Jelch's reaction to finding that she had lost the gift he had given her, the silver coin-like object. She feared his censure at her neglect.

To wipe away this thought, she asked Anand the first thing that entered her mind. "Do you miss your little sweetheart at Mr Clockwork's factory?"

He blushed and regarded his new sandals. "I would rather not talk about her, Jani-ji," he murmured.

They walked on through the pine trees; the sun was rising, warming the resin on the tree trunks and filling the air with its scent. Anand said, "And you?"

"Me?"

"Do you miss your young man?"

The odd thing was, when she thought about it, she had to admit that she did not. Events of late had swept thoughts of him away. Which was odd as, back in England, he had been constantly on her mind.

"Well?" Anand prompted.

"It's strange, Anand, but I've had so much to think about of late that I haven't had time to dwell on Sebastian."

He was silent for a time, nodding, and then asked, "Do you love him, Jani-ji?"

She laughed. "Oh, what is love? I thought I did when I was with him. Had anyone said that we would be parted like this, then I would have thought it terrible. But the reality is that it is not so terrible after all. So, perhaps, I cannot love him..." And saying these words, and seeing in her mind's eye Sebastian's face as he said farewell to her at the London airyard, she felt as if she were betraying him.

"Then again... perhaps I do love him, Anand." She shook her head. Perhaps only when she was back in England, and in his company again, would she know the true feelings of her heart?

Beside her, the boy stared at the ground and said, "Oh."

There had been a time, a few months ago, when Jani had dreamed of a life with Sebastian in England... But since returning to India she felt, more and more, that her future belonged in her homeland, working as a surgeon and ministering to the needs of her own people. She sighed; oh, how torn she was, between loyalty to her country and gratitude to Britain. Sometimes she felt as if she belonged in neither place, and wondered if a life somewhere else entirely might be the answer.

Her thoughts were interrupted when they arrived at the margin of the trees and looked down on the town. Jani took a breath and exclaimed at the beauty of the scene laid out before them.

A long, brilliant blue lake nestled at the head of the valley, and rising on the far bank was the hill station of Rishi Tal. A long promenade flanked the lake, the wide boulevard a favourite place for tourists to stroll at sunset.

At one end of the road was a square surrounded by benches, with a statue of Queen Victoria at its centre.

Jani smiled. "I first came here with my mother and father when I was three," she told Anand. "Do you see the statue?" She pointed. "Well, one day I was out walking with my mother. My father was watching from the balcony of their room in our guest house. I ran away from my mother, across the square, and just in front of the statue a horse galloped out of nowhere and knocked me down. I went tumbling under its hooves, and my mother and father thought I was dead. But by some miracle I picked myself up and toddled back to my mother, totally unharmed."

She recalled her father telling her the story many times over the years; and he never told the tale without a tear coming to his eye. Thinking of how he must have felt at the time, seeing his daughter trampled by the galloping horse, Jani felt a swelling of emotion in her chest.

Anand said, "And to think, if you had not survived, Jani-ji, I would never have known you."

She smiled, and recalled suddenly what Jelch had told her when she had asked why she should make her way to Nepal: "*For the ultimate benefit of your planet, Janisha, and all who live upon it...*"

She gasped.

"What is it, Jani-ji?"

"I know!" she said.

He stared at her. "You know what?"

She laughed. "Where I should meet Jelch." She shook her head. "The thing is, I don't know how I know. It just came to me in a flash. But... but, Anand, how could Jelch be certain? How did he know where we would meet?"

"Perhaps he has special powers, Jani-ji. But where are we to meet him?"

"Every time we came here we stayed at my father's favourite guest house. He always spoke of that first holiday he spent here with my mother... I think it was a magical time for him; he was young, and in love with my mother, and... and a year later she would be taken away from him." She looked down at the town.

"The guest house was called the Varma Singh, and it overlooked the lake. It is there that we will meet Jelch, I am sure of it!"

Jani felt a swelling in her heart as she stared across the lake, a sense of communion through time to the people her mother and father had been. And at the same time she felt a knot of fear when she made out, barrelling along the promenade on the far side of the lake, a jeep carrying khaki-clad military policemen.

She gripped Anand's hand and they set off down the track.

CHAPTER
SIXTEEN

∽

Above Rishi Tal – A conversation with Mr Knives –
The chase is on – "Prepare yourself to jump..."

DURGA DAS AWOKE from a deep sleep and sat up in
the armchair, confused for a few seconds. He recalled
landing in Dehrakesh at midnight, locating Mr
Clockwork's warehouse, and finding the place in a state
of chaos. He'd questioned a local who had been awoken
by a din, and who described seeing a mechanical giant
striding away from the warehouse.

At first light, Das had ordered his pilot to take the
airship up high above Dehrakesh – and as he'd hoped,
the trampled undergrowth wrought by the mechanical
beast was evident from on high. For a day they had
followed the route the Chatterjee girl and the boy had
taken through the dense forest, he and Mr Knives taking
it in turns to keep a lookout for the first sign of the pair.

Das blinked himself fully awake and stared around
the gondola. In the armchair opposite, the young Mr
Knives was sound asleep and snoring noisily, legs
stretched out before him, his trusty dagger lying on his
chest like an inverted silver neck-tie.

"You fool!" Das cried, pushing himself upright.

Mr Knives came awake with a start. At least he had the good grace to look guilty.

"You incompetent!" Das spat, standing over the cowering youth. "Your job was simple – stay awake while I slept, and keep a lookout!"

"But, baba-ji, I have only this second fallen asleep."

"You liar!" Das cried. He trundled across the gondola and squeezed himself into the control cabin. There, a tiny Sikh sat before the wheel.

"Thank the gods that you have not fallen asleep, Singh," Das said.

The pilot pointed through the windscreen to starboard. Far below Das made out a swathe of trampled undergrowth snaking through the forest.

"I heard the snores, Mr Das, and paid attention to the track. It is my guess that they are heading for the town of Rishi Tal."

"Excellent work, Singh," Das said, and returned to the gondola.

Mr Knives, chastened, had drawn his armchair up to a starboard porthole and was peering out intently. He pointed. "I see the track down below, baba-ji."

"It's a good job Singh is awake and alert, you fool."

Mr Knives muttered something under his breath as Das pulled his armchair across the gondola and stationed it before a porthole. He resumed his seat and stared down, hoping to catch a glimpse of the mechanical man sooner rather than later.

When they caught up with the pair, he would have Singh lower them to the forest out of sight of the girl and her accomplice; then Mr Knives would approach them with stealth, despatch the boy and capture the girl.

He outlined his plan to Mr Knives, whose complicit grin widened when Das mentioned the boy. "The boy deserves to die slowly, baba-ji. He has caused us much travail."

Das eyed the youth as if he were an insect. "You will kill him quickly and as painlessly as possible, Mr Knives: his next life awaits him. Our priority is the girl. I do not want you spending time on the boy and so allowing the girl to escape our clutches."

"And when we have the girl?"

"She has something I need, something very important..."

"And when you have what you want, baba-ji?"

Das had looked no further than obtaining the tithra-kūjī. Now he considered the Chatterjee girl and her fate. It would be a mistake to let her live, so that she might possibly incriminate himself and Mr Knives. It would be far better if she too was despatched to her next incarnation.

"When I have what I want, Mr Knives, then the girl must die."

A gleam entered Mr Knives' shifty eyes. "I will take my time, baba-ji, and make the girl suffer. I might even take my pleasure before performing a thousand cuts."

Das winced. "You will kill the girl swiftly and painlessly, Mr Knives. There is no need to inflict unnecessary suffering and cruelty. We are every one of us, when all is said and done, creatures of creation."

"But some of us," Mr Knives purred, "deserve rewards, and others retribution."

"Such rewards and retribution as we might deserve are for the gods to mete out, Mr Knives."

Das had no respect for the Chatterjee girl; as far as he was concerned, she was a traitor to her people, just as her father had been. In siding with the British in their cruel domination of India, Kapil Dev Chatterjee had signed a pact with the enemy; he had even married a white woman, an Englishwoman, and their spawn, in the form of Janisha Chatterjee, had chosen to conduct a life of western materialism and hedonism. She was beneath Das's contempt and deserved to die; for all that, however, she did not deserve to die a lingering and painful death.

A cunning look crossed Mr Knives' thin face. He said, "I wonder what your contacts in parliament would think of what you are doing, baba-ji?"

Das dragged his gaze from the porthole and stared at the young man. "What did you say?"

Mr Knives grinned. "Your contacts, the MPs you call your friends..."

"What about them?"

"They would not look kindly upon you if they found that you were responsible for the death of a minister's daughter."

Das peered at Mr Knives with mounting incredulity. "Just what are you suggesting, Mr Knives?"

The young man shrugged. "Just that, if they were to find out that you ordered her killing..." He allowed a second to elapse, then went on, "However, if you would allow me to have my way with the traitor, then the MPs might never need know about your part in the affair."

Das contained his rage. He summoned a smile and said, sweetly, "You are forgetting one thing, my friend. The blood would be on your hands, too."

"So, we would both be implicated. I do not fear the consequences. After all, I have nothing to lose. You, however, with your rich lifestyle and your ashram, with the devotion and respect you enjoy from your many followers, you have much to lose."

As he said this, Mr Knives stared down at the edge of his trusty blade, and began, insouciantly, to trim his fingernails.

"When I plucked you from the streets," Das said, "I saved your skin. I gave you a life of plenty you could but dream about. A life you took to with relish... along with my Bombay rum. Now one day, not so long ago, you were a little indiscreet after two or three too many glasses... You bragged of a ghastly murder you committed." Das gestured as the youth stared at him, wide-eyed. "I did a little research, spoke with a high-up police official I happen to know. And I learned that the police have a file on the murder, with your good self as the prime suspect. It so happened that I was feeling generous that day, Mr Knives, and proffered the superintendent a remittance if he were to close the file on the killing. However," Das went on, smiling across at the stricken youth, "that file could be opened at my say so... and will be, if you see fit to contravene my express desires. Now, Mr Knives, do I make myself understood? You will kill the girl quickly."

Mr Knives, with hatred burning in his eyes, was saved from replying by a shout from the control cabin.

"Mr Das! Down below! I see something..."

Das pressed his face against the glass. He made out the winding stretch of trampled undergrowth disappearing into the distance. He stumbled into the control cabin and peered through the viewscreen. "There, Mr Das," Singh said.

Das made out not the mechanical man he'd been expecting, but a huge brass elephant.

Singh pointed. "And there, on the path leading into town... the boy and girl you are following!"

Sure enough, there they were, trotting side by side down the steep woodland path. His heart leapt at the sight of the pair. Beyond, nestling like a vision of paradise in the wooded hills, was the lakeside hill station of Rishi Tal.

"Can you come down some distance away so that they don't hear the ship?" he asked.

The tiny Sikh peered out at the hilly terrain. "Nai, baba-ji. I cannot land. Maybe I could come down low so that you might jump out."

Das didn't much like the idea of that, but he had an idea. "Ah-cha. Do that. Is there an airyard that services the town?"

The pilot referred to his charts and nodded. "The Rishi Tal airyard is just three miles further down the valley."

"Very good."

He returned to the gondola as the motors powered down and the vessel banked and approached a parting in the treetops.

"Mr Knives, prepare yourself to jump."

"Jump?" The youth's startled expression was gratifying to behold.

"That's what I said, Mr Knives. Look..."

He took the youth by the arm and pushed him towards the porthole. "See the figures on the path down there?"

As he spoke, the airship brushed the treetops, came down even further and bobbed ten feet from the ground.

"You will leave the ship and follow them into town. Make sure you don't let them out of your sight, my friend, and ascertain where they are heading. I will meet you in the square beside the lake."

"You're not coming with me?"

"I will remain aboard the airship, then take a taxi from the airyard into town."

From the cabin, Singh called out, "I am as low as I can go, baba-ji!"

Das crossed to the hatch, swung the door open and peered out. The gondola was swaying above a dense patch of undergrowth. He took Mr Knives' arm and propelled him toward the opening. The youth goggled at the drop.

"Now follow the girl and the boy and do not let them out of your sight!" Das said. "And, if you do your job well, that murder file might remain closed... Chalo!"

And so saying, he pushed Mr Knives in the small of the back. The youth cried out and jumped into the tangle of undergrowth. He landed in a sprawl of limbs, looked up ruefully at a smiling Das, then hunted on hands and knees for his precious blade.

Finding it, he stood, gained his bearings, and set off down the hillside.

Das resumed his armchair and contemplated the rewards of the chase. "To the airyard, Singh!" he called out.

The engines powered up and the airship climbed and passed over the town of Rishi Tal.

CHAPTER
SEVENTEEN

At the Varma Singh guest house – A hot bath at last –
Jani and Anand receive visitors –
"Fear of death will loosen your tongue..."

JANI JUMPED AS she heard the sound of engines overhead.
She looked up, fearing a military airship, and gave a
relieved sigh as she made out the great bulbous envelope,
green-and-yellow-striped, of a civilian airship. The
vessel beat its way down the valley, heading south.

She and Anand entered the town, passing knots of
tourists, Indian and British alike. She glanced at Anand.
"How do you feel, brother?" she murmured.

He smiled, but nervously. "I feel like a sheep in a field
of cows, Jani-ji. I think everyone is looking at me."

She laughed and took his hand. "You'll feel better
once we've reached the guest house," she said as they
came to the square where fifteen years ago she had been
skittled by the horse.

She stood in silence and gazed up at the statue of the
dead queen, then stared at the place, described over and
over by her father, where she had been knocked down.

Then, squeezing Anand's hand, she led the way across
the square to the Varma Singh guest house.

A pair of green-painted doors opened onto an expanse of polished floorboards covered with faded rugs. Galleries on the first and second floors overlooked the foyer, their wrought-iron scrollwork also painted green. An air of faded antiquity hung about the place, as if the guest house was the relic of another age. Nothing seemed to have changed since her last visit twelve years ago.

Jani asked at reception for a twin-bedded room, and a grey, bent woman, looking as old as the house itself, showed her to a spacious, sparsely furnished room overlooking the lake. "The summer season is over," she said, "and we have many rooms available on the upper floors. This is one of the finest, with views of the lakes and hills, and I will be charging you only ten rupees a night."

"It's wonderful!" Jani said as she stepped out onto the balcony and leaned over the rail. "We will be staying for one or two nights. I wonder if food is available?"

"We have no restaurant, but if you would like to dine in your room I will arrange for meals to be delivered. There are many fine restaurants in Rishi Tal."

"That will be perfect," Jani said, and watched the old woman shuffle from the room.

She took the hot bath she had been dreaming about for days, and then went down to reception and ordered dal baht with puri, and chai, to be delivered to their room.

Later, as they ate at a table on the verandah, Anand said, "You must have wonderful memories of your holidays here, Jani-ji?"

"I remember that we stayed in rooms overlooking the lake – maybe even this one. I remember my father playing chess on a balcony with the owner, Varma Singh himself, an old man with a great white turban and the biggest moustache I have ever seen."

She imagined her mother and father renting the room on their first holiday here; she could almost see their ghosts, moving around the faded chintz bedroom like spectral actors on a stage.

"And now we wait for Jelch?"

She sipped her spiced chai. "Ah-cha. This is perfect, Anand. We have everything we need in this room. We have no need to set foot outside for anything. Although I would like to explore Rishi Tal, I would not feel safe doing so with so many police and soldiers about the place."

She gripped the balcony rail and peered down at the promenade flanking the lake. The town was a popular holiday destination for members of the Raj, and the main street was busy with tourists – among which, Jani saw, were uniformed British soldiers. She gazed down, feeling relatively safe for the first time since fleeing Delhi.

"I have been thinking..." she said a little later, watching Anand wipe his plate clean of dal with his puri. "When Jelch comes here, he will be in disguise."

"He will?"

"Well, I hope so. If not, then he will attract unwanted attention. Although he resembles a human, he looks very different. His face is flattened, his eyes large and grey – they reminded me of the eyes of a dead fish. And his legs..." She recalled him bounding away through the wreckage of the airship. Something about the articulation of his legs had put her in mind of a dog.

As she told Anand this, his eyes widened. "What kind of creature is he, Jani-ji? Where do you think he comes from?"

She shook her head. "The world is a mysterious place. There are many areas, to the north of here for example, that are unexplored. You have heard of stories about the yeti? Maybe Jelch is a creature like these."

But why, then, if this were so, had he said that he came from far away, and was here in a bid to help the human race?

"Perhaps," Anand ventured, "he is a god come to Earth?"

She smiled. "I think not. Gods exist only in the minds of those who need such things."

He stared at her. "You are so like your father! He would not allow holy men into the house. He would have no truck with anything he thought of as superstition. This worried me, and daily I prayed for him at the shrine of Shiva on Chittagar Road. I think I should pray for you, next time, Jani-ji."

She smiled. "You do that, Anand, if it will make you happy."

She finished her chai, returned to the room and lay on the bed, reading a little Tagore while Anand remained on the balcony staring down at the promenading tourists. "I will tell you when a strange-looking creature approaches the guest house, Jani-ji."

She set her book aside and closed her eyes. Minutes later, half-awake, she dreamed of a funeral pyre with her father's swaddled corpse placed atop the stacked timbers. Tears trickled down her cheeks. Three days had elapsed since her father's passing, and his funeral would have been held by now...

"Jani-ji!"

She felt a hand on her shoulder, shaking her.

Anand said, his face animated, "Jani-ji. There is someone at the door! Perhaps it is..."

She swung from the bed as the tapping sounded again. Arranging her hair, and checking her cheeks to ensure they were dry of tears, she hurried across the room and answered the summons. She had expected to see Jelch standing on the threshold, and was surprised to see the shrunken form of the old proprietor.

"You have a visitor, Miss. A most venerable gentleman wishes to see you. Shall I send him up, or will you be coming down to receive him?"

Debating what might be best, she said, "Please, send him up."

"Ah-cha." The old woman pressed her palms together before her chest and hurried off.

Anand was beside Jani. "Is it him, Jani-ji?"

"Who else can it be?" she said, stepping from the room and crossing to the gallery rail.

She stared down into the foyer. A huge holy man, his bulk swathed in a saffron robe, was climbing the stairs with considerable effort, accompanied by a thin, dark-haired youth.

Had Jelch taken on the disguise of an ash-haired sadhu? But, if so, then who was his skeletal accomplice?

Anand clutched her hand. "Jani-ji!" he hissed. "That man is not Jelch! He is a priest called Durga Das. I have heard his anti-British speeches in Delhi. The man with him is called Mr Knives – and he is a thug!"

Jani pulled Anand back into the room and locked the door. "But what can they want with us?" she said to herself.

Anand shook his head. "What should we do?" he asked.

"We should get away from here as fast as we can, Anand."

She crossed to the balcony. Her heart was thumping and she could hardly think straight. Anand voiced her uppermost thought. "But how did they know we were here?"

"I don't know. Might they have found Jelch, and somehow forced our whereabouts from him?" She stared at the boy. "And this Mr Knives? I don't like the sound of him."

"He is a criminal. He does the holy man's dirty work. Some people even say he is a murderer. The police do nothing to arrest him because he works for Durga Das, who bribes them to look the other way."

She peered over the balcony rail. The street was thirty feet below them and there was no way down, aside from a tall poplar tree whose feathery branches brushed the wrought iron scrollwork of the balcony. For a desperate second she considered jumping into the tree and trusting her safety to blind luck, but baulked at the thought.

"Jani?" Anand cried.

"We will simply refuse to answer the door," she said.

"But if they attempt to break it down?"

"Then... then we will attack them, push our way past the pair and flee from the guest house."

Anand looked far from convinced. "Ah-cha," he said.

A loud rapping sounded at the door. Jani shrank back, her heart pounding.

"Shhh," she exhorted, though Anand needed no telling.

The tapping came again, followed by silence.

A voice called out, "Janisha Chatterjee?"

The knocks started up again, more insistent this time.

"Janisha Chatterjee, I know you are within the room. Now please answer the door. We need to speak on a most urgent matter."

She turned again and stared over the rail. There was no way down, other than the tree.

The rapping upon the door became an urgent hammering. "Miss Chatterjee! I must insist!"

This was followed by an interval of silence in which Jani was aware of her thumping heart. "Jani?" Anand was wide-eyed.

Then the door shook as someone applied their shoulder to it.

Jani ran into the room, Anand beside her, and paused before the door. "Just as soon as the door bursts open," she hissed, "charge past them and sprint down the stairs. I will be right behind you."

"And then?"

"Then we will make for the hills and hide."

The door shook again and timber splintered, but held. She stood a yard from the door, watching it bulge in the frame with each blow. She looked desperately around the room for something to use as a weapon, but saw nothing – by which time, anyway, it was too late.

The door sprang open in an explosion of timber shrapnel and bounced back off the wall. The young man, Mr Knives, tumbled into the room. Anand cried out and dodged past the intruder, but at that second the corpulent holy man filled the threshold and Anand bounced off his belly. Mr Knives grabbed the boy, forcing his right arm up between his shoulder blades. Anand cried out as Mr Knives threw him to the floor.

Jani pulled the boy to her and together, defiant, they faced their captors.

Behind Mr Knives, the holy man had to turn sideways in order to squeeze his great belly through the doorway. He shut the ruined door behind him and stared at Jani and Anand with gloating delight.

Mr Knives pulled a long blade from inside his jacket and began, casually, to pare his nails, an expression of supreme satisfaction on his rat-like face as he leaned back against the door.

Jani stared at Durga Das. Everything about him, she thought, was revolting, from the long, greasy curls that hung on either side of his overfed face, with its hooked nose and full, sensuous lips, to the pendulous sack of his belly, down to the big hairy toes that protruded from his worn sandals. He exuded a malign intent as he stared at her, the reek of sweat barely concealed by rosewater.

His voice, when he spoke, was high and sweet, like a nautch girl's. "Delighted to make your acquaintance, at last, Janisha Chatterjee," he said in Hindi.

She stared at him. "What do you want with us?"

Das stared at her. "I think *you* know very well what we want, Janisha." The way he spoke the long form of her name, with cloying familiarity, turned her stomach.

"We want," he went on, "the same as the Russians want. We want the tithra-kuñjī."

The word tithra meant nothing to her; the second word, kuñjī, was Hindi for key.

"I don't know what you're talking about."

Das's cupid's bow lips puckered in mock disappointment. "Oh, but I know you do. The monster gave it to you. Or has the trauma of the Russian attack wiped that from your memory? I rather think not."

Jani shook her head. "I don't..." she began. The coin, she thought...

Das stepped forward, his gut rolling. "Now, I am a servant of my goddess," he interrupted. "My presence on Earth, the very reason for my being, is to expedite the will of Kali. My every action, my every intent, is but a manifestation of the desire of beings so much greater than ourselves that we are mere amoebas by comparison. My destiny, ordained by Kali, is to succeed in uniting the sacred realm with the mundane, this Earth with the exalted, in bringing my goddess to wreak her work on this benighted world. Nothing will stop me, nothing will stand in my way. It is written in the fates that I will succeed, that Kali will, through me, descend and destroy this evil age and renew creation..." His eyes opened wide as he stared at her. "Now where is the tithra-kuñjī!"

She shook her head, slowly, and said, "I honestly, honestly, don't know."

His eyes narrowed. "But the monster gave it to you?"

"I don't know what you are talking about!"

Anand was staring up at her. She smiled at him and gripped his shoulder.

"You make an unconvincing liar, Janisha Chatterjee," Das purred.

"It's the truth!"

Das sighed. "I have been lenient with you so far. You have been defiant, sinful even. You defy the will of the gods. But then you are but a lackey of the Raj, educated by their lie-mongers in London... You are a traitor to your nation, your people. What should I expect but defiance, and ignorance, from the daughter of a heathen like Kapil Dev Chatterjee? Now, I will give you one more chance, and if you persist in lying then I shall be forced, against my better judgement, to prevail upon Mr Knives and his trusty steel to make you see the error of your ways."

"I am telling you the truth. I know nothing about a..."

"Mr Knives!" Das barked. "Not the girl. She is too... precious. I would like to keep her alive, for a little while at least. I think you should concentrate your considerable skill on killing the boy. And Mr Knives, do it quickly." He smiled at Jani. "We will see then, as his blood flows like an offering to Kali, whether fear of death will loosen your tongue and the truth will issue from your lips. Mr Knives..."

The thin man ceased his nail-paring with a businesslike nod, smiled at Anand and stepped forward.

Jani leapt at Mr Knives with no plan other than to prevent him from hurting Anand. No sooner had she approached the knifeman than Durga Das, showing surprising speed for a man of his size, lashed out and punched her in the stomach. She cried out and fell to the floor, doubled up in pain, as Mr Knives grabbed the boy.

Anand struggled, shrieking in fear, and the look in Mr Knives' eyes as he prepared to kill the boy was one of sadistic delight.

Behind the holy man, the door swung open. Jani stared in disbelief.

Durga Das and Mr Knives turned, but too late to prevent the intrusion.

What happened next took place in a blur of motion, confusing Jani with its speed. Two figures burst into the room, one of them bearing a familiar rubber bulb. He raised it to the face of Mr Knives, sprayed, and the knifeman fell to the floor with a clatter of dropped steel. Then the intruder pivoted and pumped the anaesthetic into the horrified face of Durga Das, who cried out and collapsed like a tranquilised elephant.

Then it was the turn of Jani and Anand to suffer the same fate.

She cried out as the atomised mist enveloped her face, choking her. She sank to her knees, and as unconsciousness claimed her she stared up at the smiling face of the Russian, Volovich.

JANI SURFACED SLOWLY from unconsciousness as if through fathoms of ocean.

She opened her eyes, aware of the dull headache that pounded in her occipital region. She was lying on something soft and very comfortable in a small, beautifully furnished room, all polished mahogany fittings and brass embrasures. A high-backed armchair stood opposite the *chaise longue* on which she lay. The walls were decorated with maroon and silver flock wallpaper and... She stared. Between two watercolours of the English countryside was the round brass frame, studded with bolts, of a porthole.

She was aboard an airship, but evidently still on the ground; she detected none of the turbulence that would have denoted flight. She sat up and snagged her right hand on something. Her wrist was encompassed by a manacle affixed to the curved leg of the *chaise longue*, which was bolted to the floor. She leaned forward as far as she was able and peered through the porthole.

It was dark outside and she made out the running lights of other airships, big and small, moored across a busy yard. She saw fuel bowsers beetling across the apron and British soldiers patrolling the perimeter. Beyond, she made out the last faint glow of daylight behind a range of hills.

She looked around the room for Anand, then called his name. There was no sign of the boy, nor of her captors. A terrible thought seized her mind. Had the Russians, in reprisal for Anand's rescuing her from the warehouse in Delhi, already dealt with him? She struggled against the metal encircling her wrist but succeeded only in chafing her skin.

The headache affecting the base of her skull was wearing off and a new pain was taking its place. The skin of her face felt tight, as if badly sunburned. Intense pain needled her brow, cheeks and chin.

She gasped and slowly, as if fearing what she might find, raised a hand.

Her fingers encountered a grid of metal wire half an inch before her face. She traced the reticulation, wincing as her touch caused pressure on the supporting spokes that had been drilled into her brow, cheek bones and jaw. She gasped, more in horror than in pain, and turned towards a bulbous brass plant holder. In its convex surface she made out her face and the silver grid, and her shocked expression behind the nexus.

She called out Anand's name, hoping against hope that he might return her cry. Only silence met her call.

Judging by the dimensions of the lounge, the airship was small. She guessed that the control cabin was located beyond the green baize door. Surely, if Volovich and Yezhov were aboard, then they would have come running at the sound of her cries?

She gained a scintilla of hope from their non-appearance, followed by a grim thought: perhaps they were elsewhere, attending to Anand.

She peered through the porthole. The patrolling British soldiers seemed a long way away. Would they hear her if she cried out loud? She smiled at the irony of her situation. Hours ago she had feared capture by the British; now she would have greeted them with cries of joy.

She was about to call for help when, across the tarmac, the engines of a British India cargo airship started up, deafening her and drowning out any sound she might have made. The drone went on for an age, a steadily mounting crescendo as the bulbous airship rose slowly into the air, turned sluggishly, and moved off over the perimeter fence.

She heard another sound, the opening of a hatch beyond the baize door and an exchange of Russian voices. The gondola rocked as they climbed aboard.

Jani attempted to compose herself as the door opened and Volovich, sporting a black eye and a stitched forehead – courtesy of Anand and the Mech-Man – ducked into the lounge. Mr Yezhov followed him in, his broad face no longer wrapped in a bloody bandage. His wound had received professional attention, with a track of ugly black stitches crossing his face.

They stood over her, speaking in Russian. Something had changed in their attitude; they seemd less playful now, and more business-like, and Jani found the transformation frightening.

Volovich glared at her. "How delightful to see you recovered from your little ordeal with the Hindu. Who knows what depravities he and his henchman might have visited on you.. No, you don't have to thank me. I considered it my duty to save you from your fellow countrymen."

Volovich wedged his bulk into the armchair opposite Jani, while Yezhov stood beside him. The young man was carrying the device that resembled the innards of a radiogram – the working end of the CWAD that encaged her face. He placed it on an oak-panelled occasional table and smiled at her.

She looked from Yezhov to Volovich and, determined to keep her voice from trembling, said, "What have you done with Anand?"

"The boy?" Volovich said dismissively. "We have disposed of him."

"What have you done with him?" she cried.

Volovich cast a glance at Yezhov and snapped something in Russian.

The young man nodded and said to Jani, "The tradition of revenge is old and honoured in our country. If someone is foolish enough to slight you, then it is incumbent upon the recipient to pay back in kind. Do you understand what I am saying?"

She remained staring at him, not giving him the satisfaction of responding.

Yezhov went on, "So in the fine tradition of revenge, I slit your little friend's throat and watched the blood drain from his body until he was quite lifeless."

"And might I add," Volovich said, "that he died calling your name, Miss Chatterjee?"

At all costs, she thought, she must not break down and exhibit the terrible emotion that tortured her mind and soul. She would not, could not, allow them the satisfaction of seeing her broken. Surely, in the next few hours left to her – before they could dispose of her, too – she would have the chance to attack one of them, perhaps both, and have the satisfaction of doing them lasting physical injury. The notion was all she had now, and she clung to it.

Volovich said, "You will have noticed that we took the opportunity, while you were unconscious, of affixing the CWAD net to your face. The effect is rather fetching; the brutalist reticulation of the wires points up and emphasises your natural beauty. It could almost be a work of art. I would add that you shouldn't worry about the possibility of scarring – the supporting spikes are so thin that the punctures would heal without leaving a trace... Although in this case we have elected, after much thought, to terminate your existence after we have finished with you."

"We debated long and hard," Yezhov said, "but could really see no reason to keep you alive and risk you completing the mission – the quest? – that the creature, Jelch, started you upon when he gave you the disc. Your encounter with the injured beast was almost... touching."

"The reciprocation of the gift," Volovich said, "the disc for the offer of diamorphine... most poignant."

She stared from one to the other of the Russians. "You... you've read my thoughts already?"

"We took the liberty," Volovich said. "Why waste precious time? There you were, fitted with the fetching nexus, and sprawled unconscious, and it occurred to me that we might as well... *indulge* ourselves, hm?"

"But there was a slight problem," Yezhov went on. "You see, the subject's thoughts are never as clear, as readable, when the subject is unconscious. The thoughts are a little diffused, blurred, if you like. Oh, we read random memories of your time after the airship disaster, your meeting with Jelch, your horror at the loss of life and, with great fidelity, your loathing of my fellow Russians... which I thought rather harsh. But the precise information which we were seeking – to wit, the whereabouts of the disc – we could not read. So we must subject you to the process one more time – on this occasion, while you are fully conscious and can respond to our questioning." He smiled at her. "War is war, after all."

Her left hand was free. She would feign submission, and when one of the Russians approached she would pick up the closest object to hand and, with all the force she could muster, attempt to stave in his skull.

Volovich unplugged himself from the armchair and crossed the lounge. From his pocket, as if reading her thoughts – what irony! – he pulled a second pair of handcuffs and grabbed her left wrist. She struggled, squirming and kicking out, but Yezhov held down her ankles. Volovich shackled her left wrist to a leg of the *chaise longue*, and then assisted Yezhov in binding her legs with a thick rope. She was soon immobilised, able only to move her eyes as she watched Yezhov lift the table closer to the *chaise longue*. Volovich leaned forward and picked up the lead that dangled from the nexus pinned to her face.

He was about to jack it into the CWAD when he paused and said, "And I thought her grief for her father rather touching, too. Though her romantic feelings for young Sebastian were a little ambiguous... Does she love him, or does she not?"

"But more fascinating than all that," said the younger man, "was her ambiguous sense of *self*, or personal identity. She seemed to vacillate between thinking herself a worldly-wise, liberated English gentlewoman and a somewhat more nebulous Hindustani... though without quite being able to define herself in a cultural context as the latter. A dilemma I'm sure Dr Fraud – sorry, Dr Freud – would find endlessly fascinating. How terrible it must be, not to know where one belongs, or to whom? But what a choice! The British have a saying, do they not, 'Between the Devil and the deep blue sea'... Poor Miss Chatterjee is caught between considering herself a repressed stuffed-shirt and an ignorant savage!"

"Not that she will be perplexed by the dilemma for much longer," Volovich said. "When we leave here, and climb into the air, I will take great delight in putting the girl out of her misery by pitching her from the 'ship." Volovich smiled. "Perhaps then, as she hurtles towards impact with her homeland, will she realise where she truly belongs."

Yezhov laughed.

"But enough idle chatter. Shall we proceed?"

Volovich looked into Jani's eyes. "And now, if you would concentrate on the disc given to you by the creature called Jelch, and recall what you did with it..."

Jani stared at the ribbed ceiling of the lounge, her only comfort the thought that the Russians would never discover in her memory the whereabouts of the disc. She thought of her father; she was five again, and holding his big, warm hand as he walked down Chandni Chowk towards her favourite burfi stall.

"All set," Volovich said.

"Very well. Now, here we go."

Yezhov turned a dial on the radio-device, and a sudden, painful heat shot through Jani's skull. She gritted her teeth and tried not to cry out.

"Now, Miss Chatterjee... what did you do with the disc that Jelch gave you?"

"He gave me no–!" She screamed as Yezhov turned the dial further and the pain intensified, her face burning.

She heard a sound, a smart rapping on the outer hatch of the gondola. The Russians paused and glanced at each other, then Yezhov spoke a few words in his harsh mother tongue. He turned a dial on the radio-device and the pain in Jani's head abated.

He moved from the *chaise longue*. The knocking sounded again. Yezhov slipped through the baize door into the control cabin and a moment later Jani heard the outer hatch open.

"Awfully sorry to bother you," she heard someone say in English. "Routine identity inspection. If you'd be kind enough to allow me aboard..."

Before she could scream for help, Volovich clamped a sweaty hand across her mouth, crushing the wire grid into her flesh as he did so.

She heard Yezhov reply, and the gondola rocked as someone climbed into the control cabin. A second later the gondola swayed again, and the green baize door stood open. Jani lifted her head, despite the pressure from Volovich's hand, and stared through the doorway.

She noticed three things almost at once. Yezhov sat upright in the pilot's couch, his head twisted horribly to one side; a tall, gangling British officer, in a pith helmet, stood in the entrance to the lounge – and bundled on the floor to one side, trussed like a Christmas turkey and gagged, was Anand.

As she watched, the officer reached down and sliced Anand's bonds with a knife.

Jani wept with relief. So they had been apprehended by the British at last! But what did that matter beside the fact that Anand was alive?

The officer pulled a revolver from the holster and aimed it through the door at the surviving Russian. Beside her Volovich sprang to his feet, his expression of alarm exhilarating to behold. He backed up against the far wall, mouthing something in Russian.

The officer fired, the explosion deafening in the confines of the gondola, and a red hole appeared in the centre of Volovich's forehead. He remained standing for a second, a look of absolute incredulity on his face, before sliding down the wall and coming to rest in a comical sitting position, his fat legs splayed before him.

Anand sprang to his feet, yanking the gag from his mouth, and yelled, "Jani-ji!" He ran into the lounge and flung himself at her, sobbing. "But what have they done to you!"

She said through her tears, "Nothing that cannot be undone, Anand, and more importantly you are alive."

"I heard the lies they told you about killing me!" he said. "And there was nothing I could do to ease your pain!"

"My pain is more than eased now, Anand."

The officer stepped forward and removed his pith helmet. Jani looked up and stared at their saviour in disbelief.

"Jelch!" she said.

CHAPTER EIGHTEEN

*Evading the British – Towards Nepal –
Jettisoning the Russians –
"Think of pleasant things..."*

"Before removing the hideous mesh from your face," Jelch said, "I will get the 'ship into the air. I hope you understand this?"

"Of course, but I wonder if you might free me first?"

Anand, crouching against the wall, watched Jelch as he rooted through Volovich's pockets. The boy looked petrified as he stared at the creature, his gaze moving from its elongated legs and its attenuated torso to its oddly flattened face. Jani thought Jelch looked all the more monstrous for being garbed in the uniform of a British officer.

"Don't be afraid," she murmured. "Jelch is on our side."

Jelch looked up from the corpse. "You have nothing to fear from me, Anand."

"You know my name?" Anand said in a whisper.

Jelch gave his poor imitation of a smile. "I know your name, and I've seen how brave you've been." He looked at Jani. "How brave you've both been. I... I had no idea how much my actions would endanger you."

Jani coloured as she thought of the coin; how could she explain that she had misplaced it?

"How did you find us? And how do you know about–?"

Jelch interrupted. "I'm sorry, but the less you know, the less you can give away." He reached out towards her with his long, pale fingers and gently touched the wires enmeshing her face. "Had the Russians succeeded in reading your mind..."

She looked away and said in a small voice, "Then they would have learned that I have no idea where the coin is."

His lips became elongated again. "Jani, on some strata of your mind, subconsciously, you know very well the whereabouts of the 'coin,' as you call it."

He found the keys in Volovich's pocket and unlocked the handcuffs securing Jani to the *chaise longue*. She sat up as Jelch unknotted the rope around her ankles.

She stared at him as he worked. "I *know* where it is?" She shook her head. "But I thought I'd lost it, or that it had been stolen."

"Jani, you know where it is, though your conscious self does not know that you know – and that is how it should remain, for now."

"For now?"

He slid the looped rope from her foot and Jani stood. She was about to ask him why the need for such secrecy, but stopped herself. Of course, if the Russians were to find out about the coin, or the Chinese, or the British...

A smart tapping sounded on the outer hatch. "I say, what's going on in there?" someone called out in Sandhurst tones. "Someone reported hearing a gunshot. Open up."

Jelch, from squatting beside the *chaise longue*, sprang up like a tiger and made for the baize door. He dragged Yezhov's corpse from the control cabin and laid it on the gondola's Persian rug, then slipped into the pilot's seat and called out, "We have everything in hand. Just a little trouble with the ventilator."

"That's all very well, but I need to come aboard."

Jani sat on the *chaise longue*, clutching Anand to her as she stared into the control cabin. Jelch looked over his shoulder and hissed, "Hold on tight!"

His hands were a blur over the controls, and the gondola filled with the din of the engines as they powered up.

Jani made out a cry from the officer, "I say!" as the gondola left the ground, rocking violently. It came to a sudden halt, and Jani realised that the hawsers securing it to the tarmac had not been released. Jelch fed more power to the engines. The airship strained against the hawsers, its motor whining. A second later the 'ship shot upwards and came to a halt with a wrenching jerk. A snapped hawser whiplashed through the air and whacked the coachwork of the gondola, narrowly missing a porthole.

Jani leapt up and peered out. The second hawser tautened between the airship and the ground and the gondola tipped crazily. Anand cried out and tumbled towards her. They gripped hand-holds on the wall and stared through the porthole as Jelch fed more power to the engines. The airship circled wildly, pulling on the remaining hawser. Her heart lurched as she saw, across the airyard, the approach of a dozen soldiers armed with rifles.

Then, the engines screaming with the strain, the airship broke free of the remaining hawser; it snapped with a detonation like a cannon and this time, instead of breaking towards the gondola, lashed across the tarmac like a striking cobra. The soldiers, kneeling to take aim, scattered in fright and the airship shot into the air. Jani watched the airyard diminish beneath them, the soldiers scurrying to regroup like ants.

They took aim and fired, their rifles flaring in the twilight. Within seconds the soldiers were lost to sight amid the floodlit hulls of a dozen airships, and then even the airyard took on the dimensions of a child's toy as they climbed high into the sky and headed east.

Jani tottered across the swaying gondola towards the control cabin and ducked through the baize door. She stood beside Jelch, gripping a crossbar above her head.

"You saved my life," she said.

He glanced at her. "It was my duty to do so," he murmured.

She stared at the creature, its elongated skull rising to an egg-like dome, covered in a close-cut furze. Jade green veins pulsed beneath the pale skin; his nose was flattened, his eyes those of an old cod... He was so human in many respects, but it was his proximity to what she considered human that made him seem so alien. Had he been very different to her and her kind, she might have been able to consider him *animal*.

She peered through the viewscreen at the clouds, lit like a swirl of seltzer in the glow of the moon. "The British will send a 'ship up after us," she said.

"More than one is my bet, Jani. They had their eyes on the 'ship when the Russians landed. I think they suspected that the pair were up to no good."

"How did you find us?"

"I arrived in Rishi Tal too late, but in time to see the Russians carrying you and Anand from the guest house. They took a taxi down the valley to the airyard. I commandeered a military vehicle – which is how I came by the uniform – and followed. Don't worry, I didn't harm the officer, merely rendered him unconscious and tied him up."

She stared at him, allowing the seconds to elapse. At last she asked, "Why did you give me the coin, Jelch? What is it and why are you... using me?"

His big grey eyes regarded her. At last he said, "I *am* using you, yes, Janisha. But, please believe me when I say that the purpose for which I am using you is in the best interests of you and your kind."

"Will you tell me?"

"For your own safety, I think it best that I don't. Please believe me when I say that I have your welfare at heart."

She smiled. "For some reason, Jelch, I do believe you."

Jelch reached out and touched a control. To the right of the viewscreen a parabolic mirror moved, adjusting its angle. "And there they are," he said. "A squadron of the RAF's Sopwiths."

Her stomach turned as she made out, tiny in the curve of the mirror, half a dozen pursuing airships. They flew in v-formation, looking like wasps in the distance.

"Can we evade them?" She peered into the mirror. The pursuing airships seemed no closer now than a minute ago, and as yet they hadn't opened fire.

Jelch reached out to the controls. "I'll climb into the cloud bank above us. That won't make their task any easier." He glanced at her. "I'll need to concentrate all my attention..." he began.

"I'll go," she said, pushing herself across the rocking flight desk.

"There is one thing you could do to help."

She paused at the door and looked back at him. "Yes?"

"We're carrying excess weight..."

"The Russians?"

"Precisely," he said. "If you roll up the rug, you will find a bolted hatch in the floor. Open it with care and ditch the corpses. That is..."

"Yes?"

"If you don't object."

She bridled. "Why should I object? It is what they intended to do to me, after all. Only in my case, they promised that I would still be alive."

She ducked through the door into the lounge.

Anand was at the rear of the room, pressing his face up against a porthole and looking back in an attempt to catch sight of the Sopwiths. "We're being followed, Jani-ji!"

She hurried across to him, knelt and placed a hand on his shoulder. "Don't worry. Jelch is confident we'll get away."

He turned to her. "What is he, Jani-ji? He looks like a monster."

"But he doesn't act like one, and that's what matters."

"What does he want with us, with *you*?"

"That," she said, "we will find out in time."

He laughed. "I always dreamed of adventure, Jani-ji. I read *Treasure Island* and H. Rider Haggard, and I thought it would be wonderful to have such adventures."

"And now?"

He looked down, his big eyes hooded. "Now I would like nothing more than to be back in your father's house, working there and with Mr Clockwork."

She sighed. "Oh, I'm sorry, Anand. If it wasn't for me..."

"I didn't mean that I..." He stopped, colouring. "You needed someone to save you, to look after you."

"Because I'm a girl, ah-cha?"

He nodded. She laughed and clutched his chin, forcing him to look into her eyes. "You certainly have a lot to learn about women, Anand. Now help me throw the Russians from the 'ship."

She rolled up the rug and found the rectangular inlay of the trapdoor, secured by two sets of bolts. They took the legs of the smaller Russian and dragged him towards the hatch. Jani was about to shoot the bolts when she had a thought. "First, we'll search their pockets for money and weapons."

Anand found a wallet packed with a sheaf of rupee notes. "Look after them," Jani said.

She crossed to the bloated corpse of Volovich, a trickle of blood running from the tikka spot of the entry wound in his forehead, down the left side of his nose and around his mouth. She had a vision of him in Roopa's Tea Rooms, sympathising with her over the loss of her father – then recalled the maniacal look in his eyes just one hour ago as he described the great delight he would take in throwing her from the airship.

She went through his pockets and found a small silver pistol. She laid this to one side. She had considered pocketing any weapon she might find for possible later employment, but something stopped her: whether it was the fact that she did not want to possess something that he had in all likelihood used on innocent people, or simply because the weapon frightened her, she did not know.

She scrambled back to the trapdoor, slid the bolts free, and hauled open the heavy cover. A cold whirlwind swirled into the gondola. She peered out and saw, far below, forested peaks and troughs and the occasional lights of tiny settlements.

With Anand's help she rolled Yezhov towards the opening and pushed. He plummeted like a bomb, disappearing into the darkness. Then they dragged Volovich's corpse across the floor and, after a count of three, pushed him towards the opening. He teetered on the brink, then rolled out. She peered after him as he dwindled from sight and wondered if his body would be found by mystified villagers or if wild animals might pounce upon it first.

She slammed the hatch shut. Through the closest porthole she made out grey wisps and streamers, like ripped chiffon, enveloping the gondola in a pearly light. They were climbing steadily into the sanctuary of the cloud cover.

Anand sat on the *chaise longue*, staring in awe at the bundle of rupees. "More than five hundred roops, Jani-ji! I have never seen so much money in all my life."

She smiled as she watched him; in so many ways he was still a child at heart.

She peered through a porthole; she could see nothing to the rear but a thick padding of moon-silvered cloud.

The door to the control cabin opened and Jelch stepped through. "I have set the controls to automatic. The ship will fly itself for an hour or more. Now, I promised to take the mesh from your face."

Jani raised a hand and touched the wires, aware of numerous points of pain across her face.

She stretched out on the *chaise longue* and settled herself. Jelch instructed Anand to fetch the ship's first aid kit, and he unhooked the white box from the wall and sat beside her, taking her hand while Jelch sorted through a valise which she assumed had belonged to one of the Russians.

He found a wallet of tools, fine screwdrivers and tweezers, and laid them out on the velveteen next to Jani.

She closed her eyes.

"Jani," Jelch said, "I could find no anaesthetic, a nicety the Russians could ignore. I will be as gentle as I can, but when it comes to unscrew the pinions from your cheeks and jaw, it will be a little painful."

"I'm ready," she said through gritted teeth.

"I am with you, Jani-ji," Anand said, taking her hand. "Think of pleasant things like burfi and hot spiced chai."

She smiled. "I'll do that, Anand."

She could keep her eyes closed no longer. She wanted to see the approach of the screwdriver, rather than suffer the tension of anticipating the pain.

She saw Jelch's long, flat, alien face peering down at her, and the fine tool in his thin, oddly-articulated fingers.

She felt the connection of the screwdriver with the head of the screw, the tiny impact conducted through her cheek-bone, and then her entire face flared with pain. She gritted her teeth and moaned, and Anand squeezed her hand.

The pain mounted, and Jani closed her eyes and passed out.

CHAPTER
NINETEEN

Confrontation with a madman –
Palaver at the Varma Singh Guest house –
A little game of Russian roulette –
"My dashed British backbone…"

ALFIE SAT AT the controls, steering the 'ship low over the treetops as they approached the hill station of Rishi Tal. Alfie and Smethers had been flying all day, following the disruption in the undergrowth far below, and the occasional toppled tree that indicated the passage of something – either the mechanical elephant or the Mech-Man.

Beside Alfie, Smethers anxiously tapped his thigh with his swagger stick and peered through the side-screen to starboard while Alfie kept a lookout to port. They had lost the trail some five miles further back, but Smethers had announced his confidence that they would pick it up again.

Confined in the control cabin with Smethers for a day, Alfie had come to despise the man. His previous brief contacts with Smethers had been enough to make him realise that he had nothing in common with the overbearing colonel, and the events of the past twenty-four hours had confirmed it. It was as if everything Alfie disliked about the Raj – its jingoism, superiority and arrogance – had been distilled and poured into the character of Colonel Geoffrey Smethers. Besides which, he possessed a streak of cruelty which Alfie found abhorrent. At one point yesterday, during the hot, interminable afternoon hours, he had spoken of his exploits in Africa and bragged about 'potting a few blacks.'

"You mean," Alfie had asked naively, "you killed them?"

"Well, they were encroaching on sovereign territory, old boy."

"Armed insurgents?" Alfie asked.

"No, just nomads."

From then on Alfie had kept conversation to a minimum.

Far below he made out a gap in the canopy of the forest. It might have been the naturally occurring result of die-back, but as the airship flew overhead he saw a long swathe of trampled undergrowth in the vicinity.

"Down there, colonel. Ten o'clock."

Smethers peered. "Jolly good show. As I suspected, they *are* heading to Rishi Tal."

"How far away are we?"

Smethers consulted the chart on his knee. "Ten miles, perhaps a little less."

Alfie nodded and trimmed the controls so that the 'ship followed the trail through the forest.

After a period of silence, Smethers said, "I suppose, all things considered, we were lucky."

Alfie glanced at him. "Sir?"

"The other evening. The Mechanical Man. I mean, it could easily have killed us."

"I think that was down to the person in control of the giant," Alfie said. "He didn't *want* to kill us."

"And you think it was the boy, Anand?"

"Who else?"

"You're right. I wonder why...?"

Alfie glanced at Smethers. "Sir?"

"I wonder why he didn't just finish us off, there and then?"

Alfie just stared at the man. It was an indication of the colonel's mentality that he was perplexed by Anand's leniency: in the boy's position, no doubt, Smethers would have had no compunction about finishing off his foe.

"I think," Alfie began, "that he's the kind of person who takes no pleasure from killing, sir."

Smethers grunted. "Feared the consequences, more like. He knew he'd be strung up for killing two British officers, and funked out."

"I prefer to believe he was showing compassion."

Smethers turned and stared at him. "It really is true, isn't it?"

"What is, sir?"

"What they say in the mess. You really have gone native."

How could he even begin to state his position to a bigot like Smethers? Alfie remained silent, staring down at the emerald forest.

"The other night," Smethers said a little later, "when the Mechanical Man locked me in that overgrown jewellery box."

"Sir?"

"I called out, you know? You didn't reply."

"As I said," Alfie explained, sweating, "I banged my head on something when the Mech-Man flung me in the storeroom."

At dawn he'd crept into the warehouse and unbolted the trapdoor to release Smethers from the jewelled box – which had turned out, in the full light of day, to be the carriage of a tracked vehicle resembling a giant beetle.

"And you were unconscious all night?" Smethers asked.

"That's right. I came to my senses at dawn, and only then heard your shouts."

"And the Mech-Man had *locked* you in the storeroom?"

Alfie licked his lips and concentrated on the controls. "No, just shoved something in front of the door so I couldn't get out."

"And you climbed through a side window to escape at dawn?"

"That's right, sir."

"Ah..." Smethers said, and nodded sceptically.

Alfie shifted uncomfortably in the control chair, his grip on the wheel slick with sweat.

After a period of silence, Smethers said, "I heard about the affair at Allahabad, you know?"

Alfie's heart sank. This could only be leading to one thing. He remained silent, feigning concentration on the flight.

"In my opinion," Smethers went on, "Frobisher did the right thing. Can't have a bunch of Nationalists getting uppity like that."

Alfie thought it wise to agree. "No, sir."

"Oh." Smethers sounded surprised. "That's not what I heard you thought of the matter. Word was that you wanted no part in the action to put down the riot and ran off."

Alfie gripped the wheel, staring ahead.

"Well?" Smethers persisted.

Alfie sighed. "I did think the response was a... a little heavy-handed, sir."

"Oh, you did, did you?"

Alfie was tempted to tell Smethers that that was Brigadier Cartwright's opinion, too, but thought it diplomatic to hold his tongue.

"The thing about ruling over a people," Smethers said in a lecturing tone, "is that you must show 'em who's in control. You must clamp down on even the slightest revolt. It's a 'give them an inch' scenario, Littlebody. Remember that."

Alfie nodded.

"But you obviously don't agree, do you?"

"Ah... Not in the case of Allahabad, sir."

"Do you know your trouble, Littlebody? You have no patriotism. You don't love the flag, or what it stands for. You have no allegiance to King and Country. You're little more than a lily-livered traitor."

He knew he should bite his tongue and remain silent, but anger forced out the words, "As a matter of fact, I'll have you know that on the Allahabad matter, Brigadier Cartwright agrees with me."

Smethers' response was not the one Alfie expected. The man laughed.

"Oh, you little fool! You simpleton!" Smethers guffawed. "That's what old Cartwright *told* you, of course, to get you on his side, to win you over."

Alfie shook his head, bemused. "What?"

Smethers turned his cold, arrogant eyes on Alfie. "Why do you think you were sent on this mission, Littlebody?"

"Why..." Alfie began, flustered. "Brigadier Cartwright was impressed with my record. He said I was just the man for the job. He told me so."

Smethers was shaking his head, his expression almost pitying. "He sent you, Littlebody, because he *didn't* trust you."

Alfie was speechless for a second. "What? But... but that doesn't make sense."

"On the contrary," Smethers drawled, "it makes admirable sense. He wanted to flush you out, get you to show your true colours. He suspected you of certain *untoward* sympathies. And he sent me after you, to follow you – to keep an eye on you and to bring the Chatterjee girl back for interrogation. And along the way find out your true allegiances."

Alfie shook his head, his heart hammering.

Smethers went on, "And Cartwright was right – you're a liability, Littlebody. You can't be trusted."

"I don't see–"

"That morning in the warehouse, Littlebody, I could see through a gap in the lattice of my prison. I saw you come skulking back at dawn. You weren't locked in any storeroom. You probably went off to inform the Nationalists of the state of play."

"That's not true! I... I returned to the guest house. I didn't know where you were..."

"You found me easily enough come dawn."

"I heard your shouts," Alfie temporised.

Smethers sneered. "So you're a liar as well as a traitor, Littlebody. Where did you go?"

Alfie shook his head. "I told you, back to the guest house. I was bushed, and not a little scared."

"You liar. For all I know, you're probably in league with the Chatterjee girl, hm?"

Alfie's senses whirled. "What? But I... I mean, it was I who alerted Brigadier Cartwright to where she was heading."

Smethers stared at him. "I don't know what your little game is, Littlebody. But be warned, I'm on to you. I'll be watching you like a hawk over the course of the next few days, and if you step out of line, if you give me the slightest – the *slightest* – cause for concern..." Smethers leaned forward so that his hatchet face was within inches of Alfie's, "then by Christ I'll take great delight in blowing your brains out."

Alfie was dripping with sweat and his heart pounded. He was imprisoned in an airship with a sadistic lunatic, and he had no doubt that Smethers would indeed take great delight in shooting him dead at the slightest provocation.

"D'you get me drift, Littlebody?"

Alfie saw red. "I... I'll–" he began, gritting his teeth

Smethers stared at him, amused. "Yes? Go on, Littlebody. You'll...?"

"I... I'll report you!" he cried.

Smethers laughed. "Oh, report me, will you? To whom, and on what charge?"

"To... to Brigadier Cartwright. You... you can't threaten a fellow officer like that – threaten to... to blow his brains out."

Smethers' face turned even uglier. "You snivelling little ponce, Littlebody. You cowardly piece of lower-middle-class scum!" Without warning he whipped his revolver from its holster and pointed it in Alfie's face. "I think you fail to realise what the stakes are here, Littlebody. The Brigadier tasked me with bagging the gel and torturing the bitch for information. She might turn out to be a spy, working for God knows who – working for our *enemies*. Do you hear that, Littlebody? Our enemies! And by Christ I'll do everything in my power to apprehend the half-caste and do what I need to do to get the information. And if that involves threatening to blow the brains out of a yellow little wog-lover like you, Littlebody, I'll enjoy doing so. Now, d'you get me drift?"

Alfie stared at the madman, stared at the oiled muzzle of the revolver an inch from his nose. "You," he said with great deliberation, "you, Smethers, are insane."

The colonel barked a laugh and lashed out with the pistol. Alfie felt a searing pain across his cheek and tumbled from his seat with the force of the blow. He scrabbled across the floor of the cabin, staring up as the colonel loomed over him, aiming at his head with the pistol.

"Get up!" Smethers spat. "I said, get up!"

Terrified, Alfie scrambled to his feet and faced Smethers, trembling.

The colonel placed the barrel of his revolver in Alfie's paunch and applied pressure. Alfie felt himself sweating. Smethers leaned close and almost whispered, "I have a good mind to shoot you in your not inconsiderable gut and watch you die a slow, painful death. You're about as useful on this mission as a stopped watch, Littlebody, and the only reason I'll spare you now is that I can't face completing the paperwork your death would entail." He grinned at Alfie. "But if I hear any more mewlings about reporting me, by God I'll gladly face the paperwork. Do you understand, Lieutenant?"

Alfie stared at him, his legs weak, and refused to answer.

"Well?"

"Go to hell!" It was a feeble rejoinder, and Smethers merely laughed – then with lightning speed pistol-whipped Alfie across the cheek for a second time.

He cried out and went tumbling through the hatch into the lounge, tripping and fetching up against the far wall. Smethers strode after him, reached down and picked him up by the front of his uniform.

"I said," Smethers snarled in a hail of spittle, his face a matter of inches from Alfie's, "if I hear any more from you about reporting me, I'll puncture your gut, hm?"

"I..."

"Yes?"

I'll kill you! Alfie wanted to say, but stopped himself. Quivering, he nodded and said, "I understand."

"'I understand, *sir*,'" Smethers corrected.

Alfie swallowed. "I... I understand, sir," he said.

Smethers took a breath, let go of Alfie's shirt-front, and nodded. "Excellent. So glad you've seen sense at last, Littlebody, old boy."

Shaking, Alfie rearranged his uniform and tried to push past the colonel to the control cabin. Smethers stopped him, a hand on his arm.

"And I think that now is the appropriate time to relieve you of your revolver."

"What?" Alfie stammered

"Your revolver," Smethers snapped. "Give it to me!"

Shaking, Alfie unholstered his weapon and passed it, butt first, to the colonel. As he did so, he recalled the photon-blade Cartwright had given him, and the thought of it nestling in his tunic pocket was reassuring.

"Obliged," Smethers said, tucking Alfie's pistol under his Sam Browne belt. He returned to the cabin, leaned forward and peered through the viewscreen.

"If I'm not mistaken," he called out, "I think we've at last caught up with our quarry, no thanks to you."

Alfie joined him, looked down through the foliage and made out a glint of brass, scintillating in the sunlight. As their airship approached, the broad back of the mechanical elephant came into view. It had halted on a wooded hillside above Rishi Tal and stood amid the undergrowth like a statue. Soon, Alfie thought, Janisha Chatterjee would be in their custody. He recalled Smethers' threats to torture her for information and felt suddenly sick.

Alfie watched as Smethers steered the ship over the elephant and came down in a clearing a hundred yards away.

"Now be a good chap, hop out and make the ship secure, hm?"

Relieved to be away from Smethers, Alfie opened the hatch and jumped down. He secured two guy ropes to nearby sturdy trees and Smethers powered down the engines.

The colonel emerged from the cabin with his revolver at the ready. "Very well, Littlebody, I suggest you lead the way."

Alfie moved through the undergrowth towards the mechanical elephant, conscious of Smethers at his back with the drawn revolver.

A minute later they emerged through the trees and came upon the elephant, its cogged haunches and great jewelled flank bright in the early evening sunlight. Alfie stared up at the beast in wonder.

Smethers prodded him in the back. "Climb up, Lieutenant," he whispered, "and see if they're at home, hm?"

Alfie nodded, his mouth dry. He stood before the vast flank of the elephant, scanned the cogs rising before him, and began to scale the hind leg. He reached the broad back and saw the outline of a trap-door. He approached cautiously on hands and knees, found a handle and pulled. He turned and called down to Smethers, "It's locked."

"Then shoot the damned thing open, Littlebody!"

"But you have my gun, *sir*," he called down.

Muttering to himself, Smethers scaled the elephant's flank. "Move aside, Littlebody."

Alfie winced as Smethers drew his gun, took aim at the brass lock, and fired. The colonel hauled open the great hatch and peered inside. Alfie joined him, peering down into a sumptuous mahogany interior hung with tapestries and furnished with padded chairs and divans.

Smethers gestured, and Alfie lowered himself down a ladder and scanned the chamber. It was evident that there was nowhere to hide; an open hatch gave access to what was obviously a small control room, and this, too, was vacant. Anand and the Chatterjee girl had flown, and Alfie experienced an odd pang of relief as he looked up and said, "Empty... sir. They're not there."

Alfie climbed from the elephant's belly and both men scrambled down its great cogged flank.

"They can only have headed into town," Smethers said. "Very well, let's toddle down and make enquiries, shall we? Lead the way, Littlebody."

Obeying the command, Alfie moved away from the elephant and headed down the gently sloping hillside towards Rishi Tal.

They emerged from the trees onto a track that led to the lake and the town, basking in the light of the setting sun. The resort looked idyllic, nestled as it was in the high valley, a scattering of stone-built cottages climbing the hills on the far side of the lake. Alfie had always felt at home in hill stations, where the temperature was clement after the searing heat of the plains, and the pace of life as sedate as if it were Sunday every day. He promised himself that when this was all over, when he was free at last from the psychotic Smethers, he'd treat himself to a holiday at Simla or Darjeeling.

Smethers holstered his revolver and indicated the path. They marched into town side by side, Alfie wondering why the girl had left their transportation in the forest. He gathered his courage and asked Smethers as much.

The colonel turned an odd glance at him. "Perhaps, on their way to Nepal, they've stopped off to stock up with provisions."

"Nepal?" Alfie ventured. "But that's..."

"Of course it is, Littlebody. And that's why I think they're heading there."

"I must say... I don't really understand."

Smethers sighed. "The girl's obviously a secessionist, you idiot. She had contact with Nationalists in London, according to her dossier. Stands to reason she's heading for Nepal in order to cause a little mischief."

"It does?" Alfie said dubiously.

Smethers grunted. "Not that she'll get far. Nepal's defended like a ruddy fortress. I reckon she'll be apprehended long before she reaches the border, if we don't nab her before then."

Alfie considered the refined, intelligent girl – woman, rather – he'd shared tea with back in Dehrakesh. Try as he might, he couldn't see her in the role of a secessionist plotting subversion.

They entered the town and Smethers led the way across the square. "We'll try the Varma Singh guest house, first."

"Where?" Alfie said, hurrying to keep pace.

"Haven't you read her file, for Christ's sake? The gel came here as a child with her father. They always stayed at the same guest house. As her papa passed away a few days ago, it stands to reason she'd make a sentimental return visit, hm?"

"Ah... I suppose so."

A shrivelled old woman greeted them at reception and Smethers produced a photograph of both Chatterjee and the boy. "We're looking for this pair, ah-cha? We have reason to believe they might have stayed here." To Alfie's chagrin, Smethers' Hindi was more fluent than his own.

The woman took the photographs and squinted at them. "Ah-cha. I recognise the girl. Very beautiful, no? Yes, they were here today. They booked a room for the night, but..."

"Yes?" Smethers interrupted.

The woman spread her hands and looked woebegone. "But sahibs, palaver and mayhem ensued. Our humble guest house was invaded."

Smethers blinked. Alfie echoed, "Invaded?"

"It is a very strange story, sir. First the girl was visited by a holy man and his aide. The holy man said that he must be seeing the young lady on the most urgent business. They went up to the room and I heard a most terrible crashing and banging as the holy man's aide broke down the door."

"My word," Smethers began.

"But that is not all, sir. A minute later two Europeans entered the guest house, asking for the girl."

"Europeans?" Smethers said.

"Ah-cha. Europeans, one big man and one small. I showed them up to the room, wondering what palaver was going on there, but that was only the start of the hoo-ha, sir."

"Go on."

"The Europeans entered the room and rendered the holy man and his aide unconscious – and then the boy and girl. And they took the boy and girl away wrapped in blankets in the back of a car."

"They took them...?" Smethers began. "Where did they take them?"

The old lady spread her hands. "That I do not know, sir. They were driving away at speed."

Alfie looked at Smethers. "Europeans, one big and one small... The Russian pair?" He turned back to the woman. "And these Europeans – were they Russian?"

The woman shrugged. "Russian? European?" she said, smiling disarmingly. "With respect, sir, I cannot tell the difference."

"Christ! By Christ, what a damned farrago!" Smethers muttered, beating his thigh with his stick. "There's obviously no more we can do here... Come on, Littlebody."

Alfie nodded his thanks to the proprietor and followed Smethers from the guest house.

"So now the blasted Russians have the girl. And you know what that means?"

Alfie shook his head as he followed Smethers along the street. "No, sir."

"You haven't heard about Volovich and Yezhov? They're monsters, Littlebody. Psychopaths. They particularly enjoy torturing their victims. The girl doesn't stand a chance."

Alfie winced as Smethers led the way across the square to a taxi rank. If Colonel Smethers considered the Russians to be psychopaths, then Alfie didn't like to dwell on the depths of their depravities – or on the fate of the girl.

"There's only one road from the town, Littlebody. It's my guess that they made either for the train station or the airyard. We'll try the airyard first."

They slipped into the back of the first cab in the rank and Smethers ordered the driver to take them to the airyard at the double.

As the car tore down the main street, taking the bends at speed with little regard for life and limb, Alfie hung on and considered the girl. He saw her smile in his mind's eye, her laughing eyes, and heard her amused, educated tones as she discussed religion with him in Dehrakesh. He closed his eyes and tried not to think of her at the mercy of the Russian psychopaths.

Ten minutes later the car raced towards the dazzling arc-lights surrounding the airyard, pulled up with a screech of brakes before the main gates and juddered to a halt. Smethers threw a handful of rupees at the driver and dashed from the cab, Alfie giving chase.

An armed guard halted them at the gate. Smethers and Alfie showed their identity passes and gained admittance. As they hurried across the tarmac to the brick-built terminal building, a brigadier with pork-chop sideburns hurried out to meet them.

"Security bods, what? Dammit, you took your time, didn't you?"

"Colonel Smethers and Lieutenant Littlebody," Smethers said, saluting. "What's going on here, sir?"

"That's what I'd like to know, Colonel. Airship took off an hour ago without permission. German pair aboard, landed this morning from Delhi."

"German?" Smethers said. "You sure they weren't Russian?"

"Well, they might have been, at that," the brigadier allowed. "Anyway, a sentry heard shooting aboard, decided to have a quick recce, and next thing, the bloody 'ship takes off, snapping guy ropes willy-nilly. Nearly decapitated one of me men. I sent a few Sopwiths up after 'em, but I doubt we'll apprehend it. Bloody cloud cover, y'see."

"Which way were they heading?" Smethers asked, gazing up into the night sky.

The brigadier pointed. "East," he said. "They were aboard an old ship, but even so they'll have the cloud cover working for 'em."

Smethers requisitioned the airyard's fastest vessel and a pilot, fuelled up and, in due course, took off. Alfie watched the lighted airyard recede rapidly beneath them as Smethers steered the ship east towards the border with Nepal.

They sat in armchairs in the swinging gondola. Smethers pulled a flask from his jacket and took a swift nip.

"What I don't understand," Alfie said at last, "is why the Russians should be taking the Chatterjee girl and the boy to Nepal?"

Smethers smacked his lips. "I dread to think," he muttered.

"If the Colonel doubted that his planes could apprehend them," Alfie said, "then how will we?"

Smethers said, "I know exactly where they're heading, Littlebody. We'll go straight there and wait until they arrive. Ambush the blighters and nab the girl." He laughed. "And then the fun will begin," he finished.

Alfie turned from the colonel and stared out into the darkness.

* * *

ALFIE WOKE WITH a start.

He blinked, wondering for a second where he was. He recalled setting off from the airyard at Rishi Tal, heading east for Nepal... He was wallowing in the depths of a comfortable armchair, lulled by the drone of the airship's engines, which evidently had sent him to sleep. He sat up, then realised what had woken him.

Colonel Smethers sat in the opposite armchair, leaning forward and staring intently at him. The reek of whisky filled the room. The colonel's hip flask lay at his feet, and his face was the puce shade of the hopelessly inebriated. This, however, was not what alarmed Alfie so much as the fact that Smethers was pointing a revolver at him.

"Have... have you ever known fear, Littlebody? I mean *real* fear? The kind of gut-wrenching terror that makes a man want to... want to shit himself, hm?"

Alfie stared at the pistol. He felt sweat trickle down his face. He knew fear now, but he was damned if he was about to admit it to the colonel.

"Well, man!"

"Ah..." Alfie temporised. "Well..."

"Go on, Littlebody. Tell me."

"No, sir," he said, wondering why the hell a drunken madman was aiming his revolver at him. "No, I haven't. Not that type of fear, sir."

Smethers grunted. He sat forward in the chair, his elbows lodged on his knees. His aim wavered as he focused on Alfie. "Well, I have, Littlebody." He shook his head. "I've tasted fear, real, bowel-quaking fear, and I'll tell you this for... for nothing, I don't ever want to taste it again."

"No, sir," Alfie stammered.

Smethers grinned at him. "So... so I think it only right that you... you should have a little taster, what?"

"I don't know about that, sir," Alfie began.

Smethers blinked, belched – chewed on a reflux of single malt bile and swallowed it – then said, apropos of nothing, "You heard about Poona, 1916, Littlebody?"

"Ah, yes, sir. The rebellion."

"The rebellion. That's right. I was there, Littlebody. So was my wife."

Alfie nodded, his heart labouring. All it would take was for Smethers' trigger finger to twitch, drunkenly, and the show would be over. "Is that right, sir?" he said.

Smethers had never before mentioned that he had a wife. The thought of the maniac being married was hard to credit.

"That is right, Littlebody. I was there. Right in the bloody thick of it..." He leaned even further forward, so far that Alfie thought he was about to slip off the seat. "That's where I tasted fear, real fear, for the first time. Fear and almighty grief, Littlebody."

Alfie nodded, not at all liking where this might be leading.

"And... and I thought, you being a lily-livered little wog-lover and what have you, you should have a little taster, what?"

Alfie licked his lips. Sweat drenched his torso. "I... I'm not sure about that, sir."

Smethers laughed. "Well, I am, Littlebody. To which effect..." He raised his revolver with renewed concentration and aimed it at Alfie's chest. "Y'see, I've loaded me piece with one... one single bullet. Catch me drift? One bullet. Now... let's play a game. It's called roulette. Russian roulette, so I'm reliably informed. I first played it in 1916, in Poona..."

Alfie tried not to groan with fear. He glanced behind Smethers. The door to the control cabin, where their pilot would be sitting in happy ignorance of what was taking place here, was shut. Surely, he thought, Smethers wouldn't open fire with the pilot just yards away?

But Smethers was in his cups, he reminded himself, gripped by God knew what emotions and far from logical...

"Now... now this is how we play," Smethers went on. "You sit tight there, young Littlebody, sit tight while I... while I raise me piece, take aim and..."

Alfie gripped the arms of the chair and pressed himself back as Smethers raised his revolver and squeezed the trigger.

The hammer fell on an empty chamber and Alfie whimpered.

"One down, five to go, Littlebody. Only... tell you what, I'm a sporting man. I'll play fair. If you survive four more shots, then... then I'll let you off. How's that? Can't ask any fairer, can you, what?"

"Sir, I think..." he began.

"You think what?" Smethers snapped.

"I think this isn't a good idea, sir."

Smethers barked a laugh. The pistol wavered. "Well, I think it's a capital idea, Littlebody. Show you a little fear, what? Show *you* what *I* went through in 1916."

He raised the pistol and pulled the trigger.

Alfie cried out and jumped.

"Two down!" Smethers cried. "Funk, Littlebody. Was that funk I saw there? Heard... heard you're rather good on that score, what?"

Alfie found himself close to tears. "Please, please, sir..."

"No good. No good, Littlebody. No amount of pleading will do you any good, Littlebody. Men don't plead. I didn't plead, y'see."

Alfie thought desperately. Perhaps, if he got Smethers talking about what happened in the rebellion at Poona, then he might distract the colonel long enough so that he could launch himself from the chair and disarm the madman.

"What happened, sir?"

Smethers' gaze lost its focus as he looked back in time. "I was in me bungalow. Mary... Mary, God bless her, was asleep in the bedroom. I was burning the old midnight oil, reading something or other. Wasn't expecting a thing..." He looked up at Alfie. "Well, you don't, do you?"

Alfie gulped. "No, sir."

Smethers stirred himself, stared at the weapon in his hand and aimed it at Alfie's chest.

If Alfie launched himself at the lunatic, knocked him flying... He sat up, preparing himself.

"Sit back!" the colonel spat. "Sit back like a man and listen to what I'm saying, damn you!"

Alfie sat back, quivering.

"So there I was, midnight, the town quiet... When all of a sudden, all hell breaks loose. First thing I know, bunch of blasted sepoys – me own bloody men, most of 'em – burst into the bungalow and tie me to the blessed chair. Others... others barged into Mary's bedroom..." He blinked. Tears pooled in his ice blue eyes. "Give her this, the gel showed her mettle. Didn't cry out. Thirty minutes later... I heard the shot."

Alfie a shook his head. "God... My God, I'm sorry."

Smethers looked up and stared at Alfie as if seeing him for the first time. He raised his revolver and pulled the trigger again. Yet again the hammer fell on a vacant chamber. Alfie wept.

"Three down, Littlebody!" Smethers barked with laughter. "Two more and you live to fight another day, what? Now, where was I?"

"Poona, sir. The bungalow. The sepoys bound you to the chair."

"That's right, so they did, the dirty little cowards... So there I was. Mary dead in the bedroom and me knowing me number was up. I'd be next... But you know what, Littlebody? I was damned if I'd let the bastards put the fear of God in me. I faced them like a man. Didn't so much as flinch. Their leader, a big Sikh... he pulled up an armchair, positioned it right in front of mine and pulled out his revolver. And his men, a dozen of them, positioned themselves around the room and watched, grinning like they do, y'know?" Smethers shook his head at the recollection. "Strange thing was, he called me sahib this, sahib that, servile even when he was about to shoot me dead... 'Now we are playing a little game, you and me, sahib. Have you heard of Russian roulette, sahib?' I stared the man in the eye and told him to shoot me if that's what he intended. But no, he didn't want to do it like a man. The bastard wanted to see me quail. But I'll tell you, Littlebody, I wasn't going to give him the satisfaction of seeing me lose control."

Lightning fast, Smethers raised the pistol and squeezed off another shot. Alfie screwed his eyes tight shut as the hammer snapped on yet another empty chamber.

Smethers returned to his story, shaking his head. "So there I sat, watching Gunga Din as he slipped one bullet into his revolver and spun the cylinder. Then he aimed at me and... and pulled the trigger. And by Christ, Littlebody, I sat up proud and straight and didn't move a muscle, didn't so much as blink! Y'see, I was ready for death, after... after what they'd done to Mary, y'see...?"

Alfie licked his lips, nodded his understanding.

Four down. Two more chambers remained. Although Alfie was gripped with fear as he'd never experienced it before, he had sufficient wits to calculate that his chances – if Smethers could be relied on to keep his word – were fifty-fifty.

He gripped the arms of his chair and offered up a silent prayer.

"So Gunga Din raised his piece and pulled the trigger again, and again – and I stared straight into his evil black eyes and didn't bat an eyelid, and y'know what, Littlebody? It worked. It got to him. My stare, my defiance, my dashed British backbone showed him what a snivelling coward he was, him and all his men, standing around watching him playing games with the white man."

"What happened, sir?" Alfie whispered.

"What happened? He pulled the trigger again, and again... And I stared him in the eye, unflinching, and I knew that the last bullet had me name on it, and I was ready. I'd said me prayers and I was going to see me maker, and there was nothing Gunga Din could do to make me show me funk."

"But..." Alfie asked. Despite himself, despite the position he was in, he wanted to know how Smethers had lived to tell the tale. "But how did you...?"

Smethers rocked forward, gathered himself and sat upright. He blinked and shook himself with the theatrical shiver of a drunk attempting to instil sobriety. He focused on Alfie with evident difficulty. "Gunga Din raised his piece and I stared at him, and he wavered, his cocksure grin slipping, his eyes shifting under the gaze of his men... I just stared at him, willing the bastard to do it, to pull the... the trigger..."

Smethers mumbled to a stop, his head nodding.

Please, Alfie prayed, *please fall into a coma before...*

The colonel snapped his head upright. "And Gunga Din's trigger finger tightened, and I heard a shot – a single shot – and he topples from the chair, dead, a neat bullet hole in his left temple. And Brigadier Rogers, bless his heart, Rogers and his men burst in through the French windows and... and twenty seconds later every stinking sepoy, every man-jack of them, lay on the floor dead or dying."

He looked up, stared at Alfie and raised his revolver.

Alfie swallowed.

"Then I went into the bedroom to say me goodbyes to Mary, and then went across to the armoury, bagged meself an Enfield, joined the Brigadier and went into town and accounted for as many of the little black bastards as humanly possible."

Alfie nodded. He tried to smile. "I see, sir. Well, I must say... Jolly brave of you, and all that..." He willed himself to dive from the chair and wrestle Smethers to the floor, but he was paralysed by gut-wrenching fear.

Smethers stared at him, his head lolling. "Two more shots, Littlebody. Are you a betting man? What say the next one is the one, hm?"

He raised the revolver, closed one eye, took aim...

Alfie pressed himself into the back of the armchair, willing himself not to whimper out loud, as Smethers' aim wavered, his hand shaking, his head lolling...

Ten seconds elapsed – the longest ten seconds of Alfie's life – and then, just as Alfie was about to close his eyes and accept that the end was nigh, Smethers groaned and pitched forward, face first, onto the floor, the revolver falling from his grip and skittering across the rug.

Alfie gave a strangled cry of relief. His every limb trembling, he pushed himself from the chair and staggered across to where Smethers' revolver lay.

He picked it up in shaking fingers, snapped open the cylinder and looked for the bullet with his name upon it.

But the chamber was empty.

Weeping tears of rage and relief, Alfie staggered over to the comatose Smethers and stared down at him. "You bastard," he said. "You contemptible, sadistic, utter *bastard*..."

Then he crossed the gondola to the lavatory and locked himself in as the airship powered east to Nepal.

CHAPTER
TWENTY

*Jelch tells a fantastic story –
The threat of the Zhell – The Masters of the Cosmos –
"The less you know..."*

JANI FOUND A mirror in the tiny bathroom and examined her face. A dozen dots of blood like scarlet dewdrops marked where the pinions had pierced her flesh, and her skin was puffy and sore to the touch. She dabbed at the tiny wounds with an antiseptic gauze from the first-aid kit, wincing at the pain. Jelch had reassured her that she would not be scarred, though at the moment Jani was more concerned about the possibility of infection.

She stepped from the bathroom to find Anand curled sleeping in an armchair, his hair sticking upright in an unruly shock and his mouth open.

She looked across the lounge at the baize door, made up her mind and crossed to the control cabin. She stepped through, closing the door behind her, and perched on a ledge beside the pilot's seat.

"Is there any sign of the RAF?" she asked.

"They'll be unable to follow us through the cloud," Jelch said. "I expect they'll be turning back and dreaming of the mess and mugs of sweet tea."

She rocked with the motion of the flight, gripping the crossbar and staring at the creature.

"You admitted earlier that you are using me," she said, "and I accepted the fact. But... I would like to know by whom I am being used, and to what end? Who are you, Jelch? *What* are you?"

He affected scrutiny of the controls. "It is enough for you to know that I am not human, Jani. As to our goal – as I said, you will find out in time."

"You patronise me. On that very first occasion we met, in the wreckage of the airship, you said that my young mind would be unable to comprehend the truth. I think you owe me that, at least: the truth."

His thin lips compressed, becoming even thinner. He adjusted the controls and peered into the convex mirror.

Exasperated, she said, "Then let me guess." She took in his domed, elongated skull, his attenuated torso. "You are manifestly not human. I thought at first that you were a wild creature from north of here, a yeti or a Siberian chuchunaa. But I have revised my opinion somewhat. I think now that you do not hail from this world, as you resemble nothing I have ever seen in the animal kingdom. You are educated, intelligent..."

He made a sound like a sigh. She went on, "You are, then, evidently not of this world. Am I right?"

"Jani..."

Fury flared in her breast. "I offered you morphine, and for some reason known only to yourself you gave me a coin in return. Later you... you appeared in my dreams... or I hallucinated you... or you in some way projected yourself before me as the Russians held me captive" – he looked up sharply at this, and she thought she had guessed correctly – "and you told me to head east to Nepal, which I did, which I am doing. And in return you vouchsafe nothing! Now, please have the decency to tell me if I am correct! Do you, sir, hail from another world?"

She held her breath as he stared resolutely ahead, and finally turned to look at her. "I've said this before, Janisha Chatterjee: you are wise beyond your years."

She released a pent-up breath and nodded. "When did you come to Earth, and why?" Her thoughts swirled. She was in an airship flying towards Nepal, interrogating a creature from the stars...

He made that strange sound again, a ventilation of breath she thought might be a sigh. "What I tell you now is nothing that the British and the Russians do not already know," he said. "So even if you did fall into their hands, and they read your mind... then they would learn nothing new. Very well," he went on. "I am not of this world, but from another world. I came here fifty years ago aboard a vessel that was not mine but belonged to another race."

She stopped him there. "Fifty years?" she said. "But how old are you?"

His gelid eyes regarded her. "I am almost eighty years old," he said. "My kind often live to a hundred and fifty years, as you calculate time."

She stared at the creature, over sixty years her senior, and wondered at the strange and terrible things he must have experienced. She said quietly, "When I last saw my father, before he passed away, I asked him about you. He told me that there was another of your kind, held in London. He said that you told terrible stories of invading armies, stories – according to my father – that were the product of a ranting madman, stories that could not be believed. Is that why you came to Earth?"

"It is why we came to your planet, Janisha. I approached the Russians, and my partner the British. We told them of a race that would, if it had its way, invade your planet and enslave all upon it, or worse."

Jani stared at him, a knot of fear in her chest. "These beings?"

"We call them the Zhell, though that is our name for them. They call themselves something unpronounceable which translates as 'Masters of the Cosmos.'"

"And how do you know of these creatures?" she murmured.

"Because, Jani, they invaded my world, and enslaved my people, and slaughtered millions of us. They were merciless beyond imagining. They thought nothing of annihilating the inhabitants of a continent without warning and with no reason. They saw all who were not Zhell as inferior, and therefore expendable. In all likelihood they did not see what they did as evil, much as a human might eradicate a colony of wasps. They came from a populous world, and wanted territory, and slaves to do their work. When they came to my own world and subjugated my kind, my partner and I fled... That is a long and complex story in itself. We escaped to the world of the Vantissar, with the Zhell close behind us. From Vantissar we fled aboard a ship to Earth, with a warning to your world... a warning your leaders chose to ignore, or dismiss as the gibberings of madmen."

She stared through the viewscreen at the moonlit, opalescent depths of the cloud through which they were passing, her mind expanding as she took in the alien's words. She recalled what her father had told her on his deathbed. *There is no such thing as Annapurnite...*

She said in little more than a whisper, "Fifty years ago..."

"Jani?"

She made the connection. "Annapurnite... the reason the British are so powerful. My father... he told me that there was no such thing as Annapurnite. Now, I think, I understand."

Jelch regarded her, his thin lips stretching. "The ship landed in the foothills of the Himalayas. The Vantissar did not fare well on your world; they lived for perhaps ten years, in increasing ill-health, cared for by tribesmen who revered them as gods fallen from the skies, until viral infection killed them off. I trekked north to warn the Russians, and my partner approached the British. The tsarist Russians tortured me, until I escaped and lived a wild and terrible life, constantly on the run, for almost thirty years before being recaptured – this time by the communists, who were even more ruthless."

"And the British found the Vantissar ship, and utilised the technology they found?"

Jelch inclined his head. "The Vantissar were... are... a technologically accomplished race. Their ship was packed with wonders, even to my people. The British plundered this treasure trove, declared Nepal out of bounds, closed the border and made it protected territory and brought in legions of scientists and engineers to work through the technological wonders they found aboard the ship, though in truth they could but comprehend a fraction of what they found."

"A fraction?" she said. "But even with that, the world has been transformed!"

Jelch grunted what might have been an ironic laugh. "Transformed – but to what end, if the Zhell succeed in their plans?"

She stared at him. "But that was fifty years ago, and they are not yet here. Perhaps they have changed their minds, altered their plans? Fifty years is a long time."

"Jani, Jani... fifty years is no time at all in the grand scheme of a race which thinks nothing of quelling a world and taking a thousand years to do so, and only then moving on."

"If my father were alive," Jani said with a catch in her throat, "then perhaps I might have persuaded him to listen..."

"Your father, like those above him, chose to ignore our warnings as too fantastical, as the nightmares of madmen. Or, who knows, perhaps some in the government did give credence to our stories, but were silenced or sidelined by those more powerful? The wily machinations and power games of the human race have constantly eluded my understanding."

Jani stared down at the deck, silent. She saw movement to her left and looked up. Anand stood in the doorway, an expression of amazement on his face. She wondered how long he had been standing there, wondered how much he had heard.

She smiled at him reassuringly, then looked at Jelch and asked, "And how do I fit into your plans? You have enlisted my aid, or used me – but to what end?"

Jelch stared at her. "Jani, I have told you much. I have told you more than I ever intended. Please believe me when I repeat that, for the time being, there are some things that it is better you do not know."

She said in little more than a whisper, "The coin you gave me... That is important, is it not?"

"As I said, the less you know..."

She recalled something that Durga Das had told her. "The Hindu priest who captured me... he too wanted the coin, just as the Russians did. He called it a tithra-kuñjī. What did he mean?"

Jelch turned his head away, staring down at the controls.

"And how did Durga Das know of the key," she asked, "and why did he want it?"

"That is a mystery. I know no more than you about this so-called holy man."

"Or so you say," Jani said to herself.

CHAPTER
TWENTY-ONE

Das comes to his senses –
The Age of Kali will commence – The Goddess speaks again –
"And when we have the girl...?"

DURGA DAS CAME to his senses, sat up and stared around the room.

He'd had the Chatterjee girl in his grasp! He was *that* far from securing the tithra-kuñjī – *that* far from bringing about his life's work. And all would have gone to plan, had it not been for the intervention of the foreign pair he suspected were Russian.

Vikram, he thought. If Vikram had not sold his information about the girl to the Russians... He smiled to himself. As soon as they returned to Delhi, he would have Mr Knives flay Vikram alive.

He sat against the wall, regaining his breath. In the far corner, Mr Knives was climbing to his feet. The young man picked up his knife from the floor, then checked the lining of his jacket. He smiled when he saw that his array of blades was still in place.

Mr Knives noticed Das watching him and asked, "Who were they, and what did they want with the girl?"

"I think they were Russian," Das said, "and that they wanted the girl for the same reasons that we want her."

His heart almost stopped as a terrible thought occurred to him. Had the Russians...?

He scrabbled at the hem of his robe, revealed his expansive thighs, and slipped a hand into the cleft of his groin. He laughed with relief. The coin was still there, wrapped in its square of silk.

He knew what he had to do now. He must summon Kali, abase himself before the goddess, admit his abject failure, and ask for guidance. It went against his nature to grovel before anyone, but in the case of a goddess he would be prepared to make an exception.

He was reaching beneath his robes again when something appeared in the air before him.

Kali, apparently, was pre-empting his summons.

His heart began a laboured thudding as he watched the oval portal gain substance and the blue-faced creature stare out at him. He could not tell, from the expression on Kali's face, if the goddess was displeased. Its terrible rictus was unreadable. Across the room, Mr Knives backed away in fright.

Das pressed his hands together in supplication and said, "My apologies...!"

"The girl and the tithra-kuñjī are in the air, heading for Nepal." Kali's tone was not censorious, and Das almost wept with relief. "You will follow her aboard your airship."

Das bowed low over his belly. "Of course, of course. And then?"

"You will land in Annapurnabad," said Kali. "There, I will guide you to the girl and what she carries. You will apprehend her and obtain the tithra-kuñjī."

Das nodded, hardly able to contain his excitement as he asked, "And the third key?"

"The third key is far away. When you have obtained the second, we will turn our attention to the third."

"And then..."

"And then," said the goddess, "truly the Age of Kali will commence."

The portal closed, swirling to a point and vanishing as if it had never been. Das felt the runaway beating of his heart as he dwelt on the goddess's words...

The Age of Kali will commence...

Mr Knives cowered against the far wall, his mouth working. At last he managed. "What... what was that, baba-ji?"

"Do you not recognise Kali when you see the goddess?" Das cried. "I, Durga Das, can summon the goddess at will!"

Mr Knives stared at Das with pop-eyed respect.

"We have no time to lose," Das said, and led Mr Knives from the room.

The ancient proprietor was hovering on the landing. "Sir!" she cried. "Oh, I am relieved to see that you are unharmed. I called the police when I saw what the Europeans had done to you, but they have yet to turn up."

"I thank you for your concern," Das said, "but I assure you that we are unharmed."

"And then the British military turned up, just one hour ago, asking for the girl."

The British... That was all he needed at this juncture, the interference of the perfidious British!

He thanked the old woman once more, assured her that all was in hand, and hurried from the guest house.

They caught a taxi as the sun was going down over the hills, and Das urged the driver to make haste to the airyard.

"We are going to Nepal?" Mr Knives asked at one point.

"We are revisiting my ancestral homeland, Mr Knives. The cradle of my illustrious family. There is no vale more beautiful than that of Lokhara, as you will see – despite the city of Annapurnabad, of course, which the British built and so despoiled the land."

"And when we have the girl?"

Das thought ahead to when they would possess the second tithra-kuñjī, and then the third. "And then Kali will return, and cleanse the land of the British, destroy them as it is written! And our country will return to the people to whom it rightly belongs – and it will be my doing, Mr Knives. I will have worked with Kali to bring peace to our homeland!"

Mr Knives shook his head in wonder and Das went on, "And you, my faithful servant, will be rewarded amply."

They arrived at the airyard as darkness was falling and Das presented himself to the commanding officer. He produced his papers, his identity card, and his visa which allowed him entry into the protected territory of Nepal.

It pained him to scrape and bow to the stuffed shirt in charge of the airyard, but as always in his dealings with the British he found himself reacting to their disdain with a show of subservience. He had tried treating them with the arrogance he exhibited towards those he considered lower than himself, but the consequences had not been conducive to attaining the desired results.

The British expected their subjects to grovel... but, oh –
how the tables would be turned, one day!

The officer regarded the visa. "Nepal, hm? And
what'll you be doing there, of all places?"

"I am Durga Das, venerated High Priest of the
Temple of Kali. My ancestors hail from the once proud
Kingdom of Nepal. I return to conduct important
religious ceremonies."

"Ceremonies, hm?" the officer said. "And how long
do you plan to stay there, Mr Das?"

"My duties should not detain me for more than two
days."

"And this chappie?" the officer said, eyeing Mr Knives.

"You will see that my visa allows the entry of my
aide also."

The officer scanned the document and grunted.
"Well, it seems to be in order." He passed the visa to
his secretary. "Stamp this, Wilson. Valid for two days."

A minute later the job was done, and the officer
returned the visa to Das. "There you are, Mr Das." He
waved a dismissive hand. "Chalo, chalo, now there's a
good chap."

Das took his visa, smiled at the officer with hatred
in his eyes, swept from the office and crossed to the
waiting airship.

Thirty minutes later they were aloft and forging
through the night towards Nepal.

Durga Das ensconced himself in an armchair and
contemplated finally apprehending the girl and
obtaining the second tithra-kuñjī. As Mr Knives slept,
Das pulled the disc from its place of concealment,
stared at the mysterious script spiralling towards its
centre, and dreamed.

CHAPTER
TWENTY-TWO

∞

Towards Annapurnabad – An alien ship –
Jani's mission –
"Only time will tell..."

DAWN LIGHT GREETED the airship as it sped east.

Jani sat beside a porthole and peered out, Anand beside her.

Ahead she could see the snow-capped peaks of the Himalayas, aluminium blue and brilliant white, with the dazzling starburst of the sun rising beyond. Far below she made out crumpled foothills and the varicose squiggle of a river; they were passing above the land seemingly in slow motion, the thrum of their engines the only sound. There was no sign of pursuing British craft.

"Jani-ji, I heard what the... what Jelch told you. Is it true? Is the creature really from the stars? And will another race invade the Earth?"

From his lips, the threat did sound extraordinary. "It is true. Jelch is from another world. As for an invasion..." She shrugged. "I don't know. Jelch seems convinced, but it has been a long time since the other beings... the Zhell... threatened."

"And what does Jelch want you to do?"

"Not just me, Anand. We're all in this together. You've helped me so far. Without you..." She stopped and shook her head. "But I don't know what he wants, ultimately. You heard him say that it's best that I don't know?"

He nodded. "Can we trust him?"

"You've asked that before, and my answer is the same. Of course we can." She reached out and took his hand. "It's strange, isn't it? Here I am, trusting an alien creature above those of my own kind, above the British, the Russians, and even our fellow Indians."

Anand smiled. "I always thought Durga Das was an untrustworthy fellow. Your father called him a 'bloody troublemaker'!"

"Well, with luck we've seen the last of him."

Anand was silent for a time, and then asked, "Do you know where we're going, Jani-ji?"

"I *think* I do," she said. She'd had time to consider what Jelch had told her about the alien ship. "I think we're heading for the great ship that brought Jelch and his companion, and the Vantissar, here fifty years ago."

Even as she spoke the words, she found them hard to believe, and Anand's expression mirrored her incredulity.

The baize door swung open and Jelch ducked through. He sat on the *chaise longue*; the seat was low, and his long legs and high, articulated knee-joints jutted oddly. Jani stared at him, a being from another world.

"We are more than two hundred miles into the territory of Nepal," he said, "and I am worried."

"But I don't see any sign of our being followed," Jani said.

His lips stretched. "And that, Jani, is why I am worried. I would have expected the air to be thick with pursuing RAF airships and planes."

"Perhaps they didn't suspect that we were heading for Nepal?" she suggested.

"They wouldn't be so foolish. We were a hundred miles from the border, and heading east. They knew, all right. We might have lost them in the cloud, but they should have sent other craft up after us."

"So...?"

"It's my guess that they are tracking us from the ground."

Anand leaned forward. "So what should we do, sir?"

"What I always planned to do – land perhaps a mile or so away from our destination and continue the rest of the way on foot. If they are tracking us from below, then the lie of the land is to our advantage. They might be able to see where we come down, approximately, but the foothills are dense and hard to navigate. We would have a good head start before they caught up and found the abandoned ship."

Jani watched Jelch as she asked, "You said 'our destination'... I take it that you mean the Vantissar ship?"

Jelch inclined his head. "I do."

"And once there?"

He was silent for a stretch. Only the monotonous rhythm of the twin engines could be heard. "And once there, Jani, you will board the star-vessel."

She stared at him. "You make it sound easy. Won't the craft be guarded? I would have thought that it would be as well-defended as a garrison town."

He gave his attempt at a smile. "It will be well-guarded, Jani, which is why it would be impossible for me to enter. The British have built a bustling city around the vessel. Scientists are domiciled there, and of course – this being a British concern – administrators also. And where there is any congregation of British citizens on the subcontinent, there are also servants, Indians and Nepalese, to do the dirty work."

"Ah," Jani said.

"The British employ native men and women to ferry things to and from the interior of the ship. The vessel is vast, Jani, and at any one time there are up to a hundred scientists and engineers working within it. Of course these people need supplies, food and drink, and what they discover in there needs transporting to the outside world."

"I see."

Jelch drew a long breath. "What I suggest will be dangerous, and I will fully understand if you refuse to go through with the idea."

"Tell me."

"We land, trek towards the city that surrounds the vessel, and you and Anand will infiltrate the workers there. I have rupees with which to ease your passage, if you agree to undertake the task."

"I too have rupees," Anand said.

Jelch smiled. "And then all you have to do is buy your way into the ship. I will be on hand to assist you."

"Assist, or... *advise* from afar?" Jani asked. "Your appearance would preclude you from being present, physically."

"Jani, I once said you were perspicacious."

She smiled. "How else to explain your 'presence' in the warehouse? You were too real to be a hallucination – and anyway, if you were so, then how did I know that I would be saved, and would head east from Delhi?" She stared at the alien. "How did you do it, Jelch?"

"I am tempted to say that you would not understand, but that would be patronising, and anyway I think that you would comprehend fully. My kind have the ability to... I suppose a translation would be to 'project' ourselves, a tele-cognitive talent we use in extreme situations. To do so is taxing, and has been known to kill an individual. I am linked with you on a neurological level, can chart your presence, and if needs be project my consciousness so that you can witness it. Perhaps, in the days ahead, this might again come in useful."

She let the silence stretch as she contemplated his words, then asked, "And once I am within the ship?"

"I will tell you that closer to the time," he said. "Of course, I will fully understand if you baulk at entering the ship. The task will entail no small amount of danger, after all."

She said in barely a whisper, "I think I should make up my mind when the time comes to act, Jelch; when we have landed and approached the city around the ship, and I have assessed the situation fully. Will you accept that, for the time being?"

"Of course I will." Jelch stood. "We should be landing in fifteen minutes, I had better make preparations."

He loped off into the control cabin, and Jani watched him go in silence.

Anand stared at her. "Whatever you decide, Jani-ji, I will be with you. If you elect to enter the ship, then I will come too."

"And endanger yourself in doing so?"

He shrugged. "How could I leave you to do this alone?" he murmured.

"Thank you, Anand. But as I said, I will assess the situation later." She stood and moved to a porthole at the stern of the gondola, more to be alone with her thoughts than to see if they were being followed. The bright blue sky was as clear of pursuing craft as her mind was full of questions.

How did Durga Das know she had had the coin, or the tithra-ku⁻jī, as he called it? Why did Jelch want her to enter the Vantissar ship? And how might her doing so help combat the invasion of the Zhell?

She wondered what her father would have counselled her to do. She smiled: she knew very well what he would have said.

And, despite telling Jelch that she would make her decision later, she knew that she could take only one course of action. She had come so far, risked so much already – and she trusted Jelch wholeheartedly – that she could not in all conscience turn back now.

If humanly possible, she would enter the alien ship.

TEN MINUTES LATER the ship's engines changed pitch as they descended towards the Himalayan foothills.

Jani joined Anand and together they peered through a porthole as the forested slopes rose to meet them. Jelch called out from the control cabin that the landing was likely to be a turbulent one, and Jani and Anand found hand-holds as the airship brushed the treetops and the gondola crashed through the foliage. Jani braced herself, expecting a shattering impact to split the gondola asunder. Her surprise was matched only by her delight when the airship came to a sudden halt and the engines fell silent.

She looked out and saw close-packed trees and foliage. The gondola hung six feet from the ground, swaying slightly. Jelch emerged from the cabin. "We're closer to the outskirts of the city than I thought – less than a mile."

"Which, over this terrain, and through undergrowth like that..." Jani began.

He pulled something from the pocket of his jacket, a small golden cylinder that reminded Jani of a lipstick. "The undergrowth will be the least of our problems," he said, crossing to the hatch and pulling it open.

Jani and Anand followed. "Meaning?" she asked.

He paused, peering down. "I wouldn't be surprised if the British had a reception party awaiting us somewhere. Our first priority is to leave the airship as far behind us as possible."

He told Anand to pick up a rucksack containing food and water, then turned and climbed from the airship. The ship's collapsible ladder extended halfway to the ground. Jani followed Jelch down and jumped the last three feet, turning to assist Anand.

She gazed up at the airship lodged in the treetops high above. Jelch said, "The envelope's too damaged for the craft to take off. Not that I was planning to use it again. The British would be on the lookout for a 'ship with these markings." He looked through the canopy at the bright blue sky, still innocent of RAF airships. "We'll be forced to find an alternative means of getting away from here."

He turned and pointed through the undergrowth. "We head east. There'll be a steep climb. When we get to the crest, we should be able to see the Vantissar vessel in the far valley."

Jani's pulse quickened at the thought. She stared at Jelch, the alien; hard though it was to credit, she now had to accommodate the startling fact that out there, among the far stars, were other planets, other teeming civilisations. She had thought the contrast between

Britain and India extreme; she could hardly conceive of how totally different life on an alien world might be.

And soon she would look upon a vessel that had set out, more than fifty years ago, under the light of another sun, and she would attempt to gain access to this ship.

Jelch adjusted the golden cylinder and a thin white light sprang from it, startling Anand.

"But what is it, sir?"

"A concentrated beam of energy, Anand. Look."

Jelch swept it in an arc ahead of him, and as if by magic the dense undergrowth before them fell away.

He led the way up the incline away from the airship, clearing a path where the foliage was thickest. The air filled with the stench of ash, occasionally overcome by the perfume of bromeliads and bougainvillea. Jani heard distant birdsong. They were high up here, and the humidity of the plains had given way to a cooler, cleaner atmosphere.

They climbed steadily, stopping from time to time to peer through the canopy high above for any sign of the RAF. Jelch cocked his head to the side and listened intently. Jani knew from their first meeting that his sense of hearing was more acute than any human's. She considered his ability to project images of himself into the minds of others and wondered what other peculiar abilities he might possess.

Anand followed Jelch like a faithful dog. After his initial wariness of the alien, the boy had hung on his every word, eager to assist Jelch in whatever small task he performed. Now he offered to wield the light beam, and after a slight hesitation Jelch smiled and instructed the boy in its use. Anand marched ahead, fanning the beam to and fro before him and grinning at the results.

Jani fell into step beside Jelch and said, "And if I succeed in entering the vessel, what then? Can you tell me now?"

After a hesitation, Jelch replied, "You will be instructed what to do next, Jani."

"By whom?"

He sighed. "I can only speak in abstractions, using terms you will understand but which only approximate to the facts."

She shook her head. "I admit that I don't understand, Jelch."

"You will be met, within the ship, by an... an entity. It will appear real to you, but is in fact only a... a recording."

She shook her head. "A recording? A recording of what?"

"Of a subroutine that I installed in the ship, fifty years ago."

She glanced at the alien. "I don't pretend to comprehend your words, but no doubt you'll say that that does not matter."

He inclined his head. "Do not be alarmed when you see this... apparition. It will instruct you–"

"It can speak my language?"

"Not as such, but it will seem to you that it can."

"Again, I don't understand," she said. "But go on."

"Do whatever the apparition says."

"And then, when I leave the ship?"

"We will rendezvous, and attempt to get away from here."

She glanced at him, and voiced her puzzlement. "There is something that I don't understand about all this, Jelch. Why don't you simply go to the British and warn them of the Zhell? They didn't believe your compatriot because they thought him deranged, but surely you could convince them?"

He sighed. "Two reasons, Jani. One is that I cannot afford to be captured by the British and incarcerated while they interrogate me. That might take weeks, or even months – and as I've said before, time is of the essence. The other reasons is that I learned something while I was in Russian custody. I found out that they had spies in Delhi, high up in the British echelons. The Russians suspect that I know, and of course fear that I would inform the British. The problem is that I do not know the identities of Moscow's spies in Delhi, and I fear that if I show my hand to the British there... then there is a danger I would be signing my own death warrant."

She stare at him, shocked. "Russian spies in Delhi?" she said. "Do you think my father knew of this?"

He shrugged. "I cannot say. Certainly British security must have suspected something, given that certain sources of intelligence have been compromised of late. Certain Vantissar technologies have fallen into the hands of Moscow, and the Russians have been able to second-guess British troop movements on the border..."

"So if you cannot go to Delhi to inform the authorities there..." She stared at him. "Ah, so I think this is where I come into your plans, yes?"

He regarded her with his cold, flat eyes. "I plan to go to London with the device I hope you will be able to obtain from the ship, and I will petition the government there. Recently British scientists have perfected the CWAD device – I will consent to its use upon me – and they will see for themselves that I speak the truth, about both the Russian spies in Delhi, and the threat of the Zhell..."

She nodded, her heart thudding. A great weight of responsibility rested upon her shoulders. Not only had she to enter the ship and obtain the device, but then she would have to leave undetected and find her way back to Jelch... And then, of course, there was the small matter of how he might make the journey around the world to London.

They walked on in silence for a while. Jani glanced at him and said, "You are far from home, Jelch. Don't you miss it?"

"More than anything."

"And one day will you return?"

He stared ahead. Something hard and cold entered his expression. "That is impossible, Jani. My world was destroyed by the Zhell."

She opened her mouth to say something, but realised that no response would be adequate. She just shook her head and murmured, "I'm sorry."

"I saw the Zhell raze our principal cities, kill millions of my people and enslave the rest. That is why I had to get away, to warn the Vantissar, to warn yourselves."

She shrugged. "But even if my people, the governments of my world, were to believe you..." She shook her head. "The technology that the Vantissar possessed... it will undoubtedly be matched by that of the Zhell, will it not? So how then might a world as puny as Earth defend itself?"

Jelch was a while before replying. "There are always means, Jani, though at first they might seem impossible."

"Within the ship, perhaps, there are weapons which the British have not yet discovered, or understood? Am I right? With these, might we defend ourselves from the Zhell, beat them back from our planet?"

He gave a small grunt more like a despairing laugh. "Sadly, no weapons I know of would be a match for those of the Zhell. They have perfected technological warfare, and combine this expertise with a ruthlessness frightening to witness. No, we cannot fight the Zhell."

"But...?" she asked, sensing that Jelch was about to suggest what they *could* do.

"But perhaps we can make our... worlds proof against their invasion."

She stared at him. "But how?"

He shook his head. "Only time will tell," he said enigmatically.

She wanted to question him further, but knew that she would be wasting her breath.

She looked up the incline, to where Anand was sweeping the light beam back and forth, a fan of acrid smoke rising all around him. Ahead she made out the crest of the rise, a line of trees against the sky, and a distant line of saw-toothed mountain peaks. She guessed they had been travelling for an hour. She was tired and thirsty, and hoped that Jelch would call for a rest when they gained the summit.

Anand came to a halt, looked back at them and waved. Jani made out his awed expression before he turned again to stare down into the valley.

They hurried to catch up, then stood beside the boy and stared into the natural bowl formed by the encircling girdle of mountains.

"I didn't expect..." Jani began.

"What?" Jelch asked.

She gestured. "I never expected it to be so... so busy, so populated, so *ugly*..."

It was as if, she thought, a dark, satanic version of London had been transplanted from the heart of England and laid down in this sprawling Himalayan valley. The image that came to mind was of beauty despoiled. They had climbed through an unspoilt wilderness of natural beauty, and now they were on the threshold of an industrial hell.

She looked down on a chaos of busy streets, with grey concrete buildings like the ugliest schemes now being thrown up on the outskirts of Delhi. Surrounding the city on its outer edges was a shantytown of dwellings lashed together from whatever materials the poorest members of society could find: flattened tin and packing cases, tattered tarpaulin and woven banana leaves. The tiny figures of drafted Indian workers scurried along the streets, the cheap labour that sustained this city as it did every other one in the subcontinent. At the centre of this makeshift metropolis, by contrast, were grander, honey-coloured buildings set in emerald lawns where fountains played and officers and memsahibs, tiny figures at this distance, strolled in the light of the late morning sun.

At the far side of the city, opposite where Jani stood, was an airyard busy with a hundred 'ships. She stared as a gargantuan cargo vessel laboured into the air, its ascent so gradual she thought it might surrender to gravity and slump back to earth. The air above the distant mountain range was dotted with a pointillism of craft, thousands of them, and Jani was struck dumb by the scale of the operation going on far below.

Only then did she realise that something was missing. She turned to Jelch. "But I don't see..." she began.

He pointed.

"But..." she began, "how can that be...?"

She had expected the alien vessel to resemble something along the lines of a great gondola, sleek and streamlined and, like the latest models coming from the de Havilland factories, as silver as a bullet.

What she saw surprised her on two counts. The first was that the vessel – or the little she could make out of its superstructure that was not covered by bamboo scaffolding and walkways – was brown, like the tegument of a cockroach. In fact, the vast length and breadth of the craft, a mile long and a third as wide, looked less like something manufactured from metal than a biological entity, the pupa of some great insect. Long, curved sections of the craft's superstructure had been removed to reveal recesses full of curled, etiolated piping that put her in mind of living intestines. Towards the front of the craft – or at any rate the end which abutted the city – was a vast open maw from which emerged a procession of wheeled vehicles and lines of workers weighed down with heavy loads.

"The British call the city Annapurnabad," Jelch said. "It is where once the beautiful town of Lokhara stood. Now it's the home of ten thousand workers, and a thousand British troops and administrators."

He reached into the pocket of his jacket and passed Jani a rolled bundle of notes. "I will accompany you to the edge of the trees, and then no further."

She looked into his flattened eyes. "And when we return?"

Jelch indicated a slanting casuarina tree, laden with scarlet blooms. "I will await you there, or nearby," he said.

They continued on down the hillside.

CHAPTER
TWENTY-THREE

∽

Alfie summons his courage –
Death on the hillside – Final instructions from Jelch –
"What happened to the Russians...?"

ALFIE CROUCHED BEHIND a stand of ferns and peered out, Smethers squatting beside him. Through the treetops he glimpsed the red and blue balloon of Janisha Chatterjee's airship, perhaps a mile away.

Alfie and Smethers had landed two hours ago and made their way across the city, scanning the skies for the first sign of the fugitive 'ship. It had appeared just after midday, coming in slowly over the mountains, and, unlike all the other airships coming and going from the airyard, had flown around the city and headed for the next valley. Alfie was still exhausted from the taxi ride through the city and the subsequent dash up the hillside.

Beside him, Smethers was almost manic with excitement at the approaching culmination of their mission. His eyes were wide, staring, and his upper lip twitched nervously.

That morning, as daylight washed the gondola of their airship, Alfie had let himself out of the lavatory to find Smethers none the worse for his binge of the previous night. He had lounged in his armchair, filling his revolver with bullets and smiling across at a sheepish Alfie.

"And how are you on this fine morning, Lieutenant?"

Alfie had swallowed and said, "Very well, sir."

"Recovered from our little entertainment last night, hm?"

Alfie stared at the colonel. By Christ, he thought, the bastard will pay for that...

Now, squatting in the undergrowth, Smethers drew his revolver, nudged Alfie and said. "The VCA, Lieutenant."

"What?"

"I said, give me the VCA."

Alfie dug into his pocket for the skullcap and passed it to the colonel. His fingers brushed the cylinder of the light-beam in the same pocket, and he smiled to himself.

Smethers pulled the skullcap over his head and fastened the chin-strap. He peered through the trees at the airship, then glanced at Alfie. "As soon as they show themselves," he said, "I'll activate this and go after them. I'll bag the Russian pair first, then arrest the gel. I want you to tackle the boy. Do you understand?"

"Perfectly."

They waited, staring through the foliage. Alfie's heart was thumping fit to burst. He thought of the girl, and prayed she wouldn't do anything foolish in the ensuing encounter.

"The Russians," he whispered. "What do they want here?"

"Think about it, Littlebody. Sabotage. Annapurnabad is a strategically important city."

"And the girl? She was heading here of her own accord before being taken by the Russians," Alfie pointed out.

"Perhaps the Chatterjee gal and the Ruskies are all in it together – and the Russian pair *rescued* the gel from the Hindu earlier."

Alfie shook his head. Try as he might, he couldn't see the young woman he shared tea with in Dehrakesh as part of a Russian conspiracy. "I don't think so, Colonel. I don't have Chatterjee down as a communist sympathiser–"

"Put a sock in it, old boy. Here they come."

Alfie tensed and stared up the slope.

Through the trees he made out a flash of crimson cloth – the girl's shalwar kameez. Beside her was the boy in shorts and a white shirt. They were walking down the hillside, and Alfie guessed they would pass within ten yards of where he and Smethers were concealed. They were accompanied by a third figure, garbed in an ill-fitting British army uniform.

Alfie murmured, "I don't see the Russians."

Smethers said, "Who the hell is that?"

The third figure was tall, and almost human – but some configuration of its legs, jointed higher up than was normal, and the attenuated length of its torso reminded him of an animal.

"Christ," Smethers exclaimed under his breath, "it's the Morn."

"The what?" Alfie asked, feeling dizzy. "And where are the Russians?"

"Shut it!" Smethers snapped, fumbling with the controls on the chin-strap of the skullcap. "Stay put and don't move a muscle, Littlebody, and that's an order." And with that, he vanished.

Alfie heard a rustle beside him and sensed that Smethers was no longer squatting in the undergrowth.

Peering out, he saw the grass before him flatten as it was trampled by Smethers' passage, and charted the colonel's progress away from the stand of ferns and up the hillside.

The trio was perhaps thirty yards away. Alfie stared at the tell-tale disturbance in the grass as Smethers approached the trio. He heard a click as Smethers cocked the hammer of his revolver.

Then he heard Smethers' voice call out, "If you value your lives, then stay very still and raise your hands."

The creature, Janisha Chatterjee and the boy turned to face the sound of the voice. The strange creature's flattened, corpse-pale face remained expressionless.

"I said raise your hands!" Smethers cried.

They froze, staring around the clearing in search of the invisible Smethers. Alfie watched as the creature noticed the twin depressions in the grass, its eyes fixing on the area as it said, "Who are you, and what do you want?"

Alfie could imagine Smethers' expression as he sneered, "Don't play silly games with me, you animal. Hands in the air!"

Slowly, the creature raised its long arms high above its head.

"Very good," Smethers said. "Now, I'm going to give you a pair of handcuffs, Chatterjee. I want you to take them and manacle the Morn. I'll give you ten seconds, and if you don't do as I say I'll shoot the boy. Do you understand?"

The creature said, "Leave the boy out of this, sir. He has done nothing to warrant your threat."

"Then give yourself up and the boy will live," Smethers said.

The boy stood, hands in the air, an expression of pride and courage on his face.

Alfie felt in his pocket for the light-beam. He should do it now, he resolved, before Smethers in his lunacy became trigger happy...

Something rattled, and Alfie saw a glint of silver sail through the air and land at Janisha Chatterjee's feet. "Now take the cuffs and lock up the animal," Smethers snapped.

The creature leapt. One second he was crouching, arms raised, five paces from where Smethers stood, and the next he was flying through the air, a blur of khaki streaking towards the colonel.

Alfie winced as Smethers fired. The creature cried out and hit the ground. It rolled, grasping its bloodied thigh.

The depressions in the grass moved towards the stricken creature, which lay on its back and clutched its upper leg as blood pumped out between its elongated fingers. Janisha Chatterjee cried out, hurried across to the creature and dropped to her knees, taking its head in her lap and looking around wildly for Smethers.

The colonel made himself visible, appearing as if from nowhere a few paces from the girl and the creature. He held both his own revolver and Alfie's in his outstretched hands, aiming unwaveringly at the creature's chest.

"Take the cuffs," Smethers said, "and manacle the animal!"

Janisha Chatterjee fumbled for the handcuffs lying on the grass, tears tracking down her cheeks.

Anand ran at Smethers and leapt. Smethers lashed out with his left hand, catching the boy a solid blow with the revolver on the side of his head. Anand cried out and went sprawling, knocked senseless.

Smethers took one step forward, aiming at the creature's heaving chest with both weapons. "Hurry!" he said to the girl.

Alfie remained in the undergrowth, frozen with indecision. Something told him to turn and run, to get away from here and never look back. He was in Allahabad again, quaking with fear and revulsion. He wanted to run, he wanted nothing more than to absent himself from the proceedings, but knew that if he did so, this time, then he would forever regret his cowardice.

Finally he moved. He pulled the light-beam from his pocket and twisted its base. A lance of bright white light sprang forth, dazzling him. He rushed from his hiding place and sprinted up behind Smethers.

The girl had the cuffs in shaking fingers and was attempting to manacle the creature's wrists.

"I said hurry!" Smethers cried. "And when you've done, that, stand up and move over to the boy."

"Oh, please...!" the girl began.

"Do it!" Smethers cocked both revolvers, his face made ugly with hatred. "Or if you'd rather I finish off the animal...?"

Alfie halted two yards from the colonel, his heart beating wildly. Quaking, he cried, "If you shoot the creature, Smethers, I swear I'll kill you!"

Smethers swung round, his expression of surprise turning to one of overweening arrogance. He backed off so that he had both the prostrate Morn and Alfie in his sight.

"I might have known," he sneered. "You're a traitor and a coward, Littlebody! You're a disgrace to the uniform!"

The Morn moved. Despite the wound to his thigh – despite the gout of flesh gouged from his leg – the creature surged to its feet and dived at Smethers. The colonel cried out, swung back towards the Morn and discharged both revolvers into the charging creature's chest. The Morn staggered backwards, howling in agony as its ribcage was shredded, and Alfie expected it to fall to the ground, dead.

The Morn did fall, but only to its knees. Smethers stepped forward, his face twisted into a mask of revulsion and sadistic delight. He raised his revolvers once again as the creature launched itself at the colonel.

Smethers stepped backwards, took aim and laid down a volley of deafening fire. Alfie stared, appalled, as half a dozen shots ripped into the body of the flying Morn, ejecting gobbets of flesh and a spray of blood in all directions. Yelling, the creature hit the ground at the colonel's feet with a resounding thud.

But even then, its ribcage shattered, the Morn did not capitulate. Alfie stepped back, startled, as the creature hauled itself to its feet and reached out for Smethers.

The girl screamed as the colonel fired a further three shots into the Morn's stomach. The creature staggered and fell onto its back.

A sudden, terrible silence filled the clearing.

Smiling, Smethers swung his revolver and aimed at Alfie's chest.

"Now be a good fellow and get the boy, Littlebody."

Alfie stared at him. "What?"

"I said get the boy before he runs off."

Alfie moved. Before he knew what he was doing, he stepped forward and ran the lance of light into Smethers' stomach and up through the ribcage, slicing flesh and bone as if it were butter. With a gasp he withdrew the weapon and stared in shock at the dying man.

He would never forget the smile on Smethers' face. "Always... always had you down as a traitor, Littlebody." He coughed blood and Alfie stepped backwards, revulsion rendering him silent.

Smethers fell to his knees and slumped forward, hitting the ground face first.

The girl was kneeling over the Morn, sobbing. Miraculously, despite its mangled chest, the creature was still alive, its face a rictus of pain.

Alfie found himself saying, "I'm sorry... I'm so sorry."

Janisha Chatterjee looked up, staring at him. Recognition lit her eyes. "You?"

Alfie shook his head. "I'm sorry, Miss Chatterjee... There was nothing I could do. I tried to..." He gestured to Smethers. "I wanted no part of this. I was... I was sent after you, yes, but I wanted no part of the killing."

She stared at him. "You've got to help me!"

In her arms, the dying creature choked on its blood.

Alfie shook his head. "How?" He flicked a glance at Smethers' corpse. "Why did he want to arrest you...?"

"Please, trust me. I'm no enemy. I'm... I'm working for the safety of everyone, everyone on the planet! You must believe me."

Alfie found himself choking back a sob. "I... I honestly don't know what to believe."

She took a deep breath. "You must help me board the ship, you must!"

"The ship? I don't know what you're talking about."

Something moved to his right. He turned, thinking Anand had recovered and picked himself up. He stared in disbelief as a creature identical to the dying Morn manifested itself in the air, gradually gaining substance. It even wore the same tattered British army uniform as the Morn and, Alfie saw with horror, its chest was a shattered mess of blood and bone.

"You must believe what Janisha is saying," said the creature.

"What... what are you?" Alfie said, backing away.

The girl was staring up at the apparition, a desperate smile shining through her grief. "Please believe him, sir! Please! We are working for the good of everyone!"

The creature gestured. "Please, sit down and listen to what I have to say."

Alfie slumped to the ground and the apparition squatted beside him, its thin lips drawn into the semblance of a smile as it began. "It is imperative, for the well-being of every citizen on the planet, that Janisha is allowed to enter the city of Annapurnabad and the ship that resides there. Believe me when I stress that we work for no one side in this conflict – not the Russians, nor the Chinese, nor the British... I have come from afar to help you, the human race, and I will not have died in vain if I know that you will help Janisha complete what I set out to do."

Alfie looked from the apparition before him to its wounded double, the blood still pumping from its chest, its breathing becoming ever more shallow. He looked from the creature to Janisha Chatterjee's tear-streaked, beseeching face, and then across to where the boy Anand was kneeling, his grief-stricken expression imploring Alfie to believe the words of the enigmatic apparition.

He murmured, "But what can I do?"

The apparition smiled, or rather its lips stretched a little wider as it said, its voice fading, "Give Janisha the VCA, show her how it functions, and then be ready to take her and Anand away from here when she has done what she has to do aboard the Vantissar ship."

Alfie nodded, glancing at the girl. "Yes. Yes, I can do that."

"And then.... and then, to the best of your ability, help her get away..."

The apparition turned to the girl. "Janisha... My plan was to make my way to London, to... to warn..." His voice grew weak. "Janisha, for me – for your own people – please attempt to..."

The girl was on her knees, staring at the ghostly Morn. "I promise... I'll do whatever I can, I promise!"

"Janisha..." the apparition said, its voice a whisper.

It smiled, then faded from view, and Janisha Chatterjee wept as the creature in her arms gave a final, stuttering breath and lay very still.

Alfie climbed to his feet, numbed. He stared down at Smethers' corpse, still unable to accept that he had killed the man. He saw the light-beam where he had dropped it, scorching a line in the grass. He reached down, picked it up and twisted the base. The lance of light vanished.

He held it out to the girl. "You might need this, as well as the skullcap," he said.

She smiled through her tears. "The weapon will not be necessary, thank you. Jelch... Jelch provided me with a light-beam."

He turned to Anand. "Then perhaps you'd better keep this," he said, passing the light-beam to the boy; he could not have it in his possession a second longer.

He knelt down beside Smethers' corpse and, doing his best not to look into the dead man's staring eyes, unbuckled the skullcap and passed it to the girl.

He showed her how to operate the VCA. "I'll take Anand with me. We'll cross the city to the airyard and hire a 'ship." He looked up the slope. "We'll meet you in the next valley, when you have conducted your business aboard the ship."

He looked at the bodies of Smethers and the Morn. The girl arranged the arms of the creature – Jelch, she had called it – by its side, murmuring a few tearful words as she stared down at its frozen face.

Alfie said, "We can't leave them out in the open like this. Help me conceal them in the bushes, would you, Anand?"

Between them they heaved the bodies into the undergrowth, and Alfie arranged branches and ferns to conceal their presence. He dusted his hands, sick to the stomach as he relived the sensation of running the light-beam through the colonel's torso.

The girl smiled through her tears. "Thank you, sir."

"Lieutenant Alfie Littlebody," he said, saluting.

She pulled on the skullcap, and hugged Anand to her in farewell. Then she activated the controls on the chin-strap and vanished.

Alfie watched the depressions in the grass march down the hillside.

He gestured towards the city and, as he and the boy set off, said, "Perhaps you might be able to explain a few things to me, Anand. First of all, what happened to the Russians?"

ANAND HURRIED ALONG beside the English officer, stunned by the deaths he'd just witnessed and wondering what the future might hold. Even if they did manage to secure an airship, how might they evade the reach of the British?

He recalled the lieutenant's question and said, "The Russians were evil spies, sir. They tortured Janisha and put a metal mesh on her face in order to read her thoughts."

"By God, they did, did they? What on earth did they want to know?"

Anand shrugged. "Janisha told me that they wanted something from her – something that is vital to the safety of the world."

The officer stared at him. "This gets more mysterious by the second. But what happened to the Russians? The last I heard, the pair had kidnapped you and Janisha."

"Ah-cha," Anand said, nodding. "They did, but Jelch boarded the airship and broke the neck of one Russian and shot the other in the head."

"Good God. Death, death everywhere..."

Anand looked up at the officer. "And then Janisha and I opened a trapdoor in the floor of the airship and rolled the Russians out."

The officer winced. "Well, I suppose they had it coming." He sounded far from convinced. "A couple of sadists, by all accounts." He thought for a while, then said, "But this Jelch character... I must admit I've never seen anything like it."

Anand shook his head, recalling how Jelch had saved his life and Janisha's... and now the creature lay dead on the hillside above them.

Anand said, "Sir, I heard this in Jelch's own words. You see, he told Janisha where he came from."

"And where the deuce was it, Anand?"

Anand shook his head. "I hardly believe it myself, sir. He said he came from far away, in a vast ship. And later, Janisha told me that Jelch was an alien."

"An alien?" The officer stared at him, clearly incredulous.

Anand nodded. "Ah-cha. He came from another world, sir. Another star."

"Good God!" the lieutenant said, mopping his brow.

They came to the outskirts of the city and hurried along a street packed with pedestrians and cars. The officer glanced at Anand and cleared his throat. "I must admit, I've never met a young woman quite like Janisha."

Anand grinned. "She is very special and also very beautiful, no?"

"I'll say." The officer took Anand's shoulder and steered him through the crowds. Ahead, above the skyline of imposing buildings, Anand made out a hundred 'ships approaching and leaving the airyard.

"Do you know," the officer asked, "if she has anyone special, back in England?"

"Special?" Anand asked, knowing very well what the Englishman meant, but wondering at the reason for his question.

"I mean, does she have a sweetheart back in the Old Country?"

Anand sighed. "She is in love with a rich young man, sir. She told me so herself. At least... she thinks she is in love. But you never know..."

He grinned up at the officer, who laughed in return and clapped Anand on the shoulder.

"And here we are," said the lieutenant, staring through the great wrought-iron gates of the airyard.

Anand gaped at the bobbing vessels as some left their docking rigs and others came in to land. The yard was a hive of activity, and the noise of the engines was deafening.

The officer squared his shoulders. "Right-o. I think it might be best if you kick your heels out here for the time being. I'll be right back as soon as I've secured a 'ship."

"And then, sir?"

"And then we'll get the merry hell away from here, Anand, and with luck rendezvous with Janisha. Here goes."

With that, the dumpy little Englishman hurried into the airyard. Anand watched him until he was lost to sight amidst a crowd of bustling porters, pilots and passengers.

CHAPTER
TWENTY-FOUR

Invisible in Annapurnabad –
Inside the Vantissar ship – An amazing audience –
"From India you will return to London..."

JANI WALKED LIKE a ghost through the streets of Annapurnabad, Jelch's death weighing on her soul along with the pain of her father's recent demise.

At first she had felt self-conscious as she passed amongst the crowds. Like someone forced to divest their clothing and walk naked through busy streets, she had expected to be noticed and was amazed to find that her presence attracted not the slightest attention. The invisibility helmet really worked. As the minutes passed, she became more confident. She no longer crept along the street, but strode – careful at all times to avoid collisions, and looking ahead at the pedestrians and vehicles in order to foresee likely problems: people hurrying or running, citizens merging with the flow of pedestrians at right angles from buildings and side-streets. From time to time she looked over her shoulder for oblivious pedestrians coming up behind her. She was very aware of the possibility of discovery, or even injury.

As she walked through the city, she wondered if this was what it felt like to *belong*... No one looked at her; she was invisible. In London she had attracted many a glance and the occasional comment, and even in India she felt marked out by her dual heritage and English upbringing. No one had known that, of course, but it had had the effect in her mind of making her feel different, apart. Now she was unseen, unnoticed, and the experience was oddly novel.

At street level, no longer looking down on the city or the monstrous alien craft, she could imagine she was in any city on the subcontinent. The same noisy chaos prevailed; the same garish colours contrasted with the grey peeling buildings; the same heady scents of cooking food, wood smoke, petrol fumes, dung, incense and rosewater... The only difference she could discern was the marked absence of children. There was no-one under the age of sixteen playing cricket in the streets, flying kites or running with the inner tubes of car tyres, and there were no buses or caged rickshaws packed with schoolchildren. This was a city devoted to one thing, the extraction of technology from the alien vessel. Everyone here, she reminded herself as she passed along the bustling main boulevard towards the ship a mile away, had been brought in by the British to facilitate the ongoing supremacy of the Empire, from the most humble chai-wallah to the highest serving British officer. She wondered what the Indians and Nepalese around her had been told about the vessel; that it was a British factory, perhaps – certainly they would never have been vouchsafed the truth.

Another difference she noticed, belatedly, was the number of British on the streets, both uniformed soldiers and civilians. She wondered at the function of the latter; there would undoubtedly be a call for civil servants and administrators up here, but she suspected that a number of the well-dressed, middle-aged men in evidence were security officers on the lookout for foreign infiltrators. She wondered if they could ever conceive that among them was an Indian citizen scheming to enter the alien ship using the very technology the British themselves had taken from it.

She considered the recent turn of events, the despair of being discovered by Smethers and Littlebody, and then the surprise at Littlebody's subsequent actions. She thought of Jelch, and brought down a portcullis in her mind on that painful memory. If anything, now, she was determined more than ever to succeed in her mission within the ship. She would do it for Jelch, so that his death would not have been for nothing.

For the first time, from street level, she had a view of the distant ship. Its maw loomed over the buildings, dark and shadowy; deep within its throat she made out tiny glowing points of light. She found it hard to conceive, even now, that very soon, if all went well, she would be boarding a vessel that had made its way from the stars, fleeing merciless invaders.

She wondered if she should feel terror at what Jelch had told her about the Zhell. The odd thing was that, despite the graphic detail of his account, the idea of ravaging, invading aliens was too abstract to be truly frightening. She was still trying to come to terms with the notion that other entities existed beyond the bounds of Earth. It was like asking an innocent child, who had only just discovered the fact of playground bullies, to comprehend the existence of mass murderers.

She walked across a vast, grassed roundabout – fashioned after the centrepiece of Connaught Circus – and paused at the far side before crossing the ring road. She should not hurry, she told herself, and so increase the risk of discovery. She had all day in which to get into the ship and out again.

She crossed the ring road and took a radial road on her right. After two minutes she came to a wide road along which rumbled trucks laden with tarpaulined goods, each one escorted by a khaki-daubed military vehicle. The road ran from the maw of the alien vessel towards the distant airyard. She wondered if the hidden treasures were en route to Delhi, or beyond, to the capital city of the Empire, London.

She turned and hurried along the road towards the ship. It was mid-afternoon and the sun was hot, tempered by a breeze off the mountains. She thought of Anand and Littlebody, heading to the airyard to commandeer an airship. Was it too much to hope that, once she was away from the alien ship, all would be plain sailing?

And then? She had promised Jelch that she would continue his mission – but how might she make her way to London undetected?

She brought her mental portcullis into play again and concentrated on the task ahead.

Only when she was within two hundred yards of the ship's great opening did she fully appreciate its gargantuan dimensions. She had seen the de Havilland hangar at the London airyard – big enough to accommodate three of the world's largest cargo freighters, Sebastian had told her – but the alien ship was fully ten times its size. She stopped in her tracks and stared up, wondering at the beings who had manufactured this colossus. She saw that scaffolding had been erected within the ship as well as without; the interior was floodlit, and the tiny figures of engineers and workmen scurried about in there like ants. Directly before the opening was a vast clearing yard, milling with vehicles and people. Around the perimeter ran a barbed-wire fence, six feet high, with a centrally positioned entry and exit gate, the barrier raised to allow the passage of a dozen military trucks.

Jani approached the gate, slipped past a grumbling truck, and hurried across the clearing yard towards the ship. As she went, she was assailed by the thought of what might be awaiting her. Jelch had told her that she would be met by an apparition, a recording, a – what had he called it? – a *subroutine* that he had installed. The only word she had understood was 'apparition' – but what had he meant by that? A ghost? A spectre of the Vantissar who had brought this ship to Earth and perished half a century ago?

And how might it assist her in locating the device Jelch had told her about?

She told herself to stop worrying and concentrate on boarding the ship.

She threaded her way between the parked vehicles, the drivers, British and Indian, chatting and smoking casually. She marvelled at their nonchalance – then realised that she probably knew more about the Vantissar ship than most of the people around her.

Seconds later she passed into the shadow of the vessel.

It was as if she had stepped from one world to another – from Earthly territory to that of another race. She felt a shiver run down her spine as she increased her pace. She heard shouted commands from uniformed officers up ahead, the everyday appearance of the British soldiers contrasting with the oleaginous brown innards of the alien craft.

She came to a halt on the threshold. Before her was a long smooth lip, like a length of brown bakelite, and beyond it an expanse of ribbed decking made from the same material. She looked about her, as if expecting even now to be assailed. The workers and drivers in the clearing yard went about their business loading trucks or waiting to move off; stentorian shouts echoed in the cavern as if on an Aldershot parade ground. Smiling to herself, Jani stepped forward and climbed into the alien ship.

There was no direct sunlight in here, and she realised the necessity for the arc lights that dotted the interior. It was as if the chitinous brown material from which the ship was built absorbed the light, drank it in, leaving the vast echoing cavern in a strange, otherworldly gloom.

She walked slowly, staring about her. Just as the outer panels had been removed, so had those on the inside. Great curving sections of the chitin – or whatever it was – were missing, revealing the coiled, intestinal complexity of the tubes and pipes beneath. The true size of these coiling columns only became apparent when she saw an overalled worker high above her examining a tube three times his height.

As she walked on, she wondered if the ship was like this all the way to its stern, a great hollow shell – and she wondered if it had always been like this, or if decks and bulkheads had been removed by the British, little by little, over the decades. It was too dark up ahead to see more than a hundred yards before her; after that, the space was a blur, like looking into cloacal tunnel of a subterranean sewer.

She wondered when this apparition or 'program' might make itself known to her, and how.

From time to time groups of British workers hurried past, hauling wheeled trolleys bearing covered goods; they were accompanied by men – and the occasional woman – in white gowns, who were referring to clipboards as if inventorying the mundane stock of a London warehouse. A line of Nepalese and Indian porters, supervised by armed guards, ferried sealed containers from the shadowy interior of the ship and out to the goods yard.

She peered into the gloom before her and made out a series of ramps. They were constructed from the same sleek, brown, chitinous material as the walls, and curved up and around – each one at a steeper gradient – to a succession of tiered decks that rose before Jani in cross-section.

She felt something stir within her, an odd feeling akin to joy. It was almost a bubbling sensation of confidence, at once affirming yet disconcerting. At the same time she knew that she must approach the curving ramp to her right and ascend to the third level. She wondered where this certainty came from, wondered if the 'alien entity' was directing her with arcane mental powers.

She climbed up and around, pausing halfway up the ramp. She looked back down the length of the ship towards the proscenium of the entrance, a dazzling stage filled with sunlight and the tiny figures of the workers and their vehicles.

When she turned and resumed her climb, the receding interior of the ship appeared all the darker. She ascended, her pace slowing. There were no arc-lights up ahead, and no sign of any scientists or engineers. She felt very alone. The sensation of euphoria bubbling in her solar plexus gained in intensity.

She came to the third level and paused, staring ahead.

Before her was a wall or bulkhead, and as she stared at it she made out a pattern in the structure of the wall. It was a honeycomb, rows of large hexagonal cells, each one as tall as herself and receding from her like a tunnel. She hesitated, but something propelled her forward, the same certainty that had made her climb the ramp. She stepped forward and approached the honeycombed wall, her inclination to stop before it overridden by the command to keep on walking. She did so, and gasped as she hit the soft, yielding surface of a membrane and stepped through. She continued walking along the corridor, the walls illuminated by a soft, lambent light.

She wondered why she did not feel frightened, or even apprehensive. But the fact was that she felt only a numinous sense of awe at what she was experiencing, as well as anticipation.

She seemed to have been walking for an age when the lighting of the corridor intensified up ahead. She squinted into the brightness.

Her pace slowed as she approached the dazzling glow. She felt a familiar, cloying resistance and realised that she was passing through another membrane. As soon as she was through, the bright light dimmed and she found herself standing on the lip of an amphitheatre like a vast, white porcelain bowl.

She looked up, and the amphitheatre was mirrored above her; the entire chamber was sleek and smooth and featureless, and she had never seen anything like it in her life.

She had the conviction, then, that she had arrived at her destination.

She looked around her, turning in a complete circle, as if expecting to meet her interlocutor – or the entity or program Jelch had mentioned.

But she was totally alone in the chamber.

Something moved, down in the very centre of the amphitheatre. She stared as a slight bulge appeared in the porcelain floor. It grew slowly, domed and almost fungal, emerging from the floor at a steady rate, gaining height and breadth. When it was perhaps five feet tall, and as wide as a pillar box – but as white as the surrounding chamber – it ceased its growth.

Jani had to move towards the thing. She took a step down the shelving slope and approached the object.

She paused before the white column and became aware that a subtle transformation was taking place. The column was changing shape, taking on the form of a being, naked and pale – a being she recognised.

She murmured, "Jelch?"

A facsimile of her erstwhile companion stood before her, the same oddly articulated legs and elongated torso, attenuated ribcage and flattened face.

The being stared at her and spoke – or rather did not speak. Its face lacked animation; it merely stared at her. Its words, however, sounded in her head.

Not Jelch, but an iteration of him. A copy, if you will, which Jelch created in the vessel's nexus before he left.

She shook her head. "I'm sorry, but I don't understand."

Your understanding is not a prerequisite to your presence here.

She realised something. The being was staring directly at her. "You can see me, despite...?" She reached up and touched the helmet.

I can see you, Janisha.

"You know my name." She wondered why she was surprised by this; it was the least of the wonders she had experienced so far.

I know your name, and your exploits in getting here.

"But how can you know all this?" she asked.

Jelch was in contact with me.

"Jelch..." She felt a painful throb of emotion as she said his name. "He told me that I would be met. I didn't understand the words he used to explain who or what you were... but he said that you would instruct me, that you would tell me what to do."

That is so.

She stared at the entity before her, this copy of Jelch. It was not him, she could see now – it lacked his depth of facial features, the lines of experience that had etched his old face. It was like an ill-defined statue, granted a semblance of life.

"He told me about the Zhell, and that he and a companion – a fellow Morn – assisted the Vantissar in fleeing here. He said he tried to alert the powers-that-be on Earth to the danger approaching from the stars..."

Not from the stars, Janisha; the Zhell do not come from the stars, just as this vessel did not travel through space, from a far star, to reach here.

"But..." Jani felt dizzy; it had taken a considerable leap of imagination, not to mention credulity, to adjust her thinking to the idea that somewhere out there among the stars existed other beings. And now this iteration of the Morn was telling her that what Jelch had said was not true.

But had Jelch ever said that he came from the stars, she wondered? Or had that been her own interpretation?

"Then where?" she asked.

Janisha, the being spoke in her head, *imagine a book, a very thick book, a volume with numberless pages.*

"Very well," she said, doing just that and wondering where the explanation might be leading.

In fact, so many pages that they extend to infinity... more pages than it is possible to imagine...

She smiled. "I am trying to imagine that," she said.

Now imagine that each page of this vast book is a separate reality.

She closed her eyes, opened them and shook her head. "A separate reality?"

Imagine that everything you know of your world is in fact but a page of this vast book, separated from the next page, or reality, by nothing more than a complex weft and weave of sub-atomic particles or strings – a curtain, if you like.

She said unsurely, "I can conceive that my world, my reality, is the page of a book, yes."

Now imagine that, for the sake of argument, your reality is page eighteen, and that the Vantissar's reality is page nineteen. Now, the reality of the Morn is page twenty. Page twenty-one is where the bellicose Zhell reside... except that over the centuries they have succeeded in devising a way to pass through the pages of the 'book of reality' – or the multiplicity, as we call it – and invading various realms, both before and after their own 'page.'

"So the idea that they came from the stars...?"

Is erroneous, but an understandable mistake.

She felt weak at the knees. "So... so Jelch and his companion... they moved from their own 'page,' their own reality, to that of the Vantissar, in order to warn them?"

They did, and that peaceful race had time only to equip this ark, as they called it, and with Jelch's aid make the transfer here.

"And how did Jelch and his companion manage this?"

The race of the Morn were technologists, scientists, who had studied the fabric of reality for centuries. They invented a means by which to break down, temporarily, the fabric of the sub-atomic weft and weave of reality, in order to enable passage from one 'page' to the next, in much the same manner as the Zhell did. They also devised a means to close the fabric, and reinforce it, if you will, in such a way as to make it, briefly, impregnable to the Zhell...

Jani stared, open-mouthed, at the figure before her.

The device that allows access between the worlds, or rather part of the device, resides within the nexus of this vessel. You see, fifty years ago, when the Vantissar craft broke through into this realm, a power struggle ensued. A faction of the Vantissar demanded the 'key' for themselves, so that they could continue onwards through the book, as it were, to a place of ultimate sanctuary. Another faction, backed by Jelch and his companion, wanted to warn this world of the danger they faced. They calculated that they had fifty years to do this, before the Zhell would work out how to break down the barrier once again.

"Fifty years," Jani whispered.

Shortly after the ship landed here, the humans inhabiting this valley made contact with the Vantissar

– though they thought them gods. A Vantissar from the faction opposing Jelch fled the ship, taking with it a ventha, a disc, that was a constituent of the ventha-di, the key which facilitates the passage from one realm to the next. In its ignorance, the Vantissar rebel thought it had the entire ventha-di... Jelch and his companion left the ship and searched for the miscreant and the ventha, but without luck. Possessing their own ventha, one each, they did their best to inform the powers that rule your world of the danger they faced... In time, the Vantissar succumbed to the viruses and pathogens of your world, which proved inimical to them, and they died out, and the third ventha was lost.

In a small voice, Jani said, "And Jelch gave me his disc, his ventha – for safe keeping? But... but I lost it."

As Jelch told you, you did not lose it, Janisha. Your subconscious mind knows very well where it is.

"But..." she began.

Janisha, Jelch gave you the disc lest he should die of his wounds inflicted by the Russians. He wanted you to bring it here so that it could be reunited with the ventha-di. If he survived and found you, then he would continue his onward quest to London.

"And if he had died before reaching me, how would I have known what to do?"

In that eventuality, then the ventha would have instructed you what to do.

"It would?" she said incredulously. She shook her head and went on in desperation, "But the problem is, I don't know where the ventha is! I don't have it on me!"

But Janisha, said the entity, *you do...*

It reached out a hand to her, and a second later she felt something stirring in her stomach. She became aware of a warm glow, a sensation that travelled up from her stomach, through her solar plexus and chest. She gagged, coughed, and the warmth then resided on her tongue – a small lozenge which she took from her mouth, wiped clean on her bodice, and held before her eyes in disbelief.

"The coin..."

When you were lying in the wreckage of the airship, before the Russians found you, said the entity, *the ventha itself instructed you to take it from your pocket and place it in your mouth; this you did, and swallowed, and the ventha told you that you would recall nothing of its instructions, for safety's sake.*

"The ventha..." she said in awe.

The tithra-kuñjī, Durga Das had called it... But how had *he* known?

And now I will entrust to you the ventha-di...

Jani stared at the entity's outstretched hand, and something emerged from the porcelain smoothness of its palm: a jet black triangle, perhaps an inch and a half from base to apex, in which were three round recesses.

Take it, said the entity, *and place your ventha in one of the receivers.*

Jani took the triangle and slipped her ventha into one of the holes; it fitted perfectly and, as she watched, the disc turned from silver to the jet colour of the ventha-di.

"And now?" she asked.

Now place the ventha-di upon your tongue, Janisha.

She hesitated, then opened her mouth and inserted the ventha-di, and instantly she felt its warm glow. She swallowed involuntarily, and to her surprise the device slid down her throat like a spoonful of honey. She felt its glow travel down through her torso and come to rest in her stomach.

"And now?" she asked.

And now you will leave the ship, Janisha, and rendezvous with your colleagues. From India you will return to London.

"Jelch told me of his companion."

There you will attempt to locate the venerable Mahran; he has in his possession the second ventha. When you have successfully located Mahran, you must together endeavour to seek out and obtain the third ventha.

"I promised Jelch," she said.

And you have proved more than capable so far, Janisha Chatterjee.

"You... you said that my world had fifty years before the Zhell might break the seal and invade... That fifty years, by my calculations, are up."

That is so, and that is why your onward quest assumes utmost importance. Together with Mahran you might avert catastrophe. The Zhell are working to invade as we speak; already they are projecting avatars of themselves into this realm, in preparation.

She straightened her back and stared at the entity. "I will attempt to do my best," she said. "But how will I locate the second Morn, this Mahran?"

He is presently incarcerated in London, in solitary confinement in a gaol known as Newgate.

"I will do my very best to find the Morn," she said, "and effect his escape."

The entity inclined its head – and she was reminded, painfully, of Jelch.

Jelch, said the entity, *would have been proud of you. Now go.*

She lifted a hand in a farewell gesture, and watched as the figure before her became ill-defined, its features smoothing out as it reverted to its columnar state and then sank into the porcelain floor.

She turned, emotion blocking her throat, and hurried up the incline towards the hexagonal corridor. She passed through the membrane and moved down the corridor, emerging onto the deck of level three and squinting at the dazzle of sunlight in the distance.

She paused at the top of the curving ramp and stared down at the ant-like activity below. Her heart kicked in panic for a second before she realised that she still wore the invisibility helmet. She reached up, as if for reassurance, and touched the chin-strap.

She hurried down the ramp, eager now to be away from the ship.

She moved past the workers ferrying technological treasures from the alien ship, remembering her earlier circumspection and slowing her pace. It would be a tragedy now if she were to be hasty and reveal her presence.

The sunlight was blinding as she emerged from the maw and crossed the apron. She stared beyond to the city with its familiar architecture, cars and rickshaws and crowds of noisy citizens. How mundane all this seemed now, in light of what the entity had told her. A multiplicity of worlds like the leaves of a book, she thought, existing all at once but a hairsbreadth from each other. She found the concept almost impossible to imagine.

And the Zhell, a marauding alien race who would stop at nothing to invade, enslave and slaughter innocent peoples... How far away that threat seemed when set against the everyday reality of the bustling city.

She wondered if Littlebody had succeeded in commandeering an airship, and if at this very moment he and Anand were waiting for her in the next valley. She hurried down the main boulevard away from the Vantissar ship, retracing the steps she had taken less than an hour ago.

She avoided the people that milled along the street, ever mindful of the crowds. She still found it hard to be entirely comfortable with the notion that she could not be seen; when the errant gaze of a paan-wallah strayed her way, her heart gave a jump – until his eyes focused on a point beyond her and she breathed with relief.

She turned from the main boulevard towards the roundabout, crossed it and took the road leading to the east of the city – heading for the hills. Soon she would be passing the jerry-built hovels that surrounded Annapurnabad. The alleys and byways there were crammed with humanity going about their business, and she would have to be extra vigilant.

Before she reached the area of hovels, she passed down a quiet street devoted to vendors of leather goods and shoe-makers. The reek of tanned hides filled the air, and tiny, dark-skinned Dalits worked at outdoor stalls cutting and shaping leather with razor-sharp paring knives.

Ahead rose the forested hills, and her heart skipped in anticipation.

She saw a thin, sharp-suited man leaning against a building a few yards ahead, absently paring his fingernails. He was vaguely familiar, although his face was turned away from her. Something about the cut of his suit, the way he negligently worked at his nails with an oversized knife...

As Jani hurried past him, the man looked up and spoke to someone in a doorway beside him, and his companion moved from the recess and filled the pavement with his bulk.

The huge man barrelled into her, smiling, and behind her the knifeman fumbled his hands over her body before clutching her arm and clamping a hand over her mouth.

As they dragged her into an alleyway, then through a gate and along a passageway between the buildings, she realised that they could not see her. Durga Das had been smiling, yes, but not directly at her; he had known where she was approximately, but not exactly. And the way Mr Knives had fumbled with her suggested that he too had been unable to see her. Even as she wondered how they had managed to find her, she found hope in the fact that she was still invisible.

If she could only wrest herself from Mr Knives' grip, and lose herself down the alley...

She struggled with all her might, kicking out at her captor's shins. He cursed and threatened to slit her throat, but if anything his grip on her tightened. She felt his hand move from her mouth, reach up and grasp the rim of her skullcap. He tugged, and the chin-strap tore at her flesh as he dragged the cap from her head and cast it aside.

She yelled aloud, hoping to attract someone's attention – but Mr Knives clamped his sweaty hand over her mouth again and bundled her through another gate into a small courtyard, a patch of bright blue sky high above. He pushed her viciously and she stumbled and hit the far wall.

Durga Das closed the gate behind them and waddled forward, smiling at her. "It is so good," he purred, "to *see* you again, Miss Chatterjee. Our last meeting,

I recall, was rudely interrupted. But the gods serve those who serve the gods, as the old saying has it. We persevere, and we are rewarded. Fortune favours the righteous, and the devout."

She stared up at him and spat, "I was followed! It's only a matter of time before you're found out–"

"Be quiet, Miss Chatterjee. We know you were not followed."

Her voice faltered, "But you couldn't see me..."

Durga Das smiled, his full lips curving sensuously. "We had other means of detecting your presence," he said, "and we know that you were quite alone."

Mr Knives was leaning against a whitewashed wall, examining the blade of his knife. It was as if they had never left the guest house at Rishi Tal and were resuming their confrontation where they had left off two days ago. Only this time, she knew, her skin would not be saved by the timely intervention of the Russians, or anyone else.

This time she would have to rely on her own resources.

Durga Das leaned forward over the rolls of his stomach. "Where is the tithra-kuñjī, Miss Chatterjee?"

She shook her head. "You asked me that before, and as I answered then – I have no idea what you're talking about."

Before she could react, Mr Knives stepped forward and struck out. Pain flared across her cheek. At first she thought he'd slashed her face with his knife. Then she saw that he'd reversed the weapon and struck her with its hilt.

She fell back against the wall, holding her cheek.

"A little foretaste, Miss Chatterjee," said Durga Das, "of what is in store if you continue in this vein of wilful ignorance. We know what you were doing aboard the Vantissar ship, and that you have the ventha-di." His smile increased at her shock. "And we will, if necessary, cut you open to get it."

"Of course," said Mr Knives, "you could co-operate and give us what we want... though, speaking personally I would rather cut you open."

She shook her head wordlessly.

She was struck by a sudden thought: was it possible, she wondered, that Durga Das was in possession of one of the venthas? Was that why he wanted the device?

Durga Das turned his head slightly and muttered something; it was as if he were addressing a fourth person in the compound. She caught a brief blue flash in the air to the holy man's left and felt a stab of fear.

Das snapped, "You lie! We *know* you entered the ship and were given the ventha-di. Now, we will quite happily open your stomach and take what we want, or you can give us the device. We are humane people, Miss Chatterjee..." He glanced at his companion and added, "At least, as a man of faith, I am... and I would rather see you leave here with your life."

Her heart skipped. She had Jelch's light-beam in her pocket. She felt a sudden surge of hope and tried not to let it show on her face.

She said, "You promise? If I give you the ventha-di, then you'll let me live?"

She could see the lie in the priest's eye as he replied, "You have my word."

Mr Knives stepped forward, bringing the point of his knife to her throat. "So you admit it? You have the ventha-di!"

She tipped her head away from the blade and nodded. "I have it, but not where you think it is. I... I didn't swallow it."

"We were told..." Mr Knives began.

She reached for her pocket.

Mr Knives brandished his weapon again, making her flinch. Jani paused, her heart pounding.

Durga Das gestured. "No, let her..." he said, greed glittering in his eyes.

Slowly, carefully, planning what she would do when she had the light-beam out of her pocket, she slipped her fingers into the satin fold and clasped the tiny cylinder. She would have a split second, once it was out, to twist its base and bring forth the blade of light... and Mr Knives, she knew from recent experience, was lightning fast.

She closed her fingers around the cylinder and pulled it from her pocket. Quickly she turned the bevelled rim. A yard-long beam of rapier thin light sprang forth, and she leapt towards the pair and slashed the beam through the air.

Mr Knives screamed and something fell to the ground – his knife, with his right hand attached, its fingers still gripping the hilt. He staggered back against the far wall, his face torn with pain. Jani expected to see a fountain of blood, but the stump was cleanly cauterized, filling the air with the stench of cooked flesh.

She swung around and the light-beam tore across the holy man's belly, slicing his robes and a roll of flesh. He cried out and staggered back, and Jani dashed between the men and hauled open the gate. She saw a blue flash ignite in the square behind her as she fled along the passage, heard Das cry something unintelligible in high-pitched Hindi.

She heard a shout and turned. Mr Knives, his face a rictus of pain and rage, was a matter of yards behind her. She lashed out with the beam, screaming, and missed him by an inch. Mr Knives leapt back. Behind him she saw Durga Das emerge through the gate, holding his bloody belly as if it were an injured animal. He barrelled into Mr Knives and both men tumbled to the ground. Jani turned and ran, extinguishing the light beam as she approached the busy street.

She slowed her headlong dash lest she arouse unwanted attention, calmed herself and maintained a sedate pace as she slipped into the crowd. At the corner of the street she looked back. Das and Mr Knives appeared, frantically looking right and left.

Jani took off. She considered the blue light, which she had witnessed twice now, and then tried to dismiss it from her thoughts as she concentrated on losing herself down the warren of narrow alleys and streets of the slum area.

She headed east, using the line of the distant hills to guide the direction of her flight. She tried to maintain her poise, but was aware of suspicious glances cast her way as she hurried past impoverished families squatting in the gutter.

She passed through the sack-and-cardboard shantytown and emerged into open country. The land rose before her, a patchwork of scrubby plantations and barren fields before the treeline began some two hundred yards higher up.

She looked over her shoulder. This was where she would be most vulnerable, crossing the open land in plain sight. She could easily be seen from the hovels.

She came to the first of the trees and ran into their shade, allowing herself a relieved breath and a measure of hope. She climbed the slope between casuarina and eucalyptus trees, thinking back to her flight and wishing she had had the time, and the foresight, to cast about the alleyway for the discarded invisibility helmet. Who knew how useful it would have been in the days and weeks ahead?

She heard a sound behind her and turned. She cried out in disbelief as she saw, perhaps a hundred yards below her, Mr Knives running through the trees. He pressed the stump of his right arm to his chest, and in his left hand flashed a knife.

She sprinted. The ridge of the hill was a couple of hundred yards above her, and in the next valley – if Alfie Littlebody had managed to secure an airship – would be her salvation.

She came to the crest and hurried on without pausing to look back. She sprinted over the rise and through the trees on the other side, scanning ahead for any sign of the airship. The slope fell precipitously before her; she had a grandstand view of the shelving valley and the blue sky above, and not even so much as a cloud marred its perfection.

What to do? She looked behind her. There was no sign of Mr Knives. Should she hide behind a tree, conceal herself until Littlebody's airship came to her rescue? But Durga Das and Mr Knives had somehow located her earlier, when she had been invisible. Perhaps they had the ability to do so again? She overruled her instinct to hide and kept on running down the wooded slope.

There was still no sign of an airship, five minutes later, when she heard a shout from further up the hillside. "Flight is useless, Miss Chatterjee. We will find you even if you flee to the ends of the Earth! Be sensible now and give yourself up. We will be lenient! All we want is the ventha-di, and we will let you go with your life."

Gasping, she fumbled with the cylinder and brought forth the light-beam. She was in the valley bottom now, and cast about for somewhere to hide herself. She looked up the hillside and caught a glimpse of a dark suit through the trees. Mr Knives was no more than fifty yards away and sprinting towards her.

They could only pursue her to the ends of the Earth, she thought, if they were alive. She had the advantage over her pursuers in terms of weapons. Let Mr Knives do his best. Taking a breath, she stepped out into the open and faced the oncoming knifeman.

He emerged from the trees and stopped when he saw her. They faced each other on a broad swathe of grass beside a meandering river. He was perhaps thirty yards away and walking slowly towards her, a knife outstretched in his left hand, his right wrist a truncated, blackened stump.

She crouched, held out the light-beam, and prepared herself.

Mr Knives advanced, closing the distance between them. He was twenty yards away now, the expression on his face twisted, either in pain or hatred. Whichever, he was ugly beyond words.

"You choose to fight?" he called out, grimacing in pain. "A mistake. You were lucky once, but not a second time."

"Come any closer, and this time it will not be your hand that I lop off!" she cried.

He laughed, and continued walking.

Her heart pounded and time seemed to slow. She told herself that the light-beam was far superior to the knife, but felt a rising tide of panic even so. Where was Littlebody and his airship?

Mr Knives was ten yards from her now and steadily advancing. She held her ground. The river was behind her, and it would be a mistake to back off. She had to be brave and confront him, rather than turn and run. As soon as he came within striking distance, she would lash out, attempt to kill him. She was fighting, she told herself, for more than just her life.

Mr Knives was smiling, his blade glinting in the sun. He had dropped into a crouch and was creeping towards her little by little. Jani held her light-beam upright, her heart thumping, watching his every move.

He danced forward and lashed out. His blade swooped through the air. She leapt back, the knife missing her by inches. She swung her light-blade, but he stepped back beyond its reach like a practised fencer.

He lunged again, and she cried out in alarm and stumbled backwards, swiping her weapon through the air. He took heart, his grin turning to a sneer.

She was distracted, a second later, when something blue appeared in the air above her opponent's right shoulder. She stared in fright as she made out a devil's mask, all fangs and stunted horns and a serpentine, lashing tongue. Mr Knives took advantage of her distraction and advanced, his blade slicing her bodice and her flesh beneath. She cried out in panic and pain and brought the light-blade down, missing him by an inch, then backed towards the river.

She felt blood, warm and wet, trickle down her chest.

The airborne devil's head, eerily blue, hissed and spat at her.

She lashed out again, but her opponent danced nimbly backwards, his grin mocking her. "You will have to do far better than that to get lucky again, Miss Chatterjee."

He danced forward. She saw his knife move, but too late, and another cut bled into the material of her bodice. She stepped back, lashing out ineffectively with her weapon.

He was toying with her, taking his time.

The electric blue devil's head remained at his shoulder, as if urging him on. She heard the devil say something, the words lost to her.

Then she became aware of another sound and her heart leapt. She dared not look up to confirm with her eyes what her ears told her was approaching. The steady throb of an airship's motors beat down upon the clearing, growing ever louder. Mr Knives looked up, quickly, and did not like what he saw.

"Jani-ji!" a voice cried. Anand! "Jani-ji, grab the rope ladder!"

Mr Knives lunged again, missing her this time, and Jani chopped down with her light-beam. He howled in pain as the beam struck home and sliced through his arm just below the elbow. The severed arm, the hand still clutching the knife, dropped with a thump to the ground.

She looked up, dizzy with relief. The airship, with Anand crouching at the open hatch, was a dozen feet above her – a rope ladder dancing within reach.

She looked back at Mr Knives. He was on his knees and sobbing with pain. He was at her mercy; she could kill him now... but something stopped her. In the heat of the moment, perhaps, in the frenzy of conflict, she might have killed another human being... but she could not bring herself to do so when the man was defenceless.

She twisted the hilt of her light-beam, extinguishing the blade, reached up and hauled herself, swinging, onto the rope ladder.

"Jani-ji!" Anand cried.

She struggled up the ladder. Anand yelled again, this time in warning. She looked down; Mr Knives had leapt up at the dangling rope and grasped the lowest rung in the crook of his elbow. He lashed out at her legs with his right stump. It might normally have struck her as terrifying – but the absence of a hand at the end of his arm made his efforts blackly comical.

She kicked out and hit Mr Knives in the face with her sandal. He lost his grip with a startled cry, and Jani watched him fall fifteen feet to the ground.

She looked down as the airship gained height. Mr Knives writhed on the bank of the river, the mysterious blue devil's head staring down at him, its tongue lashing the air as if cursing his failure. Further up the slope she saw the rotund shape of Durga Das stumble from the trees and stare up at the departing airship. She had the urge to wave at him, but resisted the impulse.

She hauled herself the rest of the way up the ladder into the airship, exhausted, and collapsed into Anand's waiting embrace.

TWO HOURS LATER the airship crossed the Nepali border and headed for Delhi. Jani sat on a couch, her torso swaddled in bandages. She had dressed her wounds, which had proved to be superficial, and then Alfie Littlebody had brewed a pot of Earl Grey.

Jani finished recounting her experiences aboard the Vantissar ship, then stressed the urgency of her onward mission. Alfie and Anand had sat transfixed for the duration of her story.

"I must admit," Littlebody said, "that if I hadn't experienced what I have over the past few days, I would have found your story hard to believe."

"But you do believe me, don't you?"

He nodded. "Yes, I do. The thought of it..."

Anand said, his eyes wide, "And now we must ensure that Jani-ji gets to London!"

Alfie Littlebody sipped his tea. "Mmm. Trouble is, this crate is short haul only. Small fuel tanks, y'see. They'll only take us so far. We wouldn't even reach the first refuelling station at Karachi."

"But the authorities will be looking for us!" Anand wailed. "And so will Durga Das and other Russian spies."

Jani interrupted. "I've thought of that. I know how we can get out of India undetected."

They stared at her. "You do?" Alfie said.

"First of all, Alfie, I would like to know what your plans are."

"Mine?" He puffed out his cheeks. "Well, it looks as though I've cooked my goose with my superiors, don't you know? Killing one's superior officer is not quite the ticket, is it? So, as I'll be a wanted man, I might as well throw in my lot with your good self, if you'd accept my meagre services, that is."

Jani smiled. "Excellent. I accept. And you, Anand?"

He said, his eyes downcast, "I would very much like to go to London with you, Jani-ji. If you would like me to come."

"I would hardly leave you behind, after all you've done for me."

She crossed to a small bureau, found a pen and wrote an address on an envelope. "Anand and I will be unable to leave the airyard in Delhi when we arrive. We have no papers, no passports..."

"That might pose a problem," Alfie said.

"I hope not," she said. "As soon as we land in Delhi, I want you to go to an address with a letter I shall write. With luck, by this time tomorrow we will be on our way to London."

She proffered her cup and saucer. "I think I will take a little more tea," she said, then turned to the porthole and stared out. The flat plains of India passed far below, remote and silent. She considered Durga Das, the Russians, and the might of the Raj pitched against her.

The threat of the Zhell, she decided, was just too enormous a notion to contemplate, at the moment.

Her first concern was the small matter of leaving India without being apprehended.

CHAPTER
TWENTY-FIVE

Alfie seeks help – An anxious wait –
Aboard the Pride of Edinburgh, at last –
Set fair for London –
"To the success of our mission..."

"HE'S BEEN GONE almost two hours now, Jani-ji," Anand said.

"I know..." Jani bit her lip. For perhaps the twentieth time in the past five minutes, she twitched the curtain aside and peered through the porthole. It was midnight and the vast airyard was floodlit; dozens of airships were moored to their docking rigs and hundreds of workers scurried back and forth under the harsh illumination.

There was no sign of Alfie Littlebody out there, or the taxi which had whisked him from the Delhi airyard two hours earlier. Jani had assumed it would take no more than an hour for Alfie to do what he had to do and return, and her thoughts turned to what might have gone wrong to delay him. They had left Nepal twelve hours ago; even if the body of Colonel Smethers had been found by now, there was no way that his death could be attributed to Littlebody – so she had no reason to worry that he had been arrested on those grounds. More likely was that he had simply lost his way, or that he had been unable to locate the person whose help Jani sought.

"Come on, come on..." she fretted.

Anand stared at her. "And if the *Pride of Edinburgh* leaves without us?" he asked.

"Then we'll simply have to think of another plan, won't we?" she said, exhibiting an optimism she did not wholly feel. "So far, together, we've done rather well, ah-cha?"

He beamed and nodded.

She stared across the busy apron to where the monstrous form of the *Pride of Edinburgh* loomed over the airyard. Its triple cigar-shaped balloons, resplendent in the red, white and blue livery of the Empire Line, filled half the night sky; beneath, six vast gondolas were braced in a docking rig the size of a football stadium. The hatch of the airship's cargo hold yawned wide and dozens of vehicles came and went, loading the 'ship with supplies.

The *Pride of Edinburgh* was due to set sail for London at two o'clock in the morning. She glanced at her watch. They had a little under two hours to go before departure. Plenty of time, she told herself.

She turned to Anand. "And you won't be sad to leave India?"

"Jani-ji, I have always dreamed of travelling, of seeing England and London. I have always dreamed of adventure!"

"You won't miss your little sweetheart?"

He blushed, avoiding her eyes as he said in little more than a murmur, "I think not, Jani-ji. You see, I think our time together is over, to be honest. My feelings for Vashi are no more." He paused, thinking, then continued,

"You see, everything that has happened over the past few days has made me a different person. Do you think so, Jani-ji? I think... I think I have grown up, become a man, ah-cha?"

She smiled to herself. "I think perhaps you are right, Anand-ji."

He beamed at her. "I will write to Mr Clockwork and tell him where he can find Mel and Max."

Jani peered through the porthole again, across the yard to the massive wrought-iron gates. Even at midnight, the traffic on the road beyond the gates was busy. She willed a car to pull into the yard, and willed that car to be the taxi bearing Alfie Littlebody.

"Jani-ji," Anand said in a small voice.

"Yes?"

"I regret not being able to attend your father's funeral. I wanted to more than anything."

She smiled. "And so did I."

"I wanted to say goodbye, and pay my last respects."

She reached out and stroked his cheek. "Anand, we did that on the morning he died."

He smiled sadly. "His spirit will be willing us on our way!" he said.

She felt emotion choke her. She was about to say that her father's spirit passed away on the morning of his death, but stopped herself.

"Perhaps you're right," she said.

"Jani-ji," he murmured. "Do you think your father would have been proud of me, proud of the way I have..." He shrugged. "How I have served you, Jani-ji?"

"Anand-ji, you have been a true hero. Of course my father would be proud, and so am I."

She turned to the porthole, and her heart jumped as a taxi cab beetled across the apron and braked outside their airship. A rear door swung open and Alfie Littlebody jumped out. He trotted to the hatch of the 'ship and gave it a smart rap.

Jani crossed to the hatch and pulled it open.

"Quickly!" Alfie said. "Into the taxi. We've no time to lose!"

Jani took Anand's hand and almost dragged him from the airship, through the sultry night, and into the back of the taxi. Alfie joined them and slammed the door. Immediately the car started up and sped across the tarmac towards the *Pride of Edinburgh*.

A figure in the front seat turned, with difficulty, and smiled at Jani. "I must say, Miss Chatterjee, that if half of what Lieutenant Littlebody has told me about your exploits since our last meeting is true, then I shall have an entertaining voyage listening to you recount your numerous adventures."

Jani laughed. "Every word Alfie told you is true," she said, and went on, "I cannot express my gratitude to you, Lady Eddington."

The dowager waved a dismissive hand. "I would move mountains to assist you, Miss Chatterjee. But I must say that Lieutenant Littlebody caught me just in time: I was about to hail a cab when he turned up, red-faced and breathless."

Alfie blew, still exhausted. "My driver couldn't find the street, and I ended up running the last hundred yards and asking everyone I met where your Ladyship was staying."

"Well, all's well that ends well, Lieutenant," Lady Eddington said. "Ah, here we are. Driver, stop here if you will!"

The driver halted the cab, jumped out and rushed around to help Lady Eddington from the passenger seat. She was on crutches, and, assisted by Alfie on one side and Anand on the other, she led the way across to the steps that led up to the door of her Pullman carriage, its roof and windows repaired in the week since the crash-landing of the *Rudyard Kipling*. Jani stared at its racing green livery, scraped and battered, but obviously intact.

She looked up and down the length of the carriage, but there was no sign of any military police or port authorities who might question the right of the quartet to board the Pullman. Nevertheless, she felt greatly relived once Alfie and Anand had manhandled the dowager up the steps and into the carriage, and she was able to follow and slam the door behind her.

Lady Eddington showed them to the section of the carriage where – seemingly a lifetime ago – she and Jani had shared tea. She stomped over to the window on her crutches and drew the curtains, then turned to the trio as they sank into the cushioned seats.

"There is usually a security fellow who comes around before we embark to search each carriage," Lady Eddington said. "But don't go worrying your heads on that score. I will arrange things with the commanding officer." She waved to an overhead locker. "You'll find tea and provisions around the place; please feel free to help yourselves. I will be down to have a more detailed conflab once the *Edinburgh* is in the air. Until then, my friends..."

Jani thanked the dowager and watched as Anand and Alfie assisted her from the carriage.

The carriage shook as it was shunted along the rails towards the waiting maw of the *Pride of Edinburgh*.

Jani moved the curtain aside an inch and peered out as the carriage rolled into the cargo hold.

Alfie Littlebody located a kettle and a caddy of Darjeeling, and set about making a pot of tea. Anand found a tin of shortbread biscuits, and Jani realised that she hadn't eaten all day. Thirty minutes later, as they sat eating biscuits and sipping tea, the roar of a dozen engines announced that the *Pride of Edinburgh* was set fair for London.

Jani felt relief and exhaustion in equal measure. She looked back at the events of the past few days and wondered how she had survived half of them; and then she looked forward and wondered what travails the future might hold in store.

Alfie Littlebody was staring at her. He raised his cup. "To the success of your mission," he said.

Anand echoed his words, and added, "Am I really flying to London, Jani-ji?"

She smiled. "To the success of *our* mission," she said, "and yes, Anand, the wonder of London awaits us, and much more."